Compulsively Mr. Darcy

NINA BENNETON

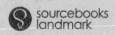

sourcebooks
landmark

Published by Sourcebooks Landmark, an imprint of Sourcebooks, Inc.
P.O. Box 4410, Naperville, Illinois 60567-4410
(630) 961-3900
FAX: (630) 961-2168
www.sourcebooks.com

Library of Congress Cataloging-in-Publication Data

Benneton, Nina.
 Compulsively Mr. Darcy / by Nina Benneton.
   p. cm.
 1. Billionaires—Fiction. 2. Obsessive-compulsive disorder—Fiction. 3. Women
physicians—Fiction. 4. Hollywood (Calif.)—Fiction. 5. Austen, Jane, 1775-1817.
Pride and prejudice—Fiction. I. Title.
 PS3602.E664426C66 2012
 813'.6—dc22

                              2011040668

                    Printed and bound in Canada
                    WC 10 9 8 7 6 5 4 3 2 1

To my Mr. Darcy and our children—
without them everything would be meaningless.

CHAPTER 1

❀

Green-Eyed Monster

"DAMN HOLLYWOOD," WILLIAM DARCY SWORE.

He was here, in this damn racket of a city, because of stupid Hollywood people and their trendsetting good deeds. Why couldn't they stick to rescuing hairless cats?

He regretted agreeing to the trip. Already, barely an hour after the Bingley's private jet had landed in Da Nang, the city's cloying dust coated his skin and clogged his pores.

The car inched through inhumanely congested streets heading to their hotel, a five-star resort on China Beach. The driver pressed his horn. Immediately, a chorus of honks answered. A constant cacophony of blaring sounds and incessant voices, in a bewildering array of pitches and tones, battered Darcy's senses.

Beside him, Charles Bingley restlessly bounced.

"Damn stupid Bingley for dragging me here." Darcy cursed under his breath. He swallowed his frustration and tried to improve his mood. Bingley was his best friend and, at this stage in his life, he didn't want the bother of training another one.

Sitting in front of them, Caroline Bingley turned to her sister, Louisa Hurst. "Did you read the latest *Us* issue on famous moms and babies? Most of my Hollywood friends were in it."

"Don't worry," Louisa said. "You'll be in it soon enough, as a doting aunt. You might even be on the cover. We're going with the best and most efficient orphanage."

"Which only accepts responsible and happily married couples," Louisa's husband Gil Hurst said dryly from his place next to the driver, "and that leaves you out of the loop, Caroline."

"That leaves you out too, Gil," Caroline returned. "And that's why we have my brother and William. They're happy and responsible."

"Yes, but who is which, tell me," her brother-in-law said with a glance directed at Darcy and Bingley. "I wouldn't want to get confused."

"Charles can't help having"—Caroline paused and faced her brother—"what did the doctor say you have?"

"Attention deficit and hyperactivity disorder," Bingley answered. "And there's nothing wrong with being happy."

The Bingley siblings and Hurst continued their family squabble. Darcy tuned them out, wondering, not for the first time, why he'd allowed Bingley to embroil him in their family's crazy expedition to adopt a trendy orphan.

"We need someone responsible in the group," Bingley had argued when he begged Darcy to join them. "No one is more responsible than you, Darce."

"Traffic here is worse than in New York City," Hurst said. "I swear the car hasn't moved in the last ten minutes."

Bingley nudged Darcy. "Look at the guy riding that bicycle. There must be close to a hundred chickens on that bamboo frame on top of his back wheel. How does he keep it balanced?"

Caroline said, "Please, Charles, didn't you see that *Crouching Tiger* movie? Asians are born with good balance. I always educate myself about the countries we visit. It's helpful to have a vast cultural knowledge of the world."

After spending hours traveling in close quarters with her, Darcy closed his eyes and briefly fantasized balancing her and her vast cultural knowledge at the business end of a catapult and pointing it toward North Korea.

"I've been doing yoga for a while. I bet I can keep my balance on that bicycle," Bingley said.

Behind closed eyelids, Darcy's eyes attempted a roll. He hoped the bouncy Tigger next to him had remembered to take his daily Ritalin. He didn't feel up to dealing with an impulsive Bingley.

"I'll be right back." Bingley leaped out of the car before anyone could stop him.

Darcy kept his eyes closed. *Let Bingley's family take care of his impetuousness.*

"Where is he going?" Hurst's voice was impatient.

"You know my brother, he can't sit still," Louisa answered.

"William, you must stop him. He's mixing with the natives, trying to make friends with them already. This is going to delay us, waiting for him to come back." Caroline touched Darcy's thigh.

Darcy opened his eyes and shifted his leg away, breaking contact. He looked out the window. Bingley was trying to lift one leg over the seat of a bicycle but was having some difficulty, hampered by the clucking chickens, all tied up by their feet and hanging upside down from the bamboo frame.

"I want to get to the hotel soon. I need a drink and a bed." Hurst yawned.

"Perhaps you should go get him, Gil," Louisa said.

"No, I'll go," Darcy said. He needed to move away from Caroline's hand, which still hovered uncomfortably close to his crotch.

By the time he reached Bingley, a large group had gathered. Bingley had managed to get himself seated on the chicken-bike and was now pedaling. He cycled a few yards, laughing along with the audience, before he rammed into a woman carrying a three-foot bamboo pole over one shoulder. Two large, straw baskets, full to the brim with strawberry-sized red fruits and dangling by strings from both ends of the pole, toppled over. Chickens, fruits, tiny market woman, and Bingley became a tangled heap in the muddy street.

Sighing, Darcy pulled out his wallet. The chicken man was happy with his reimbursement.

The unharmed fruit woman, however, glowered at Bingley until, in an attempt at peace, he reached for a fallen fruit next to his feet and bit into it while smiling at her. His immediate grimace brought laughter from the locals and, finally, a forgiving smile from the fruit woman. She selected another fruit from the ground, peeled off the outer red layer with its hairlike tentacles, and popped the white, soft center into his mouth.

The crowd gave another round of laughter when Bingley comically frowned and spit out a round, olive-sized black pit.

Darcy grimaced. He saw nothing amusing about the numerous hygienic rules Bingley had just violated. Darcy impatiently broke up the gathering and pulled Bingley away.

A curious crush followed as Darcy led a slightly limping and chattering Bingley back to the car. Darcy opened the car door.

Caroline shrieked.

Darcy glanced down and, suddenly light-headed, had to grab the car door to steady himself.

"He is not coming into the car like that. There must be at least six inches of mud on his pants!" She pointed to her brother's leg, missing the blood seeping through his pants.

"He can't go to the hotel until he gets that leg looked at by a doctor," Louisa said almost as loud.

Her husband reacted by closing his eyes and pretending to be asleep.

The horde around them informed Bingley a nice American doctor worked at a hospital a short distance away.

"A woman doctor with green eyes. Very beautiful," a small man tried to tempt them.

Darcy waved the car on to the hotel. He would take care of Bingley. Minutes later, keeping his eyes averted from Bingley's injured leg, Darcy walked alongside a cyclo, a three-wheeled-tricycle taxi, carrying Bingley to the hospital.

Oblivious to his enlarging bloodstain, Bingley chatted happily with the cyclo driver and the crowd following them. They reached a dilapidated building they were reassured was a top-notch hospital.

Bingley said to Darcy, "Wait here, otherwise you'd be washing your hands constantly the next few days. Besides, you'd be in the way. You know you're afraid of hospitals and doctors."

Darcy immediately took offense. "I'm not afraid of anything or anyone."

"I promise not to get leeched or drink lizard-tail's juice." Before he hobbled off, Bingley added with a wink, "If the green-eyed, beautiful doctor is a brunette, we'll find some excuse for you to be seen also."

Ignoring Bingley's good humor and his grinning fan club, Darcy scowled and settled next to a tree to wait. This American doctor had better be fast and efficient. He desperately needed to get to his hotel suite for some peace and darkness.

Hours later, he still stood waiting in the same spot. Bingley had developed a severe case of gastrointestinal illness, courtesy of the dirty, spiny red fruit that he had eaten, and the doctor was running behind schedule.

Silently, Darcy chanted in rhythm with the loud thumping in his head, "Hate doctors and their inability to keep to a schedule. Hate..."

"You come, I sew you," a voice broke through the chanting in his head.

He turned around. A small man with a friendly smile stood waiting.

When Darcy didn't move, the man gave him a wider smile, revealing broken and blackened teeth. "You friend, I sew. I sew you, you friend."

Darcy declined politely. "No thank you."

"Yes, yes," the man said. A small hand reached forward, and with a surprisingly strong grip, grabbed two fingers of Darcy's left hand.

In his surprise, Darcy let himself be dragged along for a short distance through the courtyard and almost into the building before he resisted, forcing the man holding tight to his two fingers to halt. "No. No. I don't need to be seen. I'm fine," he wheezed out, and wondered how the little man, whom he outweighed by at least a hundred pounds, could run so fast while Darcy was out of breath and his sides ached.

"I no seen you. I sew you friend."

"I don't need your help. No thank you."

"Friend," Friendly Face said with an earnest expression. "Come see!"

They stared at one another. A few silent moments passed. Finally, shrugging, Darcy nodded and yielded to the determined smaller man.

Not trusting his capitulation, Friendly Face again seized Darcy's two fingers and pulled him into the building. At the end of a surprisingly clean hallway, Friendly Face led him into a room.

Bingley, sitting alone in a bed near the door, gave them a wan smile.

"How are you feeling?" Darcy frowned at the paleness of Bingley's face. "They're ready to discharge you?"

"I'm fine now. The IV helped. They still have to fix the cut on my leg."

"What, you've been here for hours and they haven't even looked at it?" Darcy seethed. He noticed a crowd of medical personnel surrounding a smiling Vietnamese patient in the next bed quite a few feet away. "I want to see the doctor in charge!"

"Darce, take it easy. The doctor is busy," Bingley said to try and calm him.

Someone from the crowd moved toward them. *Finally, some attention.* Darcy fumed. Using his intimidating CEO voice, he barked, "I want this looked at now." Half turning, he lifted up the blue towel covering Bingley's injured leg. A black blind descended.

Before everything completely darkened, he caught a flash of green eyes.

He came to just as something hard tapped at his cheeks. Opening his eyes, he saw *Anna*—his late mother's name—in gold letters. The letters receded. A split second later, the letters, attached to the bottom of a black wooden clog, came at him again. *Tap, tap.* The wooden sole pressed none too gently against each of his cheeks. His mind reeled in astonishment at the audacity.

Who had the nerve to touch his face with their dirty shoes?

A pair of fiery green eyes stared down at him. "Get up. I don't have time to deal with obnoxious British pricks. Get yourself up and out of my operating room."

Stunned, he glanced to the side and discovered he was lying on the dirty floor, the floor full of germs and fluids. His stomach rolled.

"Get up and get out. You've ruined the sterile field."

"Sterile? You've got to be bloody kidding." Horrified to hear his voice sounded hoarse and weak, he quickly made sure he had his CEO boardroom face on.

"His leg was prepped and draped under sterile towels until you contaminated it with your dirty hand."

He lay on the ground, fighting nausea for another moment, before he realized no help would come from Green Eyes. Was this how they normally treated people who slipped and fell?

Unexpectedly, small fingers grabbed his arm with a strong grip and pulled him up. Friendly Face had appeared out of nowhere with his now-familiar toothy smile. He put his arms around Darcy to steady him.

Darcy stepped back from his new friend, ignored the swaying of his body, and straightened to his full height. He put on the CEO's face again and stared down at the blurry green eyes behind safety goggles. That was all he could see of her. Surgical mask and garb covered the rest of her.

"I have been waiting hours for you, Doctor, to take care of a minor injury. I guess I shouldn't be surprised at your inability to do a simple medical procedure. The fact that you're stuck working here, American Doctor," he stressed in his most sarcastic tone, "surely must mean that you had failed to gain admittance to a reputable medical school in America, or you have failed to get hired by any respectable hospital that required and demanded skill and efficiency. I have been traveling for the last twenty-four hours, and I'm in no mood to put up with your pitiful incompetence."

"Listen here, you bloody arse," she mimicked his British accent as she stressed the last two words. "I've been up for the last thirty hours working without much food or sleep, and now I have to deal with you and your insulting demands."

"Insulting demands? Simply because I request competent service?"

"Get out," Green Eyes hissed, waving something at him.

The metal smell of the blood mixed with the rotten odor of pus assaulted him. In her hand, she wielded a bloody scalpel tinged with yellow streaks. His knees wobbled.

Friendly Face's arms snaked around Darcy's waist to steady him again.

Green Eyes exchanged words with Friendly Face.

Behind Darcy, someone chuckled. Darcy turned to glare at Bingley, who avoided his eyes and tried to control himself. After a moment, Bingley lost his struggle and hearty laughter erupted from him. "Sorry, Doctor. I wanted Darcy to know I'd probably be here a while yet. I forgot he faints at the sight of blood."

Darcy tried to use the CEO face on his friend, but, as usual, Bingley was immune to it. Darcy turned back and discovered Green Eyes had disappeared amongst the group around the next bed.

Friendly Face smiled at him. "Doctor say I take you out."

"Yes, please, Oanh. Take Mr. Darcy outside before he does any more damage." Bingley turned toward Darcy. "Go get a breath of fresh air, man. You need it."

Once outside, Oanh tried to get Darcy to sit in the cyclo to rest, but Darcy, feeling he had suffered enough humiliation today, declined. He could not bring himself to sit in that contraption. He arranged for the resort to send a car and a driver.

After what seemed like another excruciatingly long wait, someone came and told him Bingley would be done in ten minutes. Darcy settled the hospital bill and clarified the discharge instructions with a nurse. He knew Bingley wouldn't remember to take care of any details and he wanted to be gone as soon as Bingley was ready to go.

On the ride to the resort, to Darcy's irritation, Bingley was back to his prattling self. "That was an amazing experience. It was like being in one of those medical shows on TV. The tough old soldier in the next bed refused all pain medication. I did too. The doctor said I must be part Vietnamese. They have a high pain threshold. She was so gentle when she worked on me. Very patient and efficient, she was."

Darcy snorted and made a rude gesture.

"You deserved what she said to you for being such an insulting, bloody arse to the poor woman. I heard a nurse say the doctor missed her dinner, again..." On and on Bingley jabbered until an evil glare from Darcy finally dampened him.

Once in his own suite, one as far away from the Bingley family as possible, Darcy immediately undressed and took a hot shower. He threw his traveling suit in the trash bin and wrote a note to the hotel staff that, yes, he did mean to discard the expensive and tailor-made suit. It was now contaminated. Infiltrated by microscopic invaders.

They'd skittered across him when he'd lain on that floor.

At that thought, he took another shower. A long one. Then one more to make sure.

Before he slipped into the king-sized bed, he checked the bedding. Satisfied at seeing his own sheets with his own monograms, he reminded himself to thank his housekeeper Mrs. Reynolds for arranging everything with the resort. He hated to sleep in linens others may have used.

At last, his head sank onto the pillow and he let the peace of the room cover him. Alone. All quiet.

As he drifted off to sleep, visions of a green-eyed monster devouring him jerked him awake. Again and again. Finally, giving up, he dragged himself out of bed and made a phone call.

He gave precise, detailed instructions for a meal to be prepared and delivered, making them repeat his instructions back to him. Mrs. Reynolds must have relayed how particular her boss would be as a guest. The hotel staff accepted his peculiar instructions without any difficulty. Sometimes there were advantages to being an obsessive control freak, he decided.

"Now, go away," he muttered to the green-eyed monster floating around him as he settled back into his bed. The pounding in his head lulled him into a much-needed sleep.

CHAPTER 2

❄

Batting for the Other Team

"YOU BLOODY ARSE!"

Hands on her throat, Elizabeth Bennet bolted up and looked around to see who had woken her up. No one. Sheepishly, she put down her hands. As usual, after a sleep-deprived on-call night, she had been talking in her sleep.

She lay back against her pillow. This was her favorite part of the day, waking up and letting the echo of life in Vietnam serenade her. She listened to the melodic music from a neighbor's radio, the singsong voices of people talking in soft murmurs, and the rhythmic chopping of a cleaver against a wooden board. The sound of lunch being prepared in the kitchen of the orphanage next door reminded her it was time to get up.

Fragrances from freshly cut fruit greeted her in the tiny dining area of the cottage she shared with her sister Jane. Elizabeth made her coffee, grabbed a medical journal from a stack, and sat down to her meal.

Two paragraphs deep in an article about post-miscarriage infections after dilation and curettage procedures, she paused, distracted by the unbidden image of a man's handsome face appearing on the page. Frowning, she swatted at the paper and refocused on medicine.

A few paragraphs later, hearing the sound of his voice reading aloud "staphylococcus," she gave up and put the journal away.

Why did she keep hearing his voice? It must be that English accent—so clear, so clipped, and so concise. Every syllable enunciated, in that public school–educated British male voice with its typical, unhurried delivery, even when giving a blistering setdown. Probably from watching too many period pieces on the BBC channel, she'd always had a weakness for snotty, male, British accents.

The phone rang. Her sister called from the orphanage's office next door. "Did you catch up on your sleep after your call night?"

"Yes, I feel rested." Elizabeth took a small bite of a jackfruit and made a face at its oversweet aroma. Jane liked the fruit, but Elizabeth thought it too sticky. "Yesterday was the worst day I've had at the hospital here. I thought I was back on-call at San Francisco General. We were short staffed. Two doctors had family emergencies."

"I'm sure you handled it fine, knowing you."

"You wouldn't say that if you were there near the end of my shift. I'm ashamed to tell you I yelled at someone in the OR."

"Staff?"

"No, a guy who came with a patient. Foreigners. Rich tourist saps."

Jane laughed. "Oh, it's one of us who was your patient."

"This guy got a bad gash on his leg from some bicycle accident in the market earlier. Any doctor in the hospital could have taken care of it, but he requested the American doctor, me. He was very friendly and seemed, oddly enough, excited to be treated in a Third-World hospital."

"Then what was the problem?"

"His partner." Elizabeth gave the details of her encounter with Mr. Darcy, ending with, "You should have heard the way Mr. Darcy carried on about the care his partner was receiving. He behaved worse than any nervous father with his wife's first delivery."

"That was terrible, what he said about you. He must have been so anxious about Mr. Bingley. They're a couple, then?"

"Yes. From the way Mr. Darcy acted, definitely."

"What happened after you yelled at him?"

"I forgot there was a bloody scalpel in my hand. I think he thought I was serious. He almost fainted again, though Mr. Bingley said Mr. Darcy always faints at the sight of blood."

"You're cranky when you're hungry. Did you remember to eat something last night?"

"Yes. When I finally sat down at my desk to finish charting, I had the nicest surprise. Net Thi Phen Resort's delivery guy handed me a basket of goodies."

"Was there a note along with it?"

"No, but I think it's from Mr. Bingley. When I finished with him, he was very apologetic for his partner's rudeness."

"That's considerate. Are you sure the two guys are together? Maybe he's flirting with you with that basket of food?"

"He's not my type. Too friendly. Too blond. Talks too much. If the dark-haired partner wasn't such a bloody arse, I might consider him. I liked his accent. And, of course, he bats for the other team. You know my track record." Elizabeth sighed. She had horrible luck with men. She was always bringing potential boyfriends home only to have them fall for her guy friends instead.

"I'd forgotten about your horrible track record." Jane laughed again. "Hmmm. Blond and very friendly, Mr. Bingley was? That's more my type. It's been so long since I had a real date, I'd even go for a green Mohawk."

"Just flash that angelic smile of yours and you'll have guys from all the hues of the rainbow lining up to be on your team," Elizabeth teased, very glad to hear Jane expressing a desire to date. As always, guilt hit her for having been too involved with her medical training to notice her sister was in an abusive relationship two years previously.

"Listen, I have to go," Jane said. "I need to track down the new investigator Aunt Mai hired and have him fax me the report on this Hurst couple who are coming tomorrow."

"Tomorrow? And you haven't done the background on the adoptive parents yet?" Elizabeth asked. Their mother's younger brother, Edward, and his Vietnamese wife, Mai, had founded Gracechurch Orphanage a few years before. When Edward Gardiner suffered a heart attack in San Francisco at the same time the orphanage's Vietnamese manager received her visa to join her son in America, Jane offered to come to Vietnam to run the orphanage temporarily. Elizabeth came along to keep her company and to volunteer as an infectious disease specialist at the local hospital.

"The pre-adoption was done during the transition from the last manager to me, and with the new investigator taking over what Uncle Ed usually handled, a few things got missed. I'll see you at lunch."

"Good luck." Elizabeth said good-bye. She glanced at the clock. She still had time to go check on a patient before lunch.

———~~~———

An hour later, as Elizabeth sat in her office at the hospital, a voice scolded her, "You're supposed to be off today, Dr. Bennet."

She looked up from reading a patient's chart and smiled at the young Vietnamese woman at her door, her friend and colleague Dr. Chau Luc. "I'm just checking on Mr. Vinh."

"You Americans are all workaholics, working all the time. You never rest."

"Speak for yourself, Chau. Aren't you always working at your father's club on your days off?" Elizabeth said. Chau was very devoted to her family.

"The only way I get to spend time with my father and brothers lately is if I help out at Merry Bar. When you and Jane have some free time, you should come and check the club out. I'll introduce you to my family."

"First chance we get," Elizabeth promised and stood. "Now, I need to go see my patient."

Mr. Vinh looked surprised to see her. "Dr. Bennet, I thought you were not working today."

"I missed you and want to see what damage I did yesterday," she said. His infection was a rare case, and she fretted about his progress.

Smiling at her teasing, Mr. Vinh replied that he was well and she need not bother herself.

Aware that Vietnamese people always said they were fine, even if they were dying, she carefully examined him anyway. Satisfied at his healing, she bid him good-bye.

He held out a hand and, in a formal manner, said, "Thank you very much, Dr. Bennet. I'm honored to have your care."

She shook his hand. "You are very welcome, Mr. Vinh. I'm glad to be able to help."

"I saw what happened with the two men yesterday. The dark-haired one insulted you. He thought you neglected his friend and he was angry. I'm honored that you put me first, though I would have been happy to wait."

"I'm so sorry you saw my undisciplined outburst yesterday. I put you first because you were the sicker patient."

"I don't have money but I have influence." His eyes serious, Mr. Vinh added, "If you want, I can make them leave the country."

She held up her hands. "No, no. He was worried about his friend. I was the bad one. You don't have to do anything. I want them to stay, please."

He pointed his finger in a commanding manner at her. "Anybody gives you trouble, you come to me. You promise?"

She quickly agreed, a little fearful if she didn't, he would do something on his own. "Don't worry, Mr. Vinh. If I have any trouble with anyone, I promise to come to you for help. Those men yesterday were tourists passing through. I'm sure I won't see them again."

CHAPTER 3

✿

Two Men and a Baby

JANE TRIED NOT TO GAWK AT THE GROUP THAT JUST ARRIVED FROM Net Thi Phen Resort.

Mr. Hurst, a forty-year-old Englishman whose family owned a Scotch and brandy distribution business, requested something stronger upon being offered tea or coffee. Mrs. Hurst, a thirty-seven-year-old woman, had simply listed "socialite" as her current and past employment history. Jane tried to recall the sparse details she had just read about the Hursts this morning. Nothing stood out.

Mrs. Hurst's brother, Mr. Bingley, and his friend, Mr. Darcy, accompanied the Hursts. Jane's eyes widened, recognizing their names.

Mr. Bingley said, "Our other sister will join us shortly, but no need to wait for her. She's reading in the car."

Mr. Bingley's infectious good humor, especially when he caught a glimpse of the children playing, more than made up for the Hursts' muted affect. His smile dimmed when Jane denied his request to join the children in the sandbox. She explained the orphanage preferred to minimize the children's exposure to potential adoptive parents, to avoid disappointment for both parties. Next, she discussed the orphanage's strict policy of first come, first adopted. The adoptive parents had no choice which child they would be given.

The Hursts showed no reaction on hearing that. Mr. Bingley simply nodded. Mr. Darcy, on the other hand, threw Jane a skeptical glance, though he remained silent and moved to stand next to a window. During her detailed explanation of the orphanage's philosophies and policies, she saw that the enigmatic Mr. Darcy was the only one who seemed to be listening intensely and carefully.

"Do you have any questions for me?" she said at the end of the interview.

Mr. Hurst asked no questions of the orphanage or of the prospective child. Mrs. Hurst asked what size clothing the child would likely wear. Mr. Bingley asked why there was no playground. After she answered their questions, Jane began to wrap up the meeting when Mr. Darcy spoke.

"If you don't mind, I have a few questions."

Mr. Darcy asked about the orphanage's founders, how it was funded, what its long-term goals were, where the orphans came from, the health history of the children prior to and during their time at the orphanage, the birth parents' continued involvement, if any, and so forth. Jane suspected Mr. Darcy knew the answers already. Though very courteous, he rarely made eye contact with her or the others, keeping his eyes fixed on the view outside the window. *Perhaps Mr. Darcy is part Vietnamese*, Jane dryly mused, thinking of the repugnance the Vietnamese culture had for direct eye contact in social interactions.

At one point, something in the courtyard distracted him and he absentmindedly repeated a question to which she had already answered. Finally, he finished with his questioning.

She stood up to again wrap up the interview.

The door to her office opened. A tall woman, wearing a white linen suit, white wide-brimmed hat, and white six-inch high heels entered. She looked like an escapee from the cover of the imaginary *Trophy Wife's Weekly.* Jane immediately felt ashamed for her unkind thought.

Click, clack. The woman's heels made stabbing sounds on the wooden floor. She marched to Mr. Darcy, grasped his arm, and nearly sliced his left eye with the brim of her hat. Mr. Darcy flinched. The woman pulled him forward. "William, you must not be so shy. You're a part of our family."

After Mr. Bingley introduced her to Jane, Miss Bingley complained, "What's taking so long with the interview?"

In a dry voice, Mr. Bingley explained, "Darcy took a while with the inquisition."

Miss Bingley looked puzzled.

After a brief moment of silence, Mr. Bingley provided the definition of *inquisition.*

His sister frowned at him and turned back to Mr. Darcy. "I know where to find the best children's boutiques in New York City. Fifth Avenue! I read about them in the car. When baby Darcy makes his or her first appearance to the world"—she winked at him—"you must get him or her a personal stylist. All the up-and-coming babies in New York and London have one."

Mr. Darcy darted a telling glance in Mr. Bingley's direction.

The latter immediately stood and, acting as if he was an adopting parent, thanked Jane for meeting with them.

Jane explained to the Hursts she would contact them soon, once she had a chance to go through their application more thoroughly and make sure all necessary paperwork was done properly. As she clarified for them, she had only that morning received the background report on them from the orphanage's new investigator, a Mr. Bill Collins.

"We met with him weeks ago. We don't understand the delay here," Mrs. Hurst said.

Jane simply apologized again and promised to do her best to minimize their waiting.

No response from Mr. and Mrs. Hurst, but Mr. Bingley smiled. "Take your time, Miss Bennet."

While Mr. Darcy subtly edged away from Miss Bingley, she turned to Jane. "I was hoping we'd learn the child's clothing size today. It takes time to put together a wardrobe."

Mr. Bingley herded his sister outside. Jane walked them to their car. Before he got in the car, Mr. Darcy kept glancing back at the courtyard. Curious, Jane followed the direction of his eyes. She saw nothing unusual except a pathway leading to her and Elizabeth's cottage. Her sister should have arrived home for lunch by now.

—⁓—

Elizabeth pointed her chopsticks at Jane. "All right, you're bursting at the seams. Spill."

Jane resisted the urge to remind her sister pointing chopsticks at people was rude in Vietnam. "Your patient Mr. Bingley and his partner Mr. Darcy just left here."

"What?" The small bowl of rice paused halfway to Elizabeth's mouth. "They're the fancy limo I saw when I arrived home?"

Jane nodded. "They were here with another couple, Mr. and Mrs. Hurst, the parents listed on the application."

"Why does your Mother Teresa–face scream complications with a big capital *C*?"

Jane described her visitors. She agreed with Elizabeth's initial impression of Mr. Bingley as a friendly fellow. When she portrayed Mr. Darcy as serious but polite, her sister snorted. Jane reminded her, "At the hospital, he was jet-lagged and anxious about his partner. He was completely different here, very courteous and controlled. He asked questions I wished the adoptive parents had asked."

"Why the hell was he the one asking questions? Shouldn't the Hursts be the ones to do that? See, that proves he's a prick, sticking his nose into everything that doesn't involve him, like he did at the hospital."

"That's just it. I think he was the right one to be asking all the questions. He did all the homework the parents usually do. His partner showed such enthusiasm at the idea of playing with a child."

"What are you saying?"

"The two men acted like expectant parents while the adoptive parents showed no emotion. Miss Bingley might have inadvertently let something slip. I heard her say 'When baby Darcy makes his or her appearance to the world.' And then she winked at Mr. Darcy."

"Ah! I see. It's the two men who are the adopting parents and the married couple are just fronting."

"It would explain the Hursts' lack of interest and the sparse background information the investigator faxed over, which revealed nothing more substantial than they're wealthy enough to financially care for a child."

"Why didn't the men apply themselves?"

"Lizzy, you know the answer to that. As much as you and I feel two men or two women can be great parents, Aunt Mai would never have been able to convince people here to accept that. She has to have married—as in a man and woman—as a requirement to satisfy the authorities."

"The 'authorities' sure made an exception for those on the covers of the gossip rags."

"You know that's good tourism publicity for the country. And it's also good publicity for the plight of orphans here. But back to my problem: I can't help feeling something's not right."

"Like?"

"The Hursts did make it this far in the adoption process. Perhaps they do want a child but aren't good at showing their feelings. I haven't had much experience with the private-jet crowd to confidently assess them. I hate to say no to them—or even the two guys—and deny a child a chance for a home because I'm not doing my job right."

"It doesn't sound like you're the one not doing your job right. This new investigator, what's his name, again? I can't believe Aunt Mai would have hired a shoddy investigator."

"Bill Collins. Aunt Sunny referred him to Aunt Mai."

Elizabeth rolled her eyes. "If Sunny Phillips from Marin County had recommended him, you have cause to worry. I bet you he's probably a flaky New Age guy who's always dabbling in various quests of self-discovery. Hell, she probably met him during one of her daily group-therapy sessions. Tell Aunt Mai he's incompetent."

Jane ignored her sister's snap judgment of a man she hadn't met. "Aunt Mai doesn't need to hear my concerns over the new investigator she hired. Uncle Ed usually does the background checks on adoptive parents, and he's not supposed to worry about anything while he's recuperating. I want to handle this myself."

"What are you going to do?" Elizabeth poured more tea into Jane's cup.

The fragrant jasmine drifted to Jane's nose and soothed her. "I need your help. I'm going to ask for another background investigation. Until I get more information, I need you to be another set of eyes and ears at my next meeting with them."

CHAPTER 4

❀

Wood Nymph

"CHARLES, WHERE'S WILLIAM?" CAROLINE'S VOICE SOUNDED TOO loud over the phone. "I keep missing him. I even made sure to wake up early this morning and he's already gone from his room. No answer."

"Why do you want him?" Bingley sleepily said before he realized the stupidity of his question. There were nine reasons why his sister always wanted the man: the row of nine zeros after the first digit in Darcy's bank account.

"I want him to join Louisa and me for a facial. They have this wonderful citrus scrub."

"Leave him alone. He's here for a rest, not to be your spa buddy. You don't know Darcy at all if you think he'd set foot in a spa, much less get a facial."

"Fine, no facial. But what he needs is a relaxing massage. He's been so tense and restless. Every time I've seen him lately, he'd fidget and move. He couldn't sit still on the plane."

"That's because he was trying to get away from you and Louisa. Your talking for hours nonstop gave him a headache."

"We were having a great bonding conversation," she insisted. "Your interrupting and telling me to leave him alone made it seem as if I was bothering him."

"You were bothering him. He was too polite to tell you."

"I don't know why he's friends with you. He's always polite and a real gentleman, and you're… you're the boy who never grows up!" she yelled and hung up on him.

"We're friends because," Bingley said to the mirror a few minutes later, shaving, "Darcy thinks I need to be taken care of, and I let him because I know he has a great need to take care of someone."

Dressed, he went to Darcy's room and knocked. Though he couldn't hear any noise inside, he suspected Darcy was silently checking the peephole to make sure it wasn't Caroline. "I'm alone. No sisters." When Darcy opened the door, Bingley asked, "Want to join me on an adventure today? See some local sights?"

"If you mean another chance of getting you out of some scrapes, no thank you. I've barely recovered from the last one."

"Took my Ritalin today; you should be safe." Bingley sat on the couch and took a guava from the bowl on the coffee table. He sniffed, appreciating its apple-pear smell. He tried not to make too much noise eating the crunchy fruit. Darcy hated hearing loud chewing.

Darcy walked toward the window. "I'll be safer here."

"By staring out of that window all day? Besides, you're not all that safe. Caroline called me earlier. She was looking for you." Bingley grinned and watched Darcy suppress a grimace at the mention of Caroline.

"I'm going to get some work done."

"You promised your sister and your cousin you'd relax on this vacation."

"I'm going to relax by making sure some work gets done." Darcy waved in the direction of his briefcase and laptop. "I hardly call this work, the little that I do now."

"You mean you'll only work twelve hours, instead of eighteen hours, today."

"Probably."

"I was being sarcastic. The only non-work thing you've done since we arrived is the visit to the orphanage."

"Have you heard from them yet? When are we going back for another meeting?"

Curious at the eager note in Darcy's voice, Bingley raised an eyebrow. "You almost sound as if you don't mind going through another meeting."

"I don't like things unfinished. It felt unfinished, the whole interview."

"I don't mind. They can take all the time in the world to fix their paperwork if it means we stay here long enough for you to learn to chill. I promised your sister and your cousin I'd have you relaxed before I brought you back to them." That was the main reason Bingley agreed to come to Vietnam with his sisters. It was the perfect excuse to get Darcy to accompany them, telling him they needed a responsible, objective person outside of the family to make sure the adoption was legit. Bingley knew Darcy couldn't resist the urge to direct something.

"I am relaxing," Darcy said in a terse, controlled voice. "As soon as the adoption is settled, I'm ready to leave the country."

"You're at a five-star resort next to a beautiful beach in the third largest city of this old country with two thousand years of history. People dream of visiting here, and you want to get stuck on a plane again with my family?"

"You sound like a bloody brochure. I can have Richard send my own plane here."

"Read about this place while I was recovering in my room the first day." Bingley ignored Darcy's threat. Darcy's cousin wouldn't send the company jet to Vietnam, no matter how much Darcy demanded it, and the chance of safety-conscious Darcy taking a commercial flight to escape this enforced vacation was too slim to worry about.

"I'll go for a walk later," Darcy allowed after a silent moment.

"Get a massage on the beach. Lie on the warm sand and let them knead your tension away." Bingley cringed at sounding like Caroline.

"I don't like strangers touching me."

"You don't even like people you know well touching you. The massage might help your headaches."

"I don't get headaches," Darcy said coldly.

"Sure, right." Bingley picked up his half-eaten fruit and started eating again, this time not caring if he was chewing loudly. "You mean you haven't sat in a darkened room for hours at a time these past few months, biting people's heads off if they even breathe too loud?"

Darcy glared at him. "Noises bother me."

"I think you should see a doctor or even an acupuncturist—" He broke off and shook his head. He'd forgotten whom he was talking to. "Fine. Go ahead and suffer in silence. Promise me, though, you won't work all day today. Just because we lost the last company doesn't mean we need to rush and look for another one now."

"I didn't lose the last company. I didn't care enough to go all out for it."

"That proves my point. You don't care enough. You're losing interest in things that used to challenge you."

"As a new challenge, perhaps I should adopt an orphan while I'm here," Darcy quipped.

"How about one a bit older, doesn't need her nappies changed, but would stick around to change yours in the future." Bingley again looked through the fruit bowl.

"Never saw the need nor met the woman who I would even want to stick around that long."

"There's always Caroline." Bingley chose an orange and started to peel it, throwing the peel on the table. That remark and the carelessly thrown peel earned him a glare.

"You, on the other hand, have not yet met a woman who didn't want to wipe your arse and your bank account clean."

"I don't have good luck with meeting nice women," Bingley agreed. "Speaking of nice women, what did you think of Miss Bennet? Wasn't she an angel?"

"She runs an orphanage in a Third-World country, of course she's an angel."

"It's not a Third-World country anymore; it's a developing country. And don't sound so suspicious. You'd have suspected Mother Teresa of being a con woman."

"Until I had her checked out, yes."

"Miss Bennet answered all your questions completely… and patiently, I might add. She was honest enough to admit she didn't have enough background information to make a decision. She was very professional, very thorough."

"Too professional. Too thorough," Darcy said. "Probably wants to know how much we're all worth before she offers up the child."

"She had the investigator's report on Hurst's financial background already."

"Which is nothing to yours or mine. I don't like it. This particular orphanage usually does extensive, exhaustive background checks on the parents. That's one of the reasons it's considered one of the best. Your angel should have had that information already."

"I wouldn't be as suspicious as you for all the coins in the world." Bingley stood. He had an appointment with his friend the cyclo driver, who'd offered to show him around the city. "I'm out of here. Try not to spend all your time working."

———— ⚬ ————

After Bingley left, Darcy moved from the window to a chair. Despite what he had said to Bingley, the orphanage and Miss Bennet's professionalism did impress him. What he heard during the interview was consistent with his research. He was still suspicious, but that was just his nature.

He slumped in his chair and stared, unseeing, at the ceiling. Much as he hated to admit it, Bingley was also correct about him. Since the fiasco with his sister, Georgiana, and that cult last winter, he'd lost interest in things that used to challenge him. For the first time in years, he had not been able to escape the tedium of his life by burying himself into work. He felt beaten. All he could manage lately was a sense of ennui he couldn't shake.

These past months, he'd been focused on helping Georgiana recover. He had failed miserably.

He loved his sister deeply, but he had never been able to find a way to bridge the indescribable chasm between them. Perhaps it was their age difference. When their father died and Darcy became her guardian at twenty-two, he was too young to be a father figure, yet too old, too weighed down with responsibility to be the playful brother a nine-year-old child needed. He wished Georgiana could have known him when he was a happy, young boy, before their mother died.

He raised a hand to cover his eyes, to block out memories better left alone.

The air felt dense and dragging. The familiar sensation of not being able to take a full breath overpowered him. Immobilized in the chair, he decided not to fight it. He dropped his hand, closed his eyes, and waited patiently for the heaviness to go away in its own time.

A moment later, he rallied. He would find a way out of this languor. That was why he was here in Vietnam, wasn't it?

He allowed his mind to wander, in search of a soothing thought or feeling.

He was suddenly at the window of the orphanage's office again. He had just asked Miss Bennet another question to which he already knew the answer. Only half listening to her reply, his eyes absently scanned the view outside.

From behind a bend in the road leading into the courtyard, a vision appeared. At first, it was like any insignificant image of a fleeting shadow. As the shadow moved closer to him, unexplainably, a surprising sensation of lightness, of delight, and of comfort enveloped him. The shadow became a figure of a woman. Left arm swinging in an enchanting wave, right hand holding the strap of a shoulder bag, the woman moved unhurriedly from under the canopy of a large tree. As she emerged from its shade, she stopped. Palms up, she slowly raised her arms and stretched them toward the sky. Face lifted to the sun, she then unexpectedly, uninhibitedly, and unself-consciously twirled.

He could almost hear the laughter he saw on her face. Long, dark hair tumbled down as she joyously danced with the warm rays. His fingers tingled, twitching in their own subconscious desire to reach out and touch that happiness.

All too soon for him the twirling stopped, and she moved with a graceful calmness toward the orphanage. She paused briefly to smell a white flower at the top of a bush. The unknown fragrance almost reached his nostrils as he watched her take a long sniff. Then she smiled again, as if showing her gratitude for the flower's gift.

He was entranced.

As quick as a blink, she passed through the courtyard and disappeared.

He did not know how long the moment lasted. It must have been as long as it took the orphanage director to respond to his question, for he knew he had repeated the question as soon as the words left his mouth.

The air had become lighter. He could hear his even, relaxed breathing as he came back to his hotel room. The grace, the joy, in the simple twirl of a woman reveling in the feel of the sun on an ordinary day, the memory of that cherished moment had helped unwind the tightness around his chest.

He smiled a thank you to the unknown wood nymph.

Embarrassed at the fanciful name he had given to her, he shook his head, glad no one could hear his thoughts and lock him up for losing his mind.

Earlier, he had halfheartedly hinted to Bingley at returning to the orphanage. He wanted to experience the vision again. No. He would not return to seek her mirage. The magic of her might dissolve into something banal, or worse, something ugly.

He chuckled. His family and Bingley were right to be concerned about him: he was afraid of a shadow. Hearing his own unexpected laughter, he laughed again. He stood and moved toward the window.

Tomorrow, perhaps he'd leave his suite and explore the beach.

CHAPTER 5

❀

Darling

"DR. BENNET, YOU HAVE AN URGENT PHONE CALL FROM AMERICA," the hospital director said.

Heart racing, Elizabeth rushed to the phone in her office.

"Elizabethy, darling!" an accented voice greeted her.

"Arrrgh! Hussein! I thought somebody had died. I ran here."

"You're in a hospital, darling. Somebody is always dying. You shouldn't rush unless you're the one at fault."

"What do you want? And don't tell me it's an emergency because I know it's not." She rolled her eyes, partly in humor and partly in frustration. "And how did you get the hospital director to be your messenger boy?"

"I always go to the top, darling," Dr. Hussein Ahmed said. "You've been ignoring my calls to your cell. Are you still mad at me for voting Republican in the last election?"

"Traitor!"

He gave a long sigh. "Darling, we've been through this before. Your childhood was warped from too many protest marches in Berkeley. The Republican Party made me a rich doctor. How can I not support them?"

"You sold out."

"You could have too if you'd listened to me and not special-ized in nasty microbes. People with fascinating infections rarely can afford to pay their bills, darling."

"What's the point of this nonurgent phone call?"

"I'm coming to your chest of the woods."

"Neck of the woods," she automatically corrected.

"Neck, chest. Who cares?" He laughed. "I'm coming to Vietnam to work at a five-star resort. And I want to treat you and your sister to some fun and relaxation. Shouldn't be much of an expense; you girls are cheap."

"What's the catch?"

"Darling, why do you always think there's a catch in my noble offers?" he said. "But you got me. I have a really good deal on a suite at the Net Thi Phen Resort for a couple of weeks. I can't be there for the first week, give or take a few days, so you'll have the whole place to yourself then. What do you say?"

"And what do I have to do for this privilege?"

"Why are you so suspicious?"

"Because there's always a twist in your offers," she returned.

"All right, I'll confess. I need you to fill in for me as a doctor at the resort next week—yes, next week, you know I tend to do things last minute—treating the VIP foreign guests." Here, his voice lowered. "I'm going to be putting some silicone on a famous up-and-coming Hollywood actress. Can't tell you her name—not ethical—but she was a lead in the movie"—he whispered a name she didn't recognize. When she didn't make any response, he gave a disappointed sigh. "I forget you're clueless about anything remotely pop culture. You don't read gossip magazines. Darling, you'd learn more about life reading the tabloids than you do reading your infectious disease journals, I keep telling you."

"Why should I bail you out? I don't want to treat rich tourists."

"I know it's hard for you to mingle and be nice to the rich and not just make fun of them," he said. "But just a little kissing-ass-service with a smile and you get a free vacation out of it, and help your best friend out here. Darling, a gay best friend adds a lot of cache when you're a single woman."

"Stop promoting yourself." She wrinkled her nose. "It's short notice. I can't take time off from the hospital here."

"It's already done. I shamelessly guilt-tripped the hospital director into clearing your schedule and let you have a little relaxation and pampering. Americans are used to being pampered. We need it, I told him."

"What? You had the audacity—" She stopped, wondering why she was surprised. Hussein did not lack impudence. That, unfortunately, was a big part of why she liked him.

"By the time you leave the resort, I'll turn you into trophy-wife material yet, my sweet."

"Fat chance."

"You're gorgeous, but you don't know that, and that's always been one of your charms." Before she could accuse him of using flattery, he continued, "Not that you couldn't use some help to turn that granola natural beauty into something trendier. Please visit the spa and get waxed or learn to shave properly during the month you're staying at the resort."

"Now it's a whole month. You're covering your ass in case you don't get here at all."

"You found me out. Yes, I'm making contingency plans in case... well, sometimes the silicone leaks, you know, and I need to be here to charm them so they won't sue my pants off," he laughed.

She smiled. It was very hard to stay upset with such a good-humored guy. She impulsively decided to accept his offer and they talked a few more minutes about the details involved. Before he rang off, he again reminded her to make sure to use the spa services to make over herself.

When she walked into their house later that day, she saw her sister bonelessly plopped on the couch.

"Bad day?" Elizabeth said and set her bag down.

Jane sat up. "I just now got off the phone with Aunt Mai. I caved and called her."

"About the gay couple adopting?"

"They're not the ones who are officially adopting, remember?" Jane sighed. "It looks like I won't get the report I want soon enough."

"What did Aunt Mai say?"

"She agreed there's not enough information to let the Hursts have a child. Neither she nor I have difficulty with the idea of the men, if it comes down to it, but we need to look at the situation more carefully."

"Sounds reasonable." Elizabeth poured herself some tea from a pot on the coffee table. "What's your worry?"

"I have to tell the Hursts we need more time and I'm not looking forward to it. I hate to have them feel they've wasted their time and money because of our inefficiency. I feel like I'm failing handling this adoption."

"Listen, the fact that you're stressing about it shows you're not failing the child." Elizabeth put her cup down and rubbed her sister's shoulder. "I say take all the time you need and be as indecisive as you want until you're sure. When you're confident that you can live with the consequences of your decision, that's when you know you've done right for the child."

A wry smile appeared on Jane's face. "Coming from my fearless, quick-to-make-snap-decisions sister, that's saying something."

Elizabeth laughed. "Yes, well, I know I have a tendency to be more impulsive and decisive than wise, but in this case, I think your instinct to go slow is on target."

Jane perked up. "You're right. I'll live with my indecision for now."

"You've been working too hard since we arrived. You need a break. I have news to share." She explained about Hussein's offer. "Knowing Hussein and how he makes his deals, there won't be much for me to do. I want you to come and stay with me there some time and get away from this place."

"I can't take too much time away, but I'll try."

"I have a meeting and a tour with the resort manager after lunch tomorrow to go over details and my duties. How about you come with me and, after my meeting, we'll go check out Merry Bar and say hi to Chau's dad and brothers? She wants to introduce us."

Jane's schedule was full the next day until late afternoon. "I'll meet you at the restaurant for a drink and meet the Lucs though."

"I'll relax at the beach and wait for you." Elizabeth drank the rest of her tea. "Let's go start on dinner. I'm hungry."

Once in the kitchen, Elizabeth gathered the ingredients for their stir-fry while Jane placed a wok on a heated stove.

"Lizzy, this is perfect. The Hursts and the men are staying at the resort. You'll have a chance to observe them and give me your impression."

"If they can all afford to stay there, you shouldn't worry then about them wasting their money waiting for your decision. The nightly rate for a room costs more than what most families here earn in a year." Elizabeth's lips curled. She was a firm believer in not overpaying for a hotel room. *Whish, whish.* She sharpened the blade of the knife against a kitchen stone and winked at her sister. "I'm prepared to face the arrogant Mr. Darcy again."

"Stop! You're making me spill the oil." Jane's shoulders shook with laughter as she drizzled drops of peanut oil onto the heated wok. "I can't believe you had the nerve to threaten him. He seemed so intimidating."

"Ha! It's hard to be intimidated by a guy who faints at the sight of blood."

CHAPTER 6

❀

Water Sprite

A MAN COULD DIE OF BOREDOM TRYING TO RELAX, DARCY DECIDED.

He had no more work. Earlier, he had checked in with Richard and Anne, his cousins and vice presidents at the company's headquarters in New York. He called Georgiana, who was currently in England at their family's old estate in Derbyshire. He even made a few calls about some failing companies he had heard about, to see if they would be worthwhile to acquire. The calls took all of forty minutes.

Perhaps he'd go for another run on the beach if it wasn't too crowded. He carried his teacup to the window. Not too crowded, but certainly more people than earlier. His eyes swept over the figures on the beach.

At the edge of the water, a woman in a white skirt performed a pirouette. She kicked the water and lifted her face to the sun.

He started. Her movement resembled the wood nymph's at the orphanage. Perhaps she had turned into a water sprite today. His lips twitched at the fanciful thoughts.

He went to get his binoculars, a useful aid to detect Bingley's sisters at a distance and avoid wherever they were. The sprite had disappeared by the time he returned. Disappointed, he almost turned away from the window but decided on a quick scan. He sighed with relief when he spotted her sitting against a palm tree, her white skirt now draping on the sand.

A small child approached. She held something in one hand to the child. Darcy raised his binoculars. As the lenses focused, a beautiful, smiling profile filled his view: warm chocolate–colored hair loosely tied in a ribbon at the neck; blowing winds had teased some strands loose to flitter and flirt against a smooth cheek tinged with pink blush. Even at this distance, he could almost see the tilt at the corner of one eye as she laughed with the child.

Her infectious joy traveled across the distance and shared some of its bounty with him. He breathed in deeply, taking in the gift. Involuntarily, his face stretched into a responding smile.

He kept the lens steady and focused on her. "Come on, turn this way."

Alas, she turned toward the ocean instead. The child walked away, having gotten something from the sprite. Darcy continued to watch for a few minutes. She seemed content to sit there, enjoying the ocean breeze.

Before he changed his mind, he left his room.

She had played on the beach too long, Elizabeth realized when she noted the time. She was late meeting Jane and Chau at Merry Bar. She grimaced at the sand clinging to the hem of her now dampened white skirt. Good thing she'd already met with the resort manager before she frolicked in the waves.

When she neared the steps to the side entrance of the resort, voices behind tall hedges reached her.

"Where are you going in such a hurry?" a man's voice sang out.

"Nowhere," a deep male voice answered.

"Then why the hurrying to nowhere?" Laughter could be heard in the first voice.

"Just going to take a look at the beach."

Elizabeth paused in her step at hearing the second speaker again. Deep voice, a somewhat familiar British accent: she wrinkled her brow, trying to place it.

"No headache today?"

"I don't get headaches," the irritated second voice spoke.

"Yes, you do. And they've been getting worse and worse," the first voice insisted.

"I don't want to talk about it."

"Fine, don't talk to me. At least talk to a doctor or somebody. Nobody here knows who you are or what you do. Once we get back, you'll be busy looking for another company to work with and you won't take care of it. You have time here."

"I don't like doctors."

About to move to pass the two men, Elizabeth stopped midstep. The irritated voice was definitely recognizable now: Mr. Darcy. Apparently, a week or so of rest and relaxation hadn't improved Mr. Darcy's mood or manner; Elizabeth was amused. Not up to dealing with an awkward scene, she quietly turned and took a different path to find another entrance to the resort.

Entering Merry Bar, she spotted Chau at the bar. As she made her way toward her friend, she passed a large group of women in elegant dresses and beautifully made-up faces. The women were subtle about it, but the full force of their scrutinizing once-over made Elizabeth feel graceless and gauche in her rumpled clothes and no makeup on her face.

"Your sister was wondering if she should go and search for you."

Chau came from behind the counter. "She thought you were probably playing in the waves and forgot the time."

"I was," Elizabeth admitted, smiling. "I was pretending I was a water sprite."

"My father needs my help at the moment. I'm sorry I can't visit."

"That's okay. I'm sorry I'm late."

"Jane's out in the patio area somewhere. She ran into some people she recognized who invited her to join them for a drink out there a few minutes ago. Come, meet my family first." Chau pulled her toward a group of men behind the bar and introduced them.

Upon hearing that Elizabeth was Mai Gardiner's niece by marriage, and that she would be working at the resort, Mr. Luc immediately assured her he and his sons would watch over her carefully.

"Sorry about that," Chau whispered when she and Elizabeth left the Luc men and headed to the patio. "My dad's protective of you because he knows your aunt Mai."

"I'm touched. Believe me, I'm used to my aunt Mai's relatives back home acting the same way," Elizabeth said.

Chau led her to Jane. Elizabeth's eyes widened when she recognized Mr. Bingley and Mr. Darcy with her sister, along with two other women.

"You found me." Jane smiled and introduced Elizabeth and Chau to the others before Chau left them.

Mr. Bingley smiled at Elizabeth. "So glad to meet you, Elizabeth. Jane told us your family's from Berkeley."

"Yes, born, raised, and educated." From his greeting, she realized he didn't recognize her. Mr. Darcy's penetrating eyes disconcerted her. Glad a table separated them and she didn't have to shake his hand, she turned back to Mr. Bingley. "How do you like Da Nang?"

Mr. Bingley said, "Such a great place. People are so friendly. I love the comfortable clothes they wear. My friend Oanh is going to get me some Vietnamese outfits."

Out of the corner of her eye, Elizabeth noted Mr. Darcy's eyes still focused on her. When she turned to face him directly, he glanced away for a second, then back at her when he thought she wasn't looking.

Miss Bingley said, "If you're going to look stupid, Charles, at least make sure the clothes are new. You don't know what kind of hygienic habits these people have."

Mr. Bingley looked embarrassed. "Caroline, people in Asia took daily baths long before it caught on in Europe."

Miss Bingley's lips curled. "I saw a travel show on TV where they showed these people drinking the same water they bathed in."

Mrs. Hurst added, "We brought our own drinking water."

"We are very careful, aren't we, William?" Miss Bingley turned to Mr. Darcy. "If you're out of yours, I can share mine with you."

Feeling like she was in junior high again, Elizabeth turned to observe his reaction to Miss Bingley's simpering offer. His expression inscrutable, he simply took a sip of his drink and didn't respond.

Jane said, "It's good to be careful if you're not used to conditions here."

"I have no intentions of getting used to conditions here. You're probably used to such conditions. Where did you say you're from? Berkeley, California?" Miss Bingley threw a pointed glance at Elizabeth's hair. "Isn't that where you'd find a lot of long-haired, dirty hippies?"

Catching the pleading message in her sister's eyes, Elizabeth swallowed the retort on her lips. She kept her tone light. "Just like Vietnam, Berkeley is not everyone's cup of tea."

Only a sniff and a slight upturn of the nose from Miss Bingley answered Elizabeth's attempt at politeness. Irritated now, she stared at Miss Bingley while she slowly raised her hand and scratched her head, then, after a few seconds, her sides. While she followed Mr. Bingley's telling of his adventure in the market with an unwashed fruit, she kept scratching, alternating between her hair and her sides.

No reaction from Miss Bingley, but Mr. Darcy slid his chair back.

Encouraged at unsettling him, Elizabeth began to scratch more vigorously until a kick under the table from Jane stopped her antics.

Mr. Darcy said to Elizabeth, "Were you out on the beach earlier?"

Surprised at the unexpected question, Elizabeth blushed and wondered if he'd seen her childish romping. "Yes."

A pointed glance at Elizabeth's skirt came from Miss Bingley. "I don't like the beach. All that sand getting into your hair and clothes, making you look stupid."

Elizabeth bit her cheeks and suppressed the urge to flick her skirt and fling a few grains in the woman's face.

"Sometimes, one can discover an unexpected, beautiful treasure on the beach," Mr. Darcy said. Holding Elizabeth's gaze, he took a small sip of his drink.

Flustered at the intense blueness of his eyes, she looked down at a plate of fruit on the table.

Miss Bingley said, "How do you know that girl Chau?"

"We work together," Elizabeth answered.

Miss Bingley turned and shared an amused glance with her sister.

With a barely concealed snicker, Mrs. Hurst said, "The tips and compensations must be quite attractive working here."

"I do get compensated obscenely well for asking people to undress"—Elizabeth's temper snapped at the sisters' bitchy attitude—"and get them to tell me secrets they wouldn't dream of revealing to their nearest and dearest—"

She was interrupted mid-sentence by Mr. Darcy's standing up. He mumbled he was expecting a phone call and abruptly left.

Elizabeth turned back to the sisters and continued, "Would you two like to make an appointment? I'd be happy to dust up what little psychiatry I know."

"You're Dr. Bennet." Mr. Bingley's eyes widened and he slapped his forehead. "Of course, the same last name. I've been trying to figure out why your voice sounds familiar. I'm sorry I didn't recognize you."

"No problem," Elizabeth said, embarrassed she'd lost her temper with his sisters. "I was masked and covered in surgical scrubs."

Jane explained to the Bingley sisters. "Elizabeth works with Dr. Chau Luc at the hospital. Though, for the next couple of weeks, my sister's going to be the in-house doctor here at the resort."

Miss Bingley studied her nails.

In a bored voice, and while looking around the patio area, Mrs. Hurst said, "Interesting."

A moment of uncomfortable silence reigned before a red-faced Mr. Bingley started a conversation with Jane about the famous snorkeling excursions at the resort.

Miss Bingley interrupted and told her brother to ask Mr. Darcy to arrange a shopping trip for them to Hong Kong while they wait for the adoption to be finalized. She turned to her sister. "Louisa, what time is my massage appointment?"

With that hint, Elizabeth and Jane said good-bye and left them.

~᷍~

Jane and Elizabeth were almost out of the resort when Mr. Bingley caught up with them. With an awkward smile, he apologized for his sisters' behavior. He gave some convoluted explanation for their rudeness, ending with, "Caroline gets possessive with Darcy when there are other women about, especially beautiful ones. She can't accept he'd never be interested in her."

Elizabeth smiled at him. She couldn't blame him for having bitchy sisters. "Please don't worry about it."

Mr. Bingley said, "I'm sorry Darcy left without saying good-bye. It must have been a very important call that he just then remembered. He's in between companies and he's anxious to hear about some new one."

Jane said, "I hope he gets good news with the phone call."

Mr. Bingley turned to her. "He can't relax unless he's working. He feels useless otherwise."

Jane nodded. "Many people feel like that."

"I had to drag him here to Vietnam, to give him a chance to regroup and relax without worrying about work and finances and all that. I told him we need him to make sure everything is fine with the adoption. He's very responsible, you see…" He trailed off and looked self-conscious, as if he had said more than he had intended.

Elizabeth bit her lip. Poor Mr. Darcy! Unemployed and stressed about it. And he and Mr. Bingley wanted to become parents soon too. Jane did say Mr. Darcy seemed to be the responsible one at the interview. For a proud man like him, it must be quite humiliating to act as a personal assistant for the Bingley family, making travel arrangements for shopping trips and so forth. "Please tell Mr. Darcy I'm very sorry for my unprofessional conduct that day at the hospital."

"Don't worry about Darcy," Mr. Bingley said. "I know he feels badly about his behavior. He usually has better manners, but it was a rough day for him, especially with my antics."

"Still, I didn't act as a doctor should," Elizabeth admitted.

"He gets these terrible headaches, and I keep telling him he needs to see a doctor, but he won't. He's been under a lot of stress and, well, he doesn't do well with doctors and hospitals. Nothing personal."

"None taken," Elizabeth assured him.

CHAPTER 7

❁

Charles Bingley Is a Lucky Whore

"Stop hiding in your room," Bingley said to Darcy. "You're coming to the club tonight. Don't shake your head at me. When was the last time you've stepped out of your room?"

Darcy said, "I'm not hiding. I don't feel like socializing lately."

"Fine, you're not hiding, you're hibernating. And when have you ever felt like socializing?" Bingley held up his hand when Darcy opened his mouth. "Not another word. My family is in Hong Kong shopping. You're safe to leave your room. Jane Bennet and her sister are at Merry Bar—"

"I'm not interested in talking with some girl working as an escort."

"An escort?" Bingley's eyes widened. "*That's* why you left abruptly yesterday. I had to make excuses for your rudeness."

Darcy moved away. "I was expecting an important phone call."

"You're such an idiot." Bingley followed. "If you'd stayed to hear the rest of what Elizabeth had said, you'd have known she's a doctor."

Darcy felt like smiling. He turned away to hide his relief from Bingley. His wood nymph, his fantasy water sprite, was not an escort.

"She was the American doctor who treated me in the hospital, you prick! The one you acted the bloody arse with."

Damn. Damn. Damn. Of course, the green eyes. "I only got a brief glimpse of her eyes through her protective eyewear. How could I have recognized her? We weren't properly introduced at the time."

"Of course you weren't properly introduced. You barged in, insulted her, threw your CEO weight around, disrupted her work on her patient in the next bed, and you only got a glimpse of her eyes because you fainted." As the last words left Bingley's lips, his irritation disappeared and he laughed.

Darcy's lips twitched. Though he felt foolish, even he had to admit it was funny. He coughed and kept his voice casual. "You mentioned Miss Bennet and uh... her sister are in the club?"

"I ran into Jane in the lobby and she mentioned she was going to be in Merry Bar with her sister. There's dancing tonight." Bingley propelled Darcy toward the door. "You don't have to dance, just stand there and hold up a pillar or two, but I want you out of this room."

Darcy scanned the crowded nightclub for a pair of green eyes.

Bingley elbowed him. "Doesn't this remind you of the good old days when you and I were regulars at all the happening clubs around the world? Remember when the tabloids caught you fondling that Victoria's Secret lingerie model dressed like an angel? How time flies. You've gotten old and staid in just ten years. Now, you're hiding in your room for days, avoiding all us earthlings, and I had to forcibly drag you out for some nightlife..."

Darcy spotted her. She was standing next to her sister at the north end of the room.

"...wings." Bingley jabbed him again. "Are you listening to me?"

Darcy nodded. "She's entrancing."

"What? Who's entrancing?"

Some girl grabbed Bingley and pulled him on to the dance floor. Another tried to grab Darcy but he declined and walked away. He stayed at a distance, far enough out of the dangerous dancing zone but close enough to keep his gaze on his enchantress.

His eyes swept over the soft curves of *her*. He allowed his imagination to wander.

Holding on to her hips, he swayed in rhythm to her body dancing. His lips tasted the softness of that tantalizing spot behind her ear. Pressing his face against her hair, he breathed in her scent. His hardness pushed against her…

"There you are. I'm surprised you're still here," Bingley rudely interrupted in the middle of Darcy's fantasy. "Jane and Elizabeth are over there. I want to go say hi and see if one of them wants to dance. Join me? You can try to redeem your previous bad manners."

Trying to appear uninterested, Darcy shrugged and stepped away from the pillar. Moments later, standing in front of his wood nymph, he could not find his tongue. Instead, while she chatted with her sister and his friend, he stared at her.

Framed by dark wavy hair, the long strands barely contained by the tie at the back, her perfect, oval-shaped face showed smooth, flawless skin, a straight impertinent nose, and a heart-shaped pair of pink, tantalizingly full lips.

Bingley asked Jane to dance and they went off.

An amused gleam in her eyes, Elizabeth seemed to be waiting for Darcy to say something.

He opened his mouth, wanting to ask her to dance, then remembered his fantasy earlier. Afraid that he would forget himself and fondle her as he did in his fantasy, he closed his mouth without speaking.

She turned toward the dance floor and moved her body to the music.

He stole a glance at her swaying backside and felt himself hardening again at the thought of how that softness would feel against him. Embarrassed, he angled his body to face away from her.

"Come, Mr. Darcy. We must pretend to have some sort of conversation." She smiled when he turned back to her. "I shall start. People seem to enjoy dancing to the music. Now it's your turn to say something equally inane."

"I don't have anything inane to say." Immediately, he winced at how lame that had sounded.

"You did just fine right there," she encouraged him. "Keep going. Say something else obvious, like how crowded it is tonight."

His lips quivered.

"Miracle. Is that almost a smile on your face, Mr. Darcy?" She clapped. "It is."

At the gleeful grin on her face, he smiled.

"Be still my heart. Mr. Darcy has dimples when he smiles." Her tone turned mock serious. "Okay, I had promised myself I wouldn't tease you. Now, help me behave. We'll both stand here and be ourselves: unsocial, uncommunicative, and unconnected. You take that side of the pillar and I'll take this side."

Bingley and her sister returned. Jane wanted to leave, as she had an early morning appointment. Elizabeth nodded.

The intoxicating fragrance of gardenia wafted past Darcy as a pair of green eyes leaned close to deliver a parting shot. "I'm going home to practice on oratorical skills. You do the same. When we meet next, we'll exchange some more witty repartee, okay?"

With that, she grabbed her sister's arm and they moved through the throng of dancers. His eyes tracked her full, undulating hips walking away from him, his senses stirred and shaken. Elizabeth

Bennet definitely intrigued him. It had been a long time, if ever, since he had felt this bewitched by a woman.

He scowled. Temporary pure lust, that was all. He'd get over it soon, like tomorrow.

—⁓—

Darcy stood in front of a door with his right hand raised to knock. He managed to stop his knuckles from touching the wood by a mere inch before he brought his fist to his mouth instead. Stepping back, he pivoted and determinedly walked away.

Bingley had been nagging at him to get himself treated for the occasional pain in his head. He did not suffer from headaches. He did not want to be told he was depressed. He did not need medicines—mood-altering medicines. He would not relinquish control of himself no matter how much his head hurt at times.

He made it past the corner before his feet dragged to a stop. He sank against a wall, defeated.

Who was he fooling? This wasn't about his headaches. He wanted to see her. His wood nymph. His water sprite. His infatuation.

Since she had gotten him to smile at the club that night, he could not get that teasing voice, those swaying hips, that seductive gardenia scent out of his mind.

—⁓—

Elizabeth heard the knock the moment she realized her next patient was quite late. She glanced at the initials on the appointment schedule the concierge had given her earlier: *F.D.* To her surprise, Mr. Darcy stood on the other side of the door.

"Hello." She wondered what he wanted. He couldn't be her patient. His first name was William. Looking up at his handsome face, she mourned womankind's loss that he batted for the other team. "May I help you?"

"Uh… Hello. How are you? Is your sister well?"

"I'm fine and Jane's fine. She's at the orphanage right now. You could call her there. I'm expecting a patient any minute now." She wondered if F.D. had gotten lost. She peered down the empty hallway.

"Uh… I'm here to see you."

Poor guy. He must be anxious about the adoption. She decided she could spare him a few minutes. "Come in. Let me call the front desk and make sure my patient didn't cancel or lose his or her way."

"I'm your patient."

"Oh. I see." She took a deep breath, inhaling a whiff of his scent—woods and something else she couldn't place. She shook her head to compose herself and put on her doctor hat. "How may I help you, Mr. Darcy?"

"Bingley wants me to see a doctor."

He looked so miserable at the idea she felt for him. Trying to appear nonthreatening, she pointed him to a chair and sat. "What worries him in particular about your health?"

"He thinks I get headaches."

At the tone of denial in his voice, she bit her lip to stop herself from smiling. "Do you have any symptoms that gave your partner such an idea?"

He looked mildly perplexed for a brief second. "No. I do not."

She waited for him to expand his answer.

Blue eyes gazed calmly back at her.

She offered, "People with headaches experience a sensation of tightness around or in their head. Sometimes a pounding, thumping, on one side of the head, or on both sides. Or the pain can be in the forehead, around the eyes, or the back of the head. Any of this sounds familiar?"

"No."

"I want to make sure, if you are having these headaches, that they're not something new and not increasing in intensity or frequency, and they're not worse first thing in the morning and get better during the day. You're not vomiting, especially in the mornings? You're not experiencing any muscle weakness, numbness?"

"No."

She wondered if the man knew another word. "Have you any behavioral changes recently that perhaps may be of concern to you or to your family and friends?"

"No." His jaws clenched visibly and she realized she had struck a nerve.

She kept her tone mild. "I'm trying to ascertain your symptoms, Mr. Darcy, to make a diagnosis. Your partner obviously noticed something to be worried. You're here because of his concern. To set his mind and yours at ease, I need to ask these questions."

The blue in his eyes became icy. "There's nothing wrong with me."

Then why the hell are you here, wasting my time? She swallowed the retort and decided on the scare tactics. "If you're not concerned about your headaches, I won't be either. But as a physician, whenever I hear the term headaches, I worry about the possibility of a brain tumor."

A twinge of guilt hit her when his eyes widened. A hiss of a quick breath escaped from him. After a minute, though, he was back to staring impassively at her.

He was certainly a tough one. She sighed. "Look, Mr. Darcy, I know you really don't want to be here. You're not answering my questions or cooperating, which makes it very hard for me to prove there's nothing wrong with you. I want a chance to say, 'You are right, sir. You have no defects!'"

His eyes gave a faint imitation of a blink.

She grinned at him. "You're going to have to pay me for my time anyway, you might as well make me work for it. Besides, I thought I told you to practice your oratorical skills. A string of no's does not count as exchanging witty repartee."

His expression softened. With a reluctant twitch to his lips, he responded to the overture. "All right, Dr. Bennet. I know you have to do your job. I'll try to cooperate as much as possible."

After this, he was less challenging, though no less of a challenge and only minimally more cooperative. Nevertheless, he answered enough of her questions that she was reassured he did not have a brain tumor, which was her main concern.

When she explained to him that she needed to examine him next, he stiffened and looked as if she'd suggested a root canal on the spot.

"You don't need to undress. I only need your shoes and socks off for me to do a brief exam." To ease his discomfort, she teased, "I don't have a scalpel here. You'll just have to suffer a few pinpricks to see if your senses are alive and intact. I promise not to draw"—she paused, leaned forward, and spelled—"B-L-O-O-D."

Humor seemed to work with him; for the second time, he fully smiled at her, revealing dimples again. Her mouth parched. She sucked her tongue and wetted her lips. *He really is a handsome devil. What a waste to…* She had to stop thinking like that. *Life is not fair,* she silently lamented instead.

She quickly but thoroughly performed the neurological exam. Though obviously uncomfortable with it, he cooperated. They were both glad when the physical exam was over.

When told everything seemed normal, he gave her a wry smile. "I did tell Bingley I don't get headaches."

"No, you only give them, I'm sure," she shot back and felt gratified at his chuckling.

He bent to pick up his shoes. She had to look away to even out her breathing. To distract herself, she reached down to gather up her tools from a low stool. When she straightened, he was standing motionless, staring at her with one shoe in his hand. Wondering at the intense expression in his eyes, she cleared her throat and told him she was ready to give him her professional opinion.

He shook his head slightly as if to bring his mind back from wherever it had gone.

"It's my opinion you suffer from recurrent migraines, likely precipitated by stress." She discussed the list of possible medicines she could prescribe for him.

His response was emphatic. "No. I don't need any."

"Somehow it doesn't surprise me you'd say that. In your case, you'd be fine with strong, over-the-counter painkillers." She gave him some additional recommendations on what he could do to treat his migraines should they worsen, though she voiced her suspicion he'd do nothing.

"Yes, you're right about that," he agreed, his eyes smiling warmly at her. "I don't have a brain tumor?"

She tried not to think of how attractive his mouth appeared when the corners were lifted with humor. "Given the number of years you've had the headaches—sorry, since Mr. Bingley thought you had the headaches—I doubt it. You'll have to give another reason for your evil ways."

He laughed out loud, looking remarkably different from the man who had entered the room. Flustered, she coughed and briefly turned away to compose herself before she concluded the visit. On his way out the door, he paused. "I'm sorry for being difficult earlier… today and well, that day at the hospital. I'm afraid I have some anger toward the medical profession."

Her heart tugged at the brief glimpse of sadness she saw in his eyes. A moment later, his face was an imperturbable mask. Gently, she tried to ease the moment with humor again. "I don't blame you for feeling that way if you had some bad experiences. Luckily, we're done for now and you're safe from any unprofessional conduct on my part."

He laughed again.

Somehow, making Mr. Darcy laugh was addictive. She teased, "I know what your defect is, Mr. Darcy. You don't laugh at yourself enough."

"And yours"—his eyes twinkled—"is laughing too much at me for precisely that particular defect." With that, he finally left.

She closed the door and leaned her back against it so she wouldn't be tempted to follow him down the hall. The warm sound of Mr. Darcy's rich laughter had made her toes curl. "Charles Bingley is a lucky whore!"

CHAPTER 8

❀

Losing My Marbles

CROUCHED LOW TO OBSERVE A SMALL CRAB CRAWLING ON THE WET sand, Elizabeth saw the pair of running shoes a split second before she heard the deep male voice.

"Hello, Dr. Bennet."

Oh my! Mr. Darcy stood four feet away, practically undressed in a maroon and gray Harvard T-shirt and black running shorts, compared to his usual slacks and buttoned shirts.

He said, "I didn't mean to startle you."

"I'm not startled. Are you running? Jane and I are taking advantage of the beautiful sand and sun of China Beach. She's over there reading on the lounge chair. I can never sit still, though. I decided to explore. Oh, and call me Elizabeth, please. I don't have my white coat on, Mr. Darcy." Out of breath from babbling too fast, she pointed to her own white T-shirt with her alma mater's Cal logo on it.

"Only if you'll call me William."

"What's the *F* in F.D. for?"

A slight tinge appeared on his cheeks.

Why, he's shy. The thought delighted her. "Fine, don't tell me. Though I have to admit now that, had I known your first initial was *F* when I first saw you at the hospital, your ears would have burned something fierce that day hearing some four-letter words." When he laughed, not wanting the dimples to disappear, she continued, "I wouldn't want to be called Freddy or Frankie either."

"Almost as bad. It's Fitzwilliam, my mother's maiden name."

"Do you run often?" How lame. Hadn't she already asked him about running? She was losing her marbles around the man.

"Every morning if I can. You're not usually out this early, Elizabeth."

She liked the sound of her name from his mouth. A soft breeze tousled his hair. When the wind blew, she smelled the musky, spicy woods scent mixed with the sea air in his sweat. She dug her bare feet into the wet sand and let the coolness of the water seep through her toes. *I need to chill down from Mr. Hottie here.* "No, I haven't been able to, though it's my favorite time of day, getting up with the sun."

"Have you got to work today? Have you got patients scheduled?"

"You mean do I have any men on my schedule who are going to give me a hard time?" she asked, amused to see a deeper flush on his neck.

"You see quite a few men? I mean male patients?"

She allowed herself a regretful sigh. Of course, he would ask only about the men. "I see whoever wants an appointment. But now that you mention it, I seem to be treating more men than women here. Most of the complaints are rather minor except for one gentleman who wasted my time with his nonexistent headaches."

As she'd hoped, he laughed. "You're busy today, then?"

"No. It's my day off."

He smiled. "If you don't have any set plans, Bingley and I are thinking of going snorkeling. Perhaps you and your sister could join us?"

She pondered the invitation. That sounded fun. It shouldn't cost too much with her employee discount. Oops. One problem.

"We'll feed you also, afterwards. Or perhaps we could bring a snack along for you, since it might be a few hours." He gave her a sideways glance. "Though, I'm sure you would never get cranky and threaten anyone when you happen to miss a meal or two."

Pleased he had teased her, she laughed. "No, it's not that. I don't know how to swim. It's embarrassing, but I've never learned. I'm actually afraid of the water. Very afraid."

"Oh? I'm sorry."

Touched at the concern in his voice, she revealed, "A bad experience. Teenage lifeguard threw me in the pool when I was three as a way to teach me to swim."

"We could do something else?"

"No. I'll come along and enjoy myself on the boat while you guys do the underwater thing. This is perfect! I want Jane to do some snorkeling but she hasn't wanted to go alone."

"Great, I shall make arrangements." He gave her a wide smile.

She pressed the tip of her tongue to the back of her teeth at seeing his dimples again and his laugh lines. "Super."

She gave him her room number and they agreed to meet once he had the details worked out. They then parted.

After a couple steps, he turned back. "Don't worry, Elizabeth, about not knowing how to swim. I'll make sure that you'll be safe."

———— ∞ ————

Exiting through the opened door, Darcy nodded to the smiling doorman and wondered if the man had noticed the eager anticipation in his gait. He had arranged for a car to take Elizabeth and him on a short sightseeing trip. Since their snorkeling excursion a few days ago, whenever they could, they spent time together. With her schedule completely free of patients, and after discovering he hadn't been out of the resort much, she was taking him to the Marble Mountains that day.

"Cyclo?"

Darcy paused.

A small Vietnamese man smiled at him. He pointed to the cyclo behind him and said something Darcy couldn't understand.

"No, No. I'm waiting for my friend."

The man began to talk in a conversational manner.

Darcy couldn't decipher a word the man spoke. He wondered how to walk away politely. Spotting Elizabeth at a distance, he breathed a sigh of relief.

"Sorry to keep you waiting." Elizabeth reached them, smiled at Darcy, and turned toward the cyclo driver. "Hello. I'm Lizzy. Are you busy today with many rides?" The driver responded and Elizabeth answered, "We go to Marble Mountain. Too far for cyclo."

The cyclo driver spoke again and pointed at the ocean.

"Enjoy the beach. It's beautiful." Elizabeth said good-bye.

Once they were settled in the backseat of a taxi and had given the driver their destination, Darcy asked, "How did you under-stand what he said?"

"What do you mean? He was speaking in English."

Distracted by the view behind her of a passing bicycle carrying tied-up pigs, he didn't reply for a moment before he confessed, with some embarrassment, "I had a hard time."

"I'm used to my aunt Mai's relatives back home. I learned to keep it simple. They don't have verb tenses or plurals. You don't say 'He walks' but 'he walk.' You don't say 'I went to the market yesterday' but 'I go market yesterday.' 'Two apples' becomes 'two apple'—details like that."

"You're amazing." He felt too shy to add she also fascinated him because she, naturally at ease in talking to people and with such simple grace, was the opposite of him. "Most of us arrogantly expect people to speak English clearly."

She patted his arm. "You're not arrogant."

He chuckled. "We both know very well that's not true. But I'm glad you don't hold a grudge."

"In English, we use our tongue and our lips when we talk. Vietnamese is a tonal language, where the sounds come from the throat with each breath. That's why sounds like *sh* or *ch* are difficult. 'Show' becomes 'sew,' and 'pushy' becomes…"

It took him a long moment before his mind supplied the word. His mouth opened.

She laughed. "You should see your face now."

"You think it's funny to embarrass me, huh? Well, let's see if you still think it's funny if I do this." He tried to tickle her. She laughed harder and squirmed.

He suddenly became aware of how close her soft, feminine body was to his. Her thigh pressed against his. Her gardenia scent announced its seductive presence. His breathing slowed. She stilled, as if she had also become aware of their nearness. The green in her eyes turned smoky and her lips parted slightly.

He bent his head…

Her face turned away at the last moment.

Mortified, he pulled back. He almost kissed her in broad daylight in the back of a car, with the taxi driver not two feet away, in the middle of a crowded city. He cleared his throat. "Elizabeth, I'm sorry—"

"For overreacting to a crude word I didn't even say by tickling me?" Her voice was its usual lighthearted tone. "I'll get you back, my sweet, when you least expect it."

Glad she had easily smoothed the awkward moment, he followed her lead and started asking about the Marble Mountains.

She instantly became the tour guide and informed him the five summits that made up the Marble Mountains were named for the five elements: earth, water, metal, fire, and wood. "There are caverns we can explore and the mountains are really marble," she assured him when they arrived at the site. "Come on, you can touch and see for yourself."

He didn't like cramped space, but he couldn't let her disappear into the caverns without him.

Two Australian women kept bumping into him. Annoyed they kept him separated from Elizabeth during one narrow passage, he gave them his intimidating face to make them disappear.

On one mountain, they explored caves containing Buddhist relics, pagodas, and temples. They climbed the steep, narrow chimney caves to reach the summit, from which they had a panoramic view of the resort on China Beach and the old airbase. She said, "During the Vietnam War, the communist Vietnamese used the caves as hospitals. Our American forces didn't know how close the enemy was."

Later, when she admired a jade bracelet, he wanted to buy it for her. She argued about his paying for it and insisted that he should save his money. He told her to hush and that he could afford the few dollars it actually cost without suffering financial hardship.

She kissed him on the cheek. "Thank you."

He wanted to turn his face and press his lips to hers, but remembering her reaction in the car earlier, he restrained himself. He reached for her hand instead.

She gently removed her hand from his grasp. "Public displays of affection are frowned upon here. I shouldn't have even kissed you earlier on the cheek. I'd forgotten. Sorry."

"No problem." He smiled, happy she had forgotten the rules and had kissed him impulsively.

"If we were the same sex, we could hold hands and even share a hotel bed, but touching or kissing between a man and a woman is considered impolite, even if they're married."

"You mean I can hold Bingley's hand in public or even share a bed with him in a room at any hotel here, but not with you or any woman I'm not married to?"

Instead of sharing his amusement as he'd expected, a strange expression crossed her face.

The rest of their time together that day, he found it difficult to recapture their earlier ease with each other. He couldn't figure out why or what he had said to have changed the tone of their interaction.

When they parted, however, she seemed to have recovered from what had bothered her and was back to her usual teasing self as she bid him good-bye.

CHAPTER 9

❁

All Mixed Up

"How was your outing with William?" Jane sat down next to her sister on the hotel bed.

Elizabeth's eyes moved from staring at the ceiling. "Great! Though, just like a little boy, he complained and pouted the whole time that he was too tall to be cramped into caves. I snapped a photo of him next to the large, marble Buddha statue to show him how small and insignificant he was next to a deity."

Jane smiled, astounded at the description Elizabeth painted of the serious man Jane had met. He must show a different side in private with her sister. "I can't believe you guys are tourist buddies now. He even got you to snorkel. You never go into the water without panicking."

"It wasn't bad with a life vest, and William holding on to me."

"He's rather handsome." Jane glanced at her sister. "I noticed he gets a lot of interested looks from women."

"They're wasting their time. Today, two very attractive, flirty Australian girls were practically falling all over him, but he wasn't interested."

"Perhaps he's not showing interest in these women because he's—"

"Because he's committed to Charles. They're adopting a baby together."

"I might be wrong about that. We've spent a lot of time with them lately, and I've yet to hear either of them make a comment about the adoption." Jane chose her next words carefully. "I'm also not certain they are together."

"Of course they are. They're not talking about the adoption to us because they don't want to take advantage of you."

"What makes you think they're more than friends?"

"I told you, the way William acted that day in the hospital. He was so upset Charles wasn't getting treated promptly. William paid the bills and everything. Charles told the nurse to give William the discharge instructions because William would make sure they would be followed. That's partner behavior."

"I take care of your finances for you, pay your bills and your school loans," Jane said. Though very frugal, her sister was notoriously terrible at organizing her finances, having no head for business or money. "I make sure you eat healthy, get enough sleep. When you get sick, I worry."

"We're sisters. Two guys who are friends wouldn't act so nurturing. They'd just say, 'Hey, man, sorry you got sick. Wanna beer?'" Elizabeth grabbed a pillow. "I don't know why, but all the nice guys I meet turn out to be gay."

"I don't think that all the nice men you meet are gay; just the ones you let get close to you."

Elizabeth's eyes met hers briefly before glancing away. "Perhaps."

Whatever William Darcy's true sexual orientation was, Jane was certain she hadn't misread the gleam of male admiration in his eyes whenever he looked at Elizabeth, nor the sexual tension between him and her sister. Bluntly, Jane probed, "Are you attracted to William?"

Elizabeth hugged her pillow tight. "You know my track record. As usual, here I am again."

Elizabeth's dating life had been rather nonexistent in the past few years, but now Jane wondered if there was some other reason besides the demands of her sister's career. "I know it's the family joke, but tell me, why do you have such a record? The three boyfriends you had all came out, and yet you never seemed upset about it."

"I didn't plan for them to change teams, but I'm glad they're happy. They were all nice guys. Hussein is still a very good friend."

"What about other guys? The ones who never made it past the first or second date?"

"Probably because they wanted to move faster than I liked." Elizabeth pressed her face into her pillow.

Jane pulled the pillow away. "How fast?"

"I've never done it," Elizabeth whispered with red cheeks then grabbed the pillow back and hid her face again.

Jane bit her lip to hide a smile. "There's nothing wrong with being a virgin. Perhaps at your age it's rare, but not unexpected."

"I'm a rare breed: a virgin at twenty-eight."

Jane rubbed her sister's back. "You'll meet the right guy and it will be very special. Actually, I'm rather envious that you still have that to look forward to."

"Please, don't be. I'm rather embarrassed I'm the oldest virgin in the family." Elizabeth lifted her face. "I'm not sure about Lydia, but I know Mary and Kitty aren't. They asked me to write them prescriptions for birth control."

"Considering some of the explicit questions you ask your patients about their sexual histories," Jane chuckled, "they'd die if they knew they were answering and getting advice from a virgin."

"I don't usually ask for a play-by-play, you know," Elizabeth said. "About William, I have these thoughts about him and these urges that aren't... well, I shouldn't."

"Why not? There's nothing wrong with feeling that way about a man, especially a handsome and sexy guy like William Darcy."

Elizabeth leaned eagerly toward Jane. "He makes you feel that way too? It's not just me?"

"I suspect Mr. Darcy makes a lot of women and men feel that way. Though, I wouldn't say he's made as big of an impression on me as he obviously has on you."

"You don't have the urge to weave your fingers in his hair? Run your hands down his bare legs? Or drown in his dimples?"

"Uh… no." Jane coughed, amused. Her sister had it bad.

<hr />

Elizabeth woke up early the next morning. Moving quietly to not wake Jane, she made her way to the tiny balcony overlooking a garden. She wished her room had an ocean view. It would comfort her to face a vast body of water and be reminded she was but an insignificant thing in this universe.

Her thoughts turned to William, probably running now. She pictured him, hair ruffled from the wind, Harvard T-shirt stained dark with sweat, and strong, muscular, tanned legs moving rapidly below his black running shorts. She resisted the urge to make her way to the beach on the offhand chance of catching a glimpse of him.

Was her sister right in her comment last night? Did Elizabeth only let "safe" men get close to her?

Unbidden, an old memory of herself at sixteen surged forth. Her stomach tightened. She'd graduated from high school early, but looking back, she saw now that she was too young, too naive, too inexperienced about life to have begun college at sixteen.

She had answered the ad that first year, when she was first

interested in archeology. The professor needed a student assistant to catalog his collection of artifacts, and there was the hint of possibly accompanying his field team out on an archeological dig. It was this hint of travel that made her take the job.

She never saw it coming. No, that wasn't quite true. There were signs, but she didn't know how to read them. She had dismissed her unease.

Until that one day, when he surprised her. Luckily, nothing happened. Hearing the sound of her jeans being unzipped had snapped her out of her shock. Repulsed at being the object of the old man's desire, she had fought him off and ran. He didn't follow. For a long while afterward, she had recurrent nightmares of fleeing.

Since then, she had been shying away from being intimate with men. Dating safe men had been a shield. Men like Hussein were definite shields. Though she loved Hussein's *joie de vivre* and his absurd sense of humor, she was never physically attracted to him.

William, she smiled wryly, couldn't really be accused of having *joie de vivre* or an absurd sense of humor. No, he was rather serious and solemn and way too uptight about everything. Yet, something about him magnetized her. She had never felt so attracted to anyone before.

William must have sensed her attraction for him. That almost kiss in the car on the way to the Marble Mountains—she had stopped him. But she had wanted it. She had wanted that kiss so badly she could almost taste the wanting this moment.

She straightened and shook her head. No. She would not come between him and his partner.

The wisest thing would be to stay away from the temptation of William Darcy, she decided.

CHAPTER 10

❀

Stirring the Poo Pot

"Are you sure there's no message for me?" Darcy said into the phone. Receiving the negative reply again, for the third time that day, he thanked the operator and rang off. He sat back, disappointed. Elizabeth hadn't been at the resort the last two days.

"Bloody hell," he muttered, "I'm acting like I've never been with a woman before."

Surely there were other women he dated who had made him feel this besotted?

After a few long, fruitless minutes, to his chagrin, he couldn't come up with a name. He could not recall the beginnings or endings with any one significant woman. Had he always been that disengaged? That shallow?

He shrugged. That was the past. That was before he met Elizabeth. She definitely engaged him. Deeply. Something about her stirred an unfamiliar yearning in him to connect with another. In every way.

He leaned back against the chair and closed his eyes.

A pair of laughing green eyes greeted him. His fingers weaved through long strands of chestnut waves, stopped atop her soft shoulders, and slid along the smoothness of her back. She lifted her face. He tasted her lips, filling himself with her sweet joy. His hands moved to the breasts rubbing against him. He unbuttoned her shirt. Delicious pink tips on full-bodied, sweet softness awaited. Breathing hard, tongue thrusting forward in anticipation of tasting, he…

Ring! His body jerked. Disoriented, his brain took a few seconds before registering the ringing of his cell phone.

"Hey, Cuz. What's up?" an annoyingly cheerful voice said on the other end.

Irritated, Darcy barked, "Don't call me that. What do you want?"

"Oh ho! I can see you're definitely not getting it up, otherwise you wouldn't sound frustrated."

"Are you calling to be annoying or do you have a reason?"

"Just checking on you, making sure you're not sitting alone in your room working or jerking yourself off."

Pissed that his cousin was more accurate than he would ever guess, Darcy lost it. "Fuck off!"

―⁓―

On the other side of the world, Richard delighted in his quick success. Nothing else made him feel as cheerful as provoking his uptight cousin into losing his composure. "I always do—with company. You need to do that. Not alone, though. They have wonderful girls there."

"You're an arse, Richard."

"You can get some of that from those girls. They know how to take care of big guys like you."

"Do you have any idea how many disgusting diseases you can get?" Darcy said. "I hope you've outgrown your penchant for visiting red-light districts when you travel. The thought of dipping into a well-used, common inkpot for a quick fuck is so bloody abhorrent."

Richard grinned. The last and only time he had been in such a place was years ago, but he liked to taunt his fastidious cousin with fabricated tales of more recent visits. "So double condom it. You can't go through life so fastidious all the time, Darce. You've got to get a smudge of dirt now and then on your little guy."

"I am not interested in getting dirty, and definitely never with a bar-girl. And my guy is not little."

"Well, big guy, roll in the mud with two or more at a time."

"Why are you so concerned with my dick?"

"Someone has got to show some interest."

"Like I said, Richard, fuck off."

Hearing the uncharacteristic curse word again, Richard decided he had teased his cousin enough. "You're starting to repeat yourself. I'll back off." In a milder tone now, he continued, "Seriously, Darce, I wanted to see how you're doing. You've had a few rough years. I worry you're going to break sooner or later if you don't let some sunshine in your life."

"I'm fine."

"How're the headaches?"

"Not too bad anymore."

Surprised at not hearing the usual denial, Richard lifted his brows. "Are they gone? You're not sitting in a darkened room anymore, whimpering?"

"I never whimper. The headaches are just simple migraines, nothing to worry about."

"Yeah, right. Like you've had a doctor tell you that!"

"She did say that."

Unbelievable. His cousin saw a doctor? Wait, *she*? Richard

rubbed his chin, thinking fast. "Is she sure about that? One never knows exactly what kind of training those doctors received over there and how competent they are."

"You arse! She's here because she's volunteering. She's brilliant. She could get any job anywhere she wanted."

Richard bit his knuckles to keep from laughing. "Her specialty is headaches?"

"No, infectious diseases."

Richard's mouth dropped. His germ-phobic cousin smitten with an infectious disease doctor? God did have a sense of humor. Richard kept his voice casual. "She must be a geek, studying something like that."

"She's not a geek. She's beautiful and... Shit!" Darcy swore.

Richard laughed. The gig was up. Darcy was onto him. "Beautiful and smart, eh? Perhaps I'll fly down and have her take a peek at my germs and wipe my brow. The resort, you said?"

"Don't even think of it. You need to stay there to keep an eye on things. You can't just leave it all for Anne to do. She's already doing too much. How are the Kethji deal and the TJean deal coming along?"

"Nice try, Cuz. I didn't call to give you a chance to discuss business. The deals are fine and your other VP's also doing fine. She thinks you've left her in charge and she's the boss of us, ignoring the fact that I happen to own a third of DDF. Technically, I'm her boss right now."

"A fact I'm sure you remind her of hourly."

"I don't want to talk about your creepy other cousin. I want to hear more about your doctor. Are you sharing germs yet? Is she sharing your room? Or are you playing doctor in hers?"

"Fuck off. None of your damn business."

"Oh ho! That means a big N-O. Otherwise, you'd sound happier. Or maybe it's not going quite as well in that department? It has been a long time for you, hasn't it? Do you need reminder pointers?"

"Leave off, Richard. And no, I don't need pointers from you, of all people. I shall be fine, I assure you."

Richard chuckled at the smugness in his cousin's voice. "I'm glad you're getting some action… or even thinking about it. You've been a hermit too long." With that parting shot, he clicked off the phone.

―――

The next day, just as Darcy tried to come up with some excuse to drop by the hospital, he received a message that Elizabeth was waiting for him downstairs. He was nervously patting down his hair in the elevator mirror when he realized what he was doing. When he reached the lounge next to a fresh water lagoon, he saw her and her sister playing with a gurgling Vietnamese baby.

"Is this one of your charges?" he said to Jane.

Hearing his deep voice, the baby let out a cry.

Elizabeth stood up and gently bounced side to side to soothe it. Darcy tried not to openly stare at her swaying hips.

"No, he's the grandson of Lizzy's patient." Jane began to make funny faces at the baby to distract it.

Elizabeth said, "His mom needs to do some personal care for Grandpa, so I offered to baby-sit. I don't want him to expose Grandpa to some new germs. I'll bring him back to them later."

Enviously, Darcy watched the baby burrow his head in Elizabeth's chest. The baby peeked at him and gave him a toothy smile. Darcy touched his finger to the baby's nose. The infant made a bubbling sound and pushed his face forward for more. Chuckling, Darcy played the game of tapping different parts of the baby's face, each time eliciting a giggle.

"William, you're good with babies. Want to adopt?" Jane teased.

"At this stage in my life, I can't afford…" Distracted by the touch of vanilla he smelled in Elizabeth's scent when she moved closer, he lost his train of thought.

"This little guy is an easy baby." Elizabeth cooed to the baby, "Aren't you, my sweetie, coochee, little man."

The baby threw back his body and laughed. He twisted his face in Darcy's direction.

Darcy reached for him. A second later, he held the happy infant in his arms. "I can't believe this little guy's family let you take him all the way here to the resort."

Jane said, "Lizzy's patients would do anything for her. If she wants the child, Mr. Vinh would probably order his daughter to give her son to Lizzy. It's a badly kept secret in the hospital that Lizzy's been paying for his medicine herself."

Darcy caught the annoyed glance Elizabeth shot in her sister's direction. "You pay for your patient's medicine? Isn't it a state-run system here?"

Elizabeth explained that as a high-ranking communist official, most of Mr. Vinh's care was subsidized but not all. "Unfortunately for him, he has a rare and aggressive infection, and he can't pay for the extra medicine."

"You're actually paying money to work at the hospital. It's negative income, then." The businessman in him found this hard to accept, especially since both Elizabeth and Jane were on a tight budget; they always carefully checked the cost of any activity.

Elizabeth grinned. "I can afford to have a negative income,

since I don't throw my money away on overpriced five-star places like this." Her smile slipped. "Here comes Charles and his family."

Bingley's eyes lit up at seeing the baby. He immediately began making funny faces at it.

Laughing at Bingley's antics, the baby bounced and Darcy had to shift his arms to hold the baby steady between them. When he glanced over at Elizabeth, a shadow crossed her face. Concerned, he raised his eyes, questioning. She gave him a small smile and glanced away.

Bingley cooed at the baby. "You look like a happy little fellow. What's your name?"

Elizabeth said, "It's Cuc."

In a peeved voice, Caroline asked, "What does 'Cuc' mean?"

Jane directed a warning glance at her sister, Darcy observed with amusement. He turned expectantly toward Elizabeth.

She didn't disappoint. A succinct word came from her as she smiled at Caroline. "Shit."

Shaking her head at her sister, Jane explained Vietnamese people called babies names they hoped would keep the evil spirits away from harming the infants. As the babies grow older, their names would be changed to something more dignified.

"Unfortunately, sometimes the nicknames stick," Elizabeth laughed. "Our aunt has a cousin whose name is Cu Ti, little wienie! And he's fifty years old."

With an unmistakable sound coming from his nappy, the baby lived up to his name right then. Darcy almost gagged.

Elizabeth took the child from him. She laid the baby down on the lounge chair and changed him. A gleam of mischief in her eyes, she offered the soiled nappy first to Hurst, then Louisa, then

Caroline, motioning for them to throw it in the nearby trash bin. None responded.

Fighting the churning of his stomach, Darcy manfully stepped up.

Bingley advanced at the same moment.

Fortunately for Darcy, Elizabeth glanced at his face and handed the offensive package to Bingley.

———— ∿ ————

Jane again read her notes on the Hursts and reached for the phone.

"Hello, sweetie," Aunt Mai answered. "Are you and Lizzy having a good time at the resort?"

"Yes, but I feel I've neglected the orphanage and Lizzy feels she's neglected her patients. She's off at the hospital right now, chasing some parasites."

"You both work too hard."

"Not really. I want to talk about the Hursts' adoption."

"What exactly is the heart of your concerns? Say the first thing in your mind now."

"They're not interested in a child," Jane said. "I mean, they're interested in a child. But they're not interested in being parents."

"Ahhh! There you go. No matter what the material advantages are, I don't think it would do the child any good to be placed with them."

"I'm waiting to talk to the investigator, Mr. Collins. He may have more to add." Jane stalled.

"If you wish, though, you should trust your judgments and instincts without depending on unreliable facts."

"You're right. I'm going to decide against." The moment she said it, Jane felt relieved.

"Good for you. Now that your uncle is better, we'll look at this Mr. Collins closely. I'm not impressed so far."

"I can't believe I dawdled over a decision Lizzy would have made in a second. In fact, from the very beginning, she told me to say no."

"Your sister can be too impulsive and tends to make snap judgments about people. For the most part she's right on, but sometimes she's not."

"Speaking of Lizzy's snap first impressions…" Jane told her aunt about her sister and William Darcy. "She finally conceded to me today perhaps the two men aren't here to adopt a baby, since William said he can't afford a child at this stage in his life. She's still convinced he's gay, though. You know Lizzy. Once that girl gets an idea in her top-heavy, mushroom head, it's hard to get her to change her mind."

"Let's hope your sister will sort it out before she shocks the guy," Aunt Mai said. "She's rather naive about men, and that worries me. Is this William a good man? He's not playing with her, is he?"

"He seems intimidating sometimes, yet a bit shy also, but it's obvious he adores her."

"You think this might get serious?"

"They've just met. I don't think either of them knows what to do about each other. It's very amusing to watch."

CHAPTER 11

❦

Bell Boy

ANNE DE BOURGH FROWNED AND LOWERED THE PHONE.

"Hey, boss lady. How's it going? Did you get a message from the Darce man?" a voice said from the doorway.

"I received a message, yes."

Whistling, Richard entered her office uninvited. He sat down on top of her desk, dislodging files and boldly pushing her laptop aside. "Our cuz is having a good time in Vietnam."

She resisted the urge to lean back. She waited, knowing he was baiting her.

"He's forgotten about us here in New York. Must have found a cure for his headaches. Last I talked to him, he mentioned something about a beautiful woman doctor at the resort there." He pointed to a file he had moved. "Did he ask you about the Chicago deal?"

"No, he said he was sure things were being handled fine here, by us." Though happy at Darcy's confidence in her, it bothered her he hadn't asked for specific details as per usual.

"Did he say when he was coming back?" When she shrugged, he whistled. "Didn't talk business and didn't give us a return date. Very unusual for our workaholic cousin. You know why? You always know what's going on with him, even before he does."

"I didn't know he was taking this trip with Charles until two days before they left."

"For whatever reason he's staying longer, perhaps he'll come back a changed man. He might even be in love." With a malicious smirk, he left her office.

She allowed herself a dart of pure hatred directed at his back before she put her laptop in her briefcase and left for home.

"Have you heard from Darcy lately?" Catherine Darcy de Bourgh noticed her stepdaughter's preoccupied mood. It must be something involving Darcy. It always was. She picked up her teacup and took a small sip, then nodded, satisfied. Earl Gray, brewed the way she liked.

"He's staying in Vietnam longer."

Catherine knew Anne hated Darcy being out of her sight. "What's keeping him there? He has a business to run here."

"Richard implied Darcy saw a woman doctor for his headaches."

"That Richard is a fool. My nephew hates doctors." The tea suddenly tasted bitter to Catherine. She put the cup down. She detested that Richard Fitzwilliam. He'd ruined everything. If only her late brother George hadn't married into that opportunistic American Fitzwilliam family and given them one-third ownership of the Darcy family's company. The one-third that should have gone to Catherine and her late husband Lewis. No matter. She and Lewis's daughter, Anne, would get back their one-third share. Soon.

Anne said, "A beautiful woman doctor."

"Since when has my nephew's head been seriously turned by a pretty face? Those beautiful women he dated, none made it from the penthouse to the townhouse. If this one steps inside of his townhouse, I'd start worrying. Until then, let him sow his oats."

Anne pressed her lips together until they disappeared.

Catherine soothed. "You know what to do; a little maneuvering and the trollop will be gone. Nothing to worry about."

"When he calls, he sounds different. Distracted. Brief."

"Unlike his loudmouth American cousin, my nephew has always been the quiet one. Like you."

"He's not so quiet around Richard. He jokes and laughs with him. They're crude with each other when they think they're alone. He never does that with me."

Anne's voice sounded wistful, which made Catherine uncomfortable. She didn't like seeing an insecure Anne. "You want him to be crude with you?"

"No." Anne's mouth tightened. "The adoption didn't go through. Bingley's sisters already left. Darcy had an appointment with the doctor. He's been spending time with her afterward."

Catherine didn't ask how Anne knew. Her stepdaughter always found a way if anything involved Darcy. "You're worrying for nothing. After what happened with his mother and that incompetent Dr. Wickham, and then the work he did with the malpractice trial lawyers to put other incompetent physicians out of business, my nephew's not going to get too involved with a doctor."

"He likes smart *and* beautiful women."

"It still doesn't mean anything." Catherine glanced across the table and swallowed a disappointed sigh. Time to gently remind Anne to make an appointment to get her mustache waxed and to trim those few hairs from that mole by her nose. Her eyes swept lower. Some work on that flat bosom wouldn't hurt, either. Still, she needed to remind the girl of her worth. "You shouldn't worry too much. He left you in charge of DDF, didn't he? That's saying quite a bit, considering how controlling he is about everything. Didn't he make you vice president of operations after only a short time?"

Anne smiled a satisfied little smile. "He did. Richard wasn't happy."

"There, you see. We'll get the *F* dropped from DDF and have the name changed to DDD soon, don't worry." Catherine smiled. With her stepdaughter Anne as Mrs. William Darcy, Catherine would reclaim a third of her father's company. That had been her and Anne's dream for years now.

"All the same, I want him back sooner than later." Anne's chin jutted out, highlighting her manly jaw and the loose folds of her neck.

Catherine curbed the urge to tell the girl to tilt her head an inch to the left to make her profile appear more tolerable to the eyes. "How are you going to do that?"

A hard gleam appeared in Anne's eyes. "My particular friend wants to visit his guru in South Korea. I'll offer to cover his expenses if he makes a detour to Vietnam. If nothing else, his showing up would make Darcy uneasy and he'd leave."

"As long as my nephew doesn't find out about it. And make sure your little friend knows exactly what to do this time and doesn't mess up like he did last year with Georgiana."

—⁓—

Elizabeth studied the man in front of her and tried not to meet her sister's eyes lest she laugh.

A short man, balding on top but with long, graying hair on the sides that he tied in a ponytail, Mr. Bill Collins had shown up unexpected and uninvited. He had a letter from their mother asking them to take care of him; he was the son of an old friend of hers. Told by Mai Gardiner last week his services as an investigator were no longer needed, he wanted to know where he had gone wrong. He wasn't upset, he informed them; he figured he just needed to learn more about the orphanage business and he would soon be hired back.

"Dr. Elizabeth, we have much in common." He smiled.

She flinched at seeing both his upper and lower gum. "Yes, we both have long hair."

"Oh, that too. I meant we both shared a common interest in medicine. Have you seen any fascinating specimens since you've been here?"

"Why yes! There's an unsightly growth, which showed up very unexpectedly, suffering from alopecia but likely to cause trichotillomania in others by contact."

He leaned forward. "The afflicted has no hair but causes hair pulling in his contacts? I have not heard of this."

"I've only been introduced to this growth very, very recently. I discovered it to be full of gas."

"I must tell you. I feel as if I am in heaven, talking medicine like this to a doctor without being accused of being a valetudinarian."

"A hypochondriac," she answered Jane's questioning glance and turned back to him. "The gas is awful smelling, but probably harmless. People who are afflicted with this... uh... growth usually have difficulty smelling the offending gas, though others can discern it quite easily."

"What's its name?"

"Billious collinititis."

He rubbed his chin and nodded, missing Jane's kick at Elizabeth. "Fascinating. I know 'billious' has to do with bile and 'collinititis' means the large bowel—the colon—is affected, which explained the gas."

After giving Elizabeth a warning glance, Jane said to him, "How did you meet our mother again?"

"Your mother and your aunt Phillips were dancers with my mother in the same show in Las Vegas years ago," he said. "My mother lost touch with them until a few months ago, when she recognized Sunny Phillips from the photo I took on a shoot. Even though it's been years, she recognized Sunny's body."

Elizabeth bit her lip. "What kind of photo shoot did you say it was?"

"An anti-war photo shoot in Marin County, in the Bay Area. Sunny was naked, as were all the other protesters. I dabble in many things and am always interested in acquiring new skills and degrees. All of us in my therapy group seek new ways to be in touch with our true selves. Must always keep learning and growing, you understand," he said.

At that Elizabeth met Jane's eyes and smirked, but Mr. Collins was too busy tapping the side of his head to notice.

Unfortunately, a phone call to their mother confirmed and corroborated Mr. Collins's story and connection, so they had to put up with him. The next day, Elizabeth couldn't shake him dogging her footstep in the hospital. He shadowed her and offered his own medical opinions to her patients. Just when she seriously contemplated taking Mr. Vinh up on his offer to get rid of unwanted foreigners, Chau took Mr. Collins on a tour of the children's ward. Grateful for her friend's help, Elizabeth agreed to return the favor by passing a message to Chau's father when she headed back to the resort later.

As she drew nearer to the resort, her heart jumped. Perhaps she'd see William.

No. No. No. She immediately scolded herself for that

undisciplined thought. *He's off limits to you, Lizzy!* She forced herself to remember that day by the lagoon. William standing next to Charles and a baby in between them, the perfect picture of a family. She was not going to disrupt that.

Since that day, Elizabeth had been very, very good. She'd avoided any alone time with William. Once, when she glimpsed him in the lobby of the resort, she managed to casually wave and dart into a room. She hoped it wasn't too obvious she was avoiding him.

After Jane denied the adoption, the Hursts and Caroline Bingley left. Yet William and Charles stayed. Of the whole Bingley family, Charles was the most disappointed with Jane's decision. Elizabeth wondered if Charles was now trying to convince William to adopt anyway and if that was why they'd stayed.

The crowd was still small in the early evening hour when she arrived at Merry Bar. The hostess sat Elizabeth at a small table to wait for Mr. Luc. She waved at Chau's brothers and caught sight of a stranger with them. The man must have thought she was flirting with him; he smiled and winked at her. Chau's younger brother said something to him.

The stranger made his way toward Elizabeth. "You're the doctor? Dr. Bennet?"

He had an English accent, she noticed. He must be a guest wanting some medical attention. "Yes, do you need to see me?"

"I always need to see someone as pretty as you. I may be developing heart palpitations, I think. I'm Wickham, George Wickham."

She tried not to roll her eyes at his cheesy line.

"You're not a Bond girl even with your looks, I see. That line didn't go over well."

Slightly pleased at being called a Bond girl—though he was

right; she wasn't a fan—she gave him a cool smile. "I'm more of a Regency period girl."

"I'm willing to wear a period costume," he offered. "A Regency militia redcoat. I've always wanted one."

"I'd prefer a dark blue topcoat." She relaxed. This could be fun, flirting with a guy she knew was harmless. He was too smarmy. She couldn't take him too seriously. He was obviously a heterosexual man, judging from the way his neck swiveled to check out the other women in the room even as he chatted with Elizabeth.

"I've always admired doctors." He sat without asking permission, but she let it go. "My father was a gynecologist. At one point, I'd planned to follow in his footsteps, but in pediatrics. I love kids."

"You didn't, though?"

"No, my father died and I had to start working. A godfather was going to leave me something to continue my schooling, but it didn't work out."

"What happened?"

"He died and his son refused to finance my medical education. He doesn't like people in the medical profession. I'm embarrassed to say I wasn't smart enough to get by on my academic strengths to attain a scholarship." He smiled a self-deprecating smile. "Enough about pitiful me. How did a beautiful woman like yourself end up here in Vietnam?"

For the next few songs, she enjoyed herself and was beginning to think perhaps she could learn to tolerate a slow dance with this particular British accent when William walked into the club with Mr. Luc.

She stopped mid-sentence, turned from the man beside her, and, forgetting that she meant to deny herself the pleasure of William's company, smiled brightly at him.

At first, he looked surprised to see her and the beginning of a responding smile appeared, but then his face froze. He rudely turned away.

Her stomach clenched. In disbelief, she stared at his disappearing back. She knew she had deliberately kept a distance from him, but still, she hadn't expected such a reaction.

"Was that William Darcy I just saw walking away?" George said.

Trying not to show her hurt over William's rejection, she swallowed and nodded. "You know him?"

"What a small world." He smiled a bitter smile. "Remember my godfather's son?"

Her mouth opened. "That's William Darcy?"

He nodded. "Darcy unreasonably blamed his mother's death on her doctors. I told you, he hates the medical profession."

George stayed with her and didn't seem to mind that she was silent. He bought her drinks. She usually didn't drink much alcohol—a sip here and there of wine—but that night she kept drinking whatever he put in front of her. George kept talking. She didn't pay attention to his words, giving a nod or two on occasion to keep him by the table so she wouldn't look stupid sitting alone drinking and ruminating about William's behavior.

He didn't have to be so rude and hateful if he didn't want to talk to her. When she avoided him, she at least had given him a friendly wave before she hid from him. He should have returned the courtesy. Was that too much to ask? She fumed and drank to the droning of George's voice.

Occasionally, she thought she saw William's face replacing George's. It was always a cold and angry one, like the one he had that first time she met him in the hospital, when he was such an ass. She kept drinking, hoping more alcohol would chase his ugly mug off. At some point, William turned from a donkey's ass into a toad, and he kissed her. She kissed back, hoping he'd change back into her prince. The kiss was unpleasant. Not wanting to get infected with warts, she pushed him away.

Abruptly, she was freed. Loud voices assaulted her ears, and blurry people moved around too damn much. She decided she'd had enough and roared she was leaving.

She floated to her room. Someone, probably a bellboy, carried her, so she wouldn't have to walk. How nice of the resort to provide such a wonderful escort service for their drunken guests, even though the bellboy was jostling her around a little too much, making her stomach queasy. Hopefully, the bellboy recognized that she wasn't Vietnamese but an American. She explained to him being drunk on occasion was acceptable in her culture, as long as she didn't drink and drive.

To the bellboy's chest, she talked all about William's rudeness and how he probably hated her and blamed her for his mother's death. She slurred it was so unfair and if she saw him again she'd vomit on him. When they reached her room, despite her nausea, good manners dictated she lift her face to thank the bellboy.

She threw up—all over his blurry face.

He didn't seem to mind. He took her inside her room, gently wiped her face clean, and, with strong arms, tucked her into bed.

"Thank you," she mumbled into her pillow. As soon as she felt better, she really must compliment the concierge for hiring such a saintly bellboy.

CHAPTER 12

❀

Strange Thoughts and Illusions

ELIZABETH WISHED THE CONSTRUCTION WORKERS WOULD WAIT until she had fully awakened and moved out of their way. The jackhammer had mistakenly been drilling on the sides of her head. She whimpered, "Stop it. You're hurting my head."

"Shhhh," a voice soothed and gentle hands stroked her head until the pain lessened. Eventually, the jackhammer moved away, though she could still hear it being used nearby. The voice coaxed her to drink some water. After taking a few sips, she opened her eyes.

William's hazy face appeared. She pushed him away. "You were rude! George said you hated me. You should wear a hard hat when you're doing construction, toad."

"You're not making sense. Here, swallow these two headache pills. You'll feel better in a while."

"No." She felt like being contrary. "I'm not supposed to take pills from men. And I'm never going to accept a drink from any man again, no matter how cute his accent is."

"I should hope not."

Annoyed at his snotty tone, she said, "Go away. My head hurts."

"I'll go away, but promise me you'll at least drink some water?"

Keeping her eyes closed, she nodded. She drifted off to sleep, lulled by the noise of the bulldozers circling around her head, but at least the jackhammer did not return.

When she woke up, her mouth felt like the construction workers had poured cement into it by accident, and her head still pounded. On the bedside table, someone had put a bottle of water, thoughtfully opened, with the cap and two aspirin next to it. She drank some water and took the pills. The effort took all of her energy, and she fell asleep again. She awoke briefly at intervals, drank some water each time, and fell back to sleep. At one point, she thought she saw William's face again and told him he was a donkey's ass. She was sure that he and his cute accent were responsible for the thumping of her head.

The pain in her head was almost all gone when she fully awakened. It took her a few moments to orient herself. A full water bottle, opened as before with a cap to the side, sat on the bedside table next to a piece of paper with her name on top.

She scanned down and saw William's signature at the bottom. Her eyes widened. She hadn't dreamt him being in her room.

He reminded her to call Jane. Her sister had called late last night to check on her. Elizabeth blushed, guessing what her sister probably concluded when William answered. He next apologized for leaving her. Charles was going diving and William needed to accompany him.

As Elizabeth read, her face flushed in embarrassment at realizing that he had witnessed her drunken behavior.

...I'm sorry to have pulled you away from your date with George Wickham last night, but you had too much to drink and I didn't want him to take advantage of you. You talked in

your sleep. From your mutterings, I can guess what he has been telling you.

Just for the record, I do not hate you, Elizabeth. I admire you greatly for your dedication and your selflessness in your work.

So that you'll understand, I will explain briefly my history with the Wickham family. George's father, Dr. Frank Wickham, was my mother's doctor and a family friend. George was named after my father, his godfather. George and I were playmates as children.

When I was fifteen and my sister Georgiana not yet two, my mother suffered a miscarriage. My father was away on business. Dr. Wickham treated her in his office. I arrived home and found my mother recuperating in bed. Though I expressed my concern at how pale she appeared, she insisted she was fine. I suspected she suffered from something related to women's problems but was too embarrassed to ask directly the nature of her symptoms. I should have, for she rapidly worsened that evening. By the time I managed to take her to the hospital and convince the busy ER doctors to treat her, it was too late.

She died within hours of arriving at the hospital.

The doctors explained bacteria had suddenly taken over her whole body, causing internal bleeding, and she couldn't fight the overwhelming infection and the blood loss.

After her death, my father withdrew into his work and I left for boarding school. My relationship with my father remained strained until his death seven years after my mother's. I suspect he and I both blamed each other, and ourselves, for not having prevented my mother's death somehow.

A few years ago, I learned a business associate's daughter had died while under the care of Dr. Wickham—in the same eerie fashion that my mother had years earlier. I investigated and discovered that this young girl—and likely my mother—had died because Dr. Wickham failed to properly sterilize his equipment. Had I asked questions years earlier, and thereby stopped Dr. Wickham from practicing unsafe medicine, the young woman's death could have been prevented.

Soon after he was forced to involuntarily retire from medicine, Dr. Wickham died of a heart attack. George blamed me for his father's death and promised revenge. I didn't take his threat seriously and dismissed it as an understandable reaction of a grief-stricken son.

That was my arrogant mistake and my little sister paid for it.

During Georgiana's first term at college, I was traveling a lot for work and didn't keep as close an eye on her as I should have. Sometime around Christmas, she told our cousin Richard—her other guardian—that she had met and fallen in love with someone. Richard assumed the guy was another college student and didn't think it necessary to inform me, since he knew that I would try to intimidate any young boyfriend of Georgiana's.

It turned out George Wickham, a man more than fifteen years her senior, was her boyfriend. He convinced her to join a cult and to turn over a significant amount of her money to them. She had planned to marry George Wickham in a mass marriage ceremony on Valentine's Day, her eighteenth birthday. (I was unforgivably away on a business trip.) Fortunately, Richard discovered her plan and prevented the wedding. George Wickham then admitted to using Georgiana to hurt me.

Though she now knows the truth about George, my sister, understandably, has been in somewhat of a depressive state since. We both have. She had to drop out of college. My work suffered.

My cousin Richard blamed himself for both of our melancholy, which was why he convinced Bingley to take me on this trip.

I am very suspicious of George Wickham's motive in befriending you. I understand now why you have been avoiding me. You may disagree with my warning, but make sure his feelings for you are true and worthy.

Bingley and I will leave Vietnam soon. Thank you for your friendship during our time here. Take care of yourself, Elizabeth.

William Darcy

She put the letter down. Poor William. Poor his young sister. She felt awful. He had been hurt by her avoidance of him these past few days. He must not leave Vietnam thinking that she was dating or even interested in George Wickham. Even if George, whose features she could barely recall that moment, wasn't completely repulsive, she could never be friends with a man who had hurt William.

The dive desk confirmed that he and Charles were on the list of divers for an excursion that would not return for a couple of hours.

Too restless to wait inside, she made her way to the dock where the dive boats came in.

A group of men hanging around a boat asked if she wanted to go for a diving excursion.

She shuddered. "No thank you. I don't swim."

"No need to be afraid," one of them said.

"We teach you," another pressed, eyeing her with an appreciative gleam.

"I don't like being underwater. I panic." She quickly moved away, lest they decide to throw her in the water for fun, as her first swimming instructor had done. She found a quiet spot on the shallow end of the dock and settled on a small stump.

One of these days, she should conquer her fear of water and learn how to swim. Suddenly, the frightening realization that William was at that moment submerged hundreds of feet deep in the ocean struck her. Her mind jumped to the image of his oxygen supply somehow being cut off by accident.

The air in her chest felt heavy. She couldn't breathe. Forcing herself to move, she stood and gulped in lungfuls of salty sea air. Not paying attention to where she was, she paced.

"Miss, careful, you're too close to the edge!" someone yelled.

Startled, she turned and lost her balance. She tumbled off the dock's edge. A shock of cold seawater hit her face. Her last panicked thought as she drowned was that she hadn't gotten a chance to tell William she loved him.

~

Thrashing, she fought the water from claiming her. Other bodies suddenly appeared next to her. She was jostled about. An octopus of arms lifted her from the sea. Her body surfed atop a multitude of strange men's hands. A whir of voices sloshed in her ears. She gasped, coughed, spit, and opened her eyes. She felt very foolish when she saw that they were all standing in waist-deep water.

She tried to tell them she was fine, but no one listened. They carried her dangling between them toward the sand.

One pair of strong arms blessedly took possession of her. A commanding, familiar voice said, "I've got her. She's fine."

Voices weakly protested.

His arms tightening around her body, William barked, "Take your hands off her!"

Her overeager rescuers backed off and walked away.

William's angry face stared down at her. "What were you doing, jumping off the dock like that and flailing about in the water?"

She cleared her throat. "I didn't jump."

His nostrils flared. "It looked like it to me."

"I was pacing and thinking and forgot where I was when I fell." She bristled at his attitude. "And I didn't flail about in the water for fun. I was panicking."

The anger left his face. He set her on the sand. "I'm sorry. I'd forgotten about your fear of water."

"You're not underwater."

He looked at her as if he wasn't sure whether she was crazy or not.

She touched his cheek. The roughness of his stubble rubbed against her palm. He hadn't shaved today. Something spicy—that illusive male scent uniquely him, now mixed with the salt of the seawater—wafted toward her. Must not be his aftershave. She shook her head and forced herself to focus. "Your note said you were going diving."

"No. I don't dive. I had planned to go with Bingley to make sure his equipment was safe, but then I decided he'd be fine without me." He frowned at her. "I went to check on you again, but you'd gone. Someone told me they'd seen you at the dive desk earlier. I came out here to search for you and saw you going off the dock."

"Thank you for rushing to save me from drowning. Though, I wouldn't blame you if you didn't." She knew she was being melodramatic, but she couldn't help herself. She was so jealous of his loving care of Charles. He was going to supervise Charles's diving equipment. What more proof did she need of William's feelings for his partner?

"You didn't need to be saved from drowning. You needed to be saved from your enthusiastic rescuers." He sighed. "And why would you think I wouldn't rush to save you if you were drowning?"

"I didn't really mean that. I mean... I know you would. It's just that... I guess I wouldn't blame you even if you didn't want to... Oh Lord, I'm not saying anything right." She wove her fingers through her hair and discovered strands of slimy seaweed on her head.

He helped her pick the seaweed from her hair. She stared at his chest and fisted her fingers so she wouldn't be tempted to rake them over the mat of hair outlined underneath his wet shirt. He was not available, she reminded herself.

He tried to pull her toward the resort. "Let's go get you into some dry clothes. You look ill."

She couldn't believe it! She wanted to explore his chest and he thought she looked ill. "I'm not ill. I'm in love with you. I love you."

Horrified at herself for blurting out her feelings, she covered her mouth and looked down at the sand. After a moment, hearing nothing from him, she glanced up.

He looked stunned. Then, with a hopeful smile, looking like a little boy who'd just been given a big ice cream treat, he reached for her. "You love me?"

She swallowed. "Yes, I do. But don't worry about it. I'll get over it. I tend to do this, you see, fall for the wrong kind of guy."

"What? I'm a wrong guy?" His face looked as if she'd knocked down his ice cream cone. "Why?"

"Because of Charles. I know you two are still in the closet about it. And I know you're a little attracted to me, but I don't want to come between you and him. I would never cheat and I wouldn't want to be with someone who would…" She trailed off, concerned.

He appeared to have stopped breathing. His mouth hung open. His pupils dilated. His face was as white as the froth of the waves around them. A man in shock, she decided. She pushed his chin up.

At her touch, he blinked. Then his mouth fish-opened again.

Afraid she'd lose her nerve if she met his eyes, she stared down at her feet. "I mean I love you. But you don't have to say or do anything. I know you've been with Charles for a long time and you're committed to him. Even though I'm very attracted to you, it's not like I expect anything to happen between us. I would never expect you to leave Charles for me." She raised her head to see if he understood her rambling.

He stood rooted, as if he'd been fossilized on the sand.

She wondered if she needed to check his vitals. Gently, she slapped his cheeks.

He stirred. No sound. After a moment, he closed his mouth, raised his fist to it, and stared.

Self-conscious she probably looked like something a whale had burped up, she tugged at her wet clothes and checked for any lingering seaweed in her hair.

He dropped his fist and opened his mouth again.

She waited.

Again nothing! He pressed his lips together and stood motionless for so long she suddenly worried. Had she misdiagnosed his past headaches as migraines? Could he suffer from temporal lobe epilepsy and was now having a paranormal experience associated with that condition? "William, are you okay? Are you having strange thoughts and illusions right now? Can you tell me your full name and today's date?"

"No. Yes. Fitzwilliam Alexander James Darcy. And today is…"

After giving her the correct date, he sucked in several shuddering deep breaths, then turned and walked in a circle.

Concerned, she followed. *He's alert and oriented. He's moving, so he's not in danger of passing out. Is he angry? Maybe he's upset I figured out his relationship with Charles? Should I have confronted him so directly?*

A mouth on hers interrupted her muddled thoughts. He'd stopped and wrapped one arm around her and brought her to that wonderful, hard chest. Her belly was crushed against a decidedly aroused male groin. A tongue parted her lips. He sucked her tongue. Her bones disintegrated. She had to clutch at him so she wouldn't slide to the sand.

He stopped and lifted his mouth. Light-headed from his kiss, she blinked and tried to focus. He lowered his mouth again. This time, she felt the slow, savoring caress of his lips. He tenderly licked at the corners of her lips before his tongue again probed. Her body shivered—a sinful, scrumptious shiver. The tips of their tongues danced. She moaned.

When he finally withdrew, they both breathed hard. He touched his forehead to hers. She pressed closer into him. Cold waves reached them and lapped at her legs, but she didn't mind, contented to stay still in the stolen moment.

The sound of a gull screeching near their heads startled them and they reluctantly parted. Holding her left hand with his right, he started walking.

She opened her mouth.

He stopped, put a finger over her lips, and shook his head. They headed toward the resort. Though, after a few steps, he paused briefly and gave her a look of disbelief before continuing.

CHAPTER 13

❀

Bloody Great!

HE DIDN'T KISS LIKE ANY OF HER OLD GAY BOYFRIENDS, THAT WAS for sure. Elizabeth smiled and touched her tongue to her lips. She took in his imperturbable profile and her smile slipped. He didn't seem too affected by the kiss, she thought. She sighed. What else did she expect? She wasn't Charles Bingley.

Once they reached the doorway to his suite, she hesitated and waved a hand at her wet clothes. Wordlessly, he pulled her inside, led her straight to the bathroom, pointed to the shower and the bathrobe hanging, and left. Shrugging, she undressed and got into the shower.

Molten, she read the engraved word on the soap bar. She took a whiff. Sandalwood and pepper. Finally, she had discovered the source of his scent. Her breathing quickened. He had used this bar. On his body. His naked body. Her pulse danced. Slowly, she circled the bar over her breasts. Closing her eyes, she leaned against the shower wall and breathed deep, letting his scent mist her…

"Elizabeth, are you all right in there? I ordered tea for you. It's getting cold."

After knocking on the bathroom door, Darcy downed a generous sip of brandy. He didn't usually drink at this time of day, but he felt a desperate need for some fortification. How? Why? What? No fathomable answer came to him how the clueless woman had come to that conclusion.

He settled on the couch and waited, willing himself not to think of her naked in his shower. Just when he was about to get up and knock again, she came out wearing his robe. She looked so beautiful, so sexy… and so vulnerable.

His heart tumbled.

Her hands fidgeted in the pockets of the robe.

To distract her from her nervousness, he said, "English Breakfast tea okay? Or would you prefer something else?"

"That's fine." When he handed her a cup, she looked surprised. "You know I take my tea plain, without sugar or milk?"

"I know a great many things about you, Elizabeth."

"Oh." Her fingers nervously tugged at her wet hair. She stared down at her tea.

"You, however, don't know much about me."

She glanced up at that. He met her eyes. She bit her bottom lip. After a moment, she straightened and a hopeful, eager look came over her.

That look told him more than any words would. He decided it didn't matter she had misread him, the how or why of it. "I'm not with Charles or any man. I'm not gay."

"You're not? Are you sure?" Her tone was hopeful.

He didn't know whether to laugh or cry. In as firm a voice as possible, he stated, "Yes. I'm sure. You were mistaken."

"Oh, William." She reached for him at the same moment he moved toward her.

Burying his face in her wet hair, he smelled the scent of his soap on her and felt a soft affectionate kiss on his neck. He closed his eyes and thanked the gods for leading him to her.

"I'm so glad."

He laughed at that. "Not that there's anything wrong with being gay if I was, but I happen to like women. I like one particular woman. I'm in love with you too."

She made a happy noise in the back of her throat. When he leaned back against the sofa, she tucked her head on his shoulder. He sighed with contentment.

After a few minutes of comfortable silence, she said, "I'm so happy."

He smiled against her hair. "Me too."

"I do know something about you, you know."

The fluttering of her breath against his neck felt better than a whole month of Sundays in Central Park, he decided. "Like what?"

"You think through things carefully before you give your opinions or make decisions. I'm a bit more snap with my opinions and decisions."

"Really? I hadn't noticed." That earned him a playful tap on the chest.

"You're responsible. That first day you arrived, you were suffering, yet you went with Charles to the hospital. Your frantic worrying about the care he needed made me think you two were partners."

"But after you and I spent some time together, did you not notice how much I liked you, from the beginning?"

"I did notice you were attracted to me, but you never pay any attention to other women... like those two cute girls at Marble Mountain or the beautiful girls at Merry Bar..."

"At the risk of sounding like a bloody vain arse, I'm used to such attention and well, I'm rather fastidious."

"As an infectious disease specialist, I'm very glad to hear that." Her voice turned shy. "If I compare myself to those ethereal and beautiful women, I always feel quite plain."

Surprised, he blurted, "But you're beautiful." Didn't she know how beautiful she was? How sexy she was? She was right, however; she was not ethereal. Even better, she was refreshingly and tangibly real both in her personality and in her appearance. He repeated, "You're beautiful."

"Really?" She gave him a bashful pleased smile that made him want to rush at her and show her how beautiful he found her.

"Yes, really." To distract himself from acting on his urge, he said, "You gave me a shock. No woman has ever been mistaken about me in that regard before."

"Not that they told you." She squeaked when he playfully lunged at her. "Okay, okay. I was mistaken. You're a big manly stud and a gift to womankind."

"I'm only interested in giving *you* my manly gift." He winked at her. To his surprise, her face turned red. Suddenly conscious she had nothing but a robe on, he coughed. "Perhaps it's best that we get you in some clothes."

He walked toward his closet and found a T-shirt and a pair of shorts for her. He turned to hand them to her but she'd disappeared to the bathroom.

She'd left the bathroom door slightly ajar. Unaware he could see her through the reflection in the mirror, she took off the robe. His eyes filled with the sight of a beautiful naked Elizabeth in side view, her full breasts swinging slightly as she gracefully bent toward her damp clothes. His breathing labored. His mouth dried. He licked his lips.

Dressed in her damp clothes, she came out smiling at him. "I need to go to my room and change into dry clothes. Are you all right? You looked flushed. William?"

He tried to shake himself out of his trance.

She gave him a puzzled look. "You'd rather I change now, into your clothes, before we go to my room?"

Not knowing what else to do, he nodded.

She took the clothes from his hands and disappeared into the bathroom again, thankfully closing the door completely this time.

—ww—

Once they reached her room, he waited outside on her balcony while she changed in her bedroom. Briefly, he pondered the possibility of getting another lucky glimpse if he walked in on her, and immediately chided himself for thinking like a hormonal teenager.

"Do you want your T-shirt back?"

He turned around. In a white blouse atop a green skirt that softly draped over her hips, she looked as refreshing as a beautiful gardenia flower.

She held up his T-shirt. "Could I have this? I like to sleep in large T-shirts." When he nodded, she ran back inside with it, as if afraid he would change his mind.

Amused, he followed her. His mood sobered when he saw his letter on her bedside table.

She kissed his cheek. "Thank you for sharing that with me."

"It's probably the first time ever I've written it all down." He wrapped his arms around her. "I wanted you to know everything. I didn't want you to be taken advantage of by George Wickham."

"I just met him last night. I can't even remember what he looks like now." She frowned. "I must have drunk a lot last night."

"Yes, you did! How could you let a man you've only met yesterday get you so drunk?"

"I was upset. I hadn't seen you for days and you threw me a disgusted glance, then you disappeared."

"I was looking at him, not you. You're the one who's been trying to avoid me for days! Don't think I didn't notice that."

"I was avoiding you," she admitted. "But that's because of Charles."

"When I saw you flirting with Wickham last night, I thought he was why you've been absent and avoiding me. And I only left to calm myself. I came back and stayed close by. I don't trust him."

"I wasn't flirting with George," she protested. He glared at her. Sheepishly, she said, "Okay, perhaps just a little flirting."

"Next time, Miss Quick-to-jump-to-conclusions, talk to me. Ask me if you have questions." He glowered. "No flirting or kissing other men."

"He was the donkey's ass I kissed? I thought it was your toad face I was kissing to… never mind."

"What? I was the toad?"

"No, no. You're a prince, always." She stroked his chest to soothe him. "Don't mind me. I'm never drinking again. You're the bellboy! And I threw up on you."

"I don't know who the bellboy was, but you did vomit on me."

"I'm sorry. I should have hurled on Wickham's face instead. You don't need to be jealous of him. I'm a very good judge of character. On first impression, I can always tell what a guy is really like underneath."

He was about to laugh when he realized she had said that last bit without any pretense of irony. He rolled his eyes instead. The crazy woman was serious.

She insisted, "I knew he was too smarmy and too smooth right away. I was in no danger of being attracted to him. All the time he was talking to me, he was checking out other women."

"Bet you didn't think he was gay because of that," he grumbled.

"No. I did not. And before you give me that pout and roll your eyes again, think of this: I was lusting after your *arse* even when his *arse* was available and right next to me." She pinched his backside.

He jumped in surprise; she did it again and ran. Laughing, he easily caught her and gently swatted her bum. She shrieked. His face was against the side of her neck when he stopped laughing. He pressed his lips against her soft skin, at the spot right behind her ear.

Her breathing changed. Their lips met. As their kiss deepened, he became conscious of her soft, full breasts pressing against him. She moaned. He raised his hands. She gasped when his thumbs caressed her nipples. Trailing his lips downward, his mouth boldly replaced his thumb. The grainy gauze of the shirt rubbed against the thin silk of her bra as his tongue dampened her pointed peaks. She shifted restlessly against him. Impatiently, she tugged at the neckline of her shirt until the top buttons loosened. She unclasped her bra. Her breast revealed, face full of anticipation, she closed her eyes.

His heart rate rocketed. God, she was as sexy and responsive as in his fantasies. He hardened and glanced at the bed. He cursed. He didn't have a condom. "Elizabeth, do you have…"

She interrupted by pushing his mouth onto her chest.

He smiled at her impatience. Bending his head, he greedily suckled. When he shifted one leg to steady himself, his thigh ended up pressing intimately between her legs. Slightly shocked at first when she began to rub herself against him, he became aroused further by her uninhibited behavior; he rhythmically pushed his thigh against her. She briefly protested when he lifted his mouth from one breast to the other. He increased his effort to help her reach her climax. Her body convulsed against his leg then she collapsed against him.

"Wow," she said a long moment later, after she caught her breath.

Chuckling at her dazed expression, he gave a little bow. "Glad to serve you, madam."

"Wow. I've never…"

"You've never what?"

Red-faced, she moved away and fussed with her clothes.

His heart rate descended. His body calmed. He kicked himself for making her uncomfortable and self-conscious. He had moved too fast. "Elizabeth, I'm sorry."

"You don't need to apologize. I've never been with anyone."

"You mean you've never experienced…" His breath caught, sure he had heard wrong. His mind refused to go further.

"No, of course I have, lots of times…"

He started to exhale slowly.

"Just not with anyone else."

The inside voice in his head screamed happily. *She's a virgin! Bloody great!*

"Some guys don't like an inexperienced woman. You don't mind, do you?"

"I don't mind at all," he managed to answer in what he hoped was a casual voice. *She's a virgin! Bloody great!*

"It's not something I'm…" She stopped and started again. "My family teases me about my love life and lack of it, and… I've only recently told Jane."

"There's no need for you to feel embarrassed," he said gently.

"I'm hungry," she suddenly said.

Amused at how red her face still appeared, he went along with her change of topic. "We shall get you fed then. Which of the five restaurants here would you like to have dinner at?"

"Could we order in? But eat in your room, on the patio? I like your ocean view."

Over dinner, they kept the conversation light. Keeping specific details to the bare minimum, she told him amusing stories about cultural differences in the practice of medicine here in Vietnam and at home. Proudly, she bragged about her recently published research on a particular parasite. He asked questions but was mainly content to listen. It was obvious how much medicine meant to her and that she loved her work.

After dinner, they sat with their arms around each other and watched the waves. They talked. He expanded on his mother's death and his guilt, and touched more on his profound regret about his relationship with his father and his hope that his sister would return to college soon.

She reassured him his sister would recover and move on soon, and told him of her own similar experience at sixteen with an older professor. He was upset for her, but he didn't interrupt while she talked. Afterward, he thanked her for trusting him enough to have shared that. It helped him understand her better.

CHAPTER 14

❀

The Blood!

JANE WATCHED ELIZABETH, IN HER UNDERWEAR AND BRA, THROW A shirt onto the floor then stick her head into a corner armoire. Her sister pulled out another shirt identical to the one just discarded. Jane laughed. "I like this new girly-girl you. I've never seen you this flustered about your clothes before."

"Arrggh. I can't find anything right to wear."

Jane eyed the frayed edges of her sister's underwear. "You need some new clothes, especially new undies, sexy ones—not grandma type."

"I hate shopping."

"How about getting a whole new wardrobe made by a good seamstress? It's not too much money. Chau's mom could help arrange it," Jane suggested. "Which reminds me, should we be better hosts and take Bill Collins off their hands?"

"No. He likes their attention and they like giving it to him. He's their American pet. They have the patience of saints." Elizabeth threw the second shirt on the floor and disappeared into the armoire again. A moment later, her head reappeared. "Jane, do you think I'm sexually unappealing?"

Jane almost laughed until she realized her sister was indeed serious. "Is it not going… well?"

"No." Elizabeth's face was the color of a pink lychee fruit. "I mean, it's just not going. I think my being a virgin inhibits him. We kiss, and I want more, but then he always stops. We've been dating seriously for days now, and we seem to have gone backward."

"Days and nothing has happened? Imagine that," Jane said dryly. Trust Elizabeth to be impatient. The girl waited all this time to have sex and now she wanted it yesterday.

"The blood! He's afraid of the blood."

"You're not thinking clearly. Your brain is clouded by lust. He's not going to be afraid of a little blood if it means he gets into your pants."

"If only I'd paid closer attention to that porn film during my human sexuality class in psychiatry, the part when they talked about reading your partner's signals."

"You sound like you're talking about an Animal Planet film on mating instead of titillating porn."

"I am titillated. By him! Every time I see him I want to rip his clothes off and feel his body and—"

"Okay, okay, stop!" Jane firmly cut in. "TMI! I get the picture. It's not a test you can prepare for by studying. Just let it flow."

"But it's not flowing. He stops. I need clear instructions on how to get him to keep going." Elizabeth's blush was now the color of passion fruit. "What if I tell you I did something so unusual that I probably disgusted him the first time we were, um… fooling around?"

"I'm sure you didn't."

"I'm thinking I did," Elizabeth insisted, still blushing. "That's why I've been waiting for him to make the first move. What if I mess up again? What if I miss an important cue or something?"

"You're being a mushroom head. Stop overthinking. It will come naturally at the right time, trust me." Jane couldn't believe she was giving sex advice to Lizzy, the intrepid, adventurous one. "They don't let unmarried people stay together in the same hotel room here. How are you going to get together with him?"

"It's not that strict at the resort. Besides, William and I have been in each other's room."

"Lizzy, you have to be discreet. You're probably being watched a bit closer than the usual tourist. You're staff there, as little as you do," Jane reminded her sister. With the orphanage next door, there was no possibility of William spending the night at their cottage.

The sound of a hammer banging interrupted. Elizabeth peered out the window into the orphanage's courtyard. "Charles has made some progress, I see."

"Yes, slowly," Jane said. Charles had offered to build a new playground for the orphanage, a one- or two-day project that had stretched much longer. Jane suddenly remembered Elizabeth planned to take William for a tour of the historical fifteenth-century town nearby. "Are you meeting William here for your trip to Hoi An this morning?"

"No, at the resort. I need to go the hospital to check on some patients first though. Did I tell you an anonymous donor from some charitable foundation in New York has paid for many of the patients' medications?" Elizabeth put on another shirt. "Speaking of New York, William has been staying up late making calls to there. I think he's looking hard for employment."

"You 'think'?"

"He's not aware I know he's unemployed." Elizabeth buttoned her shirt. "He'd feel bad if he discovered I already know Charles is covering his expenses here. Remember Charles told us about William looking for work, when he apologized for William's abrupt leaving that day at Merry Bar?"

"If William's embarrassed about being unemployed, then I guess it's too early in your relationship to be talking about a sensitive topic like that. That reminds me, you have enough money for your trip today?"

"I'm not going to buy anything. William always insists on paying if I even express the slightest interest, so I'm not even going to look at anything at all. It's bad enough he won't let me share our expenses."

"I'm sure he can still afford the occasional day trip and a trinket or two. He's on vacation, after all. What kind of work does he do? I know it's some kind of corporate business, work, right?"

Elizabeth nodded. "Something involving studying a lot of spreadsheets. He looks at numbers and sees how a company is doing financially."

"Some kind of auditing or accounting work, then. He does fit the accountant type—very methodical and detail-oriented. Do you think he's embarrassed about being an unemployed accountant while he's dating you, a doctor? Some men might have a complex about that."

"He definitely fits the type. He's a proud and prickly kind of guy." Elizabeth made a face. "Always trying to prove to me he can afford things and never looks at the prices."

Jane said, "Not everyone counts their pennies like you do. But then, technically, you're also unemployed. Oh, Mom called. There's a letter for you from Doctors Without Borders. Dad read the letter and said it's nothing. I think Mom's worried you're going to go somewhere dangerous after Vietnam."

"She worries too much."

—⁓—

"How about a break?" Chau stood in the doorway of Elizabeth's office and held two cups of drip coffee in her hands.

"Come in. I'd love some." Elizabeth smiled at her friend and accepted a cup. "I don't see your shadow."

"Bill left to meet with a friend, a Mr. Wickham."

Elizabeth almost dropped her coffee cup in her surprise. "Bill's friends with George Wickham?"

"They met in Tai Pei, on the way here. I think Bill must have told Mr. Wickham about your working at the resort. My brother said Mr. Wickham had been looking for you for a couple of days before he met up with you. Bill tried to give him some medical advice"—Chau smiled a rueful smile—"but if Mr. Wickham was looking for you, he must have needed to see a real doctor."

Elizabeth frowned. William was right: George Wickham had sought her out to cause trouble for William. "Thanks for taking care of Bill. I know he's a pain."

Chau set down her cup. "I'm going to marry him."

"What?" Elizabeth laughed and took a sip of her coffee. "I'm sorry. For a moment I thought you said you're going to marry him."

"I did... say that."

"But why?" Elizabeth said before she could stop herself. "I'm sorry. I shouldn't have said that."

"I want to get married. He's a good man. He appreciates me and my family. I think he's lonely. Though his mother is alive, he can't live with her and she won't let him." Chau's tone was both puzzled and sad.

About to explain American parents didn't feel the need to live with or take care of their grown children, Elizabeth stopped herself, ruefully recognizing the futility of explaining that concept to her traditional Vietnamese friend. Chau's culture valued filial and parental duty above all else. Instead, she simply said, "It's just the cultural difference between here and America. I haven't lived at home since I left for college, and Berkeley's only twenty minutes from Orinda, where my parents live."

"I can't imagine not living with my parents if I wasn't married."

"You're not rushing into marriage because you want to leave home, then?"

"Hardly." In a serious tone, Chau added, "I'm not in love with Bill, nor he with me. Perhaps we'll have that romantic movie-ending love some day. I'm okay if we don't. I can be a good wife to him."

"I'm sure you will." Elizabeth longed to question out loud if Bill Collins would be a good husband, but she squashed the urge.

"Bill and I can make a marriage together and support each other. He has no job, and no one who cares for him to come home to now. I want to take care of him."

Elizabeth couldn't see wanting to take care of a man, much less the annoying Bill Collins, as a good reason for marrying, but then an image appeared of William returning to New York, jobless, alone, and having no one to care for him. She reached a hand toward Chau's and said with true sincerity, "I understand perfectly."

Later, when she got to the resort, Elizabeth went first to the Merry Bar and talked to Chau's brothers. She spent some time with them, making sure she got all her facts straight.

Afterward, she found William outside the resort, talking to a cyclo driver.

"Hi, sorry to keep you waiting," she greeted William.

He introduced the cyclo driver. "This is Tri. He offered us a ride, but I told him we were taking a car to Hoi An."

As they headed toward their car, she smiled at William. "Listen to you, chatting with a local like you're Charles Bingley's twin."

He chuckled and confessed, "I didn't understand much of what Tri actually said. I guessed."

She squeezed his hand. "But you're trying, and that's why I love you."

They settled themselves into the car. Out of a corner of her eye, she caught a glimpse of a man watching them from behind a palm tree. The driver maneuvered the car away from the resort and she worked to distract William from seeing George Wickham. She was determined not to have anyone ruin William's enjoyment of the day.

She knew how to take care of Wickham. No one messed with the man she loved.

CHAPTER 15

❀

Escort Service

"YOU LOOK SO SERIOUS." ELIZABETH HANDED DARCY A GLASS. "Here you go. I brought you an iced tea, love."

"Thank you." Darcy turned from watching the waves to smile at her. He loved how the endearment easily rolled off her tongue. "Just momentarily preoccupied with work-related thoughts."

She sat down at the foot of his beach chair. "Have you been getting one of your headaches?"

He shifted his legs to make more room for her. "No. Why do you ask?"

"You're been distracted the last couple of days."

"Have I been boring?" he teased and took a sip. "I've been up late making phone calls, work-related calls, that's all."

"Tell me about these calls."

"Nothing worth talking about." He put down his iced tea and wrapped his arms around her, glad he'd reserved a private beach-side cabana this evening. A cool ocean breeze brushed over them, loosening a few strands of her hair to stroke at his face. "I don't want to waste our time together talking about my work or, as is the case lately, my not working."

She laid her hands on his arms. "About you not work—"

"Shhh. Let's enjoy ourselves and the view here," he interrupted and nuzzled her hair, delighting in the hint of vanilla he smelled. He loved the way her long hair kept falling out of the clip she used to keep it tied back. She once confessed she kept it long only because she never had the time or money to keep it maintained in a shorter, more fashionable style.

Money. He swallowed a sigh. So stubborn, so sensitive, so poor, his proud Elizabeth always insisting he not spend money on her. The difference in their financial situation must bother her.

Earlier, after carefully perusing the prices on the menu at one of the restaurants in the resort, she asserted she'd preferred a picnic on the beach. Being frugal seemed to be very important to her. He usually went along with her budgeting quirks. He didn't want to prick her pride by making an issue of it, though he hoped she'd allow him to spoil her as their relationship progressed.

Her fingers tensed atop his arms. "William, you told me to ask if I had questions?"

He wondered why she was nervous. He kept his voice light to put her at ease. "What's going on in that head of yours?"

"Jane sometimes calls me a mushroom head, so top heavy I lose my balance, my common sense."

"Elizabeth, you're stalling. What is it you're afraid to ask?" he said gently. When she remained silent, her fingers picking at his sleeves, he added in the same light tone, "Is this another question about my sexuality?"

"Yes… in a way."

He stiffened. He turned her to face him. "I thought we settled that issue. I'm not gay."

"That's not what I mean. I know you're not gay. It's just that I would like to…"

"Would like to?" he prompted.

The words rushed from her. "Why haven't you wanted to sleep with me?"

"There's nothing in the world I'd rather do now than to take you to my room and make love to you and not let you see the sun for days."

Her eyes oversized and her cheeks crimsoned. "Oh."

Chuckling, he lowered his head and briefly touched his lips to hers. "But, unfortunately, this isn't the right time or place."

"Why?"

"The orphanage. You and Jane represent the orphanage. Mr. Luc warned me not to put your reputation, and the orphanage's, in danger with my behavior. He alluded to what happened between Wickham, you, and me that night at Merry Bar. And also afterward, when I spent the night in your room."

"Your behavior? How can he talk to you when I was the one who got drunk?"

"When I first saw you with Wickham, I should have controlled myself and calmly approached you. I should have acted more decisively when I returned. I should not have just stood there, jealously thinking you were on a date and just let him buy you drinks. It was my fault, what happened that night."

"You take on too much blame that's not yours," she chided. "I was responsible for my poor judgment that night."

"Of course you're not blameless," he soothed. "I'm only admitting my part. I should have called your sister, instead of spending the night in your room."

"I thought my... uh... rubbing against you that day disgusted you." The redness returned to her face and her bottom lip disappeared.

He rubbed the soft pad of his thumb against her bottom lip to tease it to reappear. He whispered huskily, "I was very aroused by your enthusiasm and what you did."

Her mouth parted. "Oh."

He suppressed the urge to slip his tongue in between her lips to show her how much he liked what she did that day, and how much he fantasized her doing more of the same.

His phone rang. He looked at the caller ID. "My cousin," he said to Elizabeth before answering, "What do you want, Richard?"

"Hey, Cuz. How's it going? Aren't you proud I woke up early to call you? Some of us have to work hard, you know, to make up for those lazing around refusing favors from beautiful women." Richard's voice boomed loud enough to drown out the sound of the waves.

Darcy cringed and held the phone a few inches away from his ears. "Do you have some urgent news about work to tell me, or are you calling to annoy me again?"

"But annoying you is almost as much fun as doing it to Anne. Neither of you have a sense of humor."

"No, don't go." Darcy grabbed Elizabeth when she made a motion of moving away to give him privacy.

"Go? I'm not going anywhere. Darce?"

"I wasn't talking to you." Darcy kept one arm around Elizabeth.

"Are you talking to the maids? Supervising their cleaning again, eh? You need to get dirty, Cuz. Stop worrying about being clean all the time. Stop spending your time brushing and flossing yourself to death."

Embarrassed Elizabeth could hear his cousin's revealing comments about how Darcy had spent the first few days of his vacation, Darcy's tone was brusque. "If this is about the new company you wanted me to look at in Holland, the answer is no. I don't want to work with them. I want you to focus on that company we talked about last week. Check to see if they're willing to work with me long-term. They already have a big presence in New York."

"I'll give up convincing you the Holland company is better if you send me a picture of you and a beautiful babe or two at the beach, all wearing thongs. Them, not you."

Elizabeth tapped Darcy's arm and motioned for the phone. Enticed by the impish gleam in her eyes, he handed it over.

"Richard, I'm afraid Mr. Darcy can't talk business anymore." In a sleepy, sexy, low voice, she breathed, "I need him to floss his teeth..."

"What?" Darcy exclaimed.

"What?" Richard echoed. "Who are you?"

"...with my thong. I'm his paid escort," Elizabeth finished and hung up on Richard.

Darcy's mouth dropped open. Richard's mouth probably was too on the other side of the world.

She winked at him. "I always thought those thongs felt like butt floss."

The image of her in a thong sent his pulse on a roller coaster ride. He closed his eyes and groaned. "Please, could we not talk about you and thongs right now?"

"You need to return to New York soon?"

Reminded, he sobered. Anne and Richard had been covering while he and Bingley took an extended vacation, but Darcy knew he needed to return to New York soon. He nodded. "I do need to get back."

Her face fell.

He touched her cheek. "I hope not to be gone long. I'll check out this company and some others Richard wants me to look at, get everything settled, check in on my sister, then I *will* come back here."

"When do you need to be back in New York?"

"Last week," he admitted. "I couldn't go though, not while Wickham is here. I know you can take care of yourself, but I need to know that you'll be safe."

"If he moves on to some other place, you can leave?"

"It's my paranoia, but I won't make the same mistake with you as I did with my sister last year. I take the threat of Wickham very seriously now."

—⁓—

Later, as they headed back to their rooms, Darcy said, "How long are you working at the resort here?"

"Only until Hussein arrives, any day now. Why?"

He paused. "Sweetheart, I've learned your friend never had any intention of coming to replace you. From the start, you were always meant to be the doctor here the whole month."

"What?"

"He's paying for your room and expenses. The only compensation the resort agreed to for you seeing patients was deep discounts on spa services, which I know you haven't taken advantage of. Not that you need to, by the way."

"You mean I've been working here for free? They charged for my suite?" She gritted her teeth and walked faster now. "I can't believe it. I get nothing seeing stupid, rich tourists?"

He hoped she didn't include him in the group and rushed to keep up with her. "You work for free at the hospital."

"That's different. Treating poor, appreciative patients is a privilege. Treating rich and ignorant people for free really, really pisses me off. I'm going to kill Hussein."

"Tell me again about your arrangement with him? How well do you know him?"

She told him about Hussein and admitted he was one of her three previous boyfriends.

Darcy was immediately jealous and suspicious. "I'm expecting a background check report on him any day now. I ordered it as soon as I discovered your odd arrangement."

"Oh." She paused in her tracks for a moment. "I wish you wouldn't waste your money on that. He's harmless, as you'll undoubtedly discover."

Surprised at her calm reaction, he admitted, "I thought you'd accuse me of interfering in your business."

"I would have with anyone else, I suppose." She shrugged and resumed walking. "But you need to be in control of your environment. It's part of your OCD. It's a normal protective drive to make sure those you care about are safe."

"You're not angry?"

"Why would I be angry? It's not like you did it because you want to control me or make decisions for me. You need to do it to have peace. To soothe yourself. It's just like your cleaning and your hand washing."

He had to swallow the lump in his throat. Since his mother died, he'd had an obsessive need for control. He didn't let many people into the sanctuary of his private life, mainly because the urge to safeguard those he cared about took so much energy he was often left exhausted. Though he didn't want the people he loved to feel stifled, he couldn't help his compulsion. Yet, here was this free-spirited, feisty, and fearless woman who loved him enough to allow him to do whatever he needed to feel safe, even if it meant taking charge of certain aspects of her life that she was more than capable of handling. Her love and easy acceptance of him—neuroses, phobias, compulsions, and all—humbled him.

"I'll call Hussein later and chew his ass out. He'll probably give me some twisted explanation of why he did it"—she kept walking—"just like he did with his excuse of why he became a Republican..."

She had moved on to another topic, Darcy bemusedly noted. Obviously, his shameful hang-up was not a big enough deal for her to discuss further.

He smiled.

CHAPTER 16

❧

Sweet Parting

"HOW ABOUT ANOTHER EGG? I CAN COOK YOU ANOTHER." ELIZABETH wanted to stretch their time together. "Or another piece of toast?"

"I'm full, sweetheart," William said. "I can't eat another bite."

Resigned, she nodded and cleared the table. She had no appetite this morning but had forced herself to eat so he would too. She didn't want him to travel on an empty stomach.

He moved to the front door. "I'm going to test the locks one more time."

"Okay." She bit her lip to hide a smile. No one in this neighborhood had locks on their front doors, much less their back doors. After William's inspection visit last week, the new locks on both the front and the back doors of her cottage would be the envy of any bank.

He returned. "Are you sure I can't convince Jane to let me put a security system in here?"

"Yes, I'm sure Jane's firm about that." Besides the fact that she didn't want him to spend money, she didn't want to tell him Jane had threatened to throw away the keys to the house locks the minute he left the country.

His eyes swept the kitchen.

She waited.

He frowned. "Where's the fire extinguisher?"

"Here." Jane had put it atop the refrigerator, behind a box of noodles. He'd bought them one for each room of the cottage and the orphanage.

"It should always be in an accessible spot, especially in the kitchen." He placed it in a prominent place atop the counter, blocking access to their coffeemaker. "I'm going to check to make sure the carbon monoxide monitors are plugged in correctly in the back rooms."

"All right." A few minutes later, while she stood at the kitchen sink soaking the dishes, he returned and wrapped his arms around her. She leaned back against him and closed her eyes. Taking a deep breath, she inhaled his spicy scent. She squeezed her eyes tight and fought her tears.

"I don't know how I can leave you. It hurts," he whispered against a spot behind her ear. "I'm afraid something might happen to you while I'm gone and I won't see you again."

She turned. He tried to hide his face in her hair. His vulnerability embarrassed him, she realized. "I'm fearful of water, never of flying, but the thought of you on a plane today made me borrow Jane's rosary for a prayer this morning. And I never pray." She meant to kiss him softly for comfort, but her lips clung to his.

When they pulled back for air, she held on to him and tried to calm down. A few moments later, his lips sought hers again. This time, desire had replaced despondence. His tongue explored her mouth. His caresses became less tight and tense, more seeking and sensual.

Her body aching with need, she nudged him away from the kitchen. "Let's go to my room."

He resisted. "I don't want your first time to be like this, rushed."

Frustrated, she snapped, "I want to fool around a little before you take off for god knows how long. Is that too much to ask?"

Taken aback, his eyes rounded. Then he grinned and pulled her toward her room. "No, not too much to ask at all."

When she stood next to him, inches from her bed, her fingers tensed. Nervousness hit her. She wished she hadn't missed her sexuality class about foreplay. He gently kissed her cheek. She relaxed, recognizing that *he* knew what to do.

He trailed his lips down one side of her neck and whispered how he adored her scent.

Though she loved his unhurried pace, she voiced her concern about their shortage of time.

"Impatient, aren't you?" Chuckling, he stopped his kisses on her neck. Nimble masculine fingers deftly unbuttoned her shirt and expertly released the clasp of her bra.

She frowned and jealously wondered how many times he had done that before. When his hands skillfully cupped and kneaded her bare breasts, she immediately forgave him for his experience.

His mouth closed around one nipple. His tongue! What a wonderful use of lingual muscles! She purred, "Yesssss."

He pulled at her skirt. While his mouth kept busy at her breasts, his hands discarded her panties.

She pressed against his hand. Her bare legs brushed against his pants. She pulled back and complained. "You're still dressed."

He undid his shirt and unbuckled his belt. She slipped her hand into his briefs. Liking the silky feel of his hardness at her fingertips, she tried to grab more of him. At her pulling, he gasped.

Suddenly shy, she whispered, "I want to feel more of you."

He wasn't shy with his response. He immediately loosened his pants and grabbed both of her hands and placed them fully on him. Wanting to hear him gasp again, she gave another hard pull at the tip. To her disappointment, he didn't gasp. He took her hand and moved it lower, showing her how he liked it. She fondled and stroked and tugged.

He threw his head back and loudly gasped his approval.

"I want us to be together," she paused, "but we don't have a condom."

He pulled her hands off him and adjusted their positions. When he was fully on top of her on the bed, he asked with a rakish grin, "Is this what you wanted?"

She eagerly nodded. He wrapped her legs around his hips and began a gentle rubbing. Needing more, she shifted restlessly under him. He intensified his rhythm.

"Should we interrupt them?" Jane said. "What time is your flight scheduled to leave?"

Standing at the window of the orphanage office, Bingley stared at the good-bye scene between the lovers in the courtyard. "Let's give them another five minutes. My flight crew is ready. Darcy normally would have gotten to the airport hours ago and checked to make sure the pilot knows what to do. You had a taste of his inspection process."

Jane rolled her eyes. He chuckled. Darcy had finally agreed to leave Vietnam, but only after he had checked the safety of all places Elizabeth spent time at: the cottage, the orphanage, and even her office at the hospital. Elizabeth was amusedly patient through the whole process, twice, but Bingley could understand Jane's exasperation.

"I'm sorry it didn't work out with the adoption," she said.

"That's all right. I knew deep in my heart before we even arrived the adoption wasn't going to happen. I had half feared for the child who would have my sister and her husband as parents anyhow. I know that's a terrible thing to say about one's own family."

"They're not ready now, perhaps someday…"

Shrugging, he changed the topic. "How long is George Wickham expected to stay in jail?"

"At least a year before they're ready to deport him."

"How did your sister arrange it?"

"She asked her patient Mr. Vinh to check Mr. Wickham's activities. They caught him trying to lure young girls to go to South Korea to meet his cult's guru." Jane smiled a satisfied smile. "He's either too stupid to realize or remember there's no freedom of religion here."

Bingley glanced at his watch. "It's time to deal with the lovebirds."

When they approached the couple standing next to the car, Bingley turned away to hide a smile when Jane's eyes bulged at the rumpled appearance of Darcy's normally immaculate clothes. Bingley coughed. "Darce, we need to get going. The crew called. They're ready."

The couple reluctantly parted. Jane came up to Darcy to give him a good-bye hug while giving Bingley a head tilt in the direction of her sister.

As he hugged Elizabeth, she instructed him, "Charles, take care of him for me, please. Don't let him push himself too hard. Make sure he doesn't let his headaches get too bad. Caffeine would do him good at the start of one, and he needs peace and quiet."

He nodded to her and heard Darcy telling Jane, "Keep your doors locked at all time. Be careful with cooking and fire. Don't let Elizabeth near any water, she'll panic. Make sure she eats healthy and doesn't work too much. Take care of her for me. I'll be back soon."

Bingley met Jane's eyes; she looked as amused and exasperated as he was. He grabbed Darcy's arm and pushed him toward the car. Three minutes later, they were on their way.

—⁂—

As soon as they were on the jet, Darcy disappeared into the small private cabin, closed the door, and didn't come out until they stopped in Honolulu for refueling. Bingley ignored the red in Darcy's eyes, offered him some coffee, and worked to distract him.

For ten minutes, they discussed the difficulties of one of their companies. Bingley said, "What's Richard think about the Mushatt deal?"

"He thinks it's not as big of a problem as Anne made it out to be. He may be minimizing, though."

"He doesn't want you to return to the stress of your normal life yet. Your cousin is one protective mother hen with you and your sister."

"I wish he'd stop it. I'm a grown man," Darcy grumbled.

"He still feels guilty for not telling you about Georgiana's boyfriend. If he had, it wouldn't have gotten as far as it did."

"He shouldn't blame himself."

"Have you told them about meeting Elizabeth?"

"Not yet. I don't want to suffer Richard's teasing and I want to talk to Georgiana in person. She might want to come with me when I return."

"What about Anne?"

"Anne? What about her?" Darcy looked surprised. "I suppose if she wants a vacation."

"No, I meant did you tell her about Elizabeth?"

"You know I don't share details of my personal life with Anne. She lives with my aunt, remember?"

"Don't share anything."

"You usually like everybody." Darcy leaned back in his chair. "I've never understood why you've never warmed to Anne."

"It's not that I don't like her." Bingley's protest sounded weak even to him. "But it's odd how focused she is with DDF. It's all she lives for, the company."

"She's proven herself as a valuable vice president, even if I was forced by my aunt to hire her," Darcy pointed out. "Don't forget, she also handles PTF's grants process and attends functions for the foundation all over town."

"Anything that has to do with DDF and the Pemberley Trust Foundation is still work. She's not going to be happy that you plan to return to Vietnam and ignore business again."

Darcy shrugged. "Too bad."

"Why didn't you have Elizabeth come with you to New York? It's not like she has a real job."

"It's more than a real job," Darcy said in a how-dare-you-insult-my-woman voice. "She's contributing her time and commitment. She and Jane are doing more than writing checks, which is all that you and I do."

"True." Bingley turned away to hide a smile and agreed to pacify him.

"I did think about it, asking her to come with me," Darcy admitted with a sheepish smile. "But she can't leave Jane alone until something more permanent is settled with the orphanage." He stood. "I need to stretch my legs."

While Darcy paced around the jet, Bingley sat and thought

about what his friend had just said. When Darcy returned to his seat, Bingley faced him. "Listen, I'm going to help you smooth out some of the urgent problems Anne thinks we're having. As soon as things are settled at DDF, I'm thinking of taking an extended leave to go do something."

"Like what?"

Bingley shrugged. "Contribute more than writing checks. I'm in a bit of a funk and I need a change. Not another vacation, but something else."

Darcy's knowing eyes scrutinized him for a long moment, but all he said was, "All right."

Bingley switched the topic back to Darcy's girlfriend. "I can't see you handling a long-distance relationship well. You'll go nuts worrying about Elizabeth. When are you thinking of returning?"

"Hopefully in no more than a month, at most two. I might set up something so I can work in Asia until Elizabeth and Jane are done with their work there."

"Then?"

"Then I'm going to get down on my knees and beg the most beautiful, wonderful, adorable woman to take pity on me and move to New York and marry me. Then I'm going to spend the rest of my life making sure she doesn't regret it."

CHAPTER 17

❀

Help Wanted

THREE MORE HOURS. ELIZABETH GLANCED AT THE CLOCK AND absently picked at the water-spinach leaves.

"You're thinking of William, aren't you?" Jane stood beside her, peeling a cucumber.

"I know it's silly, but I've never missed anyone this much before."

"Why is it silly?"

"We only met last month."

"You've never told any guy you loved him, either," Jane said in her gentle voice. "He's special to you."

"You're going to make me cry." Elizabeth sniffed. "At least I'm not at the resort. I'd miss him even more."

"I can't believe Hussein went through all that trouble. Did you get ahold of him?"

"All I've gotten is a voice mail: 'Darling, I'll explain soon.'"

"In the end, it didn't cost him anything. William paid for it." Jane sliced a star fruit. Perfect star-shaped slices came off the knife. Tangy, fruity smell infused the air.

"Yes, my new boyfriend, who I initially thought was gay but turned out not to be, paid for the shenanigans of my old boyfriend, who I initially thought wasn't gay but turned out to be very gay.

Careful." Elizabeth removed the sharp knife from her laughing sister's hand. "It was a lot of money William paid for someone who's unemployed. I didn't know he did that until after he had already left, otherwise I would have stopped him."

"How's his job search going?"

"I don't know." At Jane's look of surprise, Elizabeth said, "He hasn't told me yet he's unemployed."

"Still?"

"I think he's waiting to get some firm offers before he does. I heard him talking to his cousin about preferring to work for some company based in New York versus Holland."

"Are you sure he's hard up financially if he's friends with Charles? They flew out of here on a private jet."

"That was Charles's family plane. The Bingley family is loaded. William must have lost his job with the last company when he took time off to take care of his sister last year." Elizabeth stole a slice of star fruit and popped it in her mouth, then smacked her lips from the sour aftertaste.

"What kind of accounting work? Auditing or tax or something else?"

"He specializes in acquisitions and mergers. I don't know what that means exactly." Elizabeth had never understood the various business terms. "He doesn't like accounting though; never wants to talk about work."

Jane laughed. "Probably because no one ever wants to hear about accounting."

"He told me once on the phone that, of all the work he's done, what relaxed him most and made him happiest was looking over grants for art and cultural foundations. Some type of nonprofit work would suit him better than being stuck in some dreary accounting department shuffling papers around."

"He strikes me more as management material, rather than someone in a cubicle." Jane pursed her lips. "Something doesn't add up. He didn't act like a man who worries about money."

"Guys are too proud to show they have money trouble, or any trouble for that matter," Elizabeth reasoned. "He's had a tough time. At the age when most guys loaf around drinking beer through their belly buttons, he was raising his sister. Little sister finally off to college, and bam, got hooked into a cult. No wonder William's been depressed. He blamed himself for working so much that he neglected her."

"True. When we first met him, he was tightly wound."

"He's going to find another unsuitable job for the money, and then he'll be back in the same grind. He's only been back there a week and he's having headaches again."

"Are you sure it's not the stress of missing you?" Jane made kissing noises.

"Stop it." Elizabeth laughed, knowing her sister was trying to cheer her up. She took a deep breath. "Listen, I've been thinking. I need to find a job."

"You mean a paying job?"

"Yes. I want to earn enough money so that William—"

"Whoa! Hold on." Jane held up her palm. "How would your getting a paying job affect William?"

"I'm going to find a job in New York. Then I can help support us both and help him with his sister's college tuition. He'd only need to take a job he'd love. Everybody will be happy." To give her sister time to adjust to her news, and to close her mouth, Elizabeth moved to the dining room and set the table for dinner.

"What?" Her sister followed. She sat down and stared blankly at Elizabeth for a few long moments. "You just met last month and you guys are talking about moving in together, consolidating finances and all that, already?"

"Not in so many explicit words. But he's mentioned he wants to grow old with me. I do want to marry him, take care of him, and help his sister." Elizabeth blushed. She sounded exactly like Chau with Bill Collins.

"You haven't discussed this with him?" Jane gave her that I-think-you-are-crazy look. "You're moving too fast here. I don't think it's going to be that simple."

Elizabeth crossed her arms. "Life doesn't always have to be complicated."

"He does not seem like a man who would let his girlfriend or wife support him financially, and I seriously doubt that he'd let you help with his sister's college tuition."

"I don't see why not."

"Lizzy, you have a sweet tendency to try to take care of people and you think you know what's good for them, and we love you for it, but he's not one of your sisters. He has his male pride—"

Elizabeth cut her sister off. "I won't be totally supporting him, only sharing his financial burden. But you're right about his pride—he has too much—that's why I'm not going to tell him until it's all done."

Jane pinched her temples. "Are you sure you've thought through this very carefully?"

"I have," Elizabeth assured her. "Remember when I did a two-month stint as a visiting fellow in New York last year? I already have an active license for the state and, more importantly, connections to a few hospitals from my time there. I've been making calls and there are definitely some good leads. The hospital where I did my rotation even asked me to give Grand Rounds."

Jane dropped her hands. "Wow, you have thought things through. That's the first time I've ever heard you carefully planning your career."

"I didn't have any reason to make plans before."

"What if you're misunderstanding the situation with William? Before you fly across the world and change your life and your whole career focus, you need to call and talk to him."

"And have him refuse my help? I'm not going to let his sensitive male pride get in the way." Elizabeth was firm. "I've made my decision. I've thought of nothing else for the last few days."

Her sister buried her head in her hands and groaned. "Most people take weeks or months to decide on something like this."

"We spend most of our phone calls talking about how much we miss each other and wishing we're together."

Jane lifted her head. "For your sakes, I hope he'll be so happy to see you, he'll agree to your crazy scheme."

That was exactly what Elizabeth hoped would happen. She refused to think beyond that—that William might not appreciate her boldness—for fear she'd lose her nerve. "Let's have Mary come and stay with you. I want to leave as soon as possible, next week if everything works out. I need to be in New York to job search."

"That soon?" Jane looked shocked, then resigned. "I shouldn't be surprised. You were always quick in making decisions, and you're even quicker with acting on them."

"About Mary, what do you think?"

"Might be a good change of scenery for her. She's at loose ends now that she's out of the tree she was living in," Jane said. "I can't believe she lasted that long, living in a tree for weeks, just to protest the logging industry. She's not going back to grad school yet?"

"She's holding off going back for a while to see if she wants to protest something else."

"Get her here quick, before she gets involved in another eco-terrorist stunt."

"I'll make some calls tomorrow." Elizabeth jumped to hug her sister. "Thank you for understanding I want to be with William soon."

Thirty minutes before ten that night, Elizabeth, wearing William's old Harvard T-shirt she had begged off him, lay in bed and counted the minutes until his nightly phone call.

Her cell phone rang and her heart skipped a beat. She frowned when it wasn't his ring. She looked at the caller ID and saw the interloper's name.

"About time, you asshole!" she shouted into the phone.

"Darling, I've been busy. I'm in between breasts, you know," Hussein calmly returned.

"Why did you waste my time? I was seeing sunburn cases at that damn resort when I could have been at the hospital treating people who could use some real medical help," she screamed the last words.

"This is the thanks I get for giving you a few weeks of relaxation?"

Not hearing outright excuses or denials, she was immediately suspicious. "You don't have a ready excuse?"

"Are you not trophy-wife material yet?"

"You have four minutes to explain, or I'll call your mother."

"Ouch. You're getting vicious. All right, since you brought my mother up, I'll tell the truth. She's been trying to set me up to marry some girl back home. I told her you and I are getting married and she's coming to plan our engagement party."

"What?"

"I thought if I gave you some relaxation time at a spa, you'd get yourself all spruced up. I knew you wouldn't go to a five-star resort without some noble purpose—you have a terrible work ethic—so I had them set up a little nothing-work for you."

"So it really was just to make me into trophy-wife material?"

"I'm desperate to get married and, of all the fake girlfriends I've had, my mother loves you the best. You're beautiful in pictures, but you're not exactly princess material. You don't highlight, you don't varnish, you don't wax. No one would believe I'd marry a granola, natural girl. I'm a plastic surgeon. You wouldn't be good advertisement."

She shook her head. He was ridiculous, but she knew he thought he made perfect sense. If it wasn't for the comic relief he gave her, she would have chucked him and his opportunistic hubris years ago. "I assume you will have a good explanation planned when the fake engagement party doesn't lead to a fake wedding."

"But, darling, nothing has to be fake. My green card status isn't all that settled. It does not help to be an immigrant named Hussein living in Arizona right now."

"You're fricking serious?" She glanced at the clock and decided she didn't have time to listen to him anymore; William would be calling soon. She got down to business and told Hussein in no uncertain terms she would never go along with his fake engagement or fake marriage or whatever else he had cooking. She threatened his life, his body, and—the scariest threat of all to him—to tell his mother everything. When he realized she meant it, he quickly changed his tune; he was a mama's boy.

After Elizabeth got him scared enough, she extracted promises of restitution from him.

She hung up satisfied. Mary's airfare would be paid for. Her own trip to New York and job search expenses would be covered. What William paid for her resort bill was about equal to what she would extract from Hussein.

Her cell phone rang again a few minutes later. Grinning in satisfaction, she flipped it open again.

"Hi, love," she said, smiling with happiness.

CHAPTER 18

❀

New York, New York

MR. DARCY WAS NOT IN A GOOD MOOD, MRS. CHING CONCLUDED, closing the CEO's office door. He was anxious about something. As his secretary for a few years now, she'd become adept at reading his mood.

Something had happened with a certain Miss Bennet. The day he arrived back at work three weeks ago, he had given her very specific instructions: he was to be available, interrupted or transferred, at any time whenever a certain Miss Elizabeth Bennet called. On a whim, Mrs. Ching Googled the name. Too many results came up. No matter. Though Miss Bennet had not called the office phone yet, Mrs. Ching suspected she'd meet the lady eventually.

After dinner that evening, Darcy asked to talk to his sister. She'd just arrived home from England earlier that day. "How was your time at Pemberley?"

Her fingers pulled at a napkin's corner. "Fine."

He sighed and wished for Elizabeth's presence. A chuckle escaped him. He was pathetic. Already, he depended on his girl-friend to help him handle the awkwardness with his sister.

Eyes guarded, Georgiana cast him a glance.

"I'm sorry, I wasn't laughing at you. I was thinking about someone." On impulse, he reached for his sister's hand and squeezed it gently.

After an initial stiffening, she gave his fingers a tiny squeeze in response. "Who?"

"Elizabeth Bennet. I met her in Vietnam. My girlfriend."

"No! Really?"

He smiled at his sister's opened mouth. "Yes, really."

"You have a girlfriend? You never have girlfriends." The napkin now carelessly discarded, she leaned forward. "Tell me about her."

Encouraged by his sister's eagerness, he began to tell her about Elizabeth.

"You sound like you really like her," his sister said when he finally stopped.

"I do like her, a lot."

"I've never heard you say that about a woman before. Does she like you?" As if realizing how that might have sounded, she hurriedly added, "I mean lots of women like you, but does she truly like you, in the same way?"

He felt his cheeks redden. "Even better, she loves me... and I love her."

She raised her hand to her mouth. "Who are you and what have you done with my brother?" She lunged at him and hugged him tight.

He hugged her back just as tightly. "And I love you, Georgiana."

"I love you too, Will," she cried into his shirt. "I'm so sorry for everything last year. I made you depressed because of my stupidity."

"I should have taken better care of you and not neglected you when you went off to college. I've been down lately because...

because of my failure, not because of you or what you did. And you are not stupid."

"I was stupid. I trusted George and I shouldn't have," she said. "Do you remember how Father was at the end?" She pulled back and wiped her eyes. "He hardly wanted to see anyone, but he always looked forward to George's visits. He made Father laugh. I remember that."

"You had good memories of George, of course you'd trust him when you saw him again."

"I should have been suspicious when he didn't want me to tell you about us dating," she said. "He explained you had cut him off after Father died because you were jealous of his relationship with our father. I should have known you had good reasons."

"I was jealous of his relationship with our father," he admitted, "and I did have good reasons to cut George off."

"I should not have given him money. He convinced me our father supported his spiritual quest for a meaningful life and had planned to leave him money to study theology. He also claimed Father was going to give him a position on the DDF board, but you denied his rights to it. I was stupid to believe him."

"Georgiana"—he shook his head—"you're not stupid. I don't want to hear you say that again."

"Yes, I was." She nodded. "I should have realized it was all lies. Even if Father did promise money, he would never give away any part of DDF to someone who isn't a family member. Richard's a part-owner and he can't even run the board meetings without your presence."

"Or yours, don't forget; you're a Darcy," he reminded her. "I don't want you to blame yourself any longer. It's my fault. I didn't take George's threat seriously and I didn't warn you. Can you forgive me?"

She accepted his apology and again tried to apologize to him;

he interrupted and insisted it was his fault. Finally, they agreed to stop apologizing to each other. She wanted to hear more about his girlfriend, and he wanted to talk more about his girlfriend.

When his sister heard his suggestion about her joining him on his return trip to Vietnam, her face lit up. "I'm not ready to go back to school yet. If you're sure I won't be in your way."

"You won't," he said firmly. "Elizabeth will love you. If you want something to do, Jane will appreciate your help at the orphanage. She's a sweet lady. You'll like her."

"Is Elizabeth a sweet lady too?"

He laughed, glad to hear the teasing in her voice. "Actually, no. She's a mischievous devil."

"Could we call them now and tell them I'm coming?"

"I'll tell her the next time I talk to her."

"Call her now. I'll leave you alone." She disappeared before he could respond.

Surprised by her eagerness, he smiled and stared after her. He called Elizabeth's cell phone. No answer. He sagged against the couch. Cell phone service and Internet connections in Vietnam were sketchy in spots, but he didn't expect her to be this out of touch. He hadn't been able to get through to her in the last few days.

"When can we leave?" Georgiana came back into the room ten minutes later. "What did she say?"

"I couldn't get ahold of her. She's traveling, giving medical lectures at various hospitals in Vietnam."

"Couldn't we get there and surprise her?"

"Hold on." He held up his hand. "We'll leave as soon as I can arrange to be away for another extended period. Anne's having some difficulty and she needs me for some tricky negotiations during the next few weeks."

"Let Richard or Charles handle them."

"It's not Richard's area of expertise and Charles left for Africa."

"All right. I'll wait," she said, disappointment in her voice. "But I'm really anxious to meet Elizabeth."

"I'm anxious to see her too," he agreed, looking down at his hands.

———

Unable to contact Elizabeth, Darcy's hands became more red and cracked over the next few days. He even tried to call the orphanage's office; some woman answered each time and refused to give him any personal information about Elizabeth or Jane. The sisters must be traveling together. He even called the hospital, but all he got each time was: "Dr. E li sa bet go home!"

"William, we're ready to start looking at the figures for Abbate Inc.," Anne said from behind him one day as he stood staring out of the window of the conference room.

For the next few hours, he dealt with graphs and figures until the meeting finally ended. Except for his two vice presidents, everyone else exited speedily when he dismissed them. He was in a bad mood and it showed. Wearily, he returned to his previous spot by the window.

Anne said, "William, the Frick Museum Board dinner meeting is tomorrow night before the reception. They acquired that painting you recommended and want your approval for the next one."

"It would be great for you to relax a bit, Cuz," Richard said. "You always enjoyed beautiful women and beautiful art. I hear Helena is organizing the reception. Give her a call."

"I've already told them you would probably be coming with me, William," Anne said. "I thought it would be more convenient to attend together."

"All right. Thanks, Anne." He didn't want to do anything except sit by the phone, but he still had obligations. Anne had been shouldering a lot of them and it was time he did his share. If he didn't hear from Elizabeth soon, the DDF jet would be on its way to Vietnam and more work would be dumped on Anne. He owed it to her to escort her tomorrow night.

Through the reflection of the window, he saw Anne glaring at a smirking Richard, who raised his middle finger. Anne quickly left the room.

"Very mature, Richard," Darcy said.

"She deserves it. She—"

"I don't want to hear it." Darcy held up his hand, not up to hearing the usual litany of complaints about Anne. He left the room, automatically checking his cell phone.

He had missed a call from Vietnam!

Jane's orphanage number. He had, out of habit, put it on silent mode during the meeting. He stopped in the hallway and listened.

Jane apologized for missing his calls. Her sister Mary—sister Mary? What happened to Elizabeth? Darcy held his breath—had not realized it was a personal call and not one related to orphanage business. Jane had bad news—Darcy's heart stopped—Wickham had been released from prison early. He reportedly had bribed his way out.

Elizabeth! Darcy's head screamed inside. He should never have left her there! The message ended with Jane telling him she was trying to get ahold of Elizabeth to inform her also. He replayed the message again. He called Jane back. No answer.

"Darce, say Darce, are you all right?" Richard appeared next to him. "You look white. Is it bad news? Georgiana? Mrs. R.?"

"I should never have left her there. I can't believe I came back

for some business deals while she was still in danger from him."
Heart pounding now, he walked rapidly toward his office. "I have
to go back to Vietnam right now."

"What? Vietnam? Who, who are you talking about?" Richard
followed and furiously whispered, "Is it the paid escort?"

Richard's assistant appeared around the corner. "Mr. Fitzwilliam,
the people from Tgruy are waiting for you in your office."

Richard held out a hand. "Wait, Darce. Let me deal with this quick."

Darcy ignored him and kept walking. He gave Mrs. Ching the
orphanage number and asked her to try to reach Jane to find out
where, exactly, her sister Elizabeth was in Vietnam and for the
DDF jet to be prepared to leave. He went into his inner office and
started planning what he needed to do.

Richard ran in and shut the door. "Darce, man. Don't go back.
Don't go crazy on me here. If I knew you were going to go this
apeshit over some casual vacation hook-up, I would never have
pushed you to get involved with one."

"Be quiet. I have to think," Darcy snapped, his mind was
already on the next item in his list. By the time he finished his
mental list, Richard had disappeared. Darcy picked up the phone.
"Mrs. Ching, get me Colonel Brandon."

—⁓—

A few short hours later, three cars pulled up to the tarmac where
the DDF jet waited. The first car had Darcy with a team of people
with him, listening as he deluged them with rapid-fire instructions.
The second car had the DDF security team traveling with him to
Vietnam. The third car had his cousin Richard, chasing after him,
still frantically trying to convince him not to go. Darcy ignored
him while he talked to Colonel Brandon, his chief of security.

A fourth car pulled up. At the sight of it, Darcy stopped talking.

Carrying a bag, Georgiana ran up to him. "If you're going to Vietnam, I'm coming with you. You promised."

His cell phone buzzed with an incoming text message: *Elizabeth Bennet found. Call office.*

"Mr. Darcy, I have a Miss Jane Bennet on the phone holding for you. I'll transfer you," Mrs. Ching said in her usual quiet efficient manner after one ring.

"William, this is Jane." Amidst the background hum of the crowd around him, her calm voice was a welcome relief. "Your secretary said you're about to board a plane to be on your way back here to Vietnam."

"Elizabeth?"

"Elizabeth is fine. She isn't here. I told her she should have told you what she was doing," Jane said. "I'm a bit frustrated with my impulsive sister for causing this panic."

"Where?" Darcy said, his heart racing too fast for him to manage more words.

"She's in New York," Jane replied.

"New York?" Darcy was shocked.

"New York?" repeated Richard.

"New York?" chorused the crowd.

"Yes, New York City. Are you anywhere near there?" Jane's raised voice could be heard clearly.

The crowd laughed, then stopped abruptly at Darcy's glare.

"Where exactly in New York City?" He ignored his staff's mumblings about their near miss of a frantic trip halfway around the world to find a woman already here in New York. He stepped away from the crowd to better hear Jane.

She answered his question, and the next, and the many more

he asked. As he listened, his hands shook. Standing apart from the crowd and next to Richard, Georgiana looked worried. Darcy gave his sister a reassuring smile as he said to Elizabeth's sister, "Thank you, Jane. Let me assure you I have enough to take care of your sister and her great-great-grandchildren's grandchildren, if I can convince that crazy, impulsive, maddening sister of yours to marry me."

He rang off after assuring Jane he would get in touch with her once he found Elizabeth. He tried the numbers of Elizabeth's new cell phone. It went to her voice mail. He closed his eyes and exhaled in relief. At least he had a working number now.

He shook his head. In a small way—a very small way—he was exasperated with her obstinate obtuseness. A large part of his heart—an overwhelming large part—however, was now filled with an unbelievable warmth. He was astounded, touched, and very humbled by the miracle of her selfless love.

It totally fit with his Elizabeth's tendency to champion the underdog. And he was the lucky dog.

He sent the security team home, canceled the flight, and gave the rest of the staff instructions. His employees began placing calls. He walked over to Georgiana and Richard.

"Darce, she followed you here to New York. Some girl followed you to New York!" Richard's panicked voice was a near shout.

"She's really here?" Georgiana asked in a hopeful tone.

"Yes. Isn't it wonderful?" Darcy impulsively picked up his sister and swung her around.

His unexpected exuberance surprised her, he saw, but then she laughed aloud and said in a near shout of her own, "I'm so happy to see you happy, William."

"Darce, you can't..." Richard paused as one of Darcy's assistants approached.

"Mr. Darcy, there is a Dr. Bennet lecturing at an Infectious Disease Grand Rounds at Lambton Medical Center in ten minutes."

CHAPTER 19

❀

Rich Man, Poor Man

"Remember, when you hear *American Sleeping Sickness* disease, they're not talking about what happened in Washington, DC, they're talking about *Chagas Disease*, a parasitic infection," Elizabeth ended her talk to the sound of laughter and applause in the hospital auditorium. "I'll take questions now."

She flipped a switch to turn the light on. Scanning the audience, she noticed a stylishly and expensively dressed blond couple she didn't recognize studying her intensely. Dismissing them as pharmaceutical sales reps, she pointed to some raised hands and answered questions. When the questions stopped and the room began to empty, she saw she had a few minutes before her dinner meeting with the residents.

Her frantic job search had paid off. Right before the Grand Rounds, the chairman of the department had offered her a one-month position, starting tomorrow; they needed someone to fill in for a pregnant attending doctor who had suddenly developed some complications. Elizabeth's application came at the right time. Since she had spent time at the hospital and her research paper was recently featured on the cover of an infectious disease journal, they were happy to offer her the temporary position on the spot.

Except for a brief break to meet with a financial planner Hussein had given her the name of—some distant cousin of his—she had been busy with job-hunting. Now that she had some good news, she wished she could skip the dinner, go back to her hotel room, and call William.

As if her wishing had conjured up a vision of him, she suddenly saw him and smiled. He seemed so real. When she straightened after bending to pick up her briefcase, the vision smiled back at her. She blinked. The vision came closer.

—⁓—

Richard observed the woman's stunned face when Darcy approached. With a hesitant motion, she reached one hand toward Darcy then paused and, instead, covered her gaping mouth. Darcy's arms enveloped her. Her small white coat–clad figure disappeared into Darcy. Richard turned away; witnessing the private moment felt intrusive. When he turned back, the couple had finished their embrace, yet they still leaned toward each other with their hands clasped.

Reassured the doctor at least appeared to have some feelings for his cousin, Richard let out a relieved breath. The next moment, he frowned. After nearly a year of being depressed, Darcy had bounced back and lost his head over a woman. And that worried Richard. He remembered the brief period of wild partying Darcy went through right after his father died, before the threat of losing custody of his sister to his aunt brought him out of his self-destructive grief.

Richard studied the doctor's appearance. Dark chestnut hair framed a lively face. Though he easily saw why his cousin was captivated, he shrugged and decided he wouldn't be too concerned.

Brains and beauty, nothing unusual there; Darcy was constantly exposed to smart and beautiful women. They were a dime a dozen, all jockeying to get at Darcy's large coin purse. Sooner or later, they'd show their tarnish and bore Darcy.

"Let's go see what's the deal with this one," he muttered and walked up to the couple. Georgiana followed.

"It's time I give you a shock, Doctor Bennet," Darcy said.

About to respond to Darcy, the doctor caught sight of Richard and Georgiana approaching. In a cool tone, she greeted them, "I'm sorry, but I'm not able to talk right now about any new antibiotics your company is promoting."

"Sweetheart, this is my cousin Richard and my sister, Georgiana." Darcy turned to them. "This is Dr. Elizabeth Bennet."

Richard's mouth fell open. *Sweetheart?*

At first, the two women greeted each other with shy smiles. Then, spontaneously and simultaneously, they hugged each other. Darcy sported a silly grin watching them.

"I'm sorry for my mistake. You both look so beautiful and stylish. Pharmaceutical reps are usually good-looking. That's how they court us doctors." The doctor tilted her head in Richard's direction. "I figured they'd sent me a pretty boy here."

While his cousins laughed, Richard winked at her. "Not handsome enough to tempt you though, Doc?"

A glower replaced Darcy's grin. Richard rocked on his heels, happy to see it.

Georgiana said, "Dr. Bennet, I enjoyed hearing your lecture."

"Please call me Elizabeth, or Lizzy. And I thank you for the compliment. I'm glad that you didn't run out when you saw the gross slides"—the doc winked at Darcy—"as someone likely did."

Darcy winked back at her. "It wouldn't do for me to faint in the middle of your lecture."

Richard reminded himself to set up a background check on the woman. Pronto.

A group of young doctors, mostly young males, approached. The doc told Darcy she had to leave for her dinner meeting with the residents. "I don't know how long we'll be."

Darcy's face fell. "I'll kill some time and drop Georgiana and Richard off, then I'll come back for you. We'll go get you checked out of your hotel and I'll take you home."

—⁓—

His cousin's last words alarmed Richard. This was serious. Darcy was going to take this woman to his townhouse and not the penthouse. Once they were in the car, Richard repeated his earlier concern. "Darce, don't you think it's odd she followed you here to New York?"

"No."

Richard could not believe what had happened to his ultra-careful cousin. "Aren't you concerned? How well do you know this girl?"

"No, I'm not concerned," Darcy said. "I know her well enough—"

"You can't know her that well, you haven't been dating her that long. You just left Vietnam a little over three weeks ago," Richard interrupted. "She probably has tons of debts from medical school and followed you here before you could get a chance to come to your senses."

"Are you done?"

Darcy's furious tone made Richard pause briefly, but he pressed on. "You're acting like Charles when he meets a nice piece of a—" He stopped, reminded of Georgiana's presence. "Once people learn of your net worth, they'll do anything. Wait for a thorough background check before you do anything stupid." At the anger flaring in Darcy's eyes, Richard leaned away from him. "You know I'm watching out for you."

"Precisely why I'm not wringing your bloody neck right now."

"Don't be taken in by a pretty face. She may be pretty and smart and a doctor, but that doesn't mean she doesn't have a hidden agenda."

"You want to know what her hidden agenda was in coming to New York? She loved my sorry arse well enough to leave her sister, drop her volunteer commitment, and come here to find a well-paying job."

"There you—"

"A well-paying job to help me."

"What? That makes no sense."

To his surprise, Darcy suddenly laughed and slumped back against the seat; all tension seemed to have left him. "She wants to lighten my financial burden. She thinks I'm unemployed. She doesn't want me to take a job I'd hate, in accounting. She thinks I'm an accountant. She wants me to do what I once told her was very relaxing work for me: looking at grants for art foundations. She thought that was a real job I had once."

"You're serious?" Georgiana said.

"You're kidding?" Richard said.

"Yes, I'm serious. And no, I'm not kidding. Her sister Jane told me all this on the phone earlier." Darcy smiled at his sister. His smile disappeared when he faced Richard. "You're right. We don't know each other that well because we haven't been together long. But in essentials, she's the most real thing I've ever met."

"Oh, Will." Georgiana reached for her brother's hand.

Darcy briefly clasped his sister's hand. "Everything fits now: her frugal behavior with money and her constant fretting about my spending in Vietnam. She kept making comments about budgeting and how one can live simply and still be happy... and I misunderstood. It never occurred to me she was talking about me."

Richard snorted. "How could she not know how much you're worth? Anyone can check..."

Darcy shook his head. "She's not one to Google a person to find out how much they're worth. A woman who volunteers at a hospital in a Third-World country is not someone who would do that."

"Don't give her any false expectations of long-term financial support or commitment from you," Richard said. "What you're telling me proves my point: you don't know each other well enough to rush into anything."

"She didn't know my monetary worth, yes, but I was worthy enough simply as the man she loved for her to want to help me. I don't need her money, but I..." Darcy paused. Eyes blinking rapidly, he turned toward the car's window.

Richard turned toward the window also, to the view outside, of New York City cabs and cars and buses whizzing by. How could he convince Darcy he was moving too fast with this woman?

Darcy faced him again. "I need her. Do you have any idea how bloody great it feels to be loved like that? To be valued simply as a man for my true worth and not my bank balance?"

Subdued by the emotions he heard in his cousin's voice, Richard swallowed his remaining protest.

"Well, I think she's wonderful." Georgiana hugged her brother. "I'm glad, Will. You deserve the best."

"She is the best," Darcy said in the tone of a man who had found a rare gem and knew it.

Georgiana giggled. "You mean, as of right now, she still doesn't know you own DDF?"

Her brother smiled at her. "Nope."

"Are you going to tell her?" Richard said.

"Of course," Darcy said. "At least she's in New York with me now. My hands can't handle any more washings, worrying about where she is."

Richard's eyes met Georgiana's briefly before turning back to her brother. "Does she know about your… uh… hand-washing habit?"

"She's a doctor; of course, she picked up on it."

"And what does she think?"

"It's not a big deal to her. She simply accepts that part of me."

Hearing that, Richard allowed a little hope in, though he still would maintain his vigilance to make sure this woman was not a good fake.

"When will you tell her about DDF?" Georgiana asked. "I want to be there when you do."

"I want to see this too." Richard tried to keep his skepticism from showing in his voice.

Darcy said, "I need to tell her soon, before she accepts a job."

"Oh, but she might go back to Vietnam to finish her volunteer work," Georgiana pointed out. "I want her to stay here."

"She shouldn't go back to Vietnam right now, regardless, because of Wickham." Darcy then told them about Wickham being in Vietnam, of Elizabeth's role in his imprisonment, and now his recent release.

"That bastard. Is that why you were frantic to go back there today?" Richard said. It made sense to him now, his cousin's panic earlier. Wickham might try to harm the doctor.

Darcy nodded. "He's probably planning some sort of revenge

on her—and me. I was told he would stay in prison for months at least. I should have foreseen he'd bribe his way out of prison. I thought he was broke."

"Now, wait a second, don't start beating yourself up. She's here now with you."

"Are you going to have security on her too?" Georgiana's hesitant question brought an instantaneous reaction in her brother.

A frantic note in his voice, Darcy immediately ordered the driver to go back to the hospital. "We left her alone there without security. I can't believe I forgot."

Richard tried to calm his cousin. "Darce, chill, man. She'll be fine. He's not here yet. What could have happened to her in the last thirty minutes?"

"You know as well as I do he has friends here who would do his dirty work for him with just one phone call." Darcy's hands visibly shook with his agitation.

"What are you going to do? Stick to her all the time, not let her out of your sight, like you do with Georgiana?" Richard impatiently asked. His cousin's reaction disturbed him. This was going backward. After the Wickham episode last year, Darcy had become too protective of his young sister. Security details constantly surrounded her and shadowed her every move. That, and the stress of watching her brother's guilt-ridden despondency and his tendency to panic over her safety, had stifled the already depressed Georgiana.

And now, Darcy had picked up another person to obsess about. Witnessing his cousin's agitation, Richard hoped this Elizabeth was made of stronger stuff than Georgiana, to withstand Darcy's compulsive controlling instincts.

"I'm going to do everything I can to make sure she's safe, just as I do with Georgiana, especially since Wickham is on the prowl again with more reasons to hate me," Darcy said in a determined voice.

Georgian stared down at her hands.

Richard sank in his seat, frustrated. The rest of the ride back to the hospital was made in silence.

They finally pulled up close to the medical center and stopped at a light. The driver prepared to make a right turn into the waiting area. A group of doctors crossed the street, heading toward the hospital's entrance. Dr. Bennet was in the middle of a sea of white coats, animatedly talking and gesturing with her hands while the others walked alongside her and listened.

When her group reached the sidewalk, Darcy lowered his window. The noise caught her attention and she turned in the direction of the car. Upon seeing Richard's cousin, her face visibly bloomed. After a long moment during which the two lovers simply smiled at each other, she turned back to her companions. She waved them off and headed toward the car.

Richard swallowed. In the thirty some years they had grown up together, he had felt many things for his cousin. He felt compassion for Darcy losing his parents at a young age and respect for the mantle of responsibility Darcy had willingly assumed as Georgiana's guardian. He felt great pity, he was ashamed to admit, for Darcy being afflicted with debilitating, compulsive habits. He felt a need, always, to protect his vulnerable cousin, a man as close to him as a brother.

But he had never felt jealousy until now, until he unwittingly witnessed that look of pure adoration in the woman's face as she caught sight of the man she loved, neuroses and all. The softened look in her eyes as she gazed at his cousin made Richard feel Darcy was the luckiest man on earth.

Richard began to understand a little why Darcy was so certain this was the real thing.

"Hi, love," she greeted his cousin.

CHAPTER 20

❀

Sweet Surrender

ELIZABETH WAS NOW SAFELY IN THE CAR WITH HIM. THE TIGHT band around Darcy's chest eased. He let out a relieved breath.

"Dr. Bennet, my cousin told me you're in New York looking for work?" Richard said.

"Elizabeth, not Dr. Bennet, unless you're paying me to give you some pain and bad medical advice," she answered, before turning to Darcy and telling him the details of her job offer. She concluded, "It's only for a month, but it's a foot in the door for a chance at a more permanent spot later."

"Hurray!" Georgiana exclaimed and blushed when they turned in her direction.

Elizabeth smiled at her. "Thank you."

"Congratulations, sweetheart. I'm sure you won't have any problem landing that permanent spot." Darcy kissed her temple. "They would be lucky to have you."

"Speaking of bad advice," Richard said, "my cousin's not happy with the company he's interviewing. I've been telling him to forget about numbers and spreadsheets in some dreary accounting department, and go for something he loves instead. You think that's bad advice?"

Elizabeth eagerly leaned toward him. "Yes. I mean, no. I think it's a great idea." She turned back to Darcy and said in an encouraging voice, "You should do something with the arts. Work for some nonprofits again."

"Are you an art connoisseur, Elizabeth?" Richard said.

"Hardly." She laughed. "I've been to museums, that's about it. I love New York. Some of the best museums are free."

"Darce here has some contacts from his... uh... previous work with some of the museums. He could get you in for free at any museum," Richard said.

"Really?" Elizabeth asked Darcy.

Not knowing how to respond, he simply nodded. When she turned toward his sister, he glared at his cousin behind her back.

Elizabeth spoke to Georgiana. "Since William can get us in for free, perhaps you could go with me on my days off?"

"I'd love to," Georgiana said.

"Darce likes looking over grants for art museums," Richard stated.

Darcy took hold of Elizabeth's hand to get her attention. "Sweetheart—"

"Nonprofits don't pay much," Richard interrupted. "Perhaps he could supplement his income. He owns a few designer duds. He would make a killing being a professional male escort. Better pay than any accounting work."

Georgiana giggled while Elizabeth stiffened and frowned at Richard.

Darcy squeezed her hand. "Sweetheart. He's teasing. Jane told me of your plans in coming here."

Elizabeth turned her frown to him. "Jane told you? Why? She knew I didn't want you to know until I had it settled."

"Your sister had to call and warn me." He explained about

Wickham. "You've been avoiding my calls and not answering my emails. Do you know how worried I've been?"

"Um... I didn't want to lie to you." Elizabeth blushed and glanced at Richard and Georgiana, obviously embarrassed they were witnessing the conversation. "My cell phone from Vietnam didn't work here. I had to get a new one. I was going to call you but I wanted to wait until I had a position settled and my financial planning done."

Richard straightened. "Financial planning?"

"Yes, I met with a financial planner. I must say, I couldn't make sense of any of that stuff he gave me to read. He gave me a binder this thick to study for homework." Elizabeth held her fingers three inches apart and made a face.

"Why did you have to meet with a financial planner?" Richard said.

"None of your business, Richard," Darcy said, not liking the suspicious tone of his cousin's voice.

"Estate planning," Elizabeth said. "To be financially responsible. They told us we should learn about it when I graduated from medical school, but I was never interested before."

"I see." Richard directed a pointed glance at Darcy.

Elizabeth caught the glance. "I wanted to understand so I can talk to William about financial matters... and his work. I'm a bit embarrassed at how little I understood terms like 'commodity and options' transactions and 'tangible personal property.'"

Darcy squeezed her hand again. "Don't worry about that, love. I don't understand your medical terms."

"Do you have much debt from medical school?" Richard asked. "Do you have many assets?"

Impatient with his cousin's doggedness, Darcy barked, "Bloody hell, Richard, leave off."

"No, it's okay, William. He's just curious," Elizabeth reassured him and turned to Richard. "I went to a state school and I received a big scholarship. My school debt is minimal. I can easily manage the payments without working too hard. I don't have any assets to speak of, however. I understood that term. But don't worry, an infectious disease specialist in a New York City hospital earns a decent salary, more than I'd know what to do with, to be honest."

"Sweetheart, we'll talk later, in private." He threw Richard a definite warning glance to cease. This time, he was clear that he wouldn't allow Richard to pester Elizabeth anymore. His cousin nodded, acknowledging the message.

They pulled up to Elizabeth's hotel a few minutes later. She took him aside, whispering, "They charged me for the night already. It'd be such a waste not to use it." She blushed and glanced at Georgiana. "You could join me. It's more private."

He resisted the temptation to immediately rush her up to her hotel room and lock the door. "Sweetheart, I'd feel safer with you at my home."

"Okay. But I insist on sharing tonight's fare. A private taxi must cost a lot."

"Shhh! We'll talk later. Let's go get you packed and checked out," he said. When she invited Georgiana to come upstairs and keep her company while she packed, he made to follow them.

Richard restrained him with a touch on his arm. "Give them some private girl time to get to know each other. Okay, I'll concede that she's probably not after your money, but..."

"But what?"

"But she doesn't know anything about art or business. I'm surprised you'd fall for someone so... so lacking in culture and sophistication."

"I had so-called cultured and sophisticated women and they did nothing to me or for me." Well aware that Richard was simply being protective, Darcy tried to check his anger. "I know why you're having a hard time accepting her. You're not used to someone like her. She may be a bit innocent and naive, I'll admit that, but she is exactly what you see, no artifice or pretense. She doesn't admit interest or knowledge in things just to impress or capture anyone's attention. I'm just lucky she's interested in me. And don't you worry. She's cultural and sophisticated enough where it counts. She knows how to handle snobby prats like you."

Darcy left his cousin and went to pay Elizabeth's bill. When she came down and discovered he had done so she became upset. She scolded him, saying he needed to save his money. She continued to harangue him on the way to the car as he carried her bags. While the car headed to his townhome on the east side of Manhattan, she refused to look at him or let him hold her hand, muttering under her breath about people who don't know how to budget and are too spendthrift for their own good.

Sighing, he ignored the snickering of his cousin and his sister and told the driver to make a detour.

They reached his office building minutes later. He pointed to the *DDF* in front. "See that? It stands for Darcy, Darcy, and Fitzwilliam."

"Cool. You have the same name as the building. Hey, have you ever gone in there and said 'Hello. I'm Mr. Darcy' and gotten a free cup of coffee?" Elizabeth immediately joked.

Georgiana laughed aloud, while Richard said, "He does that everyday, only he doesn't need to say it. They know who he is."

Elizabeth looked at Darcy. He waited. She quipped, "Wait! They have both of your names on there. You should get two cups of coffee."

He tried again. "I own the building. My grandfather was the first *D*, my father the second *D*, and the *F* was Richard's father."

She turned to stare at the building, then back at him. She furrowed her brows.

He added, "I'm rich, very rich."

Her mouth opened then closed. She squinted her eyes to make out the building's letters in the dark. She pursed her lips and frowned. After a long minute, her eyes brightened. "I don't have to meet with the financial planner again."

She was clearly more excited by this thought than the news of his wealth. Darcy bemusedly shook his head and agreed, "No, you don't."

"He's not just an accountant. He employs departments of accountants," Richard said.

"I can throw away the binder then?" she said. They all laughed at the relieved tone in her voice.

Darcy hugged her tight and buried his face in her hair. She brought laughter into his life.

She pushed him away. "Then, why was Charles paying for your trip?"

"He wasn't. I don't know what gave you that idea. I always pay my own way."

"Then, what was that about the company you lost last year that made you sad? Was that why you didn't like your work anymore? Because you lost the company?"

"I didn't lose the company. I just didn't care about it enough to acquire it. And I like my work fine. I was in a funk about it for a bit, that's all. When and what did Bingley say that gave you the impression I'm unemployed and poor?"

She told them about what Charles had said that day outside of Merry Bar, after Darcy had abruptly left.

"You misunderstood him. But why didn't you ask me about my work?"

"But I did. And you always said—"

"I always said I didn't want to talk about it," he finished, chuckling ruefully. He could see why she had concluded what she did. "I did tell you I work in acquisitions and mergers of companies. What did you think I meant?"

"That you worked in acquisitions and mergers, whatever that means."

Shaking his head, Richard laughed aloud. "It's a good thing I saw you standing in front of a whole auditorium earlier."

Angry that Elizabeth now looked embarrassed at Richard's words, Darcy challenged him. "And did you understand her stuff?"

"No, not a word. It was way above my head. I felt very stupid." Richard faced Elizabeth. "I'm sorry. I didn't mean to offend you. I was living up to my own hair." He pointed to his blond locks.

"I wasn't offended," Elizabeth said. "I should be more well-rounded in my education. I'm afraid I've spent most of my time in a laboratory and a hospital."

"Time well spent," Darcy said. "You have nothing to apologize for. You stood as an expert in front of a whole auditorium full of doctors and felt confident enough to make jokes."

"You were so brave," Georgiana said. "I could never speak in front of a large group like that."

"Nor could I," Richard chimed in. "I could make the jokes, but not say anything substantial to wow them. Darce here could wow a crowd into silence though. He has this intimidating CEO face that he—"

Darcy cut in, "Ignore him. DDF specializes in acquisition and mergers, which means I buy companies and merge or consolidate some. After I've fixed them, I turn around and sell them."

"When you say you work with numbers, you're not just a simple accountant then?"

"Hardly," Darcy said, insulted she mistook him for a common accountant.

"And when you said you enjoyed looking at grants…"

"It means he enjoys being the philanthropic stud and wearing his tux to artsy-fartsy pretentious shindigs," Richard said. "Have you heard of the Pemberley Trust Foundation?"

"Yes, of course. On PBS, they always say something like, 'Supported by a grant from the Pemberley Trust Foundation' after some show," Elizabeth imitated the commercial voice. They waited. She looked at them staring at her.

"Darcy is the Pemberley Trust Foundation, or PTF," Richard said finally. "He could easily afford to buy and sell the hotel we just left. It's like buying a cup of coffee for him."

"Just because he could afford it doesn't mean he should be wasteful and not keep track of his spending." Elizabeth turned to Darcy. "How could you pay hundreds of dollars a night for a room in Vietnam when you could spend a fourth of that and get one just as nice? You were being fleeced at that resort and you didn't even know it. You should have asked around to see how much the other guests were paying for the same type of suite. Some of them were paying a third of what you and Charles were. It was not high tourist season. You should have bargained."

Dumbfounded, he stared at her. Even after he told her how wealthy he was, she still harped on him for wasting money on a hotel room. A hotel room!

She continued, "It's been bugging me. I didn't want to say anything before, because I didn't want to make you feel bad you were wasting Charles's money, but you should always do comparison shopping."

He didn't know what to say. She was too adorable for words. He decided to agree. "I'll make sure my assistants uh… do some comparison shopping before they book me a room."

She gave him an approving smile.

After they dropped Richard off at his place, Darcy took Elizabeth and his sister home. It was late, and Mrs. Reynolds had retired for the night. Georgiana excused herself, not-too-subtly trying to give him and Elizabeth privacy.

"It's so big," Elizabeth said with unaffected awe as she glanced around. "A Third-World hospital could fit in here. But it's very comfortable, like a home should be. You have a beautiful home, William."

He wanted to tell her he wanted this to be her home too, permanently. They had never discussed marriage openly, though he had hinted at it in conversations with her on the telephone. Now that she was in his home and the words hovered anxiously on the tip of his tongue—to offer his home and his life to her—he was nervous. What if he had presumed too much? In his mind, their marrying was a forgone conclusion, but what if she didn't feel the same? What if she just wanted to shag him? Not that he'd mind obliging her, but he wanted more.

He showed her to a guest room. She gave him a puzzled glance but didn't say anything. He said good night and left her.

He performed his nightly routine, securing the house. He checked all the locks and windows on the ground floor, then set the alarm. He was halfway up the first flight of stairs when he doubled back and rechecked the doors and windows again. The third time, he made it near the landing of the second floor before he again descended. Elizabeth was now in his home. That warranted one more safety inspection.

Finally, he made it to his room. He headed straight to the bathroom sink.

After the third hand washing, about to turn off the faucet, he caught sight of his face in the mirror. The telltale nervous spasm on the right of his eyebrow—subtle and faint to others but always flashing and blaring to him like the semaphores at Penn Station—reminded him he was a man loaded with baggage.

What if she didn't want to commit herself for life to such a man?

In the crowd of white coats that surrounded her at the end of her lecture, it didn't escape his attention that most were men. One of her life's dreams was to work for Doctors Without Borders. What if one of those humanitarian doctors, a man not burdened with excess baggage, shared her humanitarian passion for saving the world? Wouldn't such a man be a better partner for her?

Lost in his anxiety, it took him a while to hear the knocking above the noise of running water. He opened the door.

A glaring Elizabeth stood on the other side. "It took me forever to find the right room." She entered and faced him with her hands on her hips. "Okay, spill. You're obviously worried about something."

He swallowed. "I... uh... I..."

"Listen, if you've changed your mind about me staying here, in your home, it's fine. But I want to know: what the hell am I doing here? Why am I here? Why did you want me here?"

"I want you here, in my home," he said through a dry throat. "I don't want you ever to leave here. Leave me."

"Then why were you so cold just now? You left me in my room so quickly—as if you couldn't stand to be around me anymore. And why the hell am I in a guest room?" she yelled.

"Because I want to marry you," he said without thinking.

"Is that a proposal?" she said with an incredulous expression. "You want to marry me, so you act cold all of a sudden and you don't want to sleep with me? Is this because I'm a virgin? I can't help that. I've been trying to get rid of it and you haven't been helping. You want to wait until we're married? Is that it? I'm fricking twenty-eight years old. I don't want to wait anymore!" She was shouting at the end.

"Do you want to marry me or do you just want to shag me?" he shouted back.

"Both," she screamed. They stared at each other for a moment before she laughed and collapsed on his bed. "That has got to be the worst proposal and acceptance in the history of mankind."

"But it's still a yes." Relieved and more than a little shocked at her easy acceptance, he grinned and joined her on the bed. She did want to marry him!

"At least you didn't begin with 'In vain I have struggled…'" She tenderly pushed a strand of hair from his forehead. "So what happens now?"

He kissed the hand caressing his hair. "You accepted me. Now I shag you."

Her hand stilled. He sat up and kissed her soft cheek. Slowly, he moved his lips to her opened mouth. Sweet heavens, he had missed how intoxicating her lips were. She wrapped her arms tight around him and enthusiastically kissed him back.

Leaving her mouth, he pressed his lips against that spot behind her ear he loved, inhaling her heady scent. She was a breath of fresh air in his stale life.

Her fingers impatiently tugged at her shirt. He pulled back and helped. Buttons popped and flew. She laughed. Her laughter abruptly stopped when his face delved into the crevice of her breasts. While she encouraged him with moans and sighs, he greedily suckled.

Aching with need, he reached down. His hand encountered her skirt. They were still dressed, he realized. He needed to calm down or he wouldn't last long. "We must slow down."

"No, no slowing," she said in a firm voice. She rose and took off her clothes with quick and decisive movements. "No stopping."

At the sight of her beautiful nakedness, all the blood in his body went south. He gawked.

She got on her knees and pulled at his shirt. He came to with her vigorous jostling and all thought of going slow left him. He pushed her hands off and stood to undress himself. She followed and hampered him with her attempts to help.

At last, naked, he pulled her body against his. They both sighed in pleasure at their first full contact unencumbered by clothes. The hard buds of her nipples rubbing against his chest felt so wonderfully arousing. Closing his eyes, he tilted his head back for a moment then lifted her so that the softness between her thighs cuddled his hardness. She wrapped her legs around his waist. When she moved her hips in a frantic movement, he groaned and laid her back down.

She reached up and pulled his head down to her chest. He nibbled and kissed her breasts before he again took a nipple in his mouth. She whimpered her pleasure. When his hand slipped between her legs, she loudly moaned her approval and pressed against his fingers. He caressed her until she thrust her pelvis frantically against his hand and her body broke with release.

A pink hue flushed over her in the aftermath. Before she completely recovered, he plunged his tongue into her mouth. As he deepened the kiss, her hand slipped between them and circled his hardness. Lifting up his hips slightly, he placed his hand over hers to guide her. He taught her to massage him in a circular motion against her, then up and down in a stroking motion. Clenching his teeth in an effort to control himself, he nudged his tip gently forward. Barely inside her, he allowed himself a few shallow thrusts. She moved her hands to his back, restlessly widened her thighs and opened herself more to him. The warmth and moistness of her undid his control. He lost it. He plunged himself fully into her. She stiffened and cried out in pain.

Embedded in her now, he opened his eyes in remorse at having been so rough. Not knowing how to undo his invasion, he stayed motionlessly suspended in her and fought the primal urge to thrust. After what seemed like an excruciatingly long moment, he began to retreat.

She shook her head, wrapped her legs tight around his hips, and tried to push him back in. "Please," she whispered. "I want you. Don't stop."

At this, he slowly pushed back into her. When he was deep within her again, he closed his eyes and stilled his body, trying to breathe slowly. The softness of her enveloping tightly around him felt so good. At the thought of how privileged he was to be her first—and God willing, her only—lover, he almost passed out. He began to move gently. After several long moments, his head against her temple, he paused and fought for control, afraid if he continued with the stronger strokes his body was demanding he would lose it and hurt her again.

Her hands lifted his head to face her. With a determined expression in her eyes, as if she was in charge, she said in a fierce tone, "Move."

A chuckle escaped him. Even in passion she made him laugh. Then laughter left him as his hips obeyed her. She whispered encouraging nonsensical words—intermittently mixed in with "my love" and "my William"—against his neck. Thrust after thrust, he entered her. With each, his body liquefied into crashing waves against the steady shore that was his beautiful Lizzy.

He forced his eyes open and locked his gaze with hers. He tried to tell her without words how wondrous she was.

At the moment of sweet surrender, he released himself into her safekeeping and spilled into her depths.

CHAPTER 21

❀

What the Frick?

Fingers twitching at Elizabeth's left breast roused her. A low-pitched rumble blew behind her ears. *He snores.* She smiled, glad, for some inexplicable reason, he was not perfect.

Quietly, she slipped out of his arms. When she returned from the bathroom, she paused at the edge of the bed to marvel at the sight of him.

Under moonlight, his long lashes laid crescent shadows over his cheeks. His lips, fuller in sleep than when awake, parted slightly, as if waiting for a kiss. She blew him a kiss before sweeping her eyes down. Soft sheets draped and outlined a very male body underneath. She hesitated for the briefest second before lifting the sheets. She sighed with appreciation.

With the sleek body of an endurance athlete and just enough well-defined muscles to convey underlying strength, he was a beautiful specimen. Slipping under the covers, she inched close to him. Even as she admonished herself for taking advantage of a sleeping man, she gently rubbed her breasts against his chest.

His eyes opened.

She stopped her rubbing. Holding his gaze, she boldly climbed atop him. "Hi."

"Are you okay?" he said, his voice full of concern. "Did I hurt you? Are you sore?"

Though she was, a little, she answered, "Do I look like I'm hurt or sore?"

She shifted and trapped his muscular thigh between her legs. His eyes flared but he remained still, though she felt him hardening against her belly. Shamelessly, she rubbed herself a few times against his leg and grinned at him. "Woof."

Growling, he suddenly moved. She was flipped over onto her back and her body covered by his.

When he was done, she barely had enough energy to utter, "Wow!"

"Wow," he agreed, kissed her cheek, and settled himself against her. Seconds afterward, even breathing emanated from him. Contented, she fell asleep to the lulling sound of his soft snores vibrating against her temple.

When she next woke up, bright sun rays beamed through the translucent drapes. She glanced at the bedside clock. "Shit!"

He stirred. "What?"

"The time!" Wincing at the soreness between her legs, she ran into the bathroom. Ineffectually, she fumbled with the shower fixture, muttering, "Damn rich sod and his fancy shower."

A male hand reached in and turned on the shower for her.

"I'm supposed to be at the hospital in less than forty minutes. I haven't had a chance to look through the patients' list this morning to prepare myself."

"I'll get you there in time," he assured her and left the bathroom. She stole a glance at his naked backside and cursed her bad luck at having to leave for work. Toweling herself dry a scant five minutes later, she walked into the bedroom and saw that he thoughtfully had her suitcase opened. He had even brought her briefcase and laid it nearby.

She wasted a few minutes looking for the right hallway to the stairs, snarling at the maze of rooms and doors in her way. Briefcase in hand, she yelled good-bye and rushed to the front door, hoping to find a taxi soon. She was about to pass through the door when, out of nowhere, he appeared and blocked her exit.

"I need to find a taxi," she said.

"The car and driver will be here shortly to take you. You'll get there in plenty of time." He put down a travel mug and a bagel on the side table in the foyer, and took her briefcase from her and placed it next to the food. "Coffee and breakfast for you."

"I'll eat in the car." She walked back and forth a few steps then stepped close to him to whisper, "Am I walking funny?"

"No, why?" he whispered back.

"I'm a little sore," she confessed. "I don't want it to look too obvious what I was doing last night and why I'm late. They all knew I was going to meet up with my boyfriend last night."

"Fiancé this morning," he corrected. "Sorry about the soreness."

She laughed at the pinkish tinge on his cheeks and teased, "I'm not. I demanded you *shag* me twice."

His face paled. "We forgot protection last night."

Jolted, she raised her finger to her lips. "I can't believe I didn't think of it."

"No, I should have thought of it. I don't think I even have any condoms here in the house." He rubbed her shoulders gently. "Sweetheart, I'm sorry. Is it a vulnerable time of your cycle? Are you in the middle?"

"No, I just had my period. It's a safe time. I'm always regular."

Disconcerted at his uncharacteristic frankness, she wondered if he was very used to discussing this topic with other women. She bit back the jealous question on the tip of her tongue and reminded herself she was an infectious disease specialist. In her best detached-professional tone, she said, "I assume you have been careful in the past about using condoms? Any history of diseases?"

He visibly shuddered. "No. And yes, I've always used condoms before. I'd be happy to get tested."

"I'd appreciate that. Okay, for now, I don't want to hear any more details about your past." She definitely did not want to think about his former lovers, most of whom she was sure had more experience than her. "You can be in charge of getting condoms."

"Call me when you're done today. Don't leave the hospital until I send a car for you."

"I can take a taxi back here." At his emphatic head shaking, she sighed. "All right, I'll wait for the car. Damn, I'm going to be late."

"The car's here." He put the coffee and bagel in her hand, picked up her briefcase and pulled her through the door. After he helped her into the car, he kissed her and whispered, "I'll kiss it better tonight, your soreness." He chuckled when she blushed and pushed him away, glancing at the driver.

The sound of his chuckles ringing in her ears kept her company all the way to the hospital.

"Come in," Georgiana answered soft knocking. She had just finished a difficult piece on the piano.

"That was beautiful." Elizabeth's smiling face appeared. "I listened outside the door. Didn't want to disturb you."

"How was your first day at work?"

"Fine. Probably the easiest day I'll have for a while. There were very few patients and I finished early, but you don't want to hear about my work."

"I do. I really do," Georgiana assured her. "What exactly will you be doing this month?"

"Starting today, any new patient who needs an opinion on any infectious issue will be under my watch. I'll be the attending physician in charge and the one to blame if anything goes wrong. My name will be the one on the chart the malpractice plaintiff lawyers would zero in on," Elizabeth said with a laugh.

"I'm sure nothing will go wrong."

"Not if I can help it." Elizabeth peered into the opening of the grand piano. "Your brother wasn't exaggerating when he bragged you're a virtuoso at the piano."

Georgiana blushed. "Oh no, not at all."

"I say you are. Besides, your brother said so, and I'm sure he would never allow himself to be wrong." Elizabeth rolled her eyes. "I just met Mrs. Reynolds. She's such a sweet lady."

"She's been humming and cleaning all day. She wants everything perfect since we now have a fiancée in the house."

"How sweet." Elizabeth's head disappeared into the opening of the piano. "Can you play some notes so I can see how things move in here?" Georgiana did as requested. When Elizabeth's head reappeared, she tugged her ears. "My, that was loud in there. What was I thinking?"

Georgiana giggled. "I can't believe you're marrying my brother. He's so serious, I was sure he'd marry someone boring." She put her hand to her mouth. "I'm sorry. It's not only Will. It's me too. We Darcys are usually serious... and boring."

Elizabeth's eyes twinkled. "So, besides you two, how many of you serious and boring Darcys are there?"

"There's my father's sister, Aunt Catherine. She's Lady de Bourgh. Her husband was Lord Lewis de Bourgh. And there's Aunt Catherine's stepdaughter Anne, Lady Anne de Bourgh. She works with William and Richard at DDF." Georgiana suddenly noticed her fingers nervously tapping at the piano keys and stilled her hands.

"With two young men as your guardians, it's good you have close female relatives, even if they do have such lugubrious titles," Elizabeth said. "Your brother hardly ever mentioned anything about your relatives, though men rarely share such details, I've noticed. What about your mother's side?"

"She only had one brother, Uncle Matt. He took over as CEO at DDF when our father died. He retired a few years ago and William became CEO. My uncle and my aunt gave their share of DDF to Richard and now they live on a yacht in Greece."

"I'm glad your brother goes by William instead of Fitzwilliam. It would be a mouthful to be yelling 'Fitzwilliam' whenever I'm mad at him." Elizabeth chuckled. "You look shocked. What? You mean to tell me you've never felt like yelling at him? Ever?"

Georgiana shook her head. At Elizabeth's raised brow, Georgiana amended, "A little, sometimes." Elizabeth's brow stayed raised and Georgiana admitted, "Maybe a lot." She took a breath. "Actually, lots of times."

"Atta girl," Elizabeth said. "As wonderful as your brother is, he can't be cheated out of his fair share of illogical male logic. Six women in my family, and most of the time we can't comprehend my father's male logic, or lack thereof."

Feeling a little like Laurie in *Little Women*, Georgiana said, "I can't imagine growing up with that many sisters. Are you the oldest or is Jane? What do they all do?"

"Jane is two years older, formerly a social worker and now an orphanage director, both perfect jobs for the quintessential very responsible oldest child. Then comes me, the ultra-responsible alpha child." She paused while Georgiana laughed. "Then Mary, who's three years younger, supposed to be in grad school studying computer science, and she's well… eccentrically responsible. Three years younger than her is Kitty, graduating from Stanford this year and who's resentfully responsible. And then there's Lydia, the youngest, who's very irresponsible for being born at all."

"Why?"

"Kitty's always complained that when she started school, Lydia slipped in and stole her spot as the youngest. Lydia's a happy, exuberantly bouncy little thing. She competes in club cheering squads."

William entered. "This is where you two have been hiding."

"You're off early? Don't rich CEOs work long hours?" Elizabeth teased him.

"I couldn't concentrate at work, knowing this bit of mischief is home already." He gently tweaked his fiancée's nose, and gave her an intense look and a gentle kiss on her cheek.

A little disconcerted at her brother's behavior, Georgiana hid a smile and pretended to be busy with the music sheets to give the couple some privacy as they chatted about their day.

Richard entered and headed straight toward Elizabeth. "My cousin here will be tied up tonight at some museum thing, Doc. But I'm free."

William turned to him. "I'd forgotten that the Frick's function is tonight. Would you take my place?"

"Sure, I'll be here with Doc." Richard gave Elizabeth a smile

Georgiana knew he considered his wow-them smile. Snorting, Georgiana wondered if he realized how ridiculous he looked. Reminded of her presence, he added, "And Georgiana, of course."

William frowned at him. "No, I mean go with Anne."

"What? Me go with Dragon Lady to some boring museum event? I don't think so. I'll be here with your fiancée." Richard turned back to Elizabeth. "Congratulations on your engagement, by the way, Doc. My cousin moved fast."

William stepped in between Richard and Elizabeth. "My swinging arm is also very fast if you don't behave."

Richard rolled his eyes. "Fine. So you wouldn't have to deal with a woman on each arm, I'll join you to even out the number. But I'm not taking Anne off your hands. I'll keep Doc company."

"But Elizabeth won't have time to get anything fancy to wear," Georgiana worried, remembering the contents of the suitcases she had helped pack at the hotel. She looked at Elizabeth's curvaceous body. "I don't think I have anything that would fit her."

"Would you mind going out tonight, sweetheart?" William put his arms around Elizabeth and turned her away from Richard, who was assessing her curves also. "We'll go shopping to get you something to wear now, if you'd like. I don't want to leave you on your first evening at home here, but I've agreed to escort my cousin Anne."

"I'm the full-blood, real cousin; she's a stepcousin with no blood connection, remember that, Doc," Richard inserted. "I'm more important than she is, no matter what she says."

"Ignore him," William said. "If he keeps flirting with my fiancée, he's going to be a distant cousin soon."

Elizabeth said, "I'll go, but I hate shopping. I might have a traditional dress from Vietnam that would do. I'm looking forward to meeting this Anne."

CHAPTER 22

❀

Hair

"Go for the jugular." Anne studied the background report in front of her.

Too bad the CEO didn't practice that. What a waste of one of the most astute business minds she'd known. No matter. Soon, she'd convince him to see things her way... once they became partners in everything. She flicked at a spot on her sleeve. She'd reduce Richard's one-third share to nothing—if for nothing else, for ruining her evening two weeks ago at the Frick.

She had been having a great evening until he'd shown up. Darcy had been so appreciative of all her hard work and apologized profusely for arriving late. He had thanked her publicly and stressed to the other museum board members he could not do without the hard work of his valuable vice president Anne de Bourgh.

Later, as they walked around the reception hall thanking the other contributors and patrons, Anne saw his one-time girlfriend Helena's eyes gleam with envy and jealousy when Darcy and Anne stood in front of Helena and her date. Two years previously, at a similar event in this same museum, the ex–beauty queen had been at Darcy's side as his date. Distracted by Richard waving at him across the room, Darcy blanked and greeted his old flame as "Elena" before correcting himself. He excused himself to talk to his cousin. Anne followed. Richard's date was some dark-haired woman wearing an oriental costume.

When they reached the couple, Darcy touched the woman's arm. "Enjoying yourself, love? Richard's keeping you entertained?"

Anne managed to prevent her gasp from escaping. It suddenly clicked for her who the woman might be, given the exotic costume. With a brightly colored chopstick sticking out from a twisted bun on top of her head, the woman looked out of place. Loose strands of hair draped across her neck, giving her a too casual appearance considering the formality of the evening.

The woman laughed. "He's trying to give me an education on art, but he knows less than I do."

"Just because I mixed up a few artists and paintings," Richard grumbled.

"Love, let me introduce you to my other cousin. This is Anne de Bourgh. She steps in as PTF's representative when I'm not around," Darcy said. "Anne, this is Dr. Elizabeth Bennet."

Anne forced herself to make pleasant talk to the woman, even when Darcy suggested that the other two stick close. "I want to introduce Elizabeth to some—"

"No way," Richard cut in. "Trust me, Doc, you don't want to meet these pretentious drones who go on and on about boring art and how their money supports it. I should know; I spend enough time with these bores at work." He grinned at Darcy's frown. "I'm going to show her the rest of the building."

"Okay, but don't leave the museum," Darcy said. "Elizabeth has to be at work early tomorrow."

"And of course, you'd want her home to bed early to get some rest," Richard said with a malicious glance at Anne. "I'll make sure Anne gets home safely so you can get Elizabeth home to have her... uh... rest."

Darcy winked and returned the woman's smile before Richard pulled her away. Darcy's eyes followed the two until they disappeared. Anne glanced around and stiffened when she encountered the pity in Helena's knowing eyes.

On the ride home, she had to suffer Richard's taunt. "Cinderelly, do you have a penthouse suite with a bevy of young princes waiting, or should I drop you off at evil Stepmama's? Is she in town now or at her castle in England?"

She ignored him.

"Speaking of the penthouse suite, this Elizabeth must be someone special, because that's not where he's taking her tonight. She's staying at his home, with his sister and Mrs. Reynolds." He whistled. "Lucky dog, a big happy family with three adoring women. Perhaps I'll talk him into deeding his penthouse suite over to me. For sure he has no further need of it."

She had to clench her fists so she wouldn't be tempted to slap him.

"Who'd ever have thought, after all that he had done to make doctors and hospitals more accountable and be a pest to the AMA, Darce is now getting tender loving care from a doc of all people. We should tell the malpractice plaintiff lawyers in town they're losing their best friend."

Richard's last words that night replayed in Anne's mind. Her eyes returned to the report in on her desk. She spotted an item: Member of American Medical Association.

She smiled. She had found a vein to draw blood from.

Elizabeth lifted up her right arm and squinted at her armpit. Using tweezers, she plucked a hair. She had learned this hair removal trick in Vietnam. Shaving irritated her skin, and she often did not bother. Who would notice or care? But now, someone would notice, and she didn't want him to.

"Next, I'm going to be getting a Brazilian wax job, whatever that is," she mumbled as she stood in the master bathroom. The natural lighting there was better than in her bathroom for peering at your armpits.

For William's sake, she had asked for a separate bathroom for herself. After one glance at the neat rows of old T-shirts hanging in evenly spaced precision in his immaculate closet, she had also insisted on separate closets.

He was out on a long run with Richard in Central Park. She decided to take this rare free Sunday morning to make herself beautiful for him, to celebrate their almost two-week anniversary of living together. With Mrs. Reynolds's help, she was also going to cook an English meal for him tonight. Now that she was getting married, Elizabeth had the urge to be like her mother, cooking and fussing over her man.

Two more weeks and her intense work month would be over. She'd be able to spend more time with him. She still had not set foot inside DDF. Once, during a rare afternoon off, she had called him at work and asked for a tour but he had said he had better things to show her at home.

And he did that afternoon—and most every night. As soon as the door to the master suite closed for the night, he would show her how much he had missed her that day. She giggled. For such a reticent man, he sure expressed himself most energetically in the bedroom.

Her thought turned to how, and likely with whom, he had come by his proficient lovemaking skills. Uninvited, the image of the slim, toned, and fit body of a beautiful woman from his past appeared—the one who'd kept staring at him at the Frick. When Elizabeth asked Richard who the woman was, he stammered she was an event organizer named Helena and tried to change the subject. Elizabeth instinctively knew then Helena had a history with William.

She studied herself in the bathroom mirror. Her breasts were too big, she decided, wishing she had the pert small chest of ballet dancers she admired. She pivoted a quarter turn and swept her eyes over her back view. Her hips protruded too much. If only she had Jane's willowy shape or the slim elegance of Georgiana.

She heard an intake of breath. Startled, she saw William's face reflected in the mirror. Mortified to be caught grooming her armpits, she blushed and tried to surreptitiously hide the tweezers.

With an indescribable expression in his eyes, he stepped into the room.

"You're not supposed to be back yet. I'm not done preparing—"

His tongue in her mouth stopped her words. When he lifted his lips from her, she melted against the counter, dazed. He turned her around so that she faced the mirror. A trail of kisses traveled down her spine. His hands cupped her soft globes and he knelt down.

"I love this bodacious bum," he whispered and traced the curves with his tongue. He gently nipped her.

Aroused, she gasped.

He immediately pulled back, concerned, "Did I hurt—"

"No." She twisted her body to press her pelvis toward him. Spreading her legs, he eagerly placed himself between them. Her head lolled against the mirror and the hard edge of the marble counter dug into her back, but she didn't complain. The dancing of his tongue as it darted and flicked between her legs had scrambled her senses.

When she at last became aware of her surroundings, she stared in surprise as she recognized the light fixture on the ceiling. Did she just have an orgasm on a bathroom counter?

"Now, you're prepared." With a self-satisfied smile, he undressed then opened a drawer. Small packets of foil flew as he impatiently reached for a condom packet.

She stood and tried to help but he shook his head. He turned her around again and positioned her face down over the counter. Her eyes widened. They weren't moving to the bedroom. Taking hold of her left leg, he lifted and bent it to rest her knee on the marble edge. One male hand reached and his fingers caressed and spread her lips.

"You're so ready for me. You drive me wild with need, my beautiful Lizzy," he whispered and withdrew his fingers. Lifting her hips slightly upward, he entered her and withdrew his fingers at the same time.

She could tell he tried to restrain himself with his gentle initial thrusting. She squeezed her pelvic muscles during one thrust to encourage him to let go, and he growled his pleasure in response. She did it again. He responded with a harder and faster pace.

She raised her head to the mirror. With his face clenching in concentration, a lock of hair falling over his forehead, and sweat running down his temple, he was a beautiful man in his passion.

Closing her eyes, she let herself suspend in the rapture of his primal mating dance. She screamed his name with her second climax. A few thrusts later, he shouted for divinity when he followed her. They both collapsed onto the counter.

Satisfied that her imperfect body could make him lose his control and his inhibition, she smiled. After a few moments, conscious of his weight on her, she wiggled.

He immediately lifted himself off her back and helped her up. He kissed her shoulder before he released her. "I'm sorry, love. I was such an animal, I didn't even give you a chance to say hello."

She touched his face. "Hello."

"You're done early today. Not too tired? Did you get some sleep? Did the patients you worried about do okay last night?"

"No, not too tired, and yes, I got some sleep in the doctor's lounge. My patients did fine. I got everyone stable." It didn't escape her notice that he was rambling a little. She kissed his neck and hugged him. The saltiness of his sweat, mixed with their love scent, wafted between.

His arms tightened around her.

"I like the way you said hello by the way. I like it when you sometimes go wild like that," she whispered into his chest, a little embarrassed herself at how much she liked it. He always apologized afterward, when he felt he had been too rough, and she wished he would not feel the need. She wondered if her inexperience made him uncomfortable.

"Once, I glimpsed you naked in your bathroom in Vietnam. The beautiful sight of your body has starred in many of my fantasies since."

"Oh?" she said, breathless at his shy confession.

"To come home today and unexpectedly see you in my bathroom, naked as in my fantasy…"

"You don't mind an intruder in your bathroom, then?"

"You could never be an intruder," he whispered tightly and clutched her body tighter.

She soothed him with gentle strokes to his back, recognizing this was one of those times when it was difficult for him to express himself with words. In the middle of the nights, she would sometimes awaken to find him staring at her with some intense, unfathomable expression in his eyes. Yet, whenever she asked him to tell her what serious thoughts had disturbed his sleep, his response was always physical and wordless. At such times, his lovemaking had a vulnerable and desperate rhythm to it. She wished she knew how to help him release his unvoiced fears.

To lighten the moment, she pulled back and teased, "If this is the kind of attention I get when I'm in your bathroom, I might move my messes in here."

"I'd like that." His expression was serious. "But I want you to be comfortable. You need privacy."

He had misunderstood her reason for wanting separate bathrooms. She rubbed his chest. "I grew up with four sisters. There was no privacy, in bathrooms or any other place at home. I'm rather untidy, and Jane had a difficult time with me when we shared a bathroom. I was just trying to spare you the aggravation."

He grinned and covered her hand with his. "Jane doesn't get the fringe benefits I get sharing a bathroom counter. I have to thank her for letting you come to New York."

"She couldn't stop me. You can thank her in person at the next Bennet clan get-together, which probably will be when we announce our engagement. I warn you, it's going to be a zoo. I have a big family."

"Did your parents mind you moving to New York, instead of going back to California?"

"Are you kidding? My parents always expected me to go off somewhere obscure and exotic to work. New York is like staying at home to them." During a phone call to arrange for her sister Mary to come replace her in Vietnam, Elizabeth told her parents she had met a wonderful man named William and was moving to New York to be with him. They immediately laughed and asked if her new guy was gay. Offended, she had childishly refused to give them any more details.

He released her. "I'd forgotten. Mrs. Reynolds wanted me to tell you she's ready anytime you want to join her in the kitchen."

She picked up her bathrobe. "I'd better go and take a shower and get down there."

"You could take a shower here, with me," he suggested with a lift of his eyebrows.

"Not now. Mrs. Reynolds is waiting for me to cook dinner with her." She ignored his pout, gave him a peck, and left the room. A few minutes later, she paused at the threshold of her own shower. What was she thinking? Turning down a shower with a sexy man to cook? Mrs. Reynolds wouldn't mind waiting. Doubling back, she crept into his bathroom, hoping to surprise him in the shower. She stopped short.

A towel wrapped around his waist, a bottle of bleach in his hand, he was hard at work wiping down the counter.

She bit her lip to stifle a chuckle and quietly backed away. Though she considered his cleaning compulsion adorable, William was very sensitive and self-conscious about it. It was too early in their relationship for her to tease him into a lighthearted acceptance of his fastidious quirks.

CHAPTER 23

❀

Dungeons and Dragons

"Tell me why we're on this new path today. We've been by here twice already," Richard said.

Running alongside his cousin in Central Park, Darcy said, "Elizabeth and Georgiana want free tickets for tonight's show at the Delacorte Theatre and I want to see if they've arrived." He ducked to avoid a low-hanging wet branch and ignored the smiles from two women runners passing him.

"Oomph."

Darcy turned and saw his cousin's head tangled in the branch. After one long look at the women's backsides, Richard caught up. "The Shakespeare in the Park show? Why can't they use the PTF's connection and get tickets?"

"You obviously don't know my fiancée if you had to ask that. She likes the idea of standing in line and getting the free tickets."

"Strange way to spend her day off," Richard said. "She still puzzles me, but as long as you're getting to know her better."

Darcy grinned. Before he left for his run, he definitely *knew* Elizabeth quite well this morning. Something about seeing him dressed in running shorts and a T-shirt made her want them off him right away. He didn't complain. Let Richard wait for once.

"How's it going really, Darcy? You're acting like a lovesick teenager with that silly grin you have on your face right now. You do that—that annoying grin—every time her name is brought up. When is the honeymoon going to be over and reality set in?"

"When my ashes are being scattered." Darcy grinned wider to annoy his cousin.

"Oh please, dear God, no! No proclaiming of undying love until the end of time, please, I beg you. You sound like Bingley in some stupid dreamland."

Darcy laughed, not missing the note of envy in Richard's voice.

"I noticed the absence of a ring on her finger still. Is there a wedding in the plans?" Richard said.

"Oh, it's definitely in the planning." Darcy smiled, imagining the perfect romantic evening when he would give her the ring and propose again, properly this time. He sighed. What a muck of it he had made with his shouting the first time.

"Why no announcement yet you're off the market?"

"I want to keep our relationship quiet for now. She's still going through the interview process at the hospital," Darcy said. The doctor Elizabeth was filling in for was expecting twins and had decided to resign. Elizabeth now had an excellent chance of being offered the woman's spot.

"Why would that matter?"

"You forget my fractious relationship with the medical establishment in this town," Darcy reminded his cousin. "They'd either want her because of my money, or not want her because of my past lobbying efforts. I'm a liability to her career."

"Because you responsibly pushed for more medical accountability and quality control? The hospital wouldn't take it out on one of their own doctors. They're in the business of healing people."

"Now you're the one living in dreamland. You said it: business. To survive, everything, by necessity, has to become a business decision sooner or later. Hospitals are not immune to that."

"You're a pessimist."

"I'm being pragmatic. I want her to be judged on her own merits. No matter how qualified and great an applicant she is, if it's known she's marrying me, any job offer they give her would be tainted with biases, for many reasons…" He trailed off. He was talking to himself. Richard had slowed down to flirt with a woman playing Frisbee with a dog on a grassy field.

His cousin was correct though, Darcy admitted as he continued alone along the tree-lined path, heading into a more wooded area. As he ran under the shade of a large elm full of vibrant green leaves, he thought about the difference between him and his fiancée. Pessimism had always been the canopy of his outlook and expectation; cynicism fertilized his roots. He preferred to stand detached, cautiously observing. In contrast, optimism was the shoot of Elizabeth's vitality; her vigor came from her passionate embrace of life and its myriad and flawed inhabitants.

And by God, he would do all he could to nurture and protect her idealism.

Wealth objectified a person in the view of others, and he could not bear for his generous and pure-hearted girl to suffer that. He could not bear to see her tainted with the patina of disillusion and cynicism.

"And become like me," he whispered and ran from under the shaded wood onto an open field heated by the harsh sun.

Lost in his thoughts, he didn't hear Richard's approach until his cousin spoke and continued their interrupted conversation. "She still wants to work? She's marrying one of the richest men in the city, and yet she's still applying for a position that pays less than the security team you're paying to watch her coming and going to the hospital. Doesn't make sense to me."

"She would have security whether she goes to the hospital everyday or spends her days doing nothing, at least until Wickham is no longer a threat. As for her salary, Elizabeth doesn't care about money—hers, mine, or anyone else's. She needs to work because she loves it."

"Your keeping quiet about your engagement explains why Anne the Dragon Lady isn't breathing fire yet."

"I don't know why you always call her that. That's unkind."

"She's unkind herself. You don't see it because she hides it from you. When you're not around and she sees me, or anyone else she considers beneath her notice, she breathes fire. She creeps around DDF like it's her dungeon and she's the dragon boss. She even looks like a dragon."

"Don't be an ass. She can't help her appearance. As to how she interacts… I think she simply lacks certain social skills. Perhaps if you can try harder to be friends with her and show her—"

"Are you fricking crazy? What are you? My mother?" Richard interrupted with an amazed look. "You're totally lacking in social skills and sense yourself if you think the woman just needs friends." He grabbed Darcy's arm, halting them both. "Both Bingley and I think that Anne has an unhealthy obsession with you."

"Oh, come on, Richard," Darcy immediately protested, not wanting to get into it. "It was a crush she had when we were teenagers, I wouldn't call that an obsession."

"It may have started as a crush, but it's an obsession now. She's always dogging your footsteps as if she's a pitiful puppy needing a pat from you. She lives for work and work alone. Even your sweet little sister finds her odd, and Georgiana has a hard time thinking badly of anyone. Anne even makes Mrs. Reynolds uneasy, and your housekeeper is a saint."

Darcy ran his fingers through his hair. Though he loathed admitting it, Richard was right about Anne not having a life outside of work. But then, neither did he until Elizabeth came into his life.

"You didn't have a life either before Elizabeth, though you weren't as pathetic as Anne. You at least had made some attempts from time to time to connect with the human race—though no one could call your past flings relationships."

"I don't see you being married with kids," Darcy shot back, annoyed his cousin had read his thoughts. "And I'm the one who's engaged now, don't forget that."

"We're talking about you, not me. Until now, you've always been indifferent to the idea of marriage."

"It's hard to remain indifferent with Elizabeth."

"Stop that silly grin. See, you do that every time her name comes up."

"You're just jealous."

"Perhaps a teensy bit. I don't know why, but she seems immune to my charms. Strange girl." Richard pointed a finger at Darcy. "Even if you don't want to deal with Anne's obsession about you, keep her away from Elizabeth. Jealous women do some crazy shit."

"You're the crazy one. You're wrong about Anne. At the Frick that night, I asked Anne not to mention Elizabeth to Catherine, and she agreed without any problem," Darcy said. "If she'd wanted to make trouble for me, I would have heard from my aunt by now about Elizabeth living with me."

"Anne got you back here from Vietnam with some bullshit excuse about needing your CEO presence. I taunted her you were seeing someone at the resort. There was nothing wrong with that Hoff situation, or the Mushatt or the Gartner deal before that, but then suddenly Anne couldn't handle them."

"I was gone a long time."

"A few weeks. Big deal. You're not indispensable, Cuz," Richard said. "I noticed the look on Anne's face when you introduced them at the Frick."

"What kind of look?" Darcy asked. He didn't recall anything out of the ordinary when the two women had met.

"Not just the meow look she was giving Helena." At Darcy's puzzled look, Richard exclaimed, "Helena, the woman you dated briefly a couple of years ago? Sheesh, if only these women knew how little you remembered them."

Darcy shrugged. "I remember. It just takes me a couple minutes."

"Yeah, right." Richard rolled his eyes "Anne had this creepy jealous look. I'm sure if Elizabeth and I had stuck around you two as you suggested, your fiancée would have noticed that."

"I introduced Anne as my cousin that night to Elizabeth," Darcy reminded him. "Elizabeth has no reason to be concerned about a cousin."

"Cousin, my ass. She's not your cousin. And another thing, haven't you wondered why Catherine always stressed Anne's your 'stepcousin' instead of plain 'cousin'? Why make that distinction? Because your aunt wants to play on your sense of family to have Anne as a 'cousin' close to you at DDF, yet she pushes for you two to get married, hence the 'step' part."

"You know that's Catherine's little obsession. She's old and has crazy ideas, but she's harmless now that Georgiana is already eighteen."

"Fine, keep on living in your dream land then, Cuz." Richard gave a snort of disgust and ran ahead.

When Darcy reached the Delacorte Theatre area, he scanned the long queue of people waiting, some in lawn chairs and on blankets; he finally spotted Elizabeth and Georgiana chatting with an older woman next to them. His eyes then scoured the area in a reflexive move to check for the security people, making note of their positions and their attentiveness before allowing himself to relax. Constant security presence was a necessity he wished they didn't need. At least Elizabeth hadn't argued with him about it.

Richard must want to die young, Darcy decided. His cousin had approached Elizabeth and greeted her with a kiss on the lips before turning around to grin at Darcy.

Elizabeth ran toward him. Too brief a kiss, Darcy thought after her brief peck on his lips. He grabbed her closer for a longer kiss.

"You know it drives me crazy to see you in running clothes, so watch it, buddy, or you'll be arrested for indecent exposure."

"What's the play tonight?" he asked, rubbing her arms.

"*Macbeth* with Jennifer Ehle as Lady Macbeth. She was the actress in that BBC production Georgiana and I made you watch."

"I thought it was the actor you guys were drooling over, not the actress." He couldn't see what was so special about some uptight guy refusing to dance that drove women crazy. He had made the mistake of saying that aloud and been kicked out of the media room. It boggled his mind there were two cinematic versions of the same story. The women in his household rapturously watched both versions repeatedly and obsessively.

"It's not the actor. It's the character from the book he played."

He didn't really want to talk about some fictional guy. "Why don't we leave Richard here in your place in the queue and you and I can go home and you can take my running clothes off again?"

Blushing, she gently slapped his arm. "No, we can't. I promised

Georgiana the full experience of waiting and getting free tickets. You go on home and shower, then you can bring us back some lunch and some cool drinks. Tell Richard to come back too. Georgiana and I can get two tickets each. He can come with us tonight if he's interested."

He frowned at her inclusion of Richard.

"And if he doesn't want to, maybe you can ask your cousin Anne. I haven't seen her since that night at the museum. I wouldn't mind getting to know her better. She works with you and I never hear much about her or see her, just that scalawag over there."

"That scalawag would love to come tonight. I don't think he has any plans," he said as he watched his sister uninhibitedly laugh at something Richard had said. Anne's presence tended to inhibit Georgiana.

CHAPTER 24

❀

Fight or Flight

Watching Georgiana struggling to wind the yarn around the knitting needle, Elizabeth wondered at the nervous vibes emanating from the younger girl. "Who was that on the phone?"

"Aunt Catherine. She invited us to her birthday dinner."

"Where does she live?" Elizabeth counted as she cast on stitches on her own knitting needles.

"She has a townhouse not far from here, though she usually spends most of her time in England, at her estate called Rosings."

"...thirteen, fourteen..." Elizabeth paused from counting. "I didn't realize she lives so close. You guys hardly talk about her. She scares you?"

"No. Well, yes, terribly. She's terrifying," Georgiana admitted. "With the excitement lately of having you here, I'd completely forgotten about the dreadful birthday dinner."

William walked in. "What a sight to come home to: my girls being domestic."

"With sharp pointy weapons, so watch it, buster." Elizabeth pointed her knitting needle at him.

He laughed and bent down to press his mouth briefly against hers. "I love this sassy mouth," he whispered. He turned to his sister. "What's wrong?"

"She's been that way ever since she got the call from your aunt about a birthday dinner," Elizabeth said.

"Bloody hell! I'd forgotten it's that time of year." William sank down on the couch and slapped his forehead.

Amused and amazed at their reaction, Elizabeth stared at the dejected pair. "I take it this is an annually dreaded event?"

"Yes, sometimes we make excuses and go out of the country, on business or something." William dropped his hand from his face. "I guess we have to attend this year."

Elizabeth laughed. "I can't wait to meet her if she terrifies you both so much that you want to leave the country."

William groaned and put his head in his hands. "She doesn't know about you."

"And why not?"

"Because she wouldn't take it well." His hand ran through his hair.

Elizabeth's finger froze. Her throat knotted. *He did not want his aunt to meet her.* She swallowed and pumped her fingers to get the blood flowing. Not counting the stitch, she blindly knitted. "I see."

"I don't tell her about any women I've ever dated." He stood and headed to the door. "I need a drink."

Elizabeth paused in her knitting and stared down at her hand, self-conscious of the bareness of her ring finger. He rarely talked about his past love life. The few times she'd broached the subject he seemed reluctant to talk.

"I have a headache. I'm going to rest." Georgiana excused herself just as William came back with a drink in his hand.

"You don't want your aunt to meet me?" The words burst from Elizabeth the moment the door closed behind Georgiana. She recoiled at the pitiful, plaintive note in her voice.

He slumped next to her and mumbled. "No. My aunt means

well, but she has odd… odd, obsessive ideas. It's not the right time yet." He stopped his mumbling and straightened. "Georgiana and I could just go by ourselves to the birthday dinner. Richard could take you out that night."

Hotness swept over her face and fingers. Anger surged through her. Her vision blurred a hazy red. Blinking, she focused on the pointy ends of her knitting needles. Concerned for his safety, she edged herself a few inches away. When she was sure her voice would not betray her, she asked, "Wouldn't Anne have told her about meeting me?"

"I asked Anne not to mention you. She knows how difficult Catherine can be. And if my aunt happens to say something, I'll deflect her."

Her heart twisted. "You'll make it sound like I'm of no consequence."

"Something like that." He downed the rest of his drink.

The red haze returned. Elizabeth closed her eyes and briefly thought about the various ramifications of having a domestic violence charge on her clean record. She put down her knitting needles. "I need to call my residents to check on some patients."

"Okay, love. I'll go wash up before dinner." He stood. "I hope Georgiana feels better soon so she can join us."

Elizabeth doubted she could sit calmly through a dinner with him tonight. "I just remembered, I have to dictate some consultation reports before tomorrow."

Her month as an attending physician on the infectious disease service had officially finished two days ago, but the doctor replacing her, Dr. Duffy, had a family emergency and asked Elizabeth to stay on a few days longer.

He said, "All right, I'll try not to bother you until you finish your work. We'll wait on dinner for you."

After he left, Elizabeth saw that she had unknowingly unraveled all the knitting she had done earlier. She walked to the office she rarely used except when she needed privacy for confidential patient discussions. When Mrs. Reynolds asked about serving dinner, Elizabeth, using the excuse of too much work, requested a tray instead.

William occasionally poked his head into her office. Each time, she ignored the ache in her heart and pretended to be dictating some medical report and couldn't be interrupted. Finally, after giving her a smoldering look and a sexy smile she refused to acknowledge, he gave up trying to distract her and went to bed. She stayed in the office, poring over various medical journals, taking notes to distract herself, and ended up falling asleep slumped over the desk.

The next morning, he woke her with a kiss on her forehead and told her she needed to get to the hospital soon or she'd be late. The tenderness of his warm lips against her cold skin made her almost want to talk to him right then. She didn't. She had less than thirty minutes before she had to meet with the team for rounds.

She put her personal problems aside and focused on medicine that morning. When her last two patients in the clinic canceled their appointments in the afternoon, she decided to head home. Mrs. Reynolds thoughtfully brought her a cup of chamomile tea as Elizabeth unwound in her favorite room in the house, William's study.

Sipping the hot tea, she took a deep breath and inhaled the smell of wood, books, and William's spicy scent all mixed. This room held the essence of him and she preferred it to the office he had set up for her. Her eyes swept over the bookshelves along the walls and dropped to the pile of books next to the chair, near the fireplace where he liked to sit and read. She perused the various titles of books he was currently reading and shook her head, bemused at his wide range of interests.

"I'm not an unsophisticated and uncultured geek. I'm interested in many things and I have a sense of humor," she said aloud to bolster her confidence. Yet, her inadequacy hovered at the edges of her bravado, whispering she was all brains and nothing else... nothing that would maintain the interest of a worldly man like William for long.

She pushed the negative thought away. She would talk to him and tell him that she was hurt he didn't want to introduce her to his aunt and ask about the women from his past. Why hadn't he wanted to marry any of them before? What had happened with Helena? And she would tell him she wanted an engagement ring, even if that would make her sound clingy and needy. Happy with her decision, she relaxed and closed her eyes.

The ringing of the phone woke Elizabeth up.

Thinking she was on duty at the hospital, she sleepily answered, "Hello. Elizabeth Bennet here."

"I'm sorry. I thought I had reached the Darcy residence," she heard a gravelly voice say in a very proper English accent. "I wish to speak to Mr. Darcy."

Elizabeth rubbed her face. "I'm sorry, Mr. Darcy is not here right now. May I take a message?"

"You answered, then I must have reached his penthouse suite by mistake. You did say your name was Elizabeth?" the elderly woman asked.

Elizabeth sat straight. "Yes, I'm Elizabeth."

"I had heard that he was dating a woman named Elizabeth. You must be his latest. He never tells me about you girls. He always hides you all in the penthouse, but I always find out. Tell me, are you enjoying yourself in the suite? Does he still have that mirror on the ceiling? Or did the last one make him take it down?"

"I... I..." Elizabeth was stumped.

"No matter how long you stay there, my dear, you must insist on making your own mark. Redecorate to suit your taste. Go for something exotic, like the Orient. I hear he was taken by the Orient recently."

"I'm sorry, I didn't catch your name?"

"Oh dear, I've rattled on. I'm his aunt Catherine. You mustn't mind me, dear. My nephew thinks I don't know anything. He thinks I won't be as understanding as Anne about his sowing his wild oats before they get married. They think I'd be upset with their modern, open relationship. Really! I was young once and my generation was the one that opened the door, so to speak." She paused as if waiting for Elizabeth to respond.

Elizabeth's stomach whorled into itself. The chamomile tea she'd drank earlier spiraled to the back of her throat. She swallowed and kept silent.

After a long moment, the aunt continued, "I can't say I blame him for playing around with you pretty girls. Much as I hate to admit it, my stepdaughter is not the most feminine looking girl, though she and William suit each other very well in all other areas. I told her to accept that men will be men. We women need to take a practical view of such matters, don't you think? Of course, I shouldn't talk so frankly to you."

Elizabeth pressed a hand against her stomach and forced herself to speak in an unaffected tone, "Was there a message you wanted to leave?"

"No, I don't need to leave a message with you. I'll try him at his office or I'll call Anne there. She'll get him for me; her office is right next to his. You take care, dear."

The moment Elizabeth put down the phone, her stomach churned and the ache she'd been suppressing all day rose and choked her breathing. She needed air.

She left the study and told Mrs. Reynolds she was going for a long walk.

Mrs. Reynolds frowned. "Are you sure you've rested enough, dear? You look peaked."

"I need some air."

"All right, then. Put a coat on. It's getting chilly." The housekeeper fussed over her. She called for security to follow Elizabeth and made sure she had her cell phone and her wallet. "Take a taxi back if you get tired, but make sure your security guy gets in the taxi also."

⌁

Keeping her mind blank, Elizabeth walked and walked and ignored the presence of the security guy a short distance behind her. She had met them all and knew their names and faces, but found them unfriendly. Both William and Georgiana assured her it was nothing personal. The guards preferred a detached working relationship; closer interactions would distract and cause them to lose objectivity. She briefly deliberated turning around and asking the security guy how many women he had trailed for William.

She found herself in front of the DDF building. She'd walked farther than she'd intended. Questions whirled in her head as she tiredly stared at the DDF letters. She looked up. Which square in the grid of opaque windows would find the answers she wanted to hear? Which one was William's office? Was it next to Anne's?

"Elizabeth, my sweet," a deep male voice suddenly spoke next to her. "I thought it was you from behind. Daydreaming?"

Happy to see the welcoming smile on Richard's face, she rushed forward and hugged him tight, finding some comfort in his friendly greeting. *Perhaps it's all a misunderstanding, just the rambling of an old woman.* "Where are you off to? It's still working hours, you know."

"I have a hot date tonight." He waggled his eyebrows. "I need to go and make myself beautiful. Most of us aren't born lucky like my cousin, attracting women like flies to honey."

Her chest tightened. She breathed a few shallow breaths. *It's just the usual way Richard talks.* "Who's this hot date now?"

He suddenly blushed. "Helena, who has finally decided to give me a chance tonight. Unless you're sick of my cousin already? Do I still have a chance?" His expression turned serious. "Are you okay? You seem distracted."

"I'm fine," she said. When he still looked concerned, she added, "And yes, you still have a chance. You're taking me out to dinner sometime this week, Friday, I think. William said he would ask you."

He whooped. "After such a dry spell, my luck must be changing. I'm going out with Helena tonight, and then you later this week. I'm da man! I might even get to use Darce's penthouse tonight." Laughing, he picked her up and swung her around.

She stumbled when he put her down.

"Hey, are you all right? You look pale. I hope I didn't swing you too hard. Elizabeth?" he asked nervously when she bent her head and breathed hard. "Can I get you a glass of water or something? You want to come inside with me and sit down? Is Darce waiting for you upstairs?"

"I'll stay here. I need fresh air," she said without lifting her head. "Water would be good."

"I'll get you a glass right away," he said. He had taken a few steps when the urge to flee hit her. She called to him and assured him she was fine now.

"Are you sure? You don't look fine. You still look pale." He headed back toward her. "Let me tell Darce you're here."

"No, don't bother him. He's not expecting me. I was going to surprise him, but I think I need to go home now and sleep instead." She backed away. "I didn't get much sleep last night."

He took his cell phone out. "Let me call a car for you."

She saw a cab driving by. Before Richard could stop her, she flagged down the cab, yelled good-bye to him, closed the door, and urged the driver to go straight. Only after the cab drove off did she realize she had forgotten about the security guy.

"The fight-or-flight response," she recited as she sat in the cab and gently rocked herself, "is the acute stress response in which animals react to threats with a general discharge of the sympathetic nervous system, priming the animal for fighting or fleeing."

"Lady, where to?" The cab driver interrupted her mumbling. "You okay, lady?"

She stared blankly at the cab driver's eyes in the rearview mirror. "I'm fine. Just drive straight for now."

Suddenly, she felt sixteen again. She needed her sisters. Her hands shaking, she called Vietnam. She couldn't reach Jane or Mary.

"I can't keep driving straight without a destination, lady," the cab driver said a few minutes later.

"Central Park, anywhere in Central Park," she finally managed to tell the cabdriver. Grateful for the foresight of Mrs. Reynolds, she slipped her hand into her coat pocket and fingered her wallet.

The familiar feel of the roughened patches and cracks of old leather comforted her and reminded her who she was before New York. When the cab dropped her off, she wandered aimlessly before finding a path leading into a wooded area. She kept walking until, just as she passed under the shade of a large elm, she heard the ringing of her phone.

It was Mary. Jane had gone to a nearby city in central Vietnam to check on some new orphans. At the sound of her younger sister's voice, Elizabeth sat down on a bench and cried. She couldn't say anything at first; she just cried and cried. When she calmed down enough to form words, she told Mary in disjointed sentences that she felt unsafe and she needed to get away but she didn't know where to go. She didn't want to go back home, to William.

"I have this urge to run, Mare!" she wailed. "I want to go back to Vietnam, to before..."

"And so you will," Mary said then calmly asked for William's house phone and told Elizabeth to stay put.

Glad someone else had taken over, even from the other side of the world, Elizabeth obediently sat still on the bench and waited. Her younger sister was very capable. She suddenly was glad it wasn't Jane who called back. Jane would ask questions and probe. Mary just listened then took charge.

Twenty minutes later, Mary called back. She had arranged with Mrs. Reynolds to have Elizabeth's passport delivered to her immediately. "I told the housekeeper there's an emergency and you need your passport pronto."

Elizabeth didn't want the security people to follow her if they delivered the passport to Central Park. She looked around but didn't see William's security detail.

When Mary heard this, she instructed, "Go to the hospital.

I'll tell the housekeeper to have the security guy deliver and leave your passport with the hospital security. It's easier for you to lose his security man from inside the hospital. Unless they follow you around there?"

"No, I insisted on no security detail when I'm inside the hospital. They usually just drop me off and pick me up when I'm done," Elizabeth said, for once grateful her eccentric sister had prior experience in outwitting security people.

"Okay. Then get to JFK. You're booked on the next flight leaving for Hanoi. You'll have a brief layover in Los Angeles. Once you arrive in Hanoi, you'll take a plane here to Da Nang. I'll arrange it," Mary said.

Elizabeth went to the hospital and called Dr. Duffy to transfer the responsibility of the service over, citing an unexpected family emergency that required her to leave for Vietnam immediately, for an indefinite period. "I'm withdrawing my application for the faculty position," she ended.

Dr. Duffy let out a big sigh and told her that it was just as well, for there had been a rumor of an ongoing argument about offering Elizabeth a faculty position.

"What kind of argument?" Elizabeth asked.

"Our hospital applied for a generous grant from the Pemberley Trust Foundation to build a community health center. A few months ago, we even received a hint we had a very good chance, and all the departments have been excited. You know that we're short of space and funds to meet our patients' needs," her friend said. "Do you know anyone at PTF?"

"No," Elizabeth lied. "Why?"

"Because, for some odd reason," Dr. Duffy continued, "they now intimated there was too much liability if someone like you were hired. I have no idea why they singled you out, but some plaintiff lawyers known to have worked closely with PTF on medical accountability issues in the past are now issuing thinly veiled threats, implying they'd closely examine the medical staff and the quality of all our work."

"The whole medical staff?"

"Actually, just the junior faculty. Their concern is that the hospital is hiring too young and too inexperienced faculty members—and they specifically gave your name as an example. Perhaps you're a visible name, since you gave that wonderful Grand Rounds last month."

"Perhaps."

"Of course, I'm telling you of a leaked rumor here, Elizabeth. We have no proof any of this is true. There might be some odd politicking going on behind the scenes that has nothing to do with you or me or any of the faculty staff and we're being used as pawns. Nevertheless, the hospital admin is nervous about our department hiring any new faculty at the present."

CHAPTER 25

❀

Liability

RICHARD FORCED HIMSELF TO FOCUS ON HIS DATE UNTIL SOME-thing stirred in his pants. *She's a beautiful woman. You've been waiting for her to give you a chance for months*, he silently reminded himself, trying to maintain his blood flow.

"Who was that woman you were with at the Frick last month?"

Richard deflated. For some reason, her well-modulated voice irritated him tonight. "That was so long ago, Helena, I don't remember."

"William seemed very interested in her."

Richard shrugged. "Was he?"

Darcy suddenly materialized next to their table. "Please excuse my interruption, miss." He nodded to Helena then turned to Richard, "I want to talk to you. Now. Outside."

They watched him walk off without waiting for a response. Richard turned to her, "I'm sure he would have recognized you if he wasn't so distracted. We've been swamped at work with…" He trailed off. From her expression, she wasn't buying his apology. "I'll be right back."

Darcy paced next to his car. Upon Richard's approach, Darcy suddenly grabbed him by his jacket and shoved him into the backseat.

Taking in the fierce, wild look in his cousin's eyes, Richard swallowed his protest at the rough handling. "What?"

"I want to know what you said to Elizabeth this afternoon, outside our office building. The security guy said you talked to her."

"What?"

"I want to know every word you said to her." Darcy's voice was very quiet, which scared Richard more than if he had yelled. "And I want to hear what she said. I want the whole conversation."

"I mostly talked about my hot date tonight, that's all. The date you're interrupting, by the way." Richard let out a relieved sigh when Darcy shifted his body back. "When she told me you'd said I could take her to dinner on Friday night, I might have swung her around a bit too fast and she got a little dizzy. But she was fine when she left in a taxi. She was going home to sleep."

"The security detail lost her when she got into the taxi. He couldn't catch up with her."

"She's missing?"

"No, he saw her later at the hospital when he dropped off her passport. She seemed fine and apologized to him that she had run off without waiting for him."

"Her passport? What? Where is she going? What about Wickham? Did you talk to Brandon?"

"Wickham's here in New York. Brandon told me Wickham arrived last week. If he had gotten anywhere near any of us, especially Georgiana or Elizabeth, I would have known it that second," Darcy said. "As to where Elizabeth's going, I'm guessing it's to Vietnam if she needed her passport."

"What? Vietnam? What did she tell you?"

"Nothing. That's the thing. She didn't talk to me." Darcy punched the seat.

Surprised by his cousin's outburst, Richard jumped. "Calm down, Darce."

"I don't exactly know for sure that she's heading back to Vietnam or I'd already be on my way there. I prepared the jet to leave, but I can't get ahold of her sisters in Vietnam to confirm anything. I would contact her parents in California, but I don't know them and I don't want to alarm them unnecessarily until I hear from her."

"This is so sudden. Must be some family emergency."

"Her sister told Mrs. Reynolds it's an emergency, but no details. I don't know why Elizabeth didn't wait for me. Whatever it is, she should know I would drop everything and go with her."

"She probably tried to call and couldn't get through."

Darcy shot him a pointed look. "Elizabeth knows she can always get through to me, no matter where I am or who I am with. Even if she couldn't reach me on my cell, she knows she could call my office."

"Maybe her cell phone was dead. If she had been receiving calls from Vietnam or wherever the emergency was, she probably ran down the battery talking," Richard offered.

"It's not difficult to find a phone to make a call in New York City, Richard," Darcy said in a tight voice. "I can't help feeling something is wrong."

"Darce, man, you're overreacting. She probably wants to talk to you in person. It may be something sensitive involving her family." He patted his cousin's knee. "Go home and wait for her call. If you're sure she's safe from Wickham, then there's nothing to worry about. I'm sure she'll call you soon. Let me end my date and I'll come to your house."

Richard went back inside the restaurant and discovered Helena had gotten tired of waiting and left. He read the message from her, shrugged at the written insult, and made his way to Darcy's townhouse. He found his cousin in the study, slumped in a chair and staring at the ceiling.

"You're being a sap, man." Richard tried to cheer up him. "She'll call soon. Don't forget, she was coming to see you when I ran into her outside DDF."

Darcy perked up slightly. "She never came to the building before. I've been waiting to give her a tour when she has more free time."

"Did Georgiana know anything?"

"No." Darcy went back to staring at the ceiling.

Richard decided to go upstairs to talk to his younger cousin. Georgiana didn't know any more than her brother. When Richard came back down to the study, ten minutes later, he found his cousin downing a generous helping of brandy. He took the tumbler out of Darcy's hand. "Hey man. You're losing it. At this rate you're going to be too sloshed to talk to her when she calls."

Darcy reached for another glass and filled it full. "She already did."

This was not good! Richard again grabbed the brandy away and pushed Darcy into a chair. "Tell me what she said."

Head plopped back and staring at the ceiling again, Darcy said in a flat voice, "She didn't get the job offer at the hospital. She decided to leave New York to think things through. There was a"—he paused for a moment to swallow—"a liability issue. She's sorry this is sudden, but she needed to figure out what she was going to do with her life."

"What the hell does she mean 'what she's going to do with her life'?"

Darcy reached for the brandy where Richard had placed it and drank it in one gulp before wiping his mouth carelessly with his hand.

Richard impatiently repeated his question.

His cousin shrugged. "A life that wouldn't involve me. She was sorry she didn't get to tell me in person, but she needed to leave right away. She'll send for her things later."

"I'm so sorry, Darce. Did she..." Richard tried to take it all in. "Did she actually say she was breaking up with you? Maybe you misunderstood her. Maybe she just wants some time—"

"She said she realized it's not going to work out between us."

"I still don't get it."

"It's simple, Richard," his cousin said in a cold voice. "Elizabeth is very dedicated to her work, to medicine. I've always known that about her."

"And? What does that have to do with leaving you so abruptly?"

"Apparently, there's no room for anything else, including me."

Darcy sounded so certain, so accepting, as if he had expected this all along. Richard couldn't think of anything else to say except to tell his cousin no more brandy and take the bottle away. The suddenness of it all stunned him. Then he remembered Elizabeth's abrupt leaving in the taxi this afternoon. Perhaps she had come to break up with Darcy in person but lost her nerve when Richard unknowingly intercepted her. That would explain her paleness and distracted manner and her sudden flight without luggage, as if she feared losing her nerve again and wanted to be far away when she told Darcy.

Over the next few days, Richard hovered at his cousin's side until he felt certain Darcy wouldn't do something rash or stupid. Darcy was not the type, but Richard worried. At times, though, he found himself wishing Darcy would do something, anything, instead of withdrawing into himself. He refused to discuss his thoughts or feelings about the breakup—not that Richard would know what to do if he wanted to talk. Still, Richard knew it wasn't healthy for his cousin to keep it all inside.

A week after Elizabeth left, two of their companies in Europe ran into difficulties, requiring DDF headquarters to send a team of troubleshooters. Richard pushed Darcy to go with the team. Darcy had lost some weight and wasn't sleeping well. Mrs. Reynolds revealed that he frequently roamed the townhouse late at night, often ending up in Elizabeth's old office or his study.

While Darcy was away in Europe, Mrs. Reynolds received a message from one of Elizabeth's sisters asking for her things to be shipped to her parents' address. Dr. Bennet needed her medical books and journals, etc., as well as the personal items she had left behind. She had accepted a position with Doctors Without Borders.

Using his contacts, Richard confirmed that a Dr. Elizabeth Bennet was on the roster for the humanitarian organization in Darfur, Sudan. After Richard informed Darcy on his return from Europe that Elizabeth had moved on, at least professionally, Darcy rallied and became his pre-Vietnam grave self. Except now, he worked constantly. He never took time off for a run, no matter how much Richard urged him to get out for some fresh air and exercise.

Worried for his cousin's health, Richard forgot himself one day and inadvertently mentioned to Anne his concern Darcy's trying to kill himself with work, now that he and Elizabeth had broken up. He kicked himself when he saw a satisfied gleam in Anne's eyes before she masked it. Of course, the bitch was happy; Darcy was now free. She even looked like she had known it all along.

Georgiana closed the door to the study, approached her brother's desk, and sat down. She had some bug with her laptop and until she got it fixed, she had to sneak down to her brother's desktop in his study. The messages from Elizabeth had been encouraging. Georgiana still didn't know exactly what had happened between her brother and Elizabeth two months ago—neither would talk about their breakup or about each other—but she was glad her brother's ex-fiancée still kept in touch. Though she felt disloyal to her brother, she needed Elizabeth's friendship. Georgiana had no other friends—probably why Elizabeth didn't abandon her. The emails had been mostly about Georgiana. Elizabeth had been pushing her to think about returning to college again, to try to meet new people, and to put her experience with George Wickham in the past.

A few days ago, Georgiana had sent an email stating she had decided to go back to school. She hadn't heard back. Clicking on her email account, she saw one new message in her inbox. She eagerly read it, laughing aloud as she got to the end. When she clicked on an attachment, a picture appeared. She was still smiling at the picture when Mrs. Reynolds informed her a big package, too big for the housekeeper to carry to the study, had arrived for her. Squealing, Georgiana excitedly ran out to see her congratulatory gift from Elizabeth. She lugged the package to her room. It was a guitar—Elizabeth's old guitar.

Tiredly, Darcy walked into his study. Georgiana's uncharacteristic giddiness during dinner baffled him. Pretending to be in a good mood so he wouldn't ruin her evening had taken much of his energy.

He sat down at his desk to do some work he had brought home. While laying spreadsheets out on his desk, his hand hit the

computer mouse by accident. He frowned at the unusual place-
ment of the mouse, two inches too far to the right. He moved the
mouse back to its usual spot. The lit computer screen cast a glare
onto his hand. He glanced up and froze.

Elizabeth's smiling face stared back at him from the computer
screen. He had not seen her for eight weeks, three days, and almost
twelve hours now. Her hair was short in the picture, an inch below
her chin. Looking tired around the eyes, and a little sad, she smiled
at the camera.

"Lizzy," he whispered and raised his hand to the screen. His
elbow inadvertently shifted the mouse; the screen blanked and she
disappeared. He frantically moved the mouse. She came back on
the screen. He didn't even stop to think before he read the email.

She'd been in touch with Georgiana. The email was brief,
mentioning that she was attaching a picture of herself with her
guitar at a Berkeley Vegan Earth Day.

> All "green" musicians got free admissions (I have no idea why)
> to the fair. That was the only time I've used the guitar in the
> last ten years, so I'm sending it to you as a gift for deciding
> to return to college. Btw, a tempeh pastrami is as nasty as it
> sounds. Couldn't complain, though. It was also free.

Darcy smiled before he could stop himself. God, how he loved
her. Even though she had broken his heart, she still made him laugh.
He sobered. *Why couldn't you have loved me enough to stay, Lizzy?*

―⁓―

Through the crack of the opened door, Georgiana swallowed a
gasp at the unguarded view of her brother looking longingly at the

computer screen. She closed the study's door as noiselessly as she had opened it. Back in her room, she called Richard.

CHAPTER 26

❀

Clue. Pattern.

LEADING MRS. REYNOLDS AND GEORGIANA, RICHARD ENTERED THE study without knocking. Darcy pushed something underneath a file on his desk and scowled at them.

Richard held up a hand. "No, we didn't knock. We're here for an intervention."

"I don't have time for your nonsense," Darcy snapped. "I have work to do."

"Yes, you do. You're going to work with us to figure out what went wrong between Elizabeth and you. Since you're obviously clueless, we're going to help."

"I don't know what you're talking about. It's over. I haven't thought about her for—" Darcy paused, a wary expression on his face as Richard edged close to the desk.

With a quick movement, Richard lifted up the file and had a photo in his hand. "It's over? Haven't thought about her? Who's this, then?"

Almost reflexively, Darcy grabbed the photo back. "Get out."

Richard motioned for Mrs. Reynolds and Georgiana to sit. "You might as well get comfortable. This isn't going to be quick." He turned back to Darcy. "You won't go see a doctor, so we're doing it this way. We're not going to leave until you talk."

Darcy's lips tightened.

Richard sighed. "We care about you, William, and we care about Elizabeth. Maybe you two aren't meant to be together, but until you figure out why it failed, it's not over and you can't move on." He watched as the anger left his cousin. Darcy sat and stared at the photo in his hand. Gently, Richard asked, "What do you think went wrong?"

Darcy threw the photo onto the desk. In a defeated voice, he admitted, "I don't know."

Georgiana reached a hand toward her brother. "It's okay, Will."

"No, it's not." Richard firmly cut off the flow of sympathy. "He thinks he knows what went wrong and blames himself. That's why he hasn't gone after her."

The anger returned to Darcy's voice. "She left me to go and figure out what to do with her life. It's simple: she discovered medicine's more important than being with me, and she realized I was a liability, excess baggage."

"Oh, come on. You don't believe that, do you?" Richard asked. "Did she actually say those nonsense words?"

"She used 'liability' and mentioned PTF in the same sentence. You and I had a discussion on this very issue in Central Park that one day, remember? What I predicted happened. She left because she didn't get the job. I didn't matter."

"I don't care, even if she did say those exact words; she's not that shallow," Richard asserted. For a while, he had lost faith in Elizabeth, but now, having heard that she was still in contact with—and obviously cared very much about—Georgiana, he wanted concrete answers before he would give up.

"I agree," Mrs. Reynolds spoke.

"Me too," Georgiana added. "Even if she did say it, I don't

believe that was her reason. You might have misunderstood because you were upset."

"I know what I heard," Darcy insisted. "She specifically asked me not to go after her."

Georgiana's face fell. "Oh."

"Perhaps so," Richard said, "but it still doesn't fit. She can't be that good of an actress to fool all of us. It doesn't fit with a woman who came to New York to get a job to help you! I was the biggest skeptic of her at the beginning, but it wasn't long before I recognized her feelings for you were genuine."

"Richard is right," Mrs. Reynolds said.

Georgiana straightened in her seat. "Yes, it doesn't fit, Will."

Richard watched as hope tiptoed into Darcy's eyes. "Yes, we all agree. She cared about you, Darce. Her face always lit up whenever you were near. But something happened. Let's figure out what. Talk it out with us, okay?"

After a long moment, Darcy nodded.

Richard suggested, "Let's start when you first met until the day she left. We might see something you missed. Well, leave out the intimate details, that'd be TMI, unless that was the problem? I knew I should have given you some pointers there."

"In your dreams," Darcy immediately shot back. His face flushed, as if he suddenly remembered the presence of his sister and Mrs. Reynolds in the room.

Her own face pink, Mrs. Reynolds smiled. Georgiana snickered. The tension in the room lessened.

"Yes, do talk, William," Mrs. Reynolds said. "It's not good to keep everything bottled up inside you."

The kind, motherly voice did the trick. Darcy talked. He ended up revealing a lot more than he had meant to while

Richard relentlessly flooded him with questions to keep the narrative going.

"And then she came to New York, and you know what happened after that," Darcy ended and waited.

Silence met him for a long moment then a titter came from his sister, followed by an uncharacteristic giggle from Mrs. Reynolds. Darcy looked offended.

"I'm so sorry, Will. I shouldn't laugh," Georgiana apologized. "You and Charles were gay partners adopting a baby. Haahaaa!" She almost fell off her chair laughing.

Mrs. Reynolds said, "She may not have known you very well, but she really loved you."

"That's it! She doesn't know you well. Do you see a pattern here?" Richard knew he had been given a gold mine of material to tease his cousin about later, but now was not the time.

Darcy's hands spread. "What pattern? I've been through it a million times trying to find the clues I might have missed."

"She keeps misunderstanding and misreading you," Richard said. "That's the pattern. Who could blame her? You're not an open book, even to us."

"She does have a tendency to act impulsively when she has decided on something. She's convinced she's right until proven otherwise." Darcy brightened, but then the hope in his eyes dimmed. "She also likes to rescue people. I was a sad sap when we met. Maybe that's all I was, a pity job."

"Oh, stop it with the pity party. She wanted you. The hospital job was an excuse to be with you," Richard pointed out.

"Then why leave me when the job didn't work out?" Darcy countered. "If it wasn't important, why would she have found another job just a week after she left here? It doesn't make sense."

"No, it doesn't." Richard agreed.

"Aunt Catherine's birthday call!" Georgiana exclaimed. "That was the day before she left. What you said might have upset her."

Darcy looked perplexed. "What? What did I say?"

"You said something about not wanting her to meet Aunt Catherine, and how you've never taken any woman you dated to meet her."

"Fitzwilliam Darcy, you told your fiancée that you didn't want to introduce her to your aunt, just as you didn't with any of the other women?" Mrs. Reynolds said in a shocked voice. "How could you?"

"I… uh… I…" Darcy turned to his sister. "Did I really say that?"

"You did, Will." Georgiana nodded. "I heard you."

"Ouch. Even I know better than to say something like that to a woman I'm dating, much less engaged to," Richard said. He started. "Engaged! Your secret engagement! Wait a minute, Anne looked too satisfied when I mentioned you and Elizabeth had broken up. Did you ever do anything about Anne? Keep her from Elizabeth? I warned you she might try something."

"Will, what if Elizabeth heard about Anne and you?" Georgiana asked. "You know Aunt Catherine truly believes you two will get married one day. And no matter how much you deny Anne's being a part of it, she has never actively discouraged Aunt Catherine."

"I knew it." Richard slapped the table. "I knew it. The damn bitch had something to do with it. They must have said something to Elizabeth."

Darcy's face turned ashen. "Oh God! I remember now… she said something about being of no consequence and I think I even agreed… I was distracted. She misunderstood me. That's why she didn't come to bed that night! Why didn't she talk to me? I would have explained what I meant."

"Because when you're hurt, you can't talk about it right then," Georgiana said. "You casually lumped her in with the women you dated, and she has her pride."

"Lumping her in with the women you dated," Richard suddenly remembered. "That day outside of DDF, I mentioned to Elizabeth about going out with one of your old flames. What's her name, now? She left me a nasty note."

"How could you tell Elizabeth about my old flames?" Darcy's hands flexed as if he wanted to strangle Richard. "I don't have any old flames to speak of."

"Helena, that was her name." Richard was triumphant. He sobered. "You're going to kill me, Darce. I might have mentioned something about getting lucky with Helena and using your penthouse that night."

"What? You told her about the penthouse? She didn't know about the penthouse. I never mentioned it to her. I'm not proud of that." Darcy shot a wary glance toward his sister.

Georgiana rolled her eyes. "Please. It's not like I think you're still a virgin."

"She received a phone call that afternoon while she was in here, this room. I heard it ring," Mrs. Reynolds said. "I don't know who called. But she went for a walk right after."

"She must have walked to DDF to talk to you. And then I intercepted her and... made it worse. I'm sorry, Darce." Richard could kick himself for his big mouth.

"She must have been so hurt... to suddenly feel she needed to leave"—Darcy raised a shaking hand to his mouth—"without talking to me."

Richard asked, "Who called her? The hospital called about the job? Or was that something she made up to break up with you?"

"No, they didn't offer her the job. I checked," Darcy said. "I even thought about offering them money to hire her and have her come back. But I didn't."

Not a bad idea, Richard thought but did not say.

Darcy covered his eyes with one hand. "I've been too focused on myself to ask questions about why they didn't want her. I should have done something to make her want to stay. She wouldn't be in a dangerous place now."

"You are not responsible," Mrs. Reynolds said in a firm voice. "Miss Elizabeth is a grown woman. She could have stayed and talked to you, no matter how hurt she was. It was her choice to leave instead and go to wherever she has gone."

The phone rang and Mrs. Reynolds went to answer it. Richard mouthed silently to Georgiana, "Where is she now?"

She mouthed back, "Don't know, still in Darfur, probably."

Darcy dropped his hand and stood. "I'm going after her."

Mrs. Reynolds hung up the phone. "That was Mr. Bingley. He called to invite you to a wedding next month."

———— ⁓⁓ ————

Richard stepped out of his rented car and glanced around. Orinda had too many trees for a city boy like him.

Elizabeth had safely left Africa last month and gone home to her parents. She still didn't want to hear from Darcy and had moved on with her life.

"Did she actually say she didn't want to hear from you and she's moved on?" Richard had asked when his cousin informed him.

Darcy admitted he didn't talk to Elizabeth personally, but a woman who answered the phone at her parents' home had— upon hearing his name—immediately screamed, "She doesn't want to have anything to do with you. She's moved on!" and hung up on him. When he called back, he discovered a block had been placed on his number to prevent his calls from getting through. His emails, text messages, and a personal letter had also been refused.

Richard had berated his cousin for giving up without talking to Elizabeth personally until Darcy threw a magazine at him and coldly told him to read page twenty. A photo, taken last month in Darfur, showed Elizabeth, with another man's arms around her, boarding a private jet. The accompanying caption read:

Is Dr. Elizabeth Bennet of Doctors Without Borders Jorge Cooley's new love? The two bonded over shared concern about the atrocities being committed in Darfur. Has Jorge finally found a woman as committed as he is to saving humanity? Yes, a close, anonymous friend reportedly confirmed.

Richard kicked a rock on the gravel driveway. He wanted to hear it straight from Elizabeth's lips she had no more feelings for Darcy. If she indeed had moved on, with or without the famous playboy actor Jorge Cooley, then Richard planned to give her hell for her callousness and tell her to stay away from Georgiana.

Some woman, obviously a crazy relative, had screamed in Richard's ear when he tried to call Elizabeth—the same treatment Darcy received. Straightening his shoulders, Richard marched to the front door. Secluded behind a large grove of trees, with some unruly purple flowers dripping down from a vine growing along the porch's frame, the house appeared homely and nonthreatening. At the last moment, he detoured a few yards toward the side window. He'd peek first before ringing the doorbell.

"Ooompph!" He landed face down on the hard gravel—with someone's foot pressed against his neck. He caught a glimpse of a dark figure before the pressure on his neck increased. His assailant twisted his left arm at a painful angle behind his back. Richard lifted his head and a blast of gas rushed at his face. His eyes burned. His face burned. His nose burned.

"What the hell?" he tried to say but only warbling noises came out. His lips and tongue felt like someone had dipped them in hot oil. He concentrated on breathing instead. *I've been Maced!*

"All right, dickhead. Why are you peeking into our window?" a feminine voice came from above. The foot pressed tighter against his left jugular, cutting off circulation to that side of his head. "Casing it? Watch it, I've got a gun on you."

When he could feel his tongue again, he managed to croak, "Dr. Bennet."

"What do you want with my father?" The foot removed itself from his neck. "Why are you coming to his home instead of his office at school?"

"Dr. Elizabeth Bennet." He massaged his neck and blinked rapidly to dispel the circling stars.

"Why?"

"May I get up? I swear I'm harmless. You have a gun," he reminded her.

"Just turn around," she ordered and poked the gun against his back. "Now, tell me why you need to see Dr. Elizabeth Bennet?"

"It's personal," he said. The gun pressed harder into his back. "Look, I've come all the way from New York to talk to her. I swear I'm not here to harm her."

"Are you the asshole who hurt her in New York?"

The crazy relative on the phone! "No, that was my cousin. No, no! I mean they were engaged, but he didn't hurt her. It was a misunderstanding. That's why I'm here, to clear it up."

"Then why did she call me crying, saying she didn't want to go home to him, she didn't want to see him?"

He pivoted. His eyes widened and his mouth fell open. A tiny woman stood in front of him holding a stick. A stick? She didn't reach higher than his armpit in height. Her eyes were huge though, almost too large for her small, gamine face. He blinked rapidly again, this time trying to dispel the strange fear this anime-ninja girl gave him. "It was my fault. I might have said things that she misunderstood."

She tapped the stick against one palm, looking as if she'd welcome another chance to knock him down.

"I just want to talk to her. You can be there if you want." His voice betrayed a tiny quiver. He glanced around to see if she had help. No one else around. He couldn't believe this tiny thing was the ninja that had flattened him.

"She's not here."

"Do you know where she is?" He hoped Elizabeth hadn't gone to Darfur again or to some other godforsaken place. "I need to talk to her, just for a few minutes. Even on the phone is fine."

"Give me your name and phone number and I'll tell her you stopped by. She's busy with the wedding."

"A wedding? Her wedding?"

"Perhaps." She crossed her arms. "I'm not saying anything else except it's none of your business."

Richard was frustrated, but he didn't have any choice. The finality of her voice and manner told him it wouldn't work trying to persuade her otherwise. He gave his number and left.

—⁂—

A week later, not hearing from Elizabeth, Richard tried calling again and discovered his number had been blocked. He gave up. Time for him to focus on getting Darcy to move on with his life. Elizabeth obviously had.

Richard needed Bingley's help. Except for that brief phone call inviting them to his sister Caroline's wedding, Bingley had not kept in touch. He called Bingley's emergency contact number and left a message.

"Where have you been, man?" Richard asked when Bingley finally returned his call. "And what the hell have you been doing all this time?"

"I'm in Zambia." Bingley's voice was cheerful. "I've been building playgrounds and teaching AIDS orphans. I wanted to do something with my life. It's been a great experience. You should try it."

Richard shuddered. Definitely something bad in the water in Vietnam, he decided. He briefly described what had happened with Darcy. "He's in even worse shape now than before Vietnam."

"I can't believe Elizabeth is marrying someone else already. Are you sure? That's a fast rebound. They were so into each other. I had a hard time getting him to leave Vietnam," Bingley said. "That's too bad. He needs some distraction. Are you guys coming to Caroline's wedding? She's marrying a plastic surgeon she met recently."

"Darcy's not keen on attending, but I'll drag him there. If the groom's a plastic surgeon, maybe there'll be beautiful women there for Darcy to have his own rebound fling with," Richard said. "Do you know much about the guy?"

"Nope," replied Charles. "Since he's brave enough to marry my sister, I don't want to discourage him by asking any questions."

CHAPTER 27

❀

Oprah Melodrama!

"DO YOU SEE WHAT YOUR PROBLEM IS HERE?" THE MAN ON THE left asked, looking straight at Elizabeth.

She hesitated then shook her head.

"Well, let me tell you. You need to get your lazy ass off your parents' couch and do something with your life. You're almost thirty, for God's sake."

Feeling ashamed, Elizabeth's eyes started to water.

"Now don't go teary eyed on me and use your troubled past as an excuse. You're smart—too smart for your own good. You can do so much more for yourself and for those less fortunate in the world. But you're lazy, that's your problem."

"But I don't feel good. I'm tired, so tired all the time now," she whispered, looking away from Dr. Phil's penetrating eyes. "I can't keep anything down."

"Don't tell me about not having energy. You're going to sit and wait for someone to rescue you. Your knight in shining armor with a bag full of coins, perhaps?"

The dark-haired woman sitting on Dr. Phil's left leaned forward. "Honey, if you think you can avoid hard work by marrying money, let me tell you, you're gonna be working hard for it anyhow in the marriage."

Fighting tears, Elizabeth protested, "But I don't want to marry him for his money. I want him, just him. I love him. But he was doubly-fiancéed!" She sobbed into her hands and heard someone else crying loudly also. A click. The crying stopped.

"Elizabeth, how many times have I told you not to watch Dr. Phil and Oprah together when they're on the same show? It's too much advice all at once. You're crying harder than the woman on the show." Jane had turned off the TV. "What was today's topic?"

"About getting my ass off the couch." Elizabeth sniffed, feeling foolish but slightly grateful for the excuse for a good cry. "And do something with my life."

Jane tucked the blanket around her. "Your ass is where it needs to be right now, and that's staying on that couch as long as you need to take care of yourself. Where's Mom?"

"She ran out to get some flaxseeds for the hockey pucks Mary wants to make for me."

"They're oatcakes and good for you to munch on. They have lots of protein and fiber." Mary entered and placed a glass of freshly made wheatgrass juice on the coffee table.

After one glance at it, Elizabeth promptly threw up into a bowl Jane had at the ready.

"I'd kill for a Snickers candy bar right now," Elizabeth said afterward. She couldn't wait for her father to come home tonight from teaching. He promised to sneak a Louisiana Hot Top Dog from her favorite grease joint on Durant Avenue in Berkeley. The women in the family had been trying to feed her healthy organic stuff.

"Do you know how much refined sugar is in each bar? Your babies will grow up to be hyperactive," Mary said. "I'll make you a soy protein drink." Mary took the wheatgrass and drank it before she left the room.

Elizabeth pressed her face closer to the threadbare old couch, seeking comfort in the musty smell of her dad's Old Spice cologne mixed with her mom's Jergens aloe lotion. "He likes doubles. Double fiancées. Double babies!"

"What?"

"Nothing. I'm just grumping." She thought Jane had left with Mary.

"Honey, if you're this grumpy during your first trimester, I'll hate to see you at forty weeks."

"With my luck I'll have to be on bed rest the whole time and never get off this couch." She heard the self-pity in her voice and felt teary again.

"You're just sick of throwing up all the time. You'll feel better soon." Jane's voice was gentle as she asked, "Lizzy, when are you going to call William?"

"'Hey, guess what? That virgin who gave you her cherry almost three months ago? She's growing some fruits now. Want to see?' Should I say that?"

"Lizzy, you need to tell him."

"I promise I'll call him when I can handle it. I can't deal with it right now. Let me have my pity moment. I only have a few more days to feel sorry for myself before the wedding." She closed her eyes and pretended to sleep. Aunt Mai arrived and Elizabeth heard Jane quietly steer her toward the kitchen.

Mary had flown home right after Elizabeth got back from Sudan; Jane had arrived a few days ago. Mrs. Luc, Chau's mother, had agreed to take over the running of Gracechurch Orphanage. Elizabeth suspected both her sisters had hustled back home once they found out she was pregnant with twins and living with their parents.

"All I've done for weeks is lie on this couch, feeling sorry for myself. I'm a bad and pathetic country song." She didn't know what was happening to her; pregnancy had turned her into a blubbering crybaby with no common sense and no pride. Despite everything, she still loved William.

Picture after picture of a younger him and various glamorous women kept replaying in Elizabeth's mind. The worst was the one of him passionately kissing a Victoria's Secret model with angel's wings—at a dance club, of all places—with his hands on the girl's breasts. After she saw that, she had impulsively signed up to work in Darfur with Doctors Without Borders. She wanted to be distracted by crimes against humanity and die a heroic death at the same time.

"Good, you're not asleep." Aunt Mai entered. "Here's the protein shake Mary made."

After drying her tears, Elizabeth sat up to drink her shake.

"What were you thinking about just now that made you look so sad?" Aunt Mai's hand brushed Elizabeth's hair gently.

"About the possibility of dying a heroic death in Sudan," Elizabeth answered honestly. "Don't mind me. I'm still in my melodramatic mood."

"How long were you there? Darfur, not the melodramatic mood."

"Long enough to throw up on everybody. I never made it out of the hotel near the airport. I was so sick from throwing up all the time they sent me straight home."

"It was fortunate Hussein was with you on the trip to Sudan." Aunt Mai wiped a drop of shake from Elizabeth's chin.

"When he ordered me to give him a urine sample, I screamed at him," Elizabeth admitted. Hussein's response was that he sure hoped she was pregnant, for if she wasn't, then he was going to kill her. She had been such an unbearable hormonal bitch on the trip over. He declared she was worse than any queen he had dated.

"What was he doing there?"

"He did a boob job on some Hollywood actress and she got him an invitation to work with some famous actor's pet project, protesting and publicizing Darfur's crime against humanity."

"That's very admirable of him."

Elizabeth snorted. "No it's not. He only did it so he could name drop his Hollywood connection. Neither of us saw any atrocities in Darfur, unless we count his meeting his fiancée."

At a star-studded reception that Hussein had dragged her to, Elizabeth spent the whole time in the bathroom throwing up and crying about what a failure she was to a very skinny woman, who she later learned was some famous actress and a Goodwill Ambassador for the United Nations. The actress soothed her and said that everything would work out. She even offered Elizabeth a ride in her private plane back to California. Some guy name Jorge Cooley helped Elizabeth onto the plane. She was so weak from throwing up, she didn't even realize who he was or what movies he had been in, though Hussein whispered Jorge was very famous.

Hussein and Caroline Bingley, who was there representing a Hollywood socialite union, bonded at the party, and were now happily planning a wedding together.

"Will you be okay for the trip to the wedding?" Aunt Mai asked. "I worry about you and all those hours traveling in the car."

"I'll be fine. I have to attend. I'm the best man." Elizabeth hoped Hussein was correct, that Caroline's brother was unlikely to be back from Africa in time for the wedding and no one named Darcy was on the guest list. She refused to admit disappointment had been her first reaction on hearing that.

"You rest now." Aunt Mai patted Elizabeth's back and stood. "I'll make you some *chao*. Bland rice soup with some beef broth will settle your stomach and give you some nutrition."

Thank God for Vietnamese aunts who didn't ask probing questions, Elizabeth thought as she watched her aunt walk out the room.

———〰———

"Did she tell you how she happened to get pregnant by accident?" Aunt Mai asked Jane, measuring some rice into a pot.

"No. You'd think being an infectious disease doctor she'd know to use contraceptives. But like most doctors, Lizzy never follows her own professional advice," Jane answered.

"We've been hoping you'd know the details of her relationship with the father."

"All I know is what Mary told me. Lizzy won't talk. Mom and Dad stopped asking her what happened, as it made her more upset each time they mentioned him." Jane helped her aunt gather ingredients for the soup. "I haven't had much more luck."

"You've met him. You even told me he adored her." Aunt Mai suggested, "Why don't you call him and ask him what happened between them?"

"He did seem to adore her. But what do I know? You know my track record with judging men," Jane said. "I'm reluctant to call him because… I'm afraid it's something Mary implied."

"What did Mary say?"

"I'm afraid Lizzy might have gotten herself into the same situation that I did with my old boyfriend."

Aunt Mai paused in lighting the stove. "What do you mean?"

"Mary said Lizzy was crying something about not wanting an arrest for domestic violence and bodily harm," Jane said. "When

234

she made the call to Mary, Lizzy said she didn't feel safe and didn't want to go home to him. That's why Mary had Lizzy leave New York that night."

Aunt Mai sighed. "I guess I can't blame Mary then, though I can't believe she was going to have Lizzy fly around the world for two days with no luggage and no word to anybody. She should have told us."

"You expect rational and practical planning from someone who spent weeks in a tree?"

"At least Lizzy came home, instead of going all the way to Vietnam."

"Only because her flight had a layover in LA and she got off the plane to call him in New York. After the phone call, she spent so much time crying in the restroom at the airport that she missed the connecting flight to Hanoi," Jane said. "She didn't hop on another plane to Vietnam because she didn't want William to worry about her being in Vietnam with Wickham loose."

"Wickham? The guy she had Mr. Vinh put in prison?"

"Yes. He got out of prison, though. That's also why she decided against going back to Vietnam. Of course, she didn't know that Wickham had already left Vietnam by then."

"She didn't want William—the man she ran away from—to worry about her safety in Vietnam, but she signed up for Darfur? Makes no sense to me," Aunt Mai said. "Do you really think this William hurt Lizzy, physically?"

"I don't know. My gut instinct says no, but I'm hoping to get the real answers from Lizzy soon, once she's calm. I'll wait until after the wedding; she says she can't deal with anything until afterwards." Jane glanced at her aunt. "Unlike me, Lizzy is not the kind to let a guy hurt her twice. She would leave after the first time. It fits her abruptly leaving New York."

"Jane, dear, you must forgive yourself. It's hard for someone with your kind nature to acknowledge the bad in people you care about. But you did eventually leave, and it's behind you. Now, let's not make any conclusion about Lizzy's babies' father until we get the facts from her."

"I'm going to be an aunt. I can't believe we're going to have babies in the family. We're all excited."

"Your mother worries that Lizzy will have a difficult time as a working, single mother."

"William's a responsible guy, whatever else he might be. He'll rush here the minute Lizzy tells him about the pregnancy, though good luck with him getting by Mary."

"For such a tiny thing, Mary is a rather militant protector," Aunt Mai agreed. "Are all you sisters going to Arizona?"

"All except Kitty," Jane answered. "We'll have some sisterly fun this weekend and help Lizzy with her duties as best man."

CHAPTER 28

❀

Dancing Queen

"I LOOK LIKE A BIKER CHICK HOOKER." ELIZABETH STUDIED HER black halter-top and low-rise leather pants. She peered at her exposed belly button to make sure it was clean. Turning sideways, she sighed. "A fat biker chick hooker."

"You don't look fat, just big-breasted chubby," Lydia said. "Are you sure you can't call up some guys and invite them to the party, Lizzy?"

Elizabeth shook her head. "Hussein doesn't want men at his bachelor party, just us."

Lydia said, "Kitty doesn't know how much fun she's missing. The bitch."

"Lydia!" Jane scolded.

"She is a bitch," Lydia said, "refusing to come and spend sisterly time with us because she disapproves of Hussein. Stupid stuck-up Stanford cow."

"Careful, Lydia," Elizabeth said, "you might decide to apply to Stanford in a couple of years."

"No way," Lydia said. "I'm smart. I have good grades. I'll get into Cal. If not, I'd rather go to Mills than Stanford."

"That would make Dad very happy, I'm sure," Jane said, "you attending a women's college."

"Hey, stranger things have happened," Lydia said. "Look at Mary, miss politically-correct-environmentalist-vegan now wearing black leather, getting her nails done, and letting us put makeup on her."

Mary shrugged. "Plumage doeth not make a womyn."

"Well I, for one, am grateful for Mary being a good sport," Elizabeth said. At one point during their long drive from Berkeley, Mary whispered she had something important to tell Elizabeth after the wedding. Elizabeth sighed. She wished her genius sister would finish her degree in computer science before indulging in any more eco-protest stunts. She glanced at the clock. "It's time to go to Hussein's room."

Jane said, "What a small world, Hussein marrying Caroline Bingley. She and the Hursts were friendly when I met them again at the rehearsal dinner last night."

"At least she stopped pretending she'd never met me before, like she did in Darfur," Elizabeth said with a small laugh. "She slipped up and asked me why I cut my hippie-long hair."

"Mrs. Hurst told me Caroline is very angry their brother's not here to walk her down the aisle tomorrow," Jane said.

Elizabeth didn't respond. She was glad she wouldn't see Charles this weekend. She wasn't quite up to dealing with the awkwardness and not asking about… she stopped the direction of her thought and put a coat on over her revealing outfit. There was no way she was parading around the hotel looking like a hooker.

Wearing a white leather suit and looking sad, Hussein opened his door.

Elizabeth hugged him. "Remember, it's not too late to back out."

"No way. My mother and all her friends are here. Besides, I'm marrying a woman whose family owns a private jet." He examined

Elizabeth's outfit. "I wish you would let me take a plaster model of your breasts now, before they go downhill and sag after you breast-feed. But I can do a lift for you then."

Elizabeth pushed him away. "No way am I ever letting you touch me with your knife."

Lydia pulled him aside and whispered in his ear. Hussein shook his head at her. "No alcohol. You know it's against my religion."

"You're going to need the alcohol for the wedding night," Elizabeth said to Hussein while Jane scolded the underage Lydia for her alcohol question.

"Don't worry, darling. It won't be much of a problem. She's frigid. That's why I'm marrying her. She'll be happy for me to leave her alone," Hussein said.

Lydia covered her ears. "Ew! TMI!" She dropped her hands. "Was Lizzy frigid?"

"She thought she was frigid, but she's not. Look at her. She's knocked down with big boobs." He shrugged off Elizabeth's glare. "Caroline thinks she's hot, but she's cold. Trust me, my bride-to-be won't be knocked down."

Elizabeth said, "It's knocked up, not knocked down. How many times have I told you that?"

He shrugged and laughed. "Up or down, doesn't matter. You look beaten. Let's dance."

Elizabeth played DJ while her sisters danced around him. She needed to rest. This trip had been a great distraction for her. It was good to finally get off her parents' couch, and her mood and her nausea had improved.

When the first song ended, Hussein ordered, "Darling, put on 'Dancing Queen' by ABBA!"

She started tapping her feet to the music at first, but after watching her three sisters uninhibitedly dancing and laughing, she decided to join them in circling Hussein.

"I love you Bennet girls!" Hussein said.

Laughing, Elizabeth lost herself in the music and the dancing.

〜〰〜

"Your sister still doesn't know you're here? And that you're bringing two extra guests to her wedding?"

Staring at the landscaped cactus garden outside the window of his hotel room, Darcy heard Richard ask Bingley the question.

"I left a message that I've arrived from Africa," Bingley laughed. "Not my fault if they don't check messages. I'm hoping to miss most of the pre-wedding festivities and just show up for the actual ceremony. And what's the big deal with two extra people at a wedding?"

"Man, that's cold, dissing your sister's wedding activities." Richard whistled. "You got some new cojones while you were in Africa, man. I had a girlfriend once who wanted me to attend her sister's boring wedding rehearsal luncheon, and when I forgot and went to play golf instead, she accused me of being passive-aggressive and broke up with me."

"No, women don't understand that," Bingley agreed in a dry voice.

"Yeah. They fuss and won't let you say no without it becoming a fight. Then they get upset when you forget to do what you didn't want to do in the first place. They call that being passive-aggressive." Richard shook his head. "You don't have to go to the rehearsal dinner tonight?"

"Missed it. Caroline would not have trusted a rehearsal done the eve before the wedding. She had it last night. I didn't arrive until this morning, remember?" Charles winked. "After spending months in Africa, I don't feel like dealing with Caroline's pretentious wedding crowd. I'm here to give her away for the ceremony, as she commanded. How hard is it to walk down an aisle?"

Darcy stopped listening to their conversation. He hadn't wanted to come to Arizona to attend—no, apparently to crash, as it turned out—a wedding of people he didn't care about, but Richard had wanted to convince Bingley to come back to work sooner, to take over some of the work previously done by Anne.

When Richard came back from California two weeks ago, he told Darcy that Elizabeth had indeed moved on. From the uncharacteristically gentle way his cousin gave him the news, Darcy knew he had truly lost her.

Bingley's cell phone rang and interrupted Darcy's thoughts from traveling down that dark road further.

Bingley grimaced. "My sisters found me. I better take this in the other room. There will be yelling." He returned a few minutes later in a surprisingly cheerful mood. "Gentlemen, I got orders. We're crashing the bachelor party. Hot-looking hooker chicks just entered my future brother-in-law's room for his bachelor party. Caroline wants me to make sure that he stays pure."

Richard stood and whooped. "Woo-hoo! We'll be impure for him. I'll do anything for your sister, man." He turned to Darcy. "Don't even think of staying away. You can just come and look, you know. I know you won't touch. You're so damn fastidious."

"And you're never fastidious enough."

"Let's not fight," Bingley intervened. "Come on, Darce. Come along and help make sure Richard stays clean."

"Yeah, you can come play den mother and pass out condoms," Richard said while pushing Bingley out of the door. "What's the room number, Charles?"

Shrugging, Darcy reluctantly followed. He wanted to make

sure that Richard behaved. They could hear loud music when they reached the fiancé's room. No one answered Bingley's knocking.

Richard pushed him out of the way and rapped hard on the door. "I want to see some skin and curves tonight."

A tiny woman in black leather opened the door. When she saw Richard, her eyes narrowed. She hissed, "You!"

"You!" Richard returned.

Darcy and Bingley glanced at each other. Darcy shook his head. He didn't recognize the woman. Richard and the woman began to argue. After peering into the room, Bingley froze. Curious, Darcy looked.

Elizabeth was dancing! She turned. Her eyes met his. Her body stilled.

Blood drained from Darcy's head. His chest suddenly felt too small for his lungs.

A smiling man in white walked in between them. He said something but Darcy couldn't hear past the loud drumming in his ears.

Elizabeth rushed past him.

Someone—Jane, Darcy dimly recognized—ran after her.

He realized then he hadn't dreamt it. It was really his Elizabeth!

The man in white leather pulled Darcy to a chair. "Sit, you look like you had a shock. Put your head between your knees."

Darcy obediently allowed the man to push his head down.

The man asked, "Tell me, are you the one that knocked Elizabeth down?"

"Shut the fuck up, Hussein!" a woman screamed before Darcy could fully lift his head at hearing the question.

"Three hot guys enter the room and immediately two of my sisters run out and the third one is screaming. Stop screaming, Mary, you know it's not ladylike to scream," a young girl said in a surprisingly firm voice. She turned to Darcy. "They're embarrassed to be caught looking like hookers. But I always say, if you got it, flaunt it. Hi, I'm Lydia Bennet."

"Shut up, Lydia! And stop flirting. These men are dangerous. They hurt Lizzy in New York. They followed her here," Mary screamed.

Darcy's heart hammered hard against his rib cage. Someone had hurt his Elizabeth. He stood and approached Mary. "Who? Tell me who."

The screamer clamped her mouth and stared back at him with a defiant look.

Richard's hand touched her shoulder. "Is this why you wouldn't let us talk to her? You think we beat her up?"

Lydia shoved his arm away. She wedged herself between them and held her fists up to Richard's face. "Don't touch my sister."

"I think there might be some sort of misunderstanding here. I'm Charles Bingley, and this is my friend William and his cousin Richard." Bingley put out his hand toward the man in white leather. "My sister is marrying the groom, and that must be you, Hassan?"

"Hussein," the groom corrected.

Darcy's head whipped toward him at hearing the familiar name again.

Mary stepped toward Darcy and bared her teeth. "You! You were the one who beat her up. Don't play innocent."

"What? I never touched her." Darcy instinctively took a step backward before he realized he had done so.

"Uh… I think that's not quite true," Hussein said with a laugh, which ended abruptly when the screamer glared at him. He too took a backward step from her.

Bingley stepped up again and within minutes managed to

unravel the story from Mary. Gasps of disbeliefs descended into loud guffaws from Richard and Bingley when Mary finished.

"Man, your relationship with Elizabeth has been one comic misunderstanding after another." Richard laughed and slapped Darcy's back.

Darcy failed to see the humor, but at least he now understood the screamer's attitude. No wonder she wouldn't let him near Elizabeth. Suddenly, realization and hope thundered through the air and struck him at the knees. He wobbled. Grabbing the back of a chair, he steadied himself. Richard was wrong. *Elizabeth had not moved on!*

"Darce, you and Elizabeth need to talk, now," Bingley said to him, then turned to Mary. "They need privacy to talk to each other. I assure you he won't harm a hair on her head."

Mary looked unconvinced, though she nodded. "We'll be close by. He better watch himself."

—⁓—

Leaving a crowd in the small sitting room of the sisters' hotel suite, Darcy quietly entered the bedroom.

Jane sat on the edge of the bed, soothing her crying sister.

He cleared his throat.

Jane gave him an assessing look. What she saw must have reassured her. She nodded at him. "Lizzy, William is here." Jane stroked her sister's hair one more time then left the room, closing the door quietly behind her.

With each little sniffle Elizabeth made, his heart flinched, though he stayed where he was and waited for her to acknowledge his presence.

After long moments, she stopped crying, hiccupped, and peeked at him over the edge of the bed covers.

He recognized pain—mixed with a flash of something—before she closed her beautiful green eyes and turned away.

When she turned back a moment later, she had composed herself. "Hello, William."

Despite her attempt to mask it, he heard the quiver in her voice. That, and the flash of love he glimpsed was enough.

He decided to trust.

He knew he would get them through this. They would make it. As long as she still cared for him, he would fight for her. No holding back. No more fear.

Feeling surprisingly calm now, he stepped closer. "Your sister Mary thought I was beating you up in New York and that's why you left me."

Her eyes widened. She sat up. The blanket fell from her body and his gaze involuntarily dropped. Had her breasts always been that full?

She said, "What? How ever did she get that idea? You would never do that."

He sat at the foot of the bed and smiled a small smile. "You would never have let me. But I'm glad you realize I would never hurt you physically"—he paused to swallow—"or intentionally."

She moved closer to him. "Will—"

He put a finger to her lips. The exquisite rush of feelings from that barest touch almost made him lose his composure. His hand trembled and he withdrew it.

Almost reflexively, she grabbed his hand back.

They both stared down at their joined hands. The rough, reddened cracks in his hand embarrassed him. He tried to pull his hand away again but she tightened her hold.

"William," she whispered. She took his other hand and

folded both together in hers. Leaning forward, she kissed his reddened fingers and palms. Gently, she laid her cheek atop their joined hands.

"Lizzy." He rested his own cheek against her head and pressed his lips to her hair. Inhaling a deep, nourishing breath, he took in the familiar fragrance of her gardenia scent. "But I did, hurt you, I know."

Her head swayed as if denying his words, but she stayed silent.

"I should have trusted in your love for me. You gave yourself so generously to me, your heart and… everything, and I was afraid."

"You were?"

"I was afraid you'd discovered I was unworthy of you. I used to stare at you when you slept, fearful you were a figment, and you'd disappear in the morning."

"Oh, William." Tearfully, she kissed his knuckles. "I'm so sorry I did disappear."

Though her tears stung the cracks in his hands, he welcomed the soothing pain. "I don't blame you, love. You didn't trust me not to hurt you, and I didn't trust you not to hurt me." He paused and lifted his head. "Can you ever forgive me?"

"Yes."

The way she had said the word without any hesitation humbled him. "I love you so much, Lizzy. I don't think I had allowed myself to love until you came into my life. You got through my defenses so easily, I was scared. I had never met, nor wanted, nor needed any one person so much until you." He blinked rapidly and turned away until he controlled himself. "I didn't, and still don't, know how to be in a relationship."

"Me either," she reminded him. "I've also never been in a real relationship."

"You asked so little of me. You didn't need my money... my name..."

"But I do need you." Her hands gripped his fingers tight. "Just you."

"When you left, I thought you had finally figured out how lacking I was as a partner, just as I had feared and expected. But you left because you were hurt—"

"No, no, you mustn't blame yourself." She touched his face. "I should have been brave enough to stay and talk to you."

"You were afraid to talk to me?"

"Yes. We were both afraid, William. Now, I want to talk about why I left so suddenly... ask you questions I was afraid to ask then, okay?"

He nodded. They heard noises from beyond the door. "I don't want to keep your sisters from their room. Could we go somewhere else to talk?"

"Let's go to your room." She reached into her toiletry bag for a small tube of something and put it in her pocket before pulling a large T-shirt on over her leather top. Taking his hand, she led him out into the small sitting room.

CHAPTER 29

❀

Cracked Hands Heal

"ELIZABETH, CAROLINE BINGLEY IS MARRYING..." DARCY PAUSED. They had left the others and were now on their way to his room.

"She's marrying my gay ex-boyfriend." She tugged his hand, urging him to keep up. "Funny, huh?"

"Does she know?"

"Hussein told me when he revealed his last relationship was with a man, and the one before that and so on, her response was he hadn't met the right woman yet and everyone experimented. And she didn't want to talk about icky intimate stuff."

He shook his head. "Sounds like Caroline."

"I'm a bit concerned about leaving Richard and Charles with him," she said. "I hope he doesn't make a pass at them. He likes blonds."

His lips twitched. "Richard was expecting strippers."

"I can't believe Mary's been running interference because she thought you were abusive to me."

"She doesn't know me. She's only being protective."

"I need to talk to her about making snap judgments without hearing all the facts. She should have at least talked to me before she acted. Why are you smiling?"

"No reason," he said, amused at her lack of self-irony.

"I'm glad you find some humor in Mary's interference."

"All your sisters have my permission and my undying gratitude to make sure no one, including me, ever harms you."

They approached the wing where his suite was. She stopped at the entrance and explored a birds of paradise plant, lightly running her hand down its stem and examining the orange bud.

"We could walk around a bit more," he offered.

"No, I'm tired."

She seemed to always have a boundless amount of energy, so her fatigue now worried him. As soon as he opened the door to his room, she went straight to the bed and crawled into it. "I'm sorry, it's been a long day with the wedding activities."

"Perhaps you should rest now."

"I'll rest after we've talked. Come." She patted the bed and pulled a small tube out of her pocket. "I want to put this on your hands." When he settled himself next to her, she reached for his right hand and dabbed a smear of cream on it. "Tell me if it stings."

Gently, she massaged the cream onto the small cracks of his knuckles. She then did the same to the other hand. He stared at her bent head while she carefully examined his hands.

"There, that should help your hands heal. We have to make sure to get you the gentle cleansing soap for when you wash your hands." She looked up. "William? Are you okay?"

He knew he should be embarrassed that his eyes had brimmed with tears, but he couldn't look away.

Her own eyes blinking rapidly, she caressed his face. "I used to wonder why you stared at me so… in the middle of the night."

He took a breath and began, "You have questions for me?"

"You aren't secretly engaged to Anne, are you?"

Despite himself, he smiled at her direct question. "No, that's my aunt's delusion. That's why you left, wasn't it? Did she tell you that?"

He had known his aunt was involved, yet when Elizabeth confirmed it with a nod, a fresh wave of rage surged through him, some of it at Catherine but mostly at himself.

Elizabeth lay down and urged him to do the same. When he stretched out next to her, she stroked his chest. Soothed by her caress, the tenseness gradually left him. In a tender voice, she said, "Tell me about your aunt. What's your relationship with her?"

"Before my father died, he asked me to watch over my sister and my aunt." He stared at the ceiling. "I've always found Catherine a rather difficult person to deal with. Immediately, we fought over custody of my sister. I admit I wasn't the best person to be a young child's guardian then, and Catherine knew it. We finally managed to come to a truce. For Georgiana's sake, I've tried to humor my aunt with duty visits, her birthday dinners and so forth, and ignore her odd obsessions and her attempts to intrude and run our lives. It became a habit to avoid confronting her directly." He met her eyes. "Now you know how weak a man I am."

The soft pads of her fingers gently tapped his chest. "No, love. You're not weak, just… loyal. Your father did ask you to care for her."

"I didn't introduce you because I was waiting for the right time to deal with her delusion about my marrying Anne. I knew she wouldn't take it well, and I wasn't looking forward to the big fight. I should have told her, though, for it cost me you."

"William"—her fingers stilled—"I thought you didn't care enough about me to introduce me. From your emotional reaction about her birthday dinner, I thought that she meant a lot to you, that you wanted her approval… and that you were ashamed of me."

He stared at her for a few seconds before he closed his eyes and grieved for the time they had lost. "How did we both come to misunderstand each other so much in New York? I was not ashamed of you, but of me; I was afraid meeting my aunt and dealing with her craziness would be another strike against me, more baggage."

"Why do you think you need to be perfect for me to love and marry you? You thought I would hold a crazy aunt against you? Did you have so little trust in my love?"

He stayed silent, not knowing how to answer her.

"All along, you really expected me to disappear somehow, some-time, didn't you?" she said. "That's why you didn't come after me."

"Your leaving proved my fear had come true," he admitted. "I wanted to so badly go after you, Lizzy. Many times, I had the jet ready to fly to wherever you were, but then I would remember the phone call and you..."

"And I asked you specifically not to follow me," she finished. "I'm so sorry, William. I was so upset that day. I regretted that so many times. Then, I thought you felt I wasn't worth it when you never came after me."

"Far from it," he paused, unable to get the words past his throat, remembering the pain of his yearning for her.

"I do know differently now." She took hold of his hands and softly kissed them again. "The state of your hands tells me you cared."

It came to him at that moment: this was what being loved and accepted felt like. His anxious habit had always been a source of shame and stress for him, but now, he saw cracked hands also heal. "I don't remember if I have always washed my hands, even when I was anxious and nervous as a child. I do remember that I was a difficult child. I didn't warm up to people very easily, or they to me."

"That's not true," she protested. "I liked you right away. I fell in love with you immediately."

He smiled at that. "My father, and a few others, had a difficult time with me, I remember that. But not my mother. After she died, I thought that no one would ever love and accept me so unconditionally or so unreservedly ever again... and I was afraid to completely trust or believe in your love for me."

"I didn't leave because you weren't perfect. I left because I was not perfect. I was scared myself."

"I guess we both were in the same state then."

She nodded. "We both were insecure about each other. We got together so quickly and came to love each other just as quickly. I think trust needs time to build, though."

"What else did Aunt Catherine say to make you leave?" His aunt had refused to tell him the details when he confronted her. Judging from the way Elizabeth now tensed in response to his question, he knew it was more than his aunt's obsession about him marrying Anne. "Richard suspected Catherine might have said something about the other women."

She met his eyes then turned to stare at the ceiling.

"Did she mention the penthouse and the women?"

Instead of answering, she put her hand over her eyes. He turned to fully face her and waited. Finally, she lifted up her hand. At the hurt in her eyes, he swallowed and collapsed back down on the bed. He too stared at the ceiling and tried to gather his thoughts and his words.

How could he tell her how ashamed he was? How could he admit to her that he had used other women, used their fascination with his looks, his wealth, and his position to take advantage of the brief moments of pleasure in their bodies, never caring how they really felt about him or how he had felt about them? He was no better than Wickham. That was why he never wanted to tell her about his previous life. How could he tell the one and only woman he loved how worthless a man he really was?

She, on the other hand, was pure in both body and heart. She gave herself to him only because she loved him—and what a gift that was, her selfless love. Each time he was in her body, he had gloried in the knowledge that he alone had the privilege, alone was the recipient of her precious gift. How could he tell her how unworthy he had felt to receive such a gift? He wished he had come to her a better man, but he hadn't expected someone like her to exist at all, much less love him so unselfishly.

He didn't know how to say all that coherently, but he tried. He must have expressed himself eloquently enough. The hurt left her eyes. She moved closer and buried her face against his neck. Wrapping his arms around her, he held her tight against his heart.

"You expect too much of yourself. You're only human, my love." They lay like that without speaking for a time before she spoke again. "Now tell me about Anne."

"I knew she was a little infatuated with me when we were teenagers. Soon after, Catherine started her obsession about Anne and me marrying."

"That must have been very uncomfortable."

"It was," he acknowledged, "and I've always tried to maintain a distance between us. I hired her at my aunt's request. It appeased Catherine enough to leave the issue of Georgiana's custody alone. Anne has proven herself very capable in business matters; otherwise she wouldn't have lasted at DDF."

"You guys never really dated? Went out?"

He barely managed to suppress a shudder. "No. Trust me, she's not my type. I thought she was as uncomfortable as I was about my aunt's matchmaking…"

"You thought? You don't think that anymore?"

"Richard and Georgiana both think Anne's not opposed to what Catherine wants."

She laughed. "You look like a nine-year-old boy who just learned some icky girl likes him in *that* disgusting way."

He smiled, glad she could laugh about it. "I've finally accepted Richard and my sister can be more astute than I am on many things."

"I'm sure they loved hearing that."

"Catherine used PTF to pressure the hospital not to hire you. The hospital denied it, of course; nevertheless, they lost the grant."

Her smile disappeared. "I'm sorry. I thought it was you. I thought you were going to break up with me sooner or later and you didn't want me to get too settled."

He sat up and stared down at her. "How could—"

"I'm sorry."

"Shhh, it's okay," he soothed when tears filled her eyes again. "You have to promise me, before you make any conclusions about me or us, you'll talk to me."

"I promise." She wiped her eyes. "But you have to talk more too. I can't read minds. You didn't tell me about your aunt or Anne. I can't ask questions if I don't know what I don't know."

"I promise to talk more," he said. "Anne denied knowing what Catherine was doing with the hospital and you, but I don't buy it, and neither does Richard."

"Why?"

"Catherine should not have any influence on the foundation's grant process at all. If Anne can't keep her stepmother out of it, then she can't be in charge of it."

"It seems rather unfair to blame Anne if your aunt was the one responsible. You yourself have trouble confronting your own aunt."

"Not anymore. I made it clear to both Catherine and Anne that even if I hadn't met you, I would never have considered marrying Anne, under any circumstances."

"And how did that go over?"

"Not well with Catherine, as expected. But it's her problem, not mine anymore. As for Anne"—he shrugged—"she seemed more upset at the loss of overseeing PTF and her reduced role at DDF. She's restricted to managing a couple of departments only. She's no longer vice president of operations."

"That's a bit harsh, for her to lose her position because of her stepmother's interference," she said. "But you must have other good reasons?"

"Not really, not yet anyhow," he confessed. "Except my trust in her has diminished. You needn't worry about her. Her negligence has damaged the foundation's reputation, even if she wasn't directly at fault. But, more important to me, you were hurt by it and I lost you."

"You didn't lose me. I've never stopped loving you."

Until that moment, he hadn't realized how much he needed to hear her say the words.

She continued, "Now that I know she means nothing to you, I trust you to do whatever you need to with Anne. We're back together and I'm happy, so I'm feeling very generous to the whole world and don't want anyone to suffer needlessly, but you know best."

"I do know that you're the best thing that ever happened to me, my Lizzy."

CHAPTER 30

✿

Mine, Yours, Ours

PEPPER SPICE. ELIZABETH RECOGNIZED THE SCENT BEFORE SHE opened her eyes. Morning was not here yet; hazy darkness still shrouded the room. She sleepily reached behind her until she made contact with a warm, male body. Reassured that he was real and she hadn't dreamt his presence, she sank back to her soft pillow.

A short moment later, a hand inching along the underside of her breast stirred her awake. Cupped palm hovered indecisively a bare inch away. She lurched her chest forward to make contact. A sensual massaging of her breast began, serenaded by a deep, satisfied sigh behind her. Soft kisses brushed on her shoulder. "Good, you're awake. I didn't want to wake you."

She let out a pleased sigh of her own. How had she survived these past months without the delicious sensation of his naked body spooning her? She'd even missed his snoring. Turning, she encountered his smiling eyes and rubbed his cheek, smiling at the fine sandpaper feel of his early morning stubble.

Exhausted, she had fallen asleep right in his arms after they had made love last night, after he told her she was the best thing that happened to him. She frowned; she hoped he'd still feel that way after hearing her big news. *Two big news! The two big news currently fluttering in her belly.*

"No frowning allowed." He moved on top of her. "A woman with beautiful breasts like these isn't allowed to frown first thing in the morning." He bent and gave one nipple a quick lick then gently blew on it.

Surprised and aroused by the warm puff of his breath on her wet nipple, she moaned.

"Moaning is allowed," he whispered. "Lots of moaning."

She decided the big news could wait. He licked and suckled and fondled her. As he made love to her, he whispered incoherent words of love and appreciation for every part of her body.

When his pacing was too controlled, too slow for her, she turned the tables. With a few tricks she'd learned from him on how to speed things up, she managed to make him cry out, "Oh God, Lizzy, so sweet!"

"Naughty girl. You made me lose control. I wanted to take it nice and slow," he murmured against her neck and tried to pull out.

Not ready to release him, she tightened her legs around him and grinned. "That was last night. I want it hard and fast now." Tenderly, she brushed a lock of hair from his eyes.

"How could you even think any other experience I had with others in the past compared to this, with you?" he asked, his face serious.

For that, she pressed her lips to his. When the kiss ended, she ran her hands down his back and caressed him. He gave a big happy sigh, lifted himself off her, and sank back against his pillow. Expectantly, she watched him. She smiled when his eyes closed seconds later. He tended to become sleepy after he climaxed.

Propping herself up on her elbow, she examined him. He felt

thinner to her. As his hands had, his body showed the physical signs of the stress of their separation. She turned her face away for a few moments, in case he opened his eyes and noticed her tears.

"I'm sorry I've been selfish," she whispered, turning back and hugging his body tight.

Only even breathing and soft snoring answered her. Contented just to lie there quietly listening to the rhythms of his body, she let him sleep and closed her eyes.

—◊◊◊—

The sun shone brightly through the gaps between the window's drapes when she awoke to the sound of loud knocking.

Richard's voice could be heard. "Darce?"

"Bloody hell!" William cursed and rolled off the bed and grabbed a robe. "This had better be good."

She glanced at the clock and gasped. It was later than she realized. The wedding. She had forgotten all about her duties as best man. "The wedding, William. I have to go back to my room and get ready."

William scowled and went to answer the door.

When she stood up too suddenly, nausea hit her hard. "Damn," she cursed as she rushed to the bathroom. The nausea subsided quickly with sips of water. She waited for a few minutes to make sure it wouldn't come back before she showered.

When she came out of the bathroom toweling dry her hair, he was already dressed and had laid out her clothes neatly, on top of the now tidied bed. He blushed when she caught sight of her red thong in his hand.

She teased, "I'll trade you that for your shorts. I don't want to put on leather pants this morning."

"Deal." He handed her a pair of shorts and put the thong in his suitcase. He closed his suitcase as if it was a treasure box.

She shook her head, amused. Men and their fascination with thongs! While she dressed, she asked, "What did Richard want?"

"He wanted to make sure we're all right before he takes off to play golf this morning."

"He's such a sweetheart."

"He is not a sweetheart. I told him if he hadn't interrupted we would be in the middle of doing 'all right.'"

"William!"

He pouted. "I was planning another make-up sex session this morning. I've never had make-up sex before now."

"Never?"

"Never." His face had a determined look. "I promise you there will never be another make-up sex session, since we're never going to fight."

She almost laughed aloud. The crazy man was serious.

He pulled his shirt out of his jeans and unbuttoned it. "Since we're never going to break up ever again, let's not waste our precious make-up sex time on other peoples' wedding."

"But—"

"No buts." Grabbing the edge of her T-shirt, he pulled it off her. "The wedding is not until late this afternoon. Hussein doesn't need you right now. I do."

She tried to still his hands. "William, there's something I must—"

"Shhh! No talking. We've talked enough already. I used up all my words last night. Back to action time," he shushed and trapped her between the bed and him. He took off the shorts she'd just put on. His gaze roamed over her. "God, you're so beautiful, even more beautiful than I remembered."

She gave up. His mind obviously was too clouded by lust now to listen to anything.

Lifting one hand over a breast, she let her thumb circle the nipple. His eyes darkened. She took a step back and brought her other hand up and did the same to the other nipple. His mouth parted. Encouraged, she began to uninhibitedly fondle herself and sensuously dance in slow circles. With an eager, anticipating gleam, his eyes tracked her movements. At one point, he had to unbutton his jeans but remained dressed, as if he was afraid to miss something if he took his attention away from her.

While laying on the couch these past weeks, she had watched hours of belly dancing on the TV, among other mindless shows. She duplicated some provocative moves she remembered. When she shimmied her behind at him, his eyes bulged. He visibly panted. Executing a few tiny pelvic thrusts, she moved closer and undressed him to his knees. When she touched his groin, his eyes rolled back and he almost stumbled.

She made him lie down on the bed. He tried to take his pants off but she shook her finger at him. Obediently, he lay back down and jutted his pelvis upward in invitation.

She gently sucked him. Animal sounds spurted from his throat. Her tongue flicked at the drop of moisture at his tip and his body vibrated and hummed in response. She closed her mouth around him and rolled her tongue. A growl turned into a purring from his throat. She sucked him harder. His hips jerked.

He pulled her head from his groin and positioned her atop him. In a frantic voice, he begged, "Please, I can't last much longer."

Accompanied by his grunts and growls, she rode him. When she collapsed on top of him after her climax, she could feel the hotness of his release exploding inside her.

"You're going to be the death of me," he wheezed underneath her.

She smirked against his neck. "Never underestimate the hormonal surge of a pregnant woman."

He stilled.

Suddenly, realizing what she had just said, she stiffened. She hadn't meant to blurt it out like that.

"Elizabeth?"

Her body still connected to him, she kept her face buried against his skin and whispered happily, "Yes. I'm pregnant."

"Is it mine?"

CHAPTER 31

❀

Dog House

"HOW COULD YOU BE IN THE DOG HOUSE ALREADY?"

Darcy ignored Richard's question and kept his eyes on the stage where the wedding ceremony would take place.

Richard continued, "Not even a full twenty-four hours, and you've already messed up again. What exactly did you say?"

"Just something stupid."

"Great. That's just great. After the trouble I went through last night reassuring that crazy Ninja sister you're a good egg, you go and say something rotten the next day. Do you know how this makes me look?"

"This is not about you," Darcy snapped.

Other guests arrived and some of the seats around them filled, putting a stop to their conversation.

He didn't know why he had asked that question. Shocked at hearing she was pregnant, he had blurted out the first thing in his mind. She had jumped up and ran. By the time he pulled his jeans up and ran after her, she had locked herself in the bathroom. He heard retching noises and anxiously waited by the door. When he didn't hear any more sound, he asked, "Are you okay? Do you need any help?"

Wrapped in a towel, she came out and headed toward her clothes. "I meant to say—"

"You've said enough. And no, I don't need any help, either; you've also done enough." A pointed glance directed at his crotch. "And yes, I was always going to tell whoever the father was about the pregnancy. I was waiting for the right time and opportunity. That, and an appointment for a paternity test."

Loud knocking again interrupted. She ignored it and continued to dress.

Irritated at the interruption and expecting Richard on the other side again, Darcy snarled as he opened the door, "What?"

Mary Bennet glared at him. "Hussein needs Lizzy to calm him. He's nervous."

"No, he's not." Elizabeth came to the door, dressed. "He probably wants to make sure I shaved and put some makeup on before the wedding."

"That too," Mary admitted. "He did mention something about that."

Darcy gently touched Elizabeth's arm. "Please, we'll talk later, after the wedding?"

She nodded, though she still refused to meet his eyes. He was encouraged, however, when he bent to kiss her cheek good-bye and she didn't turn away. "I'll wait for you here after the wedding. I love you," he whispered and tried to pretend he didn't see Mary eyeing him suspiciously.

He had spent the whole day in his room, beating himself up for being such a jerk and trying to distract himself by researching safe baby furniture.

A flurry of late-arriving wedding guests appeared. A woman, wearing a large hat, sat down in front of him and partially obstructed his view. He glared at her head. He had chosen this seat to have a good view of Elizabeth during the ceremony. The music began, signaling the start of the ceremony.

A tired Elizabeth came to stand next to Hussein.

Of course, she's tired; she's carrying a child. Your child, you bloody fool! Why did you say that? You ruined what should have been a beautiful moment! Disgusted with himself, he sighed louder than he had intended.

"Don't draw attention to yourself," Richard hissed, "not until Caroline's hitched completely. She might think you're regretting her. Wait, what were we thinking, bringing you to her wedding? If she catches a glimpse of you now, she might change her mind about marrying her trophy doctor there. Slink down and hide."

Darcy ignored his cousin. A moment later, after thinking it over, he hunched his shoulders and turned so that his face was hidden behind the rim of the large hat in front.

My child, he reverently mouthed and daydreamed of a dark-haired little girl. He saw himself teaching his little girl to ride a bicycle, with a titanium helmet on, of course. A green-eyed little girl wearing a pink tutu and dancing, just like her mummy. Well, perhaps not quite like how her mummy had danced this morning, he amended.

The music starting up again startled him. The wedding ceremony was over and he had missed it.

Skipping the reception, he waited in his room for Elizabeth. When he finally heard knocking, he leaped to the door. A stubborn expression on her face, Elizabeth stood on the other side.

Mary had accompanied her. With a warning glance directed at him, she handed him a suitcase, pushed Elizabeth gently toward him and left without saying anything. He wondered if the sister would ever talk to him, then he remembered her screaming voice and decided a silent Mary was a good thing.

"Why did you say that?" Elizabeth pounded on him the moment he closed the door. "How could you even think that?"

"I don't, I mean I don't really think that. It's just... it's just... Look, I'm an idiot. I just say things, stupid things. But to be honest most, if not all, guys think that. Even if they're on a deserted island with no other men around, the first thing that comes to their head is 'Is it mine?'"

"What?"

"It's true. We can't believe that our seed could create something so precious as a child. It's a miracle to us. It's like being on top of the world and you can't believe you're there."

"Of course you don't believe it. You men thoughtlessly scatter and sow millions of your seeds all over without ever thinking of the consequences."

"I always think of the consequences." He couldn't believe the direction of their argument. "And I don't scatter or sow my seeds all over. You may not believe this, but I have never forgotten to use a condom before you."

"Oh, yeah, you and your extensive experience with condoms. Just because you did it with all those women, in dance clubs and all, grabbing their boobs and Lord knows what else, you think I'm like you. You think I slept around with other men because we broke up." She ended up screaming the words at him halfway through her tirade. "You do! You think I did that!"

Flushing, he looked away.

She gasped. "Did that mean..." She broke off and started sobbing.

He swallowed. He'd made her cry again. Then he grasped her meaning. "No, no. Elizabeth, I've never slept with anyone else since we met. And definitely not when we were apart. In fact, I hadn't been with anyone else for well over a year before I met you." Anxious to make her understand, the words rushed out; he hardly knew what he was saying. "I stopped carrying condoms around long before I met you because I didn't feel like having sex with anyone. You, only you, are the one woman I have wanted since I first laid eyes on you. And you think after being with you, I could look at another woman, much less touch her?"

"Then why did you think I might have done it?"

"Have you taken a good look at yourself? You're beautiful and sexy and just... just... wonderful." He stepped closer. "I couldn't believe no other man had touched your heart or your body. And when you left me, I tortured myself with thoughts of other men and you. Your sister told me you had moved on and then I saw that picture of you and Jorge Cooley..."

"Who? What picture?" She looked genuinely puzzled. He explained to her about the picture and the caption he saw. Her eyes went wide. "I was in a tabloid? I was in a tabloid?" A delighted expression on her face now, she bounced and flapped her hands. "Wait until my mother hears about this. Oooh! And my sisters! Hussein will be so jealous! Which one was it? Do you still have it?"

He gaped at her reaction, though he was glad that she had stopped crying.

"What's the name of the tabloid? I want to know so I can brag to Hussein." When he told her the name of the tabloid, she said, "Never heard of it. But I don't read those things usually. Well, except when I first left New York and found all those old pictures of you. You were such a playboy."

His brain finally worked. She had mentioned him in dance

clubs and grabbing boobs. Bloody hell, she must have found those old pictures of his partying days. She was just as irrationally insecure about him and other women as he was about her and other men. At least it now made sense to him why she had so readily believed his aunt. "Those pictures were taken almost ten years ago. I was young and wild and stupid. I'm sorry for thinking that you might... some women would during a breakup. I hurt you with my insensitivity in New York; I wouldn't blame you if you had," he rambled, anxious to move past his wild past.

"Will you stop with the everything-is-Darcy's-fault blame fest? It's getting old. You can't control everything. You can't prevent everything. You're going to be a father, so you're going to have to let go of the illusion that you can control everything in life." She narrowed her eyes. "And what would you have done had it been another man's child?"

"Taken care of the child and the mother and considered it a privilege," he answered without hesitation, glad that he had spent that day thinking about this issue and could give her an immediate answer. Though he hated the idea of her and another man, he had decided he would treasure any part of her. And a child coming from her, whether his or not, would be treasured by him. Of course, he was doing cartwheels inside that she was carrying his child and the point was moot.

His answer must have done the trick because she smiled, then started crying again. She hugged him. He gratefully wrapped his arms around her and kissed her forehead.

"I'm not so sure I would be as generous if you had fathered a child with another woman while we were apart. I would have killed you," she confessed. "I'm more jealous than you are."

"I doubt that."

She told him that seeing that one picture of him in a tabloid was what had made her sign up for Darfur.

"What? How crazy is that?" he shouted. "You put yourself at risk and took years off my life with worry just because you were jealous of a woman in a picture that's at least ten years old? And whose name and face I don't even remember?"

With a sheepish look on her face, she nodded.

"You'll be the death of me!" He wasn't done with shouting. "Will you promise to talk to me before you impulsively act? Didn't we go through this once before, in Vietnam?"

"I talked to you tonight even though I was mad. I came here with my suitcase to spend the night with you even when I wanted to kick your ass. And I didn't do anything impulsive or run away even though I was hurt," she reminded him.

"Thank the gods for that. Now, are there any more things you need to ask or tell me? Any more surprises or shocks?"

"Yes. We're having twins."

CHAPTER 32

❀

Meet the Parents

"I DON'T CARE IF YOU CAN AFFORD TO PAY FOR A WHOLE FLEET OF cars to be delivered, you're not wasting your money," Elizabeth said as she and her sisters followed Darcy out of the hotel the next morning.

"Our money," he corrected. He wanted to have the sisters' car delivered to their home while his jet flew them back to the Bay Area.

"Aw, how sweet," Lydia said. "He's a keeper. Mom always said one of us girls had to marry a rich guy, and how funny it's you, Lizzy, of all people."

"How about Mary and I drive, and Lydia and Lizzy can fly with you, William?" Jane offered.

"Great idea!" Lydia clapped. "Here comes Richard. I'm going to tell him I'm flying with you guys."

"We're going to Oakland? What about Chicago? We have a meeting there," Richard said to him after hearing Lydia's news. "Surely you can part from Elizabeth for a few days."

"I'll drive home with my sisters, and you'll come to me when you're done with Chicago," Elizabeth suggested.

"Absolutely not. I'm flying you back to your parents," Darcy said. Lydia had let on Elizabeth had suffered fatigue during the long drive.

"I want to go in the jet," Lydia whined. "Come on, Lizzy, be reasonable. A pregnant woman shouldn't be traveling in the car for hours."

"You're pregnant?" Richard immediately glanced down at Elizabeth's abdomen.

"Here comes Hussein." Lydia said to him, "Hussein, Richard just heard Lizzy's pregnant, and he's wondering if it's William's babies."

"I was not," Richard protested. "I haven't said a word. Did you say babies?"

"You were so thinking it," Mary said. "I'm going to insist on my sister doing a paternity test though. The idea of them being related to you—"

"Excuse me, as if having an aunt who's a ninja nutcase—"

Jane interrupted, "Hussein, where's Caroline? We want to say good-bye."

"She's coming." Hussein turned to Richard. "At the bachelor party, I told you Elizabeth got knocked down by this guy in New York, remember?"

"Knocked up. How many times have I told you that? That means pregnant. Not knocked down," Elizabeth corrected.

"Darling, don't be bitchy," Hussein shot back. "That's how I could tell you were pregnant: your bitchiness and your knockers were getting big."

Darcy took a menacing step toward him. "Excuse me?"

Hussein hid behind Elizabeth, whispering loudly, "Oooh, darling. I see now why you're knocked over. Such a sexy, chilling voice he has when he's defending you. Too bad he bats for your team instead of mine. For him I'd be willing to break my vows." He straightened up. "Ah, here comes my lovely bride."

They watched Caroline's face brighten. She quickened her steps straight toward Darcy. "William, I was hoping you'd still be here."

Richard muttered, "I told you to hide yourself. You're not completely safe even if she's married to that jokester there."

"I want to say thank you for coming, William." Caroline arched her back to show off her silicone gift from her husband.

"Does she not see the rest of us standing here?" Lydia said in a not-too-low whisper to Hussein, "And should the new Mrs. Ahmed be flirting with another guy the day after your wedding?"

"At least she's showing she has good taste in men," Hussein whispered back.

In a louder voice, Lydia said to Caroline, "We were just discussing Lizzy's being pregnant and how your husband knew right away because he noticed her big natural boobs."

"That explains why she's fat now." Caroline turned to Elizabeth. "I hear they have great sperm banks there in San Francisco. Which one did you use?"

Hussein shushed her, "Be nice. Elizabeth is not fat; she's bloated."

Jane stepped forward. "Thank you for inviting us to a lovely wedding. It was very elegant."

Caroline barely nodded at her while Hussein pointed at Elizabeth's face. "That pigmented spot may increase in size during pregnancy—"

Elizabeth slapped his hand. "Bug off!"

Caroline pulled Darcy a small distance away from the group. "I'm sorry you have to put up with these girls this morning. They're friends of Hussein. I wished they'd leave already. The blonde was the orphanage girl who denied us. You even met her sister, the dirty hippie, in Vietnam once or twice. She had long hair then. But I'm sure you don't remember her."

"I more than remember her, I can assure you," he said.

Caroline's eyes widened at his angry tone. Looking puzzled, she stepped back to stand next to her husband.

Bingley came running up. "Sorry I'm late. Were you all waiting for me to say good-bye?"

The group began their good-byes. Mary and Jane then left. Darcy noticed Bingley's pensive staring after the disappearing car. Darcy raised his eyebrows. Bingley shrugged. Darcy shrugged back. He had enough trouble with his own love life to give advice to someone else.

While Darcy motioned to the limousine taking them to the airport to come closer, Elizabeth pulled Caroline aside and whispered something in her ear, then air-kissed her before hugging Hussein good-bye.

As Darcy helped Elizabeth into the car, he glanced back at Caroline's stunned expression. "What did you just say to her?"

Elizabeth whispered, "I told her the sperm bank I used was loaded and each and every one of my withdrawals was magnificent, especially the one this morning."

He paused in reaching for the seat belt strap and whispered back, "Naughty girl. I love you."

He double-checked a few times to make sure her seat belt felt secure before he was satisfied. He then walked around the car and kicked the tires to make sure they were all properly inflated. While the rest said their last good-byes, he asked the limo driver about his safe driving record.

"Come on, Darce, we know you think Elizabeth is precious cargo, but it's only a thirty-minute drive to the airport," Richard said. "Let's get going."

Satisfied that the driver would drive safely, Darcy settled himself next to Elizabeth. He put his arms around her and let himself relax.

"I can't wait to see Dad's reaction when you bring William home." Lydia laughed.

—⁓—

"Nervous?" Richard asked Darcy as they drove through the streets of Orinda.

"No," Darcy said. They had dropped Elizabeth and Lydia off earlier. He and Richard went to check in to a nearby hotel and were now on their way to have dinner with the Bennet family.

"Liar!" Richard laughed. "He's probably cleaning his shotgun right now."

"I doubt a professor of Women's Studies at Berkeley is a card-carrying member of the National Rifle Association."

"A man's daughter is a man's daughter," Richard said as they arrived at the Bennets' home.

Upon being introduced, Elizabeth's father gave Darcy a hard glare. Darcy asked for a private word with him. With a casual shrug, the professor dismissed his request and said there was no need. He then pointedly ignored Darcy while he chatted with Richard about sports and politics. Darcy didn't mind. In her father's shoes, he would have reacted worse.

"William, did you have any trouble getting time off…" Mrs. Bennet said.

Darcy turned to her and flushed, embarrassed that he was caught staring longingly at Elizabeth and hadn't heard the question.

Mrs. Bennet smiled and looked pleased for some reason. "I asked if you had any trouble with your boss, getting time off to come here instead of heading to Chicago. Lizzy said you inter-rupted your business trip to see her home and meet us."

While Richard laughed, Darcy cast a rueful glance at Elizabeth.

"I see your daughter didn't tell you. I own my own business, Mrs. Bennet. It was no problem to reschedule my meetings."

"That's good. I'd hate for you to get into trouble at work during these hard economic times with two babies coming. It's time for dinner. You look like you could use a good meal, young man."

Throughout dinner, Mrs. Bennet kept exclaiming he was too skinny and urged her daughter to make sure he ate more. Elizabeth would nod and follow her mother's instructions, giving him another serving of this and that until Darcy finally had to tell his fiancée he literally couldn't eat another bite.

After dinner, he pulled his fiancée aside and whispered, "Tell your mom now about planning the wedding. Whatever she wants. No limit on expenses. Tell her I'm worth billions, but tell her, as you and I agreed, we want to be married within a month."

Elizabeth took her mom to the kitchen. Minutes later a loud screech came from the kitchen, then, "Oh my goodness! Billions! My grandchildren will be well taken care of. Mrs. Long next door and her pitiful niece's wedding! Pshaw! I'll show them a wedding! Oh my goodness. A month? He can't go to Chicago for business tomorrow. We have so many details to plan and discuss with him for the wedding. What kind of fish is his favorite? Does he like beef or chicken? What about cake?"

Professor Bennet stood. "Come, gentlemen. Let's escape to my study before we're subjected to some loud cataloguing of Mr. Darcy's gustatory preferences. You can write it all down for your future mother-in-law, Mr. Darcy. You can use my favorite fountain pen."

Twenty minutes later, when his fiancée saw Darcy, she screamed, "William! Why do you have ink all over your hands and face?"

CHAPTER 33

❦

Fluorescent Microbes

"Hi, sweetheart. We've landed at Oakland airport. I'll be at my hotel in thirty minutes. Are you there yet?" Darcy said, smiling as he slipped a hand into his pocket and fingered a small box.

"Change of plans. I'm waiting for you at the airport here. We're going to the hotel. I have a surprise for you." Elizabeth laughed at a noise from him. "No need to grunt your disappointment. My surprise will involve me getting undressed."

"God, I missed you." He greeted her fifteen minutes later with a kiss and tried to cop a feel of her bosom. After three days away from her, he was horny as hell. He hoped she was taking him to some romantic hideaway. Twenty minutes later, when she pulled up in front of a nondescript office building, he complained, "This is not the private romantic place I was hoping for."

She ignored him and pushed him out of the car. "This is your surprise. We have an OB appointment. They're going to do an ultrasound today. I'm going to introduce the babies to their daddy."

"Elizabeth, I…" He turned away from her to compose himself.

Taking his hand, she led him through a narrow hallway into a big reception area. Right in the crowded large lobby, he stopped.

He kneeled down in front of his fiancée and fumbled in his pocket. "There's something I need to do before I meet my children."

"Oh, goodness, a proposal," someone in the lobby said.

"How romantic," another voice said.

Within seconds, a large crowd gathered in a circle around them. Some of the bold ones began to offer suggestions on what to say. He held up his hand to silence them, and looking up into his fiancée's green eyes, he held the ring out. "Elizabeth Bennet, I promise to love, honor, and shag you and only you until the last breath leaves my body. And then my soul will wait, search, and find yours thereafter through eternity. Will you marry me?"

With a hand over her opened mouth, she simply stared. He smiled. He had managed to shock her, for once.

"I'll take him if you don't want him," someone said.

At that, Elizabeth came to and glared at the speaker before turning back to him. "Yes, a thousand times yes. Now get up and kiss me, you silly man."

He stood and placed the ring on her finger. Then, in a sudden move, he dipped her and planted a wet, noisy kiss on her lips. Her surprised laughter was worth the prize of being the center of the now very rowdy crowd's attention. Some of the women charged forward and elbowed him out of the way to examine the ring. A few directed approving glances his way when the size and cut of the diamond was discussed.

Thirty minutes later, in rapture, he stared at the ultrasound screen where two little hearts beat rapidly. He had to clench his hands so he wouldn't touch the screen. Through the reflection of the ultrasound machine, he caught a glimpse of a man wearing a loopy grin.

"Mr. Darcy, do you have any questions?" the doctor asked.

Reluctantly, he tore his eyes away from his children's fuzzy shapes.

He cleared his throat and began. He wanted exact details about how much Elizabeth should eat daily, how much protein and so forth. After the doctor answered the question, he had more. And then more.

"William, I'm sure I can answer some of these questions for you. I'm a doctor too, you know," Elizabeth interrupted at one point. "There are other patients waiting."

Ignoring his fiancée, Darcy took another breath. "I want to know the exact steps involved in your office's sterilization procedure. I want a new set of equipment ordered and used solely for her visits. I want everything to be properly sterilized and unopened in their sterilized packaging before each of her visits. I will be inspecting each piece of equipment for the integrity of sterilization before I allow it to be used. Furthermore…" From the doctor's stunned expression, he figured his demands were not ordinary, perhaps even unreasonable, but he didn't care. "I will, of course, pay for the expenses of your office carrying out my requests."

"Requests?" Elizabeth touched his arm. "You mean impossible mandates. These are all unnecessary costs, William."

"Your health and safety are…" he stopped. Elizabeth had just opened her gown to get dressed. The sound of a door closing stirred him. He turned to find the doctor had disappeared. "Where did she go? I wasn't done. I want to talk about her office procedures with contaminated office equipment some more."

"You can talk to me." Elizabeth pushed him out of the room. "I'm an infectious disease specialist. I may know a thing or two about contaminated equipment."

Walking through the hallway, he slowed his steps to assess the cleanliness of everything. Elizabeth nudged him to catch his attention. She glanced down at his groin and whispered, "Did you know that one swab of my saliva can sterilize a certain piece of equipment particularly well? I haven't given you my special welcome home treat yet."

He barely let her enter their hotel suite before he had both their clothes off. With trembling hands, he touched her all over. She was just as frantic in her response to him, though she stopped his head descending toward her chest and tried to lead him toward the bedroom. He allowed her a couple steps before he stopped and pressed his face to her back.

"I can't wait," he whispered to the spot right between her shoulder blades then he bent her over the back of a soft armchair. He tried to be gentle at first. Yet, as soon as he was deep inside her, fear unleashed in him and he thrust blindly. Minutes later, harsh spasms coursed through his body and he shattered with unwelcome release.

Mortified, he immediately pulled himself from her. He tried to open his mouth to apologize for forgetting her, for losing control, for being fearful, but he could not breathe. His throat had closed up.

She held him and murmured soft soothing sounds until, gradually, the shaking lessened and his breathing lightened. He obediently followed when she led him into the bed and made him lie down, on top of the covers. Though the chilled air whipped at his naked body, he lay still and stared unseeingly at the ceiling and listened to the sound of her turning on the sink in the bathroom. When she returned to him, she carried a small towel. Gently, she cleansed him.

He whispered, "I'm sorry."

She shushed his apology and lay on top of him, as if by covering his body with hers, she meant to protect him with her softness and warmth. He wanted to protest that he was supposed to be the one doing the protecting. After all, he ran a business empire and was head of a world-renowned charitable foundation. But he didn't. Instead, he began to talk.

He told her he feared for her and their babies. He told her all the grief he had kept inside since the day his mother died, when he stood in that hospital, holding his baby sister and listening to the doctor tell him some virulent bacteria had taken over her body and her blood. He told of the comfort he had since found in controlling his external environment. He told her of how afraid he was of living at times, and how he despaired of ever having a normal life. He told her it terrified him, the possibility that this normalcy—of becoming a husband and a father soon—would all disappear and he would be left with darkness again.

She buried her face in the curve of his neck and kept silent. Occasionally, when the words became stuck in his throat, he would feel the lightest pressure of her lips against his neck, next to his Adam's apple. Unstuck, the words would come forth again.

Surprisingly, after unburdening himself, he felt full—not emptied as he had expected. His pain had been a part of him for so long that he had dreaded the void left behind if he let go. He talked until there was nothing left unsaid of his grief and fear, and in doing so, the jumbled, jagged pieces inside him smoothed themselves into their rightful places. He felt whole again.

～∿～

The sound of knocking woke him.

"Elizabeth?" he called out, trying not to panic at the empty room.

"I'm here." Her head appeared briefly through the doorway. "Room service knocking. I ordered some food."

When he joined her, she already had started eating.

"Sorry, couldn't wait," she said with her mouth full. "I was starving. Your children are hungry."

"Nothing I ate in Chicago tasted as good as this meal," he said to her when he finished his dinner.

"Simple pasta, with the sauce on the side, just the way you like it. Speaking of your food preferences, I can't believe my dad. Did his fountain pen really just explode on your face by itself?"

"Yes. I've told you. He wasn't near me."

"Of course he wasn't. He had rigged it to explode on you when you used it. What possessed you to listen to him and write a list when you know he was just messing with you?"

"Because, as your father, he needed to and has the right to mess with me. And I wanted to give him the satisfaction of doing so."

"I'll never understand a man's logic."

"You don't need to." He smiled. When she yawned, he added, "Let's get you to bed."

Once in bed, he reached for her, his intention obvious. "I believe I have a debt to pay."

She stilled his eager hands. "Remember, I have plans for you and your equipment. Lie down and close your eyes."

Immediately obeying, he let his body relax, anticipating. When her hair brushed his thigh, he grinned. She had settled at his groin. A light, feathery lick elicited an immediate hardening response from him. He frowned when her tongue kept that same light pressure through the next few licks. "Elizabeth." Impatiently, he lifted up his hip.

"Patience, my love," she whispered against his balls. "I'm going through the list in my mind to see which one I want to use."

"What list?"

"The list of microbes in my mouth I'm transferring to your equipment, dirtying it," she said right before her lips closed around his roundness.

His gasp turned to purring when she did the same to the other side.

"I've decided on a name." She released his ball and resumed her licking of his length. As her tongue went from the base to barely touching his tip, she paused and enunciated clearly a syllable in between each lick. "Staph." Lick. "Phyl." Lick. "Lo." Lick...

His hips moved restlessly, wondering when she would come to the point.

"*Staphylococcus epidermis*," she ended. She enclosed her mouth around his tip and sucked hard. "Next on the list is," she whispered some incomprehensible name. Again, she licked him after each enunciated syllable. Right after she pronounced the microbe's full name, she would reward him with a big long suck at the end.

His hands fisted the sheets. He hoped she had many germs in her mouth. When she lifted herself up from his groin, he whimpered a protest. "More germs."

She gave a little laugh and resettled herself on his hips. Wrapping her hand around his hardness, she stimulated herself. This time, she told him the names of the germs in her vaginal vault he would get to know intimately, and then she slid down onto him. He let out a loud sigh of contentment, happy to mingle with her microbes. She rode him to her peak and screamed something sounding like "staphylococcus" with her climax.

His subconscious mind registered her scream and later he would realize how sexy that was, his darling infectious-disease Elizabeth spewing a microbe name in her moment of ecstasy. But for the immediate moment, an urgent need took center stage. He flipped her over onto her back and, with a few thrusts, spilled his broth into her.

Satiated and utterly spent, he snuggled against her. As he drifted off, he felt a light kiss on his head.

She gave a soft laugh. "Good night, my love."

Safe in her arms, he dreamt of dancing with green-eyed fluorescent microbes that night.

CHAPTER 34

❀

Receiving the Bride

"THIS IS THE BENNET'S HOME, MISS GEORGIANA," COLONEL Brandon repeated from the driver's seat. The bodyguard abruptly stiffened in his seat and exited the car.

A teenage girl in a cheerleading outfit had bounced out of nowhere, executing perfect cartwheels as she headed in their direction.

Colonel Brandon put himself between the girl and the car.

"Hey, you're big. I bet you can lift up two girls on your shoulders easily, maybe more." Unimpressed by his intimidating glare, the cartwheeler peered into the car. "I'm Lydia. You must be William's sister. He and Lizzy are out shopping for a car. They'll be here soon. Can you get out by yourself or does this muscle-man have to carry you out?"

Embarrassed, Georgiana exited the car and waved the bodyguard off.

Lizzy's sister grabbed Georgiana's hand. "Okay, I need to practice this cheer but I can't do it alone. I need a partner. Come on. I'll show you what to do."

The younger girl's loud voice and commanding presence scared Georgiana into awkwardly copying her movements.

"It's boring." Lydia's lips protruded when she finally stopped.

"I want some voom in my routine, to stand out, but Lizzy won't let me put a pole dancing routine in my cheer. She says it's vulgar."

"I think it's a very good cheer," Georgiana offered.

Lydia's face brightened. "My friend Ashley King was going to work on this routine with me but she couldn't make it today. She had to go to some church function with her aunt and uncle. Too bad. Ashley's boyfriend was going to come and help us. He's a strong guy."

"We should have bought the SUV model for you." Darcy drove the new Volvo station wagon out of the fast-food restaurant's drive-through. "It sits higher. You can see the road better."

"I see fine right now with this car. I'm used to station wagons. If we had bought an SUV, Mary would never get into the car and I need her with me sometimes." Elizabeth unwrapped her double cheeseburger. "We agreed on the price too soon. I could have gotten the guy to come down a few more hundred dollars, or throw in a few more options."

Darcy shook his head. Naively, he had expected the car purchase to take no more than thirty minutes. He hadn't planned to quibble over the listed price. Elizabeth was scandalized. She gave him such a tirade on his wasteful ways, he was forced to endure a long wait while she drove a hard bargain with the salesman. Watching her, without shame, badgering the guy to throw in free floor mats even after the price was agreed upon, Darcy had decided if he ever had to miss a DDF board meeting, he would have Elizabeth take his place. As Mrs. Darcy, she'd automatically have full voting privilege on the board. DDF would never be the same with her bargaining skills.

Ten minutes later, he drove up on to the now familiar driveway of her parents' home. His jaw dropped.

His toughest and meanest security detail, a three-hundred-pound former secret-service agent, Colonel Brandon, was doing some sort of upside-down pyramid building routine with two blonde-headed girls, Georgiana and Lydia.

Delighted, Elizabeth laughed and clapped. She glanced at Darcy's face and laughed even harder.

He put his forehead down on the steering wheel and banged it a few times.

"Poor baby," she gurgled and patted his head before she left him. Elizabeth and his sister greeted each other. Hugging and kissing and squealing rang through the yard.

A reluctant smile on his lips, Darcy got out of the car.

Brandon walked up to him. He had set the girls down the minute he caught sight of the car. "Sorry. I forgot myself."

"Don't worry about it." Darcy surprised them both when the words came out. Brandon looked taken aback.

They discussed a few specific security plans and Brandon said, "Congratulations about the upcoming wedding, Darce. I can see she makes you very happy."

Darcy barely hugged his sister hello before the Bennet sisters, chattering nonstop about wedding details, dragged her inside.

Lydia offered to give her a tour of the house, "To show you how normal people live, not rich people like you."

"Lydia!" Elizabeth scolded.

"Sorry. I forgot," Lydia said. "We're not normal. You haven't met my sister Mary yet. Come on, I'll show you the part of the house we don't usually let guests see. It's messy."

Darcy followed Lydia and his sister while Elizabeth went to

get a drink. Five minutes later, in a hallway crammed with various objects, his foot almost kicked over a frame someone had leaned haphazardly against the wall.

"Hey, you found Lizzy's senior portrait. She hid it back here the day we got back from Arizona. She was afraid you'd see it and be scared off," Lydia said.

Darcy studied the portrait. Long, straight, dyed black hair blended with a black trench coat over a few inches of black skirt atop black Army boots. Heavy, dark makeup outlined her eyes and lips. He laughed at the expression on her face. Despite looking like a raccoon, she had that adorable stubborn look on her face.

"Oh God. I didn't want you to see that," Elizabeth said, coming up behind him.

"Is that really you?" Georgiana said.

"Yes, it's her. And she complains that some of my cheer outfits look ridiculous," Lydia said. "At least I look like a normal sixteen-year-old."

Elizabeth laughed. "Yeah well. That was my Goth stage."

Jane appeared. "I thought I heard noises up here."

"That's Jane. She's the oldest, but it's Lizzy who's the bossy one." Ignoring Elizabeth's vocal protest, Lydia continued, "It's a pain being the younger sister of a bossy and controlling older sibling, eh?"

Darcy pretended he didn't see his sister avoiding his eyes as she gave an imperceptible nod. Instead, he looked down at the portrait.

"Hey, look at William. He's staring at Lizzy's picture and he got a dopey smile on his face. Love is blind." Lydia laughed.

Elizabeth took the portrait from him and handed it to Jane. "He didn't run away, so you might as well put it back in the living room."

Jane handed it back to him. "I think William deserves to have it, for the good work he did in Vietnam. I just heard about the Operation Smiles team you've sponsored and the medicine for the hospital."

Darcy frowned. "I thought I could trust Mr. Luc."

"Of course, you're the foundation from New York." Elizabeth hugged him. "I can't believe I didn't make the connection. Why didn't you tell me?"

"It wasn't Mr. Luc," Jane said. "Your cyclo-driver friend Oanh now smiles all the time, showing off his pearly whites. He tells everyone about it. Charles told him you're behind everything, but to keep it a secret because you don't like the attention."

"You are the best of men." Elizabeth kissed Darcy's cheek. "And that's why I'm marrying you."

Jane said, "Speaking of marrying, we need to get some plans firmed up."

Besides the church ceremony in the afternoon, Elizabeth's mom decided to add a touch of cultural flavor with a Vietnamese wedding ceremony at home in the morning. He didn't care what ceremony or how many he had to endure, as long as at the end of each, he was married to Elizabeth. Darcy had to suffer through a long, tedious discussion over the myriad minutiae of wedding details. His mind wandered until something about the wedding invitations caught his attention, puzzling him.

"But they might give you something with Mr. and Mrs. Darling engraved," Jane was saying.

"What do I care? Besides, remember we're inviting a lot of Aunt Mai's relatives. They won't give gifts. They'll give money. Ka-ching!" Elizabeth imitated the cash machine motion then high-fived Lydia.

Bemused, he stared at his fiancée. She did a little dance around the couch with her younger sister. He wondered if he would ever fully understand his frugal fiancée. Elizabeth had unlimited access to his billions—a fact he knew hardly entered into her consciousness—yet here she was, gleefully happy at the prospect of fleecing the wedding guests.

"Aunt Mai has a boatload of relatives," Elizabeth said. "Mr. and Mrs. Darling are going to rake in some coins, baby."

Reminded of what had puzzled him about their wedding invitation, Darcy asked his fiancée, "Who are this Mr. and Mrs. Darling?"

"Didn't I tell you? That's who we are."

—◦◦◦—

"Why do we have to wear dresses while the groom gets to wear a tux, a fucking debonair black tux?" Richard growled and gestured to their matching, dark blue Vietnamese wedding outfits.

"Because uptight Darce would never survive wearing something so ethnic like these *ao dais*," Bingley said. "You and I are from a tougher breed of men."

"We're tough all right. We're both wearing silk dresses over what look to me like pajama pants." Richard pulled the front flap of the dress from between his legs. The dress split on the side from the waist down. At least he had insisted on wearing his tuxedo trousers underneath the flowing silk pants.

"Richard, stop talking and lagging behind, boy," his father yelled loudly down the line. "We're going to do this properly, this receiving-the-bride ceremony. Carry your box upright. Don't drop it. You're the best man. Why can't you have a happy smile on your face like Bingley there does?"

"Because the idiot is happy playing dress-up," Richard muttered under his breath and quickened his steps. "Damn Bingley and his corporate cultural-sensitivity training."

Behind him, in a single file, the procession continued with five men recruited from Elizabeth's Vietnamese connections, carrying boxes and trays of various traditional gifts. The last man, a Mr. Collins, carried a roasted pig.

Just ahead of Darcy and behind two little boys carrying brightly colored silk umbrellas with long fringes, Richard's father also had on a traditional Vietnamese dress, in a darker shade of blue. On his dress, imprinted with gold, the imperial symbol of the phoenix was displayed prominently, signifying his status as the respected eldest in the groom's family. An honor that had gone to his father's head, Richard concluded, observing the strut in his father's stride.

Firecrackers going off welcomed the groom's party as they arrived at the front of the bride's house. They handed the procession of gift boxes to a beaming Mrs. Bennet and an amused Mr. Bennet. Richard's father made a long speech, asking permission to receive the bride, and someone named Uncle Two responded with an even longer speech before inviting the groom's party inside.

Darcy endured some ribbing by the bride's side when he was caught looking eagerly around for her.

Elizabeth, beautifully dressed in a traditional red-silk *ao dai* embroidered with gold, entered the room.

Richard gawked at the red flying saucer headdress atop her head. Turning to his cousin, the quip on Richard's tongue died. Darcy's eyes had lit up at the sight of his beaming bride. Feeling generous, Richard patted his cousin's back and said simply, "You deserve it, you old dog."

On one side of the room, surrounded by flowers and incense burning, large photographs of the late Anna and George Darcy sat on easels. The bridal couple knelt in front of the portraits, quietly asking for a blessing for their marriage and future family from the groom's late parents. At one point, the bride's hand grasped and squeezed the groom's—a breach in protocol, touching in public by the bridal couple, but no one said anything.

The ceremony was not as solemn as Richard had expected, consisting mainly of speeches—some humorous, some serious—given by the elders in the room. Every married person then felt compelled, it seemed to Richard, to give some sort of long-winded marital advice to the couple.

When the bridal couple lit the candle to symbolize the joining of the families, Georgiana's sniffling overpowered those of the bride's mother. The latter won the next round. Mrs. Bennet cried openly, loudly, and uninhibitedly when the bridal couple served tea to her and her husband. After they served Richard's father his tea, Elizabeth placed two cups in front of the late Darcys' portraits. The room silenced and the groom turned away to compose himself. Even Richard had to look down and blink his eyes rapidly.

The mood of the room lightened when friends and relatives handed the couple red envelopes of money. Darcy looked embarrassed as he accepted them. The smiling bride, however, shamelessly held out her hands.

The jewelry box Richard carried earlier as a gift from the groom's side was brought out and opened. The bride's mother seemed more excited than her daughter. The bride, who merely glanced at the gleaming rubies and diamonds, declined the traditional custom of guests pinning jewelry on her with the explanation that, with the headdress, she felt off balance already. She did, however, allow her groom to place a small garnet cross necklace on her.

"The receiving the bride ceremony is now over," Uncle Two proclaimed at the end.

When the bride stared up at the groom with an adoring smile, the groom leaned toward her. Richard had to cough loudly and nudged his cousin to remind him, "No kissing allowed during the Vietnamese ceremony."

Darcy ignored him and kissed his bride.

CHAPTER 35

❀

Half-Empty

"William Darcy stole my woman!" Jorge Cooley was overheard exclaiming bitterly. The former Dr. Elizabeth Bennet of Doctors Without Borders, last seen leaving Darfur in Jorge's arms, has reportedly married the billionaire William Darcy. Sources close to Mr. Darcy revealed he and the good doctor have been secretly dating on and off for months, but it was not until the appearance of Jorge Cooley during an off period that the businessman-philanthropist was prompted to propose.

CHUCKLING, ELIZABETH SAT ON THE BED AND PUT DOWN THE tabloid Hussein had sent her. "They're using that old picture of me with that actor. My face is hidden and all you see is my hair," she said loudly to her husband in the next room. "At least this tabloid got my name and my profession right. I've been called Lisa Bend, Isobella Benitez, and Betty Benet in various publications. Nobody seems to know who you married, or if you're even married."

"And that's how I wanted it. Nobody knows anything about my private life, Mrs. Darling." Bare-chested, a towel wrapped around his waist, her husband came into the room and gave her a rakish smile. "Good. You're not dressed yet. I don't know how you get any work done. If I had breasts like those, I'd stay home all day, lie on the couch, and play with them."

She tried to hold him off when he joined her on the bed. "You'll be late for work, again. Mr. Darling."

"I'm the boss," he mumbled against the middle of her spine. His hands snaked around to cup her breasts. "Know what I would wish for most in the world now? More arms to touch you. That's what I would wish for."

"Shall we call Jorge? That would make two extra."

He stilled his fingers, growled, and flipped her on her back. "Teasing me, eh? Thinking of other men touching what's mine? Mine. Mine." With each, he kissed her nipples briefly. She arched up, wanting him to take them in his mouth. He held back. Instead, he looked up at her and stuck out his tongue, twirling it in a circular motion over her nipple without making contact. He did the same tease with the other breast. She arched her back and spread her legs wide to trap him, a little difficult to do with her protruding tummy, but she managed. She squeezed her legs together and lifted her hips to rub herself against him. Though he growled his pleasure, he still stubbornly refused to touch her nipples. Mouth hovering over her breasts, his eyebrows remained raised as he waited expectantly.

She capitulated. "Yours, yours, only for you." He rewarded her with the sweet wetness of his tongue. When he was a little too enthusiastic, she reminded him, "Gentle."

"They're darker." He pulled back and examined her nipples. "They're more smoky."

"Don't stop. And be gentle," she ordered and pulled his head back down to where it was.

"Yssss, m'mmmmm," he said, his mouth now full.

Unmindful and uncaring of the time, she kept her husband's mouth and body busy following her orders.

—◦◦◦—

Whistling, Darcy left the master suite. His wife's last order was for him to start breakfast without her.

"Don't worry if you have to work late." Elizabeth waddled in twenty minutes later. "We're having a girls' night in."

"I suppose that's a hint I should work late. You want to drool over the two Regency blokes on those DVDs all evening long."

"I'll reward you tonight." She sat on his lap.

He coughed to hide a grunt. Now nearing her third trimester, she seemed to have ballooned overnight, something she was very sensitive about.

She gave him a disgruntled look. "I didn't hear you complaining earlier when I was on top of you."

He licked his lips and leered at her chest. "I love every bit of you, on top or bottom or sideways or bent over. All positions. All the time."

Eyes sparkling, Elizabeth tipped her head.

He turned and jumped.

Mrs. Reynolds's red face was inches away from him. "You need to get going or you'll be late. Again. Mrs. Darcy needs to rest before she's expected at the free clinic."

"Yes, ma'am," he meekly replied.

After the housekeeper handed Elizabeth a glass of milk and left the room, his wife laughed and moved off his lap. "Did Anne leave? She wasn't in your Oakland office very long for her briefing with you, was she?"

"She went back to Chicago yesterday." Though Elizabeth was

willing to move back to New York, he knew she wanted to be close to her family now that babies were coming. He'd relocated to the Bay Area and left Richard and Charles to manage their New York headquarters. Georgiana also moved west and now shared a house with Mary. Both had returned to school.

"Isn't the Chicago thing about done in a few weeks?" His wife buttered her toast. "What are you going to do with her next?"

"Everyone in Chicago has been satisfied with her."

"Do I hear a note of reservation in your voice?"

"Yes," he admitted. "Though, I double-checked everything she's done lately and everything is fine."

"If you're still having doubts after all these months, why don't you just fire her straight out?"

"She still runs a couple of crucial departments Richard and Charles can't spare the time to oversee right now. If I let her go, I would need to restructure internally and many jobs would be affected. I have no wish to uproot my other employees on a suspicion. I need more concrete reasons."

"All you have on her is an uneasy feeling?"

He stared hard into her green eyes. "In my experience, once someone slips and slides with their ethics in one area, they tend to do it in other areas of their life also."

"That's a very black-and-white way of looking at the world. It's hard for you to trust and forgive, isn't it?" Her voice was gentle, accepting.

"I'm learning, my love." He gave a wry smile. "I'm afraid there's more than a touch of truth to my reputation, a glass half-empty guy."

"That's because your glass hasn't been filled for a while." She grasped his hand. "But now, you got a hefty wife on your plate."

295

"And you, my love, are ever an optimist. And I love you for it." He squeezed her hand, grateful that his wife didn't deny him his pessimism. "We went through hell. What if something had happened to you in Darfur?"

She moved her hand to his arm. "We can't blame it on Anne or your aunt. I was responsible for running away without talking to you. We need to move on, my love."

He kissed her hand and put his chin on top of it. "I saw some disturbing pictures of Anne yesterday."

"What kind of pictures?"

"Pictures of her in compromising positions."

"Compromising positions, indeed. You sound like such a Regency prude."

"She was tied up in bondage."

"Bondage? Oh." Her mouth opened. "How? I cannot imagine the woman I met at the museum…"

"She left her briefcase open, near the edge of the table. When she left the room, she closed the door too hard and her briefcase toppled over. These pictures came tumbling out."

"Must be pretty interesting pictures if you're grimacing and shuddering even now talking about them. What did you do then?"

"I shoved the pictures back in her briefcase and pretended nothing happened when she returned."

After spending a few moments laughing at him, his wife narrowed her eyes. "And how would you have known it was bondage? Personal experience? At the penthouse perhaps?"

"Sweetheart, any red-blooded male over fifteen knows about bondage. And no, it was not something I was into in my single days. But now that I have a sexy, adventurous wife"—he waggled his brows—"bring it on, isn't that what you always say?"

"Please." She pushed him away. "I'm in bondage already, pregnant with twins and big as a hospital. I cannot imagine being tied up anymore. And I want to know what you were into at that penthouse. Your aunt said you had a mirror on the ceiling."

"What? There was no such tasteless thing. I should have taken you there before I sold it so you could have seen the place for yourself, the way you keep carrying on about it." He wished he had never had the damn penthouse. "I definitely never had any woman setting up house there. I hate to disillusion you from thinking I was such a stud before you, but my dates at the penthouse were boring. I barely remember anything."

"Why have a separate place? You have a big townhouse."

He stared at her, amazed at her questions. "I had Georgiana. There was no way I was going to bring a woman into my own home and have her invade my privacy or expose Georgiana to that. And..." He stopped, embarrassed.

"And you're too damn fastidious to have the woman sleep in your bed and use your regular sheets." She laughed. "My God, you must have had piles of new sheets there at that penthouse that you got rid of after each date."

"No one told me being married meant I should be a source of amusement for my wife," he complained, though he was thankful she could joke about his checkered past now.

"You were such a damn spoiled billionaire with too much money."

"And that's why I have you as a wife now, to laugh at me and keep me in line." He stood and kissed her good-bye. "Remember, no more than two hours on your feet today at work, your doctor said."

"She only said two hours after you harassed her for a specific number, but I'll be good."

When he arrived home late that evening, he smiled at the sounds of feminine laughter coming from the media room. Lydia bounced out and greeted him with a big hug. Not used to the exuberant way some of the Bennet women showed their affection, he awkwardly returned it.

"Hey, did you hear my good news? I'm going to be on a new show called *Cheering with the Stars*. They saw me at an anti-war protest and liked my protest cheer. They're going to match me up with a star. I hope it's going to be some cute guy." On and on she chattered and she led him to his wife, who greeted him with a look in her eye that told him she hadn't forgotten her promise to reward him that night.

CHAPTER 36

❀

Bondage

"Next, we chop up everything." Elizabeth put the onions, garlic, and carrots in the food processor.

"We're making a mess," Georgiana said.

"We'll clean up before Mrs. Reynolds gets home," Elizabeth said. Something had been worrying Georgiana. She seemed jumpy lately. It usually took half a day to make fried egg rolls, hopefully long enough for Elizabeth to find out what was going on. "Now add the shrimp, the ground pork there, and the eggs."

"Did your mom teach you to cook?"

"No, Aunt Mai did. You'd think that I was out doing wild things dressed all in black as a Gothic chick, but I actually spent most of my free time in my aunt's kitchen cooking the angst out of my tortured young soul."

Instead of laughing at Elizabeth's joke, Georgiana said, "Did you ever do anything then you now regret?"

Here was the opening, Elizabeth realized. "I spent years looking like Morticia from *The Addams Family*. Don't you think that's enough of a reason to regret my youth?"

A weak smile appeared on Georgiana's face.

Gratified to see that, in a serious tone, Elizabeth talked of her experience with the college professor, leaving nothing out, including how lost she'd felt. She ended with, "Lydia is much more savvy than I was at her age."

Georgiana started crying.

Elizabeth rubbed her back. "Sweetie, talk to me."

"If I tell you, I'm afraid you'd think…"

"You're afraid I would think you're not perfect like your brother, and I won't love you? Wait, he's not perfect. Darn it." She wiped Georgiana's tears. "Why don't you just tell me what's been going on with you lately, and I'll decide whether or not I can live with another imperfect Darcy?"

"I'm being threatened because of some pictures."

Elizabeth sucked her breath in. "What kind of pictures?"

"Porn pictures, of me."

"By whom?"

"I don't know. It started last year then stopped, but it started back again."

"And what do they want? Money?"

"They haven't asked for money yet, but they keep reminding me they have embarrassing pictures of me. When I hadn't heard from them for months, I thought I was safe."

"You are still safe," Elizabeth said. "I won't let anything happen to you."

The rash promise seemed to relieve Georgiana. "The pictures were taken when I was seeing George Wickham."

"I see. Pictures of you two?"

"No, just me."

"I'd forgotten about his existence for the last few months."

"I wish I could." Georgiana made a face. "I was terrified about making friends on campus. Then, George showed up, and I didn't have to work to make new friends. He knew all about me and where I came from; it was comfortable and easy to be with him and his friends. They were so nice, so friendly, so welcoming; it didn't seem like they were a cult at all. That's how stupid I was. I was excited about belonging..."

"Everybody wants to belong. Don't be hard on yourself."

"Luckily, my brother found out in time. I had invited Richard to the wedding... and that's how Will learned of it."

"Subconsciously, you must have wanted your brother to know if you invited Richard."

"I wish I could say I was that smart, but the truth was George told me to. Richard already knew I was dating someone."

"I see." But Elizabeth didn't see at all. She could not fathom why George Wickham told Georgiana to invite Richard. Surely, Wickham knew that likely the wedding would be stopped. Unless, he wanted it stopped. "George's the one blackmailing you then."

"No. That's the thing. He swore it's not him. He claimed someone must have broken into his apartment and set up a hidden camera."

"If that's true"—Elizabeth could not keep the skepticism from her voice—"then it must be someone who knew him well. Very well."

"I don't know for sure it's not him," Georgiana admitted, "but when I confronted him, he was shocked and looked very scared. This may be stupid, but I don't think he faked that."

Elizabeth pursed her lips. "The cult might be behind this, with or without Wickham's cooperation. That may explain why he's scared."

Georgiana's eyes widened and a small gasp escaped her. "The cult?"

"It seems logical. We need to talk to your brother, honey. You know that, right?"

"Lizzy, he's going to freak." Georgiana was now panicking.

Elizabeth tried to soothe her. "Sweetie—"

"Now that he has you to worry about, he's finally giving me some breathing room. I don't want to move backward." Georgiana's voice turned firm. "I don't want to hurt William by fighting with him, but I like my freedom. A lot."

Elizabeth clucked sympathetically but she didn't argue the point. She loved her husband dearly—even with all his obsessive quirks—but she had to admit being his wife was easier than being his younger sister. "How do they contact you? You get letters?"

"No. Emails."

"Emails? That's not very smart. More easily traced than letters. I hope you didn't delete the emails?"

Georgiana hid her face in her hands.

"Georgiana! You didn't!"

"I did," Georgiana confessed. "I still have the last one they sent me though, in my trash file."

"Let's see it." Elizabeth stood and half dragged, half pushed Georgiana to the office. "Even if you did delete them all, I bet Mary could figure out how to get them back. She's a genius with computers." Three minutes later, staring at the screen, she exclaimed, "That's not porn! I've seen more on tabloid covers."

Georgiana looked hopeful. "You think so?"

Elizabeth rolled her eyes. "Sweetie, all the pictures show is you wearing a leather outfit with a chain around your neck and a whip in your hand. That one there of you touching yourself between your legs is a little provocative but you don't look any worse than any ad in *Vogue*."

"You don't think it's embarrassing?"

"Are you kidding? If these got published and it became known they weren't staged, you'd be the hottest male fantasy. A classy, edgy, and sexy blonde heiress in black leather and bondage."

"I don't want to be an edgy, sexy blonde. I'm going to dye my hair black and be Goth."

"I don't think you have to go that far and go Goth," Elizabeth soothed. "Nobody is going to be shocked by your pictures. Again, you're sure George Wickham is not involved in threatening or blackmailing you?"

"Not completely sure, but my gut says no. He's not smart or patient enough to not do anything all these months anyhow."

Elizabeth reluctantly nodded and agreed. "That's a good point. But who else's behind this?"

"The cult, you said?"

"Now that I've seen these pictures, I doubt they'd involve themselves in an amateur thing like this to mess with a Darcy. They have got to know your brother would whoop their asses." She smiled to see Georgiana giggling at that. "Okay, that's more my trashy style, I admit. Your brother would probably hire a whole team of useless lawyers to deal with it and make them rich, wasting money."

"Lizzy, if it might not be the cult, could we not involve William yet? Please?" Georgiana pleaded.

Elizabeth sighed. "Before I agree to anything about keeping it from my husband, let's think it through first. And I have to ask this: Only dressing up for him? Nothing more? Like S and M sex? Did he do anything strange sexually?"

"I never went all the way. I wanted to, but he said he liked the idea of me being a virgin and wearing those sexy clothes. He… um… said it would make the anticipation greater for when we got married; it would have been a double present then, my um… wedding gift and my birthday gift."

Ignoring the girl's red face, Elizabeth pressed, "We need to figure out what's the worst that this unknown photographer might have also taken. I'm very used to hearing about my patients' sexual exploits so don't worry. I won't be shocked. Okay?"

William's sister bit her lip then nodded. "Okay."

The answers she gave in response to Elizabeth's explicit questions reassured her somewhat that there wouldn't be pictures that would be considered overtly obscene pornographic material. More importantly, she suddenly realized something. "Wait. These pictures were taken before your eighteenth birthday on Valentine's Day. That's when you were set to get married?"

Georgiana nodded. "Thank God Richard showed up the day before my birthday. I can't believe I almost married George in a mass wedding."

"But you didn't," Elizabeth reminded her. "If you were truly under his and the cult's power, you would still have gotten married the next day, no matter who had shown up to stop it. You showed self-preservation."

Georgiana's face relaxed. "I hadn't thought of it that way."

"Let me think about this and see what we can do. Meanwhile, why don't you talk to Mary when you get home tonight?"

"You don't think she'd be shocked?"

"Mary? Are you kidding? She's gotten into trouble much worse than this. She might be able to talk to you about how to deal with the stress. I'll talk to her too tonight also."

Georgiana hugged her. "Thank you. I wanted to tell you… and even Mary. It's just that Will—"

She cut Georgiana off, "I won't involve your brother yet, not until we figure out exactly what's going on. Quite frankly, I'm not in the mood to deal with his panic attacks." She began to talk of other subjects to distract the younger girl. William would be home soon and she wanted his sister calmed before then. "We should get back to the kitchen. I'm hungry and the babies are hungry. Did I tell you that your brother is having the cribs custom-made so he could supervise the production? He worries the ready-made cribs would collapse. Can you believe that?"

CHAPTER 37

❀

Showbiz

As Elizabeth sat charting in the free clinic's office on a late Tuesday afternoon, her cell phone rang. She smiled. "Hi, love."

"Are you almost done? You've been there over three hours. It's getting late."

She ignored the worried note, closed her eyes, and savored her husband's sexy accent.

"Elizabeth, are you there?"

"Hmmm, yes. I was just thinking how sexy you sound."

"Don't change the subject. I don't want you on your feet for too long. The OB said two hours a day."

She rolled her eyes. "I'm leaving now. Are you back home from Los Angeles?"

"Unfortunately, no. I'm stuck here twenty-four seven for now. Why don't you have one of the sisters come and stay with you until I get back?"

"Mary and Jane just left to... uh... they're out of town." She cringed, remembering. Before her husband started asking questions, she added, "I'm not alone; Georgiana's staying over tonight. Besides, there are so many bodyguards around I can't even sneeze without them reporting to you."

"I need to have you safe." His voice was full of guilt. "I'm sorry."

"It's okay, love. You know I don't mind the security. I'm just hormonal." Hiding his sister's situation from him stressed her more than she wanted to admit. While she missed him, his unexpected business trip to Los Angeles the day before was fortuitous timing.

"I miss my hormonal wife."

"Better stay away from all those skinny LA actresses or I'll come down there and scratch their eyes out," she teased.

Her husband laughed. "I love you, my little jealous wife."

"Speaking of actresses, Lydia is down there in Hollywood with my mom—"

"I have to go, love. I'll call later," her husband abruptly interrupted and ended the conversation.

Lydia glanced at her backside in the mirror of the hotel's lobby. Satisfied her cheerleading skirt showed enough but not too much, she continued toward the rehearsal room. She spent a few delicious moments imagining the jealous look on her sister Kitty's face watching Lydia on TV doing a cheerleading routine. Kitty had been impossible lately, complaining all the time to their parents that Lydia's being on a TV show had taken attention from Kitty's graduating magna cum laude from Stanford.

When Lydia entered the rehearsal room, a man with a baby face smiled at her. "Rehearsal won't start for a while. Nothing to do but sit and wait. Welcome to showbiz! There's no business like show business!" He frowned when she didn't join in his lame singing. "Are you sure you're old enough to be in this show?"

"I'm sixteen," she said.

Her friend Ashley had some difficulty getting permission from her uncle to be in the show before succeeding, but Lydia had no problems with her parents. Her mother was excited by her opportunity and her father simply muttered something about the failure of feminism. Only Lizzy openly objected, raising a stink and throwing a temper tantrum about the evil of reality TV shows, but she was pregnant and hormonal and everyone—except her husband—thought she was overreacting, so she was ignored.

"Where are you from?" Without waiting for an answer, babyface began to talk about his previous reality show. She tried to appear interested, but after a while, she wondered if all Hollywood people were this boring. Luckily, other cheerleaders began to arrive and the man had new audiences to bore.

Ashley arrived with Ury, the producer of the show. "There's Lydia. I told you she'd be early. She takes cheerleading very seriously."

Ury winked at Lydia. "And that's why we wanted her as a contestant on our show. She's got great kicking legs."

Ashley pouted. "What about me? Why do you want me?"

Ury turned and whispered something in her ear.

Watching them, Lydia's insides felt queasy, just as she had this morning, when she had overextended herself too far forward during the arabesque foldout routine and she lost her balance.

When Ury moved off to talk to a production assistant, Ashley said to Lydia, "Ury thinks you and I could use some extra private coaching to appear more natural on camera. Aren't we lucky, Lydia? He's giving us personal attention."

Unable to sleep, Darcy sighed and got out of bed. He walked over to the sink. A quick glance in the mirror confirmed what he suspected. He looked guilty. He hated sleeping away from his wife and he hated keeping secrets from her. Yesterday, when she mentioned Lydia and her mother being in Hollywood, he had to cut short their phone call.

When he saw his hands red and wrinkled, he forced himself to stop and return to bed. He might as well get an hour or two of sleep before meeting with Colonel Brandon and the FBI.

Closing his eyes, he tried to imagine his wife next to him in bed.

The phone rang just as he drifted off. He jerked awake. His heart skipped. It was her ring tone. This was too early in the morning for her to be calling. "What's wrong?"

"Nothing, except I miss you like crazy and wanted to hear your voice," Elizabeth said. "I knew you were probably awake, worrying and obsessing about something trivial, so I decided to call you. Did I wake you?"

"No, I've been up." He relaxed. His wife's teasing voice was exactly what he needed to hear.

"You're up, already? I miss that."

"No, I wasn't"—the image of Elizabeth in their bed at home made his voice lower—"but I'm starting."

"Hmmmmmm."

"What are you doing?"

"Rubbing my tummy."

His fingers stretched, wanting the tactile connection to his babies. "Are they kicking?"

"No, they're quiet for now."

When no further sounds came through, he asked, "Are you still rubbing?"

"Uh-huh."

"How about moving your hand up to one of those scrumptious breasts, the right one, and squeeze it gently for me." He heard background noises crinkle through the connection when she put the phone on speaker. "Are you naked?"

"No. I'm wearing one of your old T-shirts. I can smell you on it."

"Take it off."

"Okay, it's off." Her voice sounded breathless now. "You put yours on speaker too."

"No, I want to focus on you." He ignored the tenting of his sheet and tugged at his pajama bottoms.

"Uh-uh! I want us together."

He lifted the sheet aside.

"Your pajama bottoms too."

He smiled at the bossy tone and undressed. Immediately, cool arousing air brushed against him.

"Ahhhh!" Her satisfied sigh came through the speaker.

"What? You started without me?"

"No, not yet. I was thinking of your naked body and your hard cock."

For a woman who was a virgin until a few short months ago, his wife was uninhibited and adventurous in the bedroom. Occasionally, she liked to talk dirty during sex, mostly to shock him. "Are both your hands on your breasts now?"

"Yes. I want you between my tits," she moaned.

He squeezed his eyes shut at what her words had conjured. "I don't think it would be a safe position for me right now, on your tummy."

"It's phone sex. We can have any position we want. Pretend we're circus performers with flexible and weightless bodies." She purred, "Let my breasts stroke you."

He reached one hand down and stroked himself.

"I feel your balls hitting against the bottom of my breasts."

His other hand reached down and caressed.

"I'm lifting up my head and sucking at your tip."

His thumb moved up to rub his tip.

"I'm sucking and squeezing. I'm swirling my tongue around your tip. My hands are squeezing your tight ass. Rub harder, faster between my tits."

His hands madly rubbed and stroked.

"Fuck my tits harder!" she barked.

Head thrown back, his chest arched and his hips cranked.

"I'm sucking you hard. Come into my mouth!"

Wrapped in her moist, hot mouth, he exploded with a loud howl. Breathing hard and deep, he gulped air to recover from the force of his orgasm.

His wife gave a delighted, satisfied giggle through the speaker.

"You naughty girl," he scolded when his breathing normalized. "I was in charge starting out."

"Are you complaining?"

"No, on the contrary. But what happened to 'together'?"

"A bit awkward to maneuver around my large stomach."

"I shall pay my debt in person then."

"You bet your sweet ass I'll make you," she laughed.

At the sound of happiness in his wife's voice, his throat tightened at his good fortune. "I'm a lucky dog, Mrs. Darcy."

"I love you too, Mr. Darcy."

They talked a few more minutes, but then she suddenly had to ring off just as he was asking where Mary and Jane had gone.

CHAPTER 38

❦

Mistaken Identity

THE NEW YORK CITY YELLOW CAB SLOWED DOWN AND THE DRIVER looked for a spot to stop. Jane checked her makeup one more time. Mary chuckled. Blushing, Jane snapped it shut.

Once on the sidewalk, Mary said, "Don't be embarrassed. You're supposed to be alluring."

"I'm only following orders. This is so out of my comfort zone. I can't believe I let you and Lizzy talk me into this."

"You'll do fine."

"Easy for you to say. Why am I the one who has to distract him?"

"Because we wouldn't have any success at all if I was the one doing it," Mary returned calmly. "As Mom always says, you couldn't have been born that beautiful for nothing."

"Very funny. I wish Lizzy or Lydia could take my place in this caper. They'd definitely think it's a lark."

"Lizzy is too big, too pregnant, too married, and Lydia is too silly, too young, and too unpredictable. Besides, she's in Hollywood with mom. It's you and me, partner." When Jane didn't respond, Mary added, "Think of Georgiana; we're doing this for her."

That was the one reason why, dismissing all rational reasons why it wouldn't work, Jane had agreed to the crazy scheme.

Yesterday, Georgiana told them she had received another email from the blackmailer on Monday. Within hours, Mary discovered the email was sent from a computer with an Internet protocol address registered to DDF. Jane didn't even want to know how Mary had figured that out, though Jane suspected it involved some of her genius sister's computer hacker friends.

They approached a building with *DDF* on the front. Mary said, "This is it. You go and distract Peter Pan, get his permission, and I'll do the rest."

"Are you sure this plan is going to fly?"

"Relax. It's a simple plan." Mary paused right outside the entrance and flicked her fingers over Jane's face. "There. You have some pixie dust. That's a must," she sang softly as she pushed Jane through the door. "Just remember, Wendy, 'You can fly! You can fly! You can fly!'"

Somehow, in the face of her sister's supreme confidence and silliness in singing the Disney movie song, Jane's nervousness lessened. Giving their names as Tina and Wendy Darling, they had called DDF and asked if Mr. Bingley was free to talk about the orphanage in Zambia. Elizabeth didn't want someone to recognize the name Bennet.

"We have to be suspicious of everyone. Charles or even Richard might be the blackmailer," Elizabeth had said when she suggested they use aliases. "After all, who would have thought Georgiana's blackmailer would be someone from DDF? The only person from DDF we can be certain to rule out is William. You'll start at the executive floor."

Though Jane had privately wondered if some of her brother-in-law's paranoid quirks were beginning to rub off on his wife, Jane had to agree with Elizabeth's caution. Jane had suggested telling her brother-in-law, currently in LA on some business, but everyone vetoed that.

In the elevator, alone with Mary, on the way to the executive floor, Jane said, "Are you sure this isn't illegal?"

"Of course it's illegal."

Stunned by her sister's calm answer, Jane said, "William could—"

"Yes, he could. But by the time he gets back here, whoever it is will have changed the Internet protocol addresses," Mary said. "For security reasons, companies change their executives' IP addresses frequently. That's why we had to get here pronto, incognito, and unannounced, so we have a better chance to catch the blackmailer before the IP address changes."

"William may be owner and head of DDF, but he has a board of directors who—"

"Wouldn't look kindly upon his sisters-in-law hacking into the company's computer system, I know. But then, one of them might be the blackmailer," Mary interrupted again in her maddeningly even voice. "If it makes you feel better, Georgiana is part owner of the company and she gave us permission, so technically, it's not breaking or entering."

"Tell that to the judge!"

"You go and do your Mata Hari thing. I'll be flitting around stealing shadows."

———

Bingley took off his glasses and rubbed his eyes. Before his next appointment, he decided he needed a little pick-me-up. He skulked to the closet where he kept a secret stash. Just another small sip, he told himself. He reached for the bottle on the high shelf. His fingers curved around a two-litter bottle.

The door opened. "Mr. Bingley, Miss Wendy Darling and Miss Tina Darling are here."

Startled, he turned and accidentally knocked the two-liter bottle down. The lid popped off and Mountain Dew doused him.

"Mr. Bingley, you did it again," his secretary said in an exasperated voice. She grabbed some paper towels off a nearby counter. "You're supposed to be off sugar and caffeine."

"Are you okay?" Jane Bennet's angelic voice asked. "Here, let me help you." She took the paper towels from his secretary's hand and started to pat his face and his shirt.

He opened one eye and waved his secretary off.

Jane apologized, "We didn't mean to startle you."

"No, I was careless. How are you? How is your sister Elizabeth?" He had heard all about Elizabeth ad nauseam from Darcy daily, but he couldn't think of anything else to say at the moment. "Do you have sisters name Wendy and Tina I didn't know about?"

"No." She blushed. "I'm… uh… called Wendy sometimes. My sister Mary… uh… I mean Tina… I mean Mary is here with me."

He looked. Tina-Mary was at his desk, touching his computer. "Do you mind if I check my emails?" she asked while her fingers moved rapidly on the keyboard.

"Sure." As long as her angelic sister was ministering to him, he didn't care what Tina-Mary wanted to do in his office. He turned to Jane-Wendy. "How long are you staying in New York?"

"A few days. I was wondering if we could talk about your experience in Zambia. Compare notes on orphanages?"

Happily, he nodded. "Yes, we should. We didn't get a chance to at the wedding. Perhaps we can go for a cup of decaf coffee?"

Jane-Wendy smiled. "I'd love to."

Tina-Mary, still fiddling with his computer, spoke up. "I don't do coffee. I'll work on my emails here while you guys go off. I might wander around a bit if that's all right with you, Peter... I mean, Charles."

"Uh... sure, of course." He had no idea what she had just said, something about wandering and emails. His angel's soft smile distracted him.

—⁕—

Richard walked into his office and stopped short.

Mary Bennet was sitting at his desk smirking. "My brother-in-law knows you spend your working hours looking at porn? It's not even good porn. You can see more skin than this on TV."

"Do you mind? This is private!" He wondered how he got so careless and left the porn site on.

"You didn't leave it on." She read his mind. "I hacked into it."

"You... you... you!"

She ignored his stuttering, took a pencil from his desk, and tapped it, a thoughtful look on her face.

He sighed and sat across the desk. "Why are you here on a Wednesday afternoon, bothering me? Aren't you back in school?"

She took out her cell phone. "It's me. We're here and the two men are clear. At least their computers are." She gave him a sly glance. "Just some boring smut, but nothing exciting or incriminating."

"What the hell? Who is that?"

"Okay, I'll clue him in." She hung up and in a surprisingly calm voice, told him about Georgiana's being blackmailed, ending with, "And we can't let William know yet because both his wife and sister are afraid he'll freak and put them both in bubble wrap."

He opened his mouth, only to close it immediately. She was right. Darcy would freak.

She said, "I need to get access to your IP log. I prefer not to have to look through it to find the match, though. Lizzy has a suspect in mind already, but she won't tell. She doesn't want us to zero in on one person and miss others."

"This is not a game!" He grabbed his phone. "She damn well better tell me who—"

"She said to ask you why Wickham would have Georgiana invite you, her cousin and co-guardian, to her mass wedding."

"I don't know." Surprised at the question, he put the phone down. Cousin! He stood. "Damn it! I know who!"

"Who?"

"Mistaken Identity." His brain clicked through the clues. "Could Wickham have meant Anne and Georgiana thought he meant me? It's so obvious. I can't believe I missed the connection."

"You're saying you're suspecting Anne and Georgiana's cult-boyfriend worked together?"

"Yes, and Catherine."

"The aunt?"

Richard paced, thinking out loud. "My uncle's will left Catherine with no real power over Pemberley Trust Foundation or DDF, but most importantly, no guardianship of little Georgiana, as Catherine had expected. When Darcy named me co-guardian instead of her, she threatened an ugly custody fight."

"I'm beginning to see..."

"She had a good chance of winning custody. Darcy's tabloid behavior after his father died didn't help him. He sobered up and stopped partying. But she held that threat of a public custody fight over them throughout the years. Georgiana would have been traumatized."

"The timing makes sense now. She was losing the leverage to pressure William to marry Anne, so she and Anne targeted Georgiana right before she turned eighteen." Mary stood. "Where is Anne?"

"She was here briefly Monday but she returned to Chicago. She won't be back until our board meeting next week."

"Does she have a computer here?"

"There should be a desktop computer in her office here. Both her laptop and her desktop are DDF property…"

He was speaking to an empty room. Rushing after her, he pointed to Anne's office.

Within minutes, Mary had hacked into Anne's desktop and discovered Georgiana's pictures, as well as pictures of Anne and Wickham in various bondage poses. She deleted Georgiana's but left the couples' on the screen.

Richard had to turn away to fight waves of nausea.

Mary clicked on a particularly explicit picture of Anne and nudged him. "Now that's what I call good, dirty porn. Not that cheap, lightweight stuff you had on your computer."

One glance and he emptied his lunch into the nearby trash can.

Showing no concern for his state, she left the room.

After heaving a few more times, he scrambled after her. He found her in Darcy's office. He gasped. "That's the chairman of DDF's computer with classified information!"

"Then he should have had better safeguards so I wouldn't be able to hack into it so easily. Besides, I don't give a fuck what chairman he is. He's married to my sister and I want to see if he has kinky taste too." Her fingers flew over the keyboard. "What do you know? All the smut is at the VP's level. The chairman is boring. No porn, nothing."

"Darcy is going to cough up a cow when he hears how easily you've breached the security system."

"Never mind that now." She drummed her fingers on the desk. "So, what to do about slutty, wicked, greedy Anne?"

CHAPTER 39

❦

Bang Bang

ANNE'S CELL PHONE RANG THE MINUTE SHE ENTERED HER hotel suite.

"There's a way for you to get rid of the two clowns and be back at DDF headquarters," her stepmother said in greeting.

"Tell me how." Anne put down her laptop. "I can't stand it here in Chicago anymore."

"I know it's been hard, but it's wise to keep a low profile until my nephew forgets the hospital business."

"He didn't even say anything personal to me when I saw him in Oakland. He treated me like I was a regular employee, giving my report." She had tried to tempt him with provocative pictures of herself—her best pictures, she must admit—but she detected no spark of interest. The man behaved, as usual, like an asexual piece of rock around her.

"Never you mind that," Catherine advised. "Focus on his weak area instead, his sister. Time to send her another email to keep her off balance."

"I sent one Monday from New York," Anne said. Richard and Charles were in her office looking over her figures from Chicago. Angry at being supervised by them, she had impulsively sent an email to Georgiana. "That's only two days ago. It's best to wait a while before sending another. If we overwhelm her, she might go running to Darcy and we'd lose the chance to pressure her to sell her voting shares of DDF to us."

"Good thinking. Has that fool in Los Angeles sent you anything good yet?"

"Not yet, but I'm expecting it soon. He has it set up." Anne had received an email the day before from Wickham telling her he would move soon. He sent her sample pictures taken with some other girl to assure her he knew what to do with the Bennet girl.

"Email the sample pictures to me," Catherine ordered when Anne told her. "And tell him I also want to see all the pictures he takes of the Bennet girl before he leaks them to the tabloids. I want my nephew embarrassed good by his wife's family. I want him sorry he married into trash. Are you sure Wickham got the right girl?"

"Yes. I told him to target the Bennet sister who's graduating from Stanford."

"Good. She's of age then. I paid a lot of my money for them and I want to make sure he's not wasting my money this time indulging in his perversion with girls too young for him."

"Don't worry. He's not messing with underage girls," Anne soothed, then reminded her stepmother, "though, don't forget that his perversion was what got us the pictures of Georgiana."

"Be very specific with him in your instructions. If only he hadn't messed up last year. If only he'd specified you, not that fool Richard."

"It wasn't completely George's fault," Anne defended Wickham. "We didn't know she'd told Richard she had a boyfriend. And I myself should have thought of some work emergency somewhere to send Richard off that week, as I did Darcy."

"I still say that fool Wickham ruined it for himself and for us with that mistake. He could be collecting alimony right now from my nephew for agreeing to divorce Georgiana, and you would be Mrs. Darcy right now and on the company's board."

"There was no guarantee Darcy would have married me."

"Of course he would have." Catherine's voice was confident. "He would have done anything to have you help get Georgiana released from that Wickham fool and his cult. You have leverage with Wickham."

"I do." Anne knew Wickham wouldn't be able to resist getting Georgiana into some bondage getup, even if he was able to stick to the agreement that he couldn't touch the underage girl until her eighteenth birthday. Hiding herself in his apartment and doing a little subterfuge photography had been fruitful. With those photos, she had been able to control both Wickham and Georgiana.

"About my news"—excitement returned to Catherine's voice—"those two clowns in New York called a board meeting tomorrow instead of waiting until next week."

"Go on."

"Remember the company bylaws about board meetings? The one my father had put in to ensure that the DDF board couldn't meet in secret and outvote a Darcy if the family's ownership of the company's shares dipped?"

"Yes?"

"Any member who called such a board meeting and knowingly didn't inform or exclude a Darcy would be ousted. My nephew's never missed a meeting."

Anne leaned forward. "And?"

"He'll miss this one. A little bird told me he's tied up with some emergency with his wife's pregnancy, and the two clowns aren't going to bother him."

Restless with excitement, Anne paced.

"Without him, it's an illegal board meeting and you'll have reason to force their hands. Show up and remind them all of the bylaws. I bet they forgot about it."

"Brilliant."

"Darcy will have no choice but to dismiss or suspend the two clowns from the board. They're not expecting you at the meeting. You need to get to New York tomorrow and surprise them. Just show up and tell them you're there to report to the board about Chicago."

"I'm going to check on flights right now." Happily, she opened her laptop.

—⁓—

"Damn Hollywood." Darcy leaned his elbows on his legs, clasped his hands, and fought the urge to get up and wash them again. He'd been away from his wife since Monday, and already it was Wednesday evening. His hands were now red and raw. He hated not being able to control the situation, though he had no choice but to stay put. Lieutenant Denny of the FBI didn't want to run the risk of having him accidentally run into Wickham in the hotel. He turned to the large man sitting beside him. "Are you certain Denny knows what he's doing?"

Brandon answered, "Denny's a little young and eager, but he's well supervised. I know his boss very well. Eleanor Dashwood is a sharp and sensible agent."

"Then why isn't she here supervising?" Darcy said, peeved.

"Because, like many brilliant people, Eleanor's also a bit eccentric," Brandon replied in a dry voice and a pointed glance at

Darcy. "She's attending a *Star Trek* convention." He shrugged in response to Darcy's disgusted snort. "When you're head of the Law Enforcement Unit of the Anti-Child Pornography Task Force, you need to chill sometimes and have a hobby in order to deal with this kind of situation day in and day out."

"While she's playing dress-up with some Vulcans, that bloody whelp Denny is going to falsely charge my mother-in-law."

"You know it's not Mrs. Bennet Denny's after. He's only using the threat of charging her as Wickham's accomplice to keep you in line and get you to cooperate."

"She's silly and starstruck, and that's all she is. No nefarious, deeper thoughts or complicity with Wickham's ugly doings."

"I'm sure Denny knows that. Why do you think he arranged for her to be touring a few exclusive movie sets around Hollywood today? He wants her out of the way."

"Damn Hollywood," Darcy muttered again.

"I should have picked up Wickham's trail when he re-entered the country."

"Don't blame yourself. I had our guys watch him to make sure he didn't get close to my wife and sister, not to track his whereabouts once he left the country."

"Wickham's too much of a small-time guy to have the resources he's suddenly acquired, bankrolling a reality TV show. Eleanor is certain it's not the cult money behind this. Someone else is financing his child pornography."

Brandon lapsed into silence after that, leaving Darcy to his thoughts. When Lydia and her mother went to Hollywood, Darcy automatically had Brandon check out whether or not the show was a legitimate operation as a routine precaution. After Brandon informed him Monday morning George Wickham was the director behind Lydia's show, going under his Dutch name of Ury, Darcy immediately flew down to Los Angeles.

They discovered the FBI had also been watching Wickham. With the FBI involved, it wasn't that simple to extract Lydia from the show without first proving to the FBI that Lydia's mother wasn't involved, for Mrs. Bennet appeared to be friendly—too friendly—with Ury/Wickham.

Darcy made a deal with Lieutenant Denny. He would cooperate and provide all necessary help with the operation if Mrs. Bennet would not be pursued legally when the FBI found no cause to charge her. He didn't trust the ambitious FBI agent not to trump up something to implicate his innocent, if exasperatingly silly, mother-in-law.

The door opened. An eager look on his face, Denny entered. "Bang bang. It's game time, gentleman. He has the two girls in the room and the equipment set up. We're sure it's not only cheerleading pictures he's planning."

Irritated with the agent's manner and anxious about Lydia, Darcy ignored him.

Denny put his hand out. "We won't let any harm come to your sister-in-law, Mr. Darcy."

Darcy headed toward the door.

"We're going to let him hang himself a little before we swoop in." Denny raised his voice. "I'm in charge of the FBI operation here, Mr. Darcy."

At that, Darcy dropped his hand from the doorknob and faced the agent. "I don't give a bloody damn if you're in charge of the presidency of the United States, I'm not going to let Wickham or you or even her put herself in jeopardy so you can call this operation a success."

After a brief second meeting Darcy's stare, the agent nodded and backed down.

They walked in silence toward the hotel room where Wickham's supposed studio was set up. When they neared it, Darcy noticed undercover men already in place. A mere three yards from the room, they heard a loud scream from inside.

Darcy sprinted. Brandon pulled him back and shoved him behind. Undercover men appeared with guns drawn.

"You motherfucker asshole dirty old man! Ew! Ew! Gross! No way am I doing any of that with you! Gross!" Lydia's voice rang loud and clear. "Yuck! Yuck! Ew! Get somebody your own age! You pervert!"

A loud scream of a man in pain followed.

Denny opened the door to Wickham's suite. He stood still... and laughed.

Darcy escaped Brandon and lunged to join Denny.

Wickham was on the floor, wearing nothing but crotchless black leather pants, writhing and screaming with his hands over his groin. "Owwwwww! Help me! The bitch kicked me!"

"Don't call me a bitch!" Lydia, dressed in a cheerleading outfit, screamed back and lifted her leg to deliver another blow.

Brandon placed himself between her and Wickham.

She screamed at Brandon, "He did something to Ashley over there. She's all loony toony now. Look!"

Ashley, half lying, half falling from a couch in a corner of the room, idiotically smiled and waved.

Lydia noticed Darcy then. She ran to him. "Ew! William, he was gross!" she half sobbed, half shouted. "We were supposed to be posing for another set of cheer pictures when he ripped off the flap of his pants and tried to get me to... Ew! He's old! He must be over thirty at least!"

"Shh. You're all right, now," Darcy soothed.

"Ew! Yuck! I'm going to get Mary to kick his ass. He bared his hairy ass and his old wienie. Gross! Gross! Yuck! I am never ever going to have sex with a man! So gross!"

The FBI men laughed quietly. Brandon motioned for him to take Lydia away while they dealt with the scene.

Darcy calmed his sister-in-law and arranged for Ashley to be observed at a hospital until her guardians arrived. When he later met up with Brandon for debriefing, he learned Wickham had to be taken to the hospital by ambulance. Lydia, with her strong cheerleader legs, had kicked the man so hard his genitals developed painful swelling and bleeding.

CHAPTER 40

❀

Caught in a Pickle

MRS. CHING PRESSED A TISSUE TO HER NOSE AND FOLLOWED THE hostess into the back room of Carnegie Deli.

The hostess stopped. "I'm sorry. My mistake. There's no free table back here."

"I'd be happy to share my table," a young lady sitting alone said. "But I'm not sharing my pickles. She has to get her own."

Gratefully accepting the friendly offer, Mrs. Ching sat. After she ordered the matzo ball soup, she turned to her companion. "Why, you're pregnant! Oh, I feel bad sitting here when I have a cold. I don't want you to get sick."

"Why? I told you I'm not sharing my food." The young lady's hand covered her pickle plate. "I'm teasing. I'm Elizabeth."

"Lorna," Mrs. Ching introduced herself. What a sweet, friendly thing. A waiter brought two giant-sized pastrami sandwiches for Elizabeth.

"I was very hungry when I ordered," Elizabeth said when she saw Mrs. Ching's reaction. She pointed to her stomach. "Twins."

"That's a lot of meat." Mrs. Ching was stunned at the amount of food in front of Elizabeth.

"These days, I eat everything. I'm also supposed to report my dietary intake to a very worried husband so he can graph it. He loves to work with numbers and graphs. Some days I make up a healthier diet to appease him. It's our first pregnancy."

Mrs. Ching smiled. "He sounds like a devoted husband."

"He is. He's trying to get as much work done as possible before the babies arrive. He's a workaholic. It's a good thing I met him when he was an unemployed accountant on vacation."

Mrs. Ching wondered why Elizabeth had laughed at the end. "Please, eat your food before it gets cold."

"Yumm. Nothing beats a New York pastrami sandwich. I've been craving this and the pickles the whole plane ride here this morning." Elizabeth added she was in New York to take care of some family business. "Why are you out and about instead of at home resting when you're sick?"

"There's an important meeting at work this afternoon. My boss is not in town at the moment. He can be such a bear if things aren't done right. I don't trust these young assistants they have covering for me."

"You must be a treasure then."

Over lunch, they chatted about pregnancy food cravings. Mrs. Ching revealed she used to crave Chinese dim sum. Elizabeth agreed that sounded good and that it might be her next craving, after pickles.

Mrs. Ching asked, "Are you prepared for the little ones with supplies?"

Elizabeth made a face. "Everything is so expensive. I can't believe some of the babies' outfits cost more than my own clothes."

Mrs. Ching hoped Elizabeth's husband job was secure, with two babies coming. Thank goodness DDF was in good shape from Mr. Darcy's diligence. Though he kept in touch with her daily by phone and email, she hadn't seen him since he relocated to the

West Coast. His employees had yet to meet or see a clear picture of the illusive Mrs. Darcy. That surprised no one. Mr. Darcy was fanatical about his privacy. "If you want to shop while you're here, I know the best bargain places for children's clothes."

"Thanks, I'd appreciate the stores' names."

Mrs. Ching wrote the names of the stores and added her home number. "Call me if you have a craving for dim sum too. I know the best place in Chinatown. Now, I need to head to work."

"Thanks, Lorna." Elizabeth pocketed the slip of paper without looking at it. "Good luck with the meeting. Tell your boss to go suck a pickle if he's too much of a bear."

Chuckling at the thought of the serious Mr. Darcy sucking a pickle, Mrs. Ching left.

Two hours later, Mrs. Ching positioned herself near the door of the DDF boardroom and observed the sea of serious faces. Elizabeth's pickles would do some good for this crowd, Mrs. Ching decided. Mr. Fitzwilliam and Mr. Bingley appeared grave and the meeting hadn't even started yet. A tiny young woman with unusually large eyes sat next to Mr. Fitzwilliam at the conference table in the center of the room.

Assistants arranged themselves along the perimeter of the room, ready to take notes or run errands. Mrs. Ching saw a couple new assistants, like that one who seemed to be hidden from view, sitting behind Wendy, Mr. Bingley's newly hired assistant. Mrs. Ching reminded herself to say hello to the new assistants after the meeting.

The door opened behind her. Anne de Bourgh entered. Mrs. Ching glanced at the agenda to double-check; just as she'd thought, Miss de Bourgh's name appeared nowhere.

Miss de Bourgh coolly took a seat directly across from Mr. Bingley. "I thought we could talk about our new acquisition in Chicago. I see you don't have that on the agenda. We'll add it to the end of the meeting."

The meeting started. Mr. Bingley formally announced he would chair the meeting in place of Mr. Darcy. The CEO was stuck in California for personal reasons. After taking care of some routine business, Mr. Bingley gave Mr. Fitzwilliam the floor. The latter announced a new plan to revamp computer security at DDF. A long question and answer session ensued with some board members in favor and some against.

"We need more concrete proof of why and how our security system is not safe," Miss de Bourgh stated.

Some board members nodded in agreement. One said, "Has there been a breach, Richard?"

"There's no overt breach. We simply want to be cautious and upgrade to the highest level there is," Mr. Fitzwilliam said.

"You're going to have to do better than that to prove to us why the expense would be worth it before we vote," added another board member. "You moved the board meeting from next week to today for it. There must be a good reason. How about a demonstration?"

Murmurings around the room rose in agreement with the last speaker's statement.

"I can give you a demonstration. I'm Tina Darling and I'm the computer expert Mr. Fitzwilliam has been consulting with. I can show you how easily it is for me to break into your current computer system in just a couple of minutes." The young lady walked up to a board member sitting next to Miss de Bourgh and pointed to his laptop. "May I?"

"Sure, sugar. I've got nothing dirty in there," he drawled and winked. The crowd tittered.

Ms. Darling returned to her seat and worked with the laptop. She bit her lip and flipped her bangs, looking more nervous as the minutes ticked on. Mr. Fitzwilliam began to shift in his chair and Mr. Bingley's hands fidgeted with the papers in front of him.

Miss de Bourgh leaned back in her chair and smiled. "Ms. Darling, if you don't get through his DDF laptop in the next decade, you can try some of our other ones. Or do you need a password for security clearance?"

As if she had been waiting for such an opportunity, Ms. Darling eagerly reached across the conference table for Miss de Bourgh's laptop. "No password needed, but I'll try yours."

A few minutes later, with a satisfied tone, Miss de Bourgh said, "Stumped, Ms. Darling?"

"Just give me a few more minutes," Ms. Darling said. "It's harder than I thought."

"Of course it is. I myself recommended the security system to our CEO." Miss de Bourgh laughed aloud. A handful of the other board members joined in.

In the midst of the increased din in the room, the door opened behind Mrs. Ching again. She started when Elizabeth from the deli slipped in. Her entrance was unnoticed by almost everyone else in the room.

Eyes widening in surprise when she saw Mrs. Ching, Elizabeth came and sat right beside her. In her hand, she carried a paper bag with the Carnegie Deli logo. She whispered, "Pickles."

"What—?"

"Shh!" Elizabeth put her finger to her lips and turned toward the action.

Miss de Bourgh motioned Ms. Darling to turn the laptop around. "Time's up. Let us see what you've discovered."

"Are you sure?" the computer expert asked.

"Yes."

Shrugging, Miss Darling turned the laptop to face Miss de Bourgh.

A loud gasp escaped from the board member sitting next to Miss de Bourgh.

Immediately, everyone else lurched close, including both Mrs. Ching and Elizabeth. Gasps reverberated throughout.

"Oh my! No wonder you didn't want to miss the meeting," Elizabeth whispered to Mrs. Ching. She returned to her chair and focused her attention on opening the twist tie of her Carnegie Deli bag.

"That's my private stuff." Miss de Bourgh ran around the conference table and fought to get through the huddling mass. "How dare you! Give me back my laptop!"

Mr. Fitzwilliam grabbed the laptop. "You gave her permission to break into it, and this laptop is DDF's property."

Miss Darling took the computer from Mr. Fitzwilliam, her fingers flying on the keyboard again, and taunted, "Besides your icky pictures, you have what looks like child pornography on your laptop, and that's a crime, sugar."

"The girl's over eighteen," Miss de Bourgh screamed. "There is no Darcy present. The bylaws says those who called the board meeting will be dismissed."

A small voice spoke up, "They have a Darcy here."

A young woman stepped forward. Mrs. Ching's mouth opened. Why, Miss Darcy had been sitting hidden behind Mr. Bingley's new assistant Wendy the whole time!

"Some of you may remember meeting Miss Georgiana Darcy years ago," Mr. Fitzwilliam introduced his cousin. "She's grown up."

Miss Georgiana looked petrified, then she glanced in Mrs. Ching's direction and her face relaxed. Mrs. Ching smiled and gave a little wave. She hadn't seen young Georgiana for years and didn't think the young lady even remembered what she even looked like. With some embarrassment, Mrs. Ching saw Elizabeth copy her greeting.

After waving and smiling at Miss Georgiana, Elizabeth noisily ferreted around her pickle bag. Oblivious that she now had the whole room's attention, she pulled out a pickle and took a big bite. *Crunch. Crunch.* The sound of Elizabeth munching the pickle was the only one heard for a long moment.

Self-conscious that people might think she had brought an uninvited guest to a board meeting, Mrs. Ching nudged Elizabeth on the shoulder, trying to get her to leave.

Elizabeth swallowed. "I'm sorry, am I making too much noise chewing? My husband hates it when people do that, though he pretends he doesn't mind when I do it. I just have this craving for crunchy, green, dill pickles. I don't like it when they're yellow and mushy and old. I like them green and fresh and have a snap when you bite into them. These Carnegie Deli green pickles are the best." *Crunch. Crunch.* Again, Elizabeth took another bite and munched happily.

"You! Why you!" Miss de Bourgh said. "What are you doing here?"

"I invited her," Mrs. Ching defended Elizabeth. She didn't know why Elizabeth was here next to her chomping noisily on a pickle, but Mrs. Ching wasn't going to let anyone harm the pregnant lady—even if she herself thought her new friend must be very odd. *Oh dear, she followed me here*, Mrs. Ching worried. One never knew about people with mental problems who may be off their medications during pregnancy.

Elizabeth nodded. "Yeah, she told me she knew the best place for dim sum in Chinatown. I have a craving now. Hey, after the meeting, let's all go for some. You get a better deal if there's a large crowd to share." She frowned at Miss de Bourgh. "Well, at least those of us who aren't going to be arrested for child pornography could go."

Miss de Bourgh moved toward Elizabeth.

"You touch one hair on my wife's head, and you're dead," a steely voice said from the doorway.

At the fury in Mr. Darcy's eyes, Mrs. Ching's hand went to her heart.

Miss de Bourgh's face paled and she stood rooted.

Elizabeth waved her half-eaten pickle at Mr. Darcy. "Hi, love. You've made it."

Mrs. Ching needed to sit down, quick. She was too old for this kind of shock, she decided. Elizabeth gently patted her on the shoulder.

Mr. Darcy ignored everyone else and walked toward his wife. With his back to the rest of the room, he bent and carefully inspected her. Elizabeth reached in the bag and pulled out another pickle. With a quirk of her eyebrow, she offered it to Mr. Darcy. Lips twitching, he shot her a warning glance. He then turned and decisively dismissed the board meeting.

His employees and the board members filed out. Mrs. Ching stood to follow.

Elizabeth placed a hand on her arm and whispered, "Lorna, you stay."

"Mrs. Darcy?" Mrs. Ching felt compelled to confirm. When Elizabeth smiled and nodded, Mrs. Ching whispered, "But you told me you wanted to go bargain shopping for baby clothes."

"I do want to go bargain shopping for baby clothes. I've always been a bargain shopper," Elizabeth whispered back. "What a coincidence, you working here. Who's your bear of a boss? I'd like to offer him a pickle."

"You just did." Mrs. Ching allowed herself a tiny smile and nodded when Elizabeth's eyes widened and mouthed, "Mrs. Ching?"

The next moment, they both sobered as they turned back to the near-empty room.

Three people Mrs. Ching didn't recognize approached Miss de Bourgh.

"Anne de Bourgh, I presume?" an unfamiliar young woman asked. Miss de Bourgh responded with a haughty look, which turned ashen at the sight of the badge the young lady flashed. "I'm Eleanor Dashwood of the FBI Anti-Child Pornography Task Force. You are now under arrest for possessing and transmitting child pornography…"

"My word!" Mrs. Ching whispered when Miss de Bourgh screamed she was set up.

Mr. Darcy approached and, without words, simply stared at her. The screaming abruptly stopped. Miss de Bourgh's gaze dropped to the floor.

After the agents and Miss de Bourgh left a few minutes later, heavy silence hung in the room. Mr. Darcy walked to the window and stared out, his body stiff. Elizabeth put down her pickle and signaled for everyone else to leave. Silently, they did as she requested.

Right before she closed the door, Mrs. Ching glanced back into the room. Elizabeth had her head on her husband's shoulder and her arms around him.

As they viewed New York City below them through the window, Elizabeth gently rubbed her husband's back. Gradually, the stiffness left his body.

He turned to face her. "I feel so responsible."

Her heart broke at the sadness in his eyes and the guilt in his voice. She gave him a few more minutes to blame himself before she comforted him with a kiss. His lips clung to hers. When he finally broke contact, she said, "I know you do, my love. I wish I could make you see it's not your fault."

"Thank you for calling me. I got here as fast as I could. I'm going to have nightmares from the thought of what could have happened to you and Georgiana flying on a commercial plane—"

"Shhh," she interrupted, amused that with everything that had happened, he'd chosen to perseverate on that detail. "We couldn't take the risk of someone at DDF learning and leaking to Anne that Georgiana and I were flying here this morning if we had used the company's jet."

"I wished you had listened to me and stayed away from here today and let—"

"And miss all the fun?" she cut him off again. "I did try to stay away, but when I saw that you hadn't shown up by the time the meeting started, I couldn't let Georgiana be the only Darcy there."

"If anything had happened to you—"

"Nothing did," she soothed. They had lured Anne to DDF with the leaked news of a secret board meeting. William was supposed to have arrived before the meeting and surprised Anne with an order to see her laptop. "I'm so sorry it got public and involved your whole board. We didn't count on you being late, so the meeting had to go on as scheduled and then things just happened—"

"Sweetheart, I need to tell you that..."

"I told my parents not to let Lydia get involved with a reality TV show!" she shouted when he finished telling her what had happened in Hollywood. She spent a few minutes ranting and ignored her husband's attempts to calm her. Then the humor of it got to her. She shook her head. "Both of us were protecting each other's little sister without telling the other."

A wry smile appeared on his face. "Great minds think alike."

She sobered. "So that was why you had the FBI here. I didn't expect them. Gosh, what a mess this is going to be."

"After your phone call about Georgiana and Anne, I knew I had to immediately talk to the FBI agent in charge, Ms. Dashwood. That's why I was late."

"I'm a bit confused why. It defeated the purpose of us protecting Georgiana by deleting the pictures on Anne's computer."

"I knew the FBI would soon make the connection between Anne and Wickham and track her down. I didn't want any of us to be charged with tampering with evidence or impeding an investigation. Brandon convinced me that Ms. Dashwood is a reasonable, sensible person and to lay everything up front on the table."

"So you did, I see."

He nodded. "In exchange for not including any photos of Georgiana as evidence—"

"That is, if they can find any after Mary's done with the computer."

"I know you have great faith in your sister's skills on the computer, but I can't take that risk," he pointed out. "As I was saying, in exchange, I gave Ms. Dashwood open access to DDF. I will not use my resources and have lawyers involved to hinder her investigation."

"Mary said the authorities wouldn't be able to really prove..." She stopped. "You're right. As usual, you thought through everything carefully."

"If it hadn't been for my blindness—"

She put her fingers on his mouth. "Okay, buster. Here's the deal. I won't blame myself and you don't blame yourself. Agreed?"

He kissed her fingers. "Agreed. I love you, Mrs. Darcy."

Though she knew he agreed only to humor her, she let it go. "I love you too, Mr. Darcy. Now, I have had enough of this ugly business for today. You finish what you have to do here and then come home. I know how to make you feel better."

CHAPTER 41

❀

Love and Acceptance of Mr. Darcy

ELIZABETH TURNED A PAGE AND LAUGHED ALOUD. SHE GAVE THE tabloid to her aunt and pointed. In the background of a photo taken at a Hollywood premiere of Jorge Cooley's latest movie, Hussein and Caroline, standing behind the actor, smiled into the camera.

"Are you okay?" Aunt Mai put aside the magazine when Elizabeth shifted uncomfortably in her chair. "Are they kicking you too hard?"

"I'm fine." She ignored the wave of the gentle contraction lolling over her abdomen. "My appointment time was thirty minutes ago. I'll be late calling William. He's going to be more anxious and difficult."

"Yes, very likely," Aunt Mai's voice was dry.

"He has reasons to be anxious and difficult," Elizabeth defended her husband.

"No need to explain." Aunt Mai rubbed Elizabeth's forearm. "It's understandable William and you feel guilty and responsible, but remember the woman was actually beating her lawyers with her cane when she suffered a fatal stroke. They caught it on video at the courthouse."

Elizabeth sighed. It was such a dramatic way for William's aunt to have died, just as she was being charged with trafficking child pornography. The authorities didn't buy her or Anne's defense that the women had meant for Wickham to target Kitty, not Lydia.

"Your uncle suspects Mr. Wickham, as this is not his first offense, will likely get three consecutive life sentences with no chance of parole, and Miss de Bourgh a few years."

"I hope they rot in prison."

"Don't get yourself upset," Aunt Mai soothed. "Focus on what's coming, like these two precious babies. I'm surprised you managed to get their father onto the plane yesterday."

"They need him in New York. They haven't yet found a computer security system Mary can't hack into. He plans to be back in a couple of days."

"He made a schedule of who—along with the backup person—was to be with you at all hours while he's gone. He has called us all repeatedly to make sure we all know our shifts and what to do if you even hiccup." Aunt Mai laughed. "We took bets that he wouldn't leave."

"New York is only a five-hour flight away. Jane's there. She'll keep me posted if William gets too stressed. I'm glad she accepted his offer to have her oversee the Pemberley Trust Foundation. He needs someone he can trust and Jane needs to be in New York to get to know Charles better."

"How's that romance going?"

"He worries that he's not good enough for her, and she worries that she's got too much baggage from her old relationship, but they're progressing."

"And your sister Mary and Richard? Are they progressing?"

"Now that's a relationship I'm not even going to comment on." Elizabeth shook her head, bemused. "Who'd ever have thought—" She suddenly felt short of breath.

"Lizzy?" Her aunt's face looked concerned. "You look like you're in labor."

After her breathing normalized, Elizabeth reassured her aunt, "False labor contraction. Nothing to worry about."

Her aunt ignored her and took out her cell phone. "I'm calling your husband. I value my life."

—⁓—

Darcy carefully placed the phone down. He stood and walked slowly at first until he reached the hallway. His stride lengthened. He weaved through desks and cubicles. The startled faces of his employees flashed by him. Spying the lit *down* triangle above the elevator door, he broke into a run. He launched himself through the doors just as it opened, clipping the shoulder of the man walking out.

"Darce, where are you going? The meeting with the computer people is starting now."

"Elizabeth, my babies," was all the response Bingley got before the elevator doors closed on him.

Jane was at a meeting across town. He should wait for her. No. The precious seconds the elevator took to descend to the ground floor convinced him he could not wait for anyone or anything. The elevators opened. He tore through the lobby, not caring he was scattering a group of his employees as if they were bowling pins.

Thirty minutes later, when the DDF car couldn't maneuver past a New York City traffic jam—a pregnant woman delivering her seventh child in the middle of the roadway a few miles up ahead was rumored to be the cause—he unbuckled his seat belt. Barking a series of last-minute instructions to his bodyguard and driver, he took off his jacket and tie and exited the car, shutting the door on their protests.

He raced through the streets, dodging pedestrians and cars, and reached the cause of the traffic jam. The sight of an ambulance parked next to a car, out of which he swore he could hear the loud wailing of a mother and infant, spurred his legs to a faster speed. Glimpsing a flash of yellow ahead, he sprinted and grabbed the door handle of a cab that had just pulled up to a group waiting at a corner.

"Wife, twin babies born now, must get there," he gasped to the astonished faces of the people whose cab he was stealing.

Their scowls turned into beaming smiles. He shut the door on them, in the middle of their congratulatory wishes.

With the promise of a tip twice as big as the man's yearly income, he persuaded the cab driver to break an unprecedented number of traffic laws to deliver him to the waiting DDF jet in record time.

The cross-country flight was agonizing. Despite his repeated urgings to fly faster and faster, the DDF pilot refused.

"Mr. Darcy, we are going as fast as the aircraft can, at maximum cruising speed. Your hovering in the cockpit, peering over my shoulders isn't—"

"Helping, I get it." Darcy interrupted impatiently.

"Perhaps before Mrs. Darcy next gives birth, you might look into buying a supersonic jet."

He had no better luck with the helicopter pilot who flew him from the Oakland airport to the hospital's roof. Darcy refused to wait for the hospital representative, now delayed by an elevator, to greet him and take him to his wife. His instincts would lead him to his wife quicker, Darcy was convinced. He charged down the stairs.

Five minutes later, cursing the incompetence of whoever had designed the maze of the hospital corridors, he managed to find the

Labor and Delivery wing. He burst through its double doors and ran smack into his mother-in-law.

"William! You shouldn't be running in a hospital."

Fearful, he could only manage a small whisper. "Elizabeth?"

His mother-in-law must have recognized his state. Her expression softened and she gently led him into a room.

Friends and relatives crowded the room, but the only person he saw clearly was his wife.

———

One glance at her husband's face and Elizabeth waved everyone out.

After everyone had left, her husband still hadn't moved an inch.

Spreading her arms wide, she waited. After another paralytic moment, he flew toward her. She could feel tremors coursing through his body as he buried his face in her neck. She pressed harder into him, offering comfort with her body.

"I... I..." his voice stumbled against her neck.

"I know, my love." She stroked his arms and waited.

At last, his body stopped shaking and his breathing calmed. "How are you feeling?"

"Fine. I've been having strange sensations but it's all normal."

He pulled back and gently rubbed her abdomen. "What sort of sensations?"

One of the babies kicked at his hand and he smiled. She thought that was the most wonderful sight, her husband's delighted smile. Describing her contractions as best she could, she ended, "I'm not uncomfortable at all."

"I should never have left you."

She caressed his sweat-drenched hair. "Shhh! I made you go to New York. You needed to be there to deal with the security problem. Think of it as securing DDF for our babies' inheritance. I'm fine. We're all fine."

"I was so afraid I wouldn't see you again," he whispered. "You're as necessary to me as breathing, my Lizzy. Without your warmth, I can't... I've only begun to live."

She closed her eyes and inhaled, letting his pepper scent infuse her. "You're my air, William."

"I remember that first day I arrived in Vietnam, how I resisted going inside that hospital when Bingley injured himself. Today, I couldn't get to you inside this hospital fast enough."

"I'm cuter than him, that's why." She was gratified to see her husband smile at that.

"Will they be okay?"

"They'll be fine. Now, it's time to think of names."

"No. No names yet."

She laughed at the firmness in his voice. He was more superstitious than Aunt Mai's Vietnamese relatives. They had convinced him it would be bad luck to have the baby names before birth; the gods would be jealous.

"You're only at thirty-four weeks," he said.

To distract him from his worrying, she groped him. "I know a way to pass the time while we wait for your children, Mr. Darcy."

Groaning, he pulled her hand away. "We're in a hospital room and you're in labor."

"Likely just false labor. I'm here as a precaution because my OB is afraid of you." Per doctor's orders, she'd had to abstain from sex for weeks. She'd refused, however, to give up the one sure way she knew would relieve stress for her husband. She smirked. "You know I do some of my best work with my hands and mouth lately."

He blushed. "Naughty girl. I don't want it without you."

"We'll see how long you'll last."

"I'm willing to be patient."

For the next two weeks, their babies sorely tested William's patience by refusing to be born. Her labor did not progress until a day shy of her thirty-sixth week of pregnancy, when she awoke one night more uncomfortable than usual.

Her husband, who had been sleeping in a cot next to her bed, instantly joined her when she restlessly moved. "You want me to rub your back?"

"Yes." Her hand took advantage of his proximity. When he tried to move her hand away, she snarled at him. He stopped resisting. Despite her discomfort, she smiled at having gotten her way; she wasn't in the mood to behave and she was glad he recognized that.

Occupied, they didn't hear the quiet entrance of the night nurse coming to check Elizabeth's vitals. William's gasp echoed the embarrassed nurse's gasp. The woman quickly retreated. The sight of his mortified face made Elizabeth laugh so hard, her water broke.

She was now in active labor.

Immediately, her medical training took over. She barked orders at the staff. She wanted perfection and prompt responses. No way was she going to accept anything less, not with her children's lives at stake.

"Sweetheart, everyone is trying hard. Please calm down," her husband said at one point.

"Why the hell are you the easygoing and calm one now?" she shouted at him, irritated that the staff had turned to him for guidance on how to deal with her.

"Because I, we, have done everything possible to make this experience safe for you and our babies," he answered, his tone even. "I can't promise you nothing bad will happen, but you and I have done everything in our power to prevent what we could. The rest is up to fate."

"For a man who doesn't usually say much, you can talk pretty when you need to, Mr. Darcy."

"With your total love and acceptance of me and my neuroses, how could I not at least learn and grow a little, Mrs. Darcy?" He bent and kissed her forehead. "Besides, I did promise to talk more. That's all I can do right now, talk. You're the one who has the hard work ahead."

And she worked hard the next few hours. Their baby boy was born first, followed minutes later by his sister. As soon as their daughter's lusty cries followed their son's hearty howling, Elizabeth's husband promptly fainted.

Acknowledgments

The best part of writing this novel is the friendships I have gained. Besides the numerous readers who kept asking for more, I owe a big debt of gratitude to: my sister and Maria for being there from the first word, laughing; Kendra, Mary Anne, TJean, and Susan for their invaluable encouragement and help with the first draft; Mischa, Dawn, and Teresita for cheering and reading the finished first draft; Linda, Francesca, Carol, and Josephine for cheering and reading the ninth draft; and Sharon, Catherine, and Patricia for cheering and tirelessly proofreading the nth draft.

A special thank you to my critique partner and guardian angel, Pamala Knight, who encouraged, pushed, and threatened me with bodily harm if I didn't pursue publication.

Thank you to my editor Deb Werksman for finding it a compulsive read and for her sharp editorial insights.

Thank you to my agent Jill Marsal for believing in my writing voice.

Lastly, thank you to my husband and children for bemusedly tolerating my Jane Austen addiction and my tabloid addiction.

Nina Benneton

❀

About the Author

When Nina Benneton and her family first arrived in America years ago, she took one look at the front lawns of her new neighborhood and thought, *Gosh, these Americans are indeed a blessed race. They even got the gods to give them the power to grow trees in perfect geometric shapes.* Inspired, she spent years making her family proud by trying to achieve the American dream—college, graduate school, gainful employment, then conquering the world and winning a Nobel Prize in something. A wonderful husband and a gaggle of beautiful children interrupted her attaining the last two goals, though the family promised she could resume her campaign once the nest is emptied.

Meanwhile, armed with a laptop, a stack of tabloid magazines, and a dog-eared Jane Austen novel, Nina started writing. On the same week that she learned *Compulsively Mr. Darcy* would be published, she went to the local nursery to look for trees with perfect geometric shapes to plant in her yard. She is hard at work on her third novel.